# *BALLERINA*

Women and men, gay and straight, soaring for stardom, heading for heartbreak, in the greatest ballet novel since *The Red Shoes* . . .

*"Rumor has it that galleys of this book were being passed around backstage at the New York City Ballet just the other week, and no wonder. Stewart has put together the quintessential ballet novel, long overdue . . . bound for as much success as a book as* Turning Point *achieved in films!"*

— PUBLISHERS WEEKLY

# Ballerina

## EDWARD STEWART

BERKLEY BOOKS, NEW YORK

This Berkley book contains the complete
text of the original hardcover edition.
It has been completely reset in a type face
designed for easy reading, and was printed
from new film.

BALLERINA

A Berkley Book/published by arrangement with
Doubleday & Company, Inc.

PRINTING HISTORY
Doubleday edition published 1979
Berkley edition/March 1981.

ISBN: 0-425-04272-3

A BERKLEY BOOK® TM 757,375
Berkley Books are published by Berkley Publishing Corporation,
200 Madison Avenue, New York, New York 10016.
PRINTED IN THE UNITED STATES OF AMERICA

**For Gary Combs,**
**for keeping me on my toes**

# one

Anna Lang fidgeted in her eighth-row-center seat. She squinted at her watch. In two minutes and thirty seconds the curtain would go up on Act One of *The Sleeping Beauty*. In eight minutes her little girl would be an international star.

Tonight was the answer to all Anna Lang's prayers. Tonight was the reward for all her struggles.

And Anna Lang was scared stiff.

The last bell sounded. Stragglers came drifting back to their seats. At two hundred and fifty dollars a ticket, you didn't hurry. The theater was packed with society, ballet potentates, celebrities. Conversation buzzed like a hive of excited hornets.

The house lights dimmed. Anna pulled in her knees to let people squeeze past. A jeweled dowager glanced at her curiously, probably wondering why she was alone, why she'd spent intermission in her seat.

*I'll tell you why, Mrs. Whoever-you-are: because it's taken me a lifetime to get this far, and I'm not taking any chances on slippery stairs or falling chandeliers. This is the moment I've lived my life for, and I'm damned well going to stay alive for it.*

The Prologue had gone smoothly. The whispers in Anna's vicinity had been approving.

1

"Stunning production."

"Never saw them dance so well."

These people hadn't seen anything yet. They hadn't seen Stephanie Lang.

Anna peered again at her watch. She frowned. Either her watch had suddenly speeded up or Act One was late. She peered at the orchestra pit. Tips of bassoons, the curved necks and upper pegs of double basses, a golden sweep of harp jutted into visibility.

The musicians were ready.

The audience was ready.

What was holding up Act One?

The curtain fanned out and seemed to part slightly. Anna braced her feet against the floor, preparing herself for the announcement of some backstage disaster. The curtain dropped back, like lips that had been on the verge of whispering a secret and then lapsed again into silence.

Her dowager neighbor was still staring. Anna wondered if her hair was out of place or if she was sweating through her makeup. The dowager leaned across her escort and touched Anna's hand. Anna smelled Joy.

"Excuse me, aren't you Anna Barlow?"

Anna stared back. The woman was wearing two thousand dollars' worth of Dior and five of Cartier, easily. She had a Palm Beach tan and a Beacon Hill accent and she probably had a Rolls-Royce waiting to take her home. And she remembered Anna Barlow.

"I used to be," Anna said, smiling.

"And didn't you dance with...?" The woman threw a nod toward the stage, toward the curtain that still hadn't budged.

"I used to dance with them, yes. Long time ago."

The couple introduced themselves, somebody-or-other Dickerson. They said they'd been balletomanes for years and asked what Anna thought of tonight's gala.

"I'm biting my nails, waiting for my little girl to come on."

"Your little girl?" Mrs. Dickerson said, fascinated.

"Stephanie Lang. She's dancing Aurora. You'll see her in this act." *If they ever get that damned curtain up*, Anna thought.

She squinted again at her watch. Three minutes late.

Someone in the third ring began clapping and someone

shushed, but the clapping broke through the shush barrier. In fifteen seconds the gala audience had turned into a carnival mob. The theater vibrated like a prison on the brink of rebellion. Every nerve in Anna's body screamed: *Get that curtain up!*

Suddenly, mercifully, the house lights dimmed down. A follow spot picked out the conductor's white-fringed head and tracked him to the podium. The clapping became generous, forgiving.

Anna tried to relax.

She sat through the orchestral prelude. The curtain hissed up and she sat through the scene with the three crones and their spinning wheels. She sat through the dance of the peasant girls and she wondered how the hell Tchaikovsky could have crammed so many repeats into one little waltz.

A spot clicked on, stage right, and Anna's hands readied to applaud Aurora's entrance. There was absolute silence in the theater and absolute stillness on the stage. And one empty spot. Anna's throat tightened.

Aurora stepped onstage. The audience burst into applause.

Anna did not applaud. She sat frozen in a rush of shock. *It's the light*, she thought. *I'm crazy.*

But she wasn't crazy. What she saw on that stage was a million times worse than any empty spotlight. She shot to her feet, pushed her way past jutting knees and surprised faces. She ran up the aisle, stumbled. She picked herself up off the carpet, ignored the stares, kept running.

"What's the fastest way backstage from here?"

The speechless usherette managed to point.

Anna plunged down the deserted corridor. Her heart was pounding and the walls rippled past like water. It was happening exactly as it had happened twenty years ago. She was drowning, drowning all over again, and she knew from what she'd just seen on that stage that this time nothing could save her.

# two

It was five years ago that Anna had brought Steph to New York.

The doorman was one of those Fifth Avenue snots, didn't want to let them wait. Anna said they were friends of Mrs. Amidon's, which she was, and they were expected, which they weren't, and she marched Steph over to the bench and sat her down.

The doorman kept watching as though they'd try to steal the potted palm.

They waited a half hour. Steph kept pressing her feet against the floor, second position, first position, fifth. Anna began to wonder if she should have phoned. No. On the phone Dorcas would have turned her down.

A woman came into the lobby leading a white terrier on a leash. Dorcas Amidon—still crisp, still brisk, still young. She didn't so much as glance at Anna and Steph. She pushed the elevator button and frowned at the gold sliver of a watch on her wrist.

Suddenly Anna felt scared. Her dress was a J. C. Penney pattern. She'd made it herself on the Singer. Did she dare talk to this woman in tailored silk?

She had to. For Steph.

"Dorcas! Hi!"

Anna waved and sprang to her feet.

Dorcas stared, blank and astonished. The terrier growled and pawed tile.

"I'm sorry," Dorcas said, "you must be mistaken."

"It's me. Anna. Anna Lang."

Still no reaction.

"Anna *Barlow* Lang."

Dorcas gasped. Her teeth were tiny and perfectly even and every one of them looked real. "Anna—darling! You've changed—"

They hugged.

"Well, I'm a little older," Anna said. "And I can tell you, I've had my ups and downs. But you're looking just great. I love your hair."

The hair was softly waved chestnut; not a fleck of gray. The skin was pale and unlined. Boy, the things you could do with money nowadays. Dorcas Amidon didn't look a day older than when Anna had walked out of NBT.

"Why, thank you." Dorcas' eyes shifted a degree. "And who's this young lady?"

"This is my daughter Stephanie."

Anna gave Steph a little nudge forward. Steph's dress was store-bought, manufacturer's close-out from Lerner's. It was pale green, simple, but it looked expensive on her. Everything looked expensive on Steph. She had a dancer's posture.

"Marty's little girl?" Dorcas cried.

"Marty's and mine."

Dorcas fluttered out a hand. Anna counted a diamond and two rubies. "How do you *do*, Stephanie? I knew your father." She hesitated. "Do you two have a moment to come upstairs?"

"We have a moment," Anna said. "Sure."

They rode up in the oak-paneled elevator. Some building. Even the elevator man had air conditioning. Dorcas sifted through the mail in a cloisonné bowl on the foyer table. She unleashed the dog and handed the leash to the maid. They went into the living room.

The dove-gray walls were like a backdrop for one of Dorcas' dance galas, setting off ripe plum chairs and sofas, mahogany tables dotted with crystal and silver and cut flowers. There were carved glass fishes on the marble mantelpiece. A pyramid of birch logs had been laid across brass andirons. You could have parked a car in that fireplace.

"Wow," Anna said.

"Coffee?" Dorcas offered.

"Terrific," Anna said. She could stretch a cup of coffee to ten minutes' discussion or better.

Steph was looking around the enormous room. Her little nose crinkled. "Its beautiful here," she said quietly.

"Thank you," Dorcas said. "But I don't know about that rug."

The rug looked fine to Anna: a few thousand dollars fine. The maid brought coffee. They sat, and Dorcas poured.

"Are you visiting New York?" she asked.

"Visiting?" Anna laughed. "This nuthouse? No, we moved here. Yesterday."

Dorcas handed Anna her coffee. The white china cup seemed dangerously thin, like the top of a newborn baby's skull.

"Why?" Dorcas said. "Did you get tired of Cincinnati?"

"Cincinnati was seventeen years ago. Don't ask the cities we've been—Wichita, Sioux City—would you believe Butte, Montana? Mining town. One breath and there's soot on your nose."

"But why New York?" Dorcas said.

"There's nowhere else. Not for dance."

"You're still—dancing?"

"Me? Relax. I'm teaching exercise at Arden's. Starting Monday. Stephanie's the dancer in the family now."

Dorcas stretched smoothly to hand Steph a cup. Anna couldn't see an ounce of flab on the upper arm. A few sun freckles, but those would fade in the fall.

"You dance, Stephanie? Where?"

"That depends," Anna said. "We're keeping our fingers crossed. She auditions tomorrow."

"Is that so."

"We're staking a lot on that audition," Anna said.

"Is that wise?"

"You tell us. You're judging, aren't you?"

"Stephanie's auditioning for *us?*" Dorcas sipped.

"Frankly, we're hoping she'll get a scholarship. The tuition's murder at New York Ballet School. I couldn't swing it on my own. No way." Anna shuddered.

"There aren't many scholarships these days. Funding is very tight."

"Maybe you could put in a good word. We'd appreciate it." After all, Dorcas was on the boards of the school and of NBT. It wasn't any skin off her knuckles.

Dorcas stirred her coffee. "I'm afraid my word doesn't carry much weight. I'm only one vote out of four."

"I thought you ran those auditions."

"It's gotten a little large for one woman to handle. Patricia McBride and Jean-Pierre Bonnefous will be helping at the finals."

"And who's the fourth judge?"

"Marius."

Anna jerked forward. "Volmar? But how can he? Isn't he busy running NBT?"

Dorcas looked down at her hands, smooth and narrow and peaceful in the pale blue folds of her skirt. "He's running a great many things. You must know he advises the President's council for the arts. He's a powerful man."

Anna considered the implications of Volmar's judging her daughter. "He's not doing so well with the critics. That Chabrier Symphony thing got creamed."

"He didn't choreograph the Chabrier, Mom," Steph said softly. "He only staged it."

"It still got creamed. So how is Volmar? Does he still hate me?"

Dorcas tipped her head to the side. Chestnut waves spilled. "I can't imagine anyone's hating you, Anna. Especially with such a lovely daughter."

Anna was worried now but she managed to smile. She felt proud of the little girl sitting so straight and pretty and calm in the big maroon armchair.

"Now you've got me thinking, Dorcas. Maybe Steph should change her name for that audition. Volmar might not like the sound of 'Lang.'"

"Don't be silly. Marius loved Marty. We all did."

Anna took a swallow. The coffee was much too strong. Maybe it was her nerves.

"I still remember Marty's Albrecht," Dorcas was saying. "Those lifts in the Act Two adagio. He made Hildie soar."

"If anyone could make *her* soar, Marty could. He had muscle."

Dorcas angled toward Steph. "Did you ever see your father dance, dear?"

"I wish I had."

Anna looked at her daughter and suddenly it struck her that Steph's spoon was in her saucer. Dorcas' spoon was in her saucer. Anna's spoon was not. She took it out of her cup. It was a tiny silver spoon with a twisting thread of a handle. She laid it in the saucer, softly so it didn't clink.

"Steph's father died when she was eleven months old," Anna said. "She can't even remember him. To her he's just a name and some photographs."

Steph's eyes seemed to retract suddenly, to examine distant objects one by one—the long black Steinway piano, the mysteriously lit shelves of pearl-colored vases built into the wall, two sofas, deep and silken and curving, placed near the terrace doors. For no reason at all Anna felt sad. She realized she would never be able to give her girl anything as pretty as even an ash tray in this apartment.

"It's a pity," Dorcas said. "So many of our American *danseurs nobles* cut down in their prime. Now we have to import them all from Russia. You've seen Rudy Nureyev?"

"Once," Anna said. "Must have been one of his off nights."

You'd have thought Nureyev was a personal friend from the way Dorcas' jaw hung open. It was Steph who broke the silence.

"Mother likes Edward Villella. We saw him in *Prodigal Son*."

"Now *he's* a dancer," Anna said. "Not just a show-off."

"You danced the Siren for us, didn't you?" Dorcas asked Anna. As if she didn't know.

"A lot of walking if you ask me." Anna shrugged. Coffee spilled. Damn. She moved the saucer to her lap to cover the spot. "I wish I could have done that one with Villella."

"It would have been stunning," Dorcas said. "Eddy's such a considerate partner. And you, Stephanie—whom do you like?"

"If you mean men," Anna said, "she doesn't know they exist."

Small spots of color flared up in Steph's cheeks.

"Whom do you prefer of the current male dancers, Stephanie?" Dorcas asked.

"There are so many good ones," Steph said.

"Such as?" In two minutes Dorcas got more opinions out of the girl than Anna had in two years. Nureyev was stunning, but who except Fonteyn could stand up to him? D'Amboise was god. Erik Bruhn was fantastic but on toe Steph was an inch too tall for him. Delibes didn't score for male dancers as well as female. Anna had never thought of it that way. Then they were talking about Balanchine's Stravinsky ballets, why Mr. B. hadn't ever touched *Sacre* or *Petrouchka*.

Anna felt by-passed, left out. She sneaked a peek under the saucer, daubed at the stain with her napkin. She sat listening through another cup of coffee. Then Dorcas apologized and said she had to meet a woman from Texas for lunch—a terrible bore, but NBT was hoping she'd give sets for the gala.

Anna realized she hadn't straightened out the question of the scholarship. She began to bring it up again, but Steph gave her an odd look and she stopped.

Dorcas bustled them into the foyer. Steph asked where the bathroom was. Now was Anna's chance to settle that scholarship, but Dorcas kept talking and didn't give her an opening.

"What a perfect little lady. Did you send her to school?"

"Dance class since she was seven."

"But did you send her away?"

"Why would I send her away? She's a wonderful kid—never gives me any trouble."

"You never remarried?"

"Are you kidding? Once around that dog track was enough for me. Anyway, I had my hands full."

"How I admire you, Anna. How I admire you both."

"Wait till you see her audition. That'll really give you something to admire."

Dorcas took Anna's hands. "Darling—whatever happens— we're friends now, aren't we?"

"Of course we're friends. Didn't you get my Christmas cards?"

"I loved your Christmas cards."

"Well, yours were nice too."

Steph was standing there. Dorcas wished her good luck and kissed her.

Going down in the elevator, Anna thought about Volmar and her stomach made a fist. "Get some sleep tonight, honey. Tomorrow you're going to knock those idiots dead."

\*     \*     \*

Steph's eyes worried Anna. Those studios had tall windows, natural light, and nothing made a face look more washed out. Anna sat Steph down in the hotel room and tried a few strokes of water-insoluble brown liner.

Steph pulled away. "It's an audition, I'm not supposed to wear stage make-up."

"This isn't stage make-up. It's just so they'll notice you a little better. Hold still."

"Mom, it's not a performance."

"You got four hundred kids going against you for ten scholarships. Today's a performance. You remember your variation?"

Steph nodded. Anna had made her prepare a short solo with a gorgeous backward hop in arabesque. Maybe she'd need it, maybe she wouldn't. Better safe than sorry.

"These lids look like dropsy. Someday when we're rich I'm going to give you surgery for Christmas."

Anna remembered her own auditions and she knew the traps. In the taxi she tested Steph.

"They'll shout combinations at you ten miles long. You have to remember and you have to be ready."

Anna made up combinations of steps. Steph tried to recite them back.

"You won't have time and you won't have breath. Use your fingers—mark the combinations. Its the only way they'll stay with you."

Steph marked. When Anna made up crazy combinations Steph marked those too, which showed she was reacting, not thinking, and that was exactly what a dancer had to do.

They arrived at the school good and early. Anna knew auditions: you never had time to warm up. That was another of the traps. Steph was going to be warmed up and ready today.

They went to the desk, where a receptionist gave Steph a piece of cardboard with two holes and a string.

"Wear it around your neck. That's your number."

The number was 32, which told Anna there were thirty-one little girls and thirty-one moms ahead of them. It looked more like eight million when they pushed through the door.

"Where the hell are we going to warm you up?" Anna muttered. "Never mind. Go change. I'll find somewhere."

Steph went to the girls' dressing room. With nervous, fumbling fingers she changed clothes and put her number on. The girls who already had scholarships were watching the others. They seemed sleek and worldly and enviably grown up as they sipped coffee and smoked cigarettes, and slightly cruel as they talked, not caring if they were overheard.

"Baby pink hand-knit—do you believe it?"

"Volmar hates leg warmers—he'd puke."

Steph's leg warmers were green, machine-knit. She took them off anyway.

"Oh, God—*she'll* never get in, not with that flouncy skirt."

Anna had bought Steph the flouncy skirt especially for the audition. But these girls knew the judges better than her mother, and Steph took the skirt off too.

"Where's your skirt?" Anna cried.

"I don't want to wear it."

Twelve dollars and fifty cents and she didn't want to wear it. "And your leg warmers!"

"I don't want the judges to see me in leg warmers."

Too late now to argue. Anna pulled Steph into the ladies' room and slapped her hand down on the edge of the sink. "Profile to the mirror and *plié*. Come on. If you don't stay warm you'll never hold your turn-out."

"Mom, you're embarrassing me."

Anna tossed a nod at a girl who was warming up two sinks down. "She's not embarrassed, why should you be?"

The other girl was so deep in concentration her eyes could have been fastened to her reflection with wires. She had hair a little less blond than Steph and eyes a little darker.

Anna clapped her hands, driving Steph through *pliés* and *tendus*. Girls dashed in and dashed out, peeing, washing hands, needing the sink, but Anna kept clapping and she kept her little girl warm right up till the moment the voice on the loudspeaker called, "Numbers 1 through 40, rehearsal room 4."

"That's us. Now remember, don't try to do it by watching the other girls. Half of them are wrong and the other half are copying someone else. Do exactly what the teacher says and do it fast." Anna pushed Steph through the mob and into rehearsal room 4. She waved good luck and Steph waved back.

The dance teacher had braced himself in the doorway. He funneled the girls past with flicks of the hand, ready to block any momma or friend who tried to crash the audition. *My God*, Anna thought. *Hugh Williams. Ballet Caravan.* She'd seen him just after World War II in *Til Eulenspiegel.* So that's what had happened to Hugh Williams: dyed hair and a mouth stitched into a tight little pout and he was running the cattle auction for NBT.

Anna wondered if Marty would have ended up like that. Fat chance.

And then she noticed the other girl going in too, the blonde from the bathroom, and she thought, *Uh-oh, two blondes, same height, and that one has a better turn-out, why the hell couldn't Steph have drawn a number over 40?*

\*    \*    \*

The teacher closed the door. He clapped his hands for attention.

"All right, boys and girls—excuse me, *boy* and girls—take your positions at the barres. Numerical order, please."

It took a half hour's jostling and Steph could see the teacher getting more bored and more bad-tempered with each wasted minute. When numbers 1 through 40 were finally straight he put down his coffee and called the first exercise.

"*Plié* combination first second fourth fifth position. Reverse it yourselves." He snapped it out as though it were one word, almost too quickly to grasp. *He did that on purpose*, Steph realized. It was his revenge for the fumbled half hour.

The pianist oompahed the 2/4 *plié* rhythm. He obviously had a grudge against anything with a keyboard.

*Ronds de jambe* piled up on top of *pliés*—"Reverse it yourselves!" and then came the leg-stretching *tendus.* "*Demi-*

*plié, tendu devant,* up, *demi-plié* in fourth, *tendu,* close." The teacher stalked up and down the barres. He had the disgusted look of a farmer inspecting rows of blighted corn.

"*Battement* right leg; open to side; balance *à la seconde.*"

The *battement*—a fluttering movement of the foot, like beats of a bird's wings—required speed, but most of the girls were up to it. It was at the first balance that candidates began failing. The floor thudded with falling bodies. Some girls could not let go of the barre. Others let go and had to grab it again. Some let go and staved off a fall by a quick close into fifth position.

"Reverse into *battement à la seconde;* half *pointe;* bring legs together—"

The movements became complex now, and the dancers marked with their hands, pressing the directions into their memory.

"In fifth standing, *soutenu* into reverse."

Failures came more and more rapidly. Some girls did *en dedans* instead of *en dehors,* inward instead of outward. Some didn't bring their legs up before the turn. Others brought them up after the *rond de jambe* and fell off their balance. Some got as far as the balance but couldn't keep their turn-out.

Sweat was running into Steph's eyes. Her center was wobbling and her leg muscles were screaming but she stayed balanced and she stayed turned out. The teacher's eyes gave her a flick up and a flick down. He clapped.

"Girls put on *pointe* shoes, please."

As Steph was changing shoes a girl sat down beside her. Steph recognized the little blonde who had warmed up at the other sink in the ladies' room. There was a sweetness in her expression that made Steph say, "Hello. My name's Steph. For Stephanie."

The girl looked at her and smiled. "I'm Chris. For Christine." The number on her cardboard was 7. They were lacing up their shoes and there was no time to shake hands.

"What a rush," Steph said. "I've never auditioned before. What about you?"

"I'm not auditioning."

That baffled Steph. "Then why are you here?"

"It's a trick on my parents—kind of. They could pay to send me to school, only they don't think ballet's important. But if I'm good enough to win a scholarship they'll change their minds and let me stay in New York. I hope."

All sorts of wondering went through Steph. It sounded nice to have two parents and to have rich parents. But parents who didn't want you to dance sounded awful.

"I'm sorry you have parents like that."

"They're all right—they're just idiots when it comes to ballet."

"I hope you make it."

"Thanks. I hope you make it too. *Merde*." It was bad luck to say "Good luck" in ballet, so you said "*Merde*" instead, which was French for *shit*. Steph had learned that from her teachers. Chris pronounced the word as though she had studied French.

"*Merde*," Steph said.

For center work the teacher divided the candidates into odds and evens. Steph was even. She watched the odds' adagio, the slow, flowing movements. Some of the girls had flawless arabesques and extended their leg in *développé* straight to their ear.

*I'm not that good*, she thought, but when it came evens' turn she tried harder than she'd ever tried in her life, and she was almost that good.

The teacher put them through pirouette combinations and the little jumps of *petit allegro* and the great leaps of *grand allegro*. "Here's where we separate the boy from the girls," he said, and he gave the girls *fouettés* and hops *en pointe*. Then it was the boy's turn to do pirouettes *à la seconde*. The girls sat against the walls and watched.

"It's too bad he's not better," Chris whispered.

"It's too bad he's not even good-looking," Steph whispered.

"He'll pass, though, won't he?"

"Sure. There are never enough boys in ballet school."

The audition went on an hour. The teacher consulted his notebook. "Please step to the left as I call off your number."

He did not call off 7, and Steph felt a pang as Chris was left standing on the right. But he didn't call off 28 either, and the boy stayed on the right, and he didn't call off 32, and Steph was left with them. The teacher glanced at the larger group.

"You may go."

And then at Chris and Steph and the boy and the twelve others standing on the right.

"Come back Thursday, same time."

\*     \*     \*

Thursday, on the reception desk, a huge sign with hasty-looking letters reminded visitors that points beyond were absolutely off limits. No one else paid it any attention; Anna didn't see why she should.

She pressed past the desk with its one frantic attendant, squeezed through the churning mob. The narrow stairway opened onto a corridor of gray-carpeted walls with observation windows that looked down into the studios.

"Coming through, please! Let me through! I've got a girl down there!"

She pushed her way to a front position at the studio 3 window. Four free-standing barres had been placed like police barricades across the floor. Six dozen girls in tights and leg warmers were limbering up. All she could hear were the muffled strokes of a piano, fistfuls of the "Pizzicato Polka" from *Sylvia* that seemed to come from two blocks away.

Her eye searched for Steph.

A clear slanting sun fell through the windows, flattening the girls to silhouettes with bands of light flickering around the edges. They all looked the same. Anna squirmed to a better position, squinted down at the mirrored wall. Suddenly a movement at the center barre tugged her eye.

*There she was!*

That frail little girl all by herself, practicing quick, tiny jumps—that had to be Stephanie. Her golden hair was drawn back, fastened with a tortoise-shell barrette.

Anna could feel the child's concentration, her hope and terror. She wished she could reach and touch her and whisper, "It'll be all right—you'll make it!" But it was a mother's business to know such things—and to keep silent; for the moment, the girl needed all the terror she could muster.

It was beautiful to watch Steph's feet. They fell so lightly, not even striking the floor, but skimming it like a breeze.

Now Steph stood free of the barre. Even with her hands on her hips, her arms were rounded, the hands continuing the delicate line. She *relevé*'d up onto the toe of the left foot. The right leg lifted and bent inward, the foot curving up to touch the left knee. How many students, Anna wondered, could curve their feet like *that!*

The arms extended up and out like arcing wings. *Plié* now—the body dipped, the supporting leg bent at the knee. The free leg whipped out to the right. The girl spun clockwise, full circle. Anna counted the *fouettés:* one, two, three . . .

*Six fouettés!* Six *perfect fouettés*—for *practice!*

Anna wished Volmar had seen *that!*

The dazzling blur that was Steph spun to a stop, came to rest in fourth position: right foot *sur la pointe*, left foot perfectly turned out, arms arched overhead with hands barely grazing fingertips.

The girl turned. Her profile was clear and sharp against the window.

Anna's heart gave a painful thump against her ribs. It was not Steph, not her girl at all. It was that pug-nosed, chicken-breasted little creature who'd been hogging the other sink in the ladies' room before audition.

It took a long moment for the shock to subside and then Anna was able to smile at her mistake. What a laugh, she thought. That kid would never make it. Terrible arms. No *port de bras*.

\*   \*   \*

In studio 3, sixty-five girls and ten boys nervously warmed up for the final audition. The barres were overflowing with dancers, and anything else that could stand still was pressed into service—the piano, chairs, window sills, even girls and boys offering shoulders and hands to one another. The room was a jungle of stretching limbs and bending torsos and waving arms and bodies that popped twirling into the air.

On the stroke of ten the door opened.

Through the jungle, clearing a narrow path of stillness, came the judges, single file. They took their places on wooden chairs in the front of the room, blocking the mirror.

"Who's that?" Chris pointed unobtrusively.

"Dorcas Amidon," Steph said. "She's on the board."

The two girls recognized the others from photographs: Marius Volmar, whose face seemed to relax naturally into a scowl; and Jean-Pierre Bonnefous and Patricia McBride, the husband-and-wife team from New York City Ballet—he was even handsomer than his pictures; she had a girlish beauty and a kind smile, yet neither of them looked as though they wasted a minute or a judgment.

"I never believed they were *real*," Chris whispered.

"I still don't," Steph said. She could feel waves of authority radiating from the four. Nervousness began creeping up from her feet.

A dapperly dressed man strode to the front of the room.

"He's the dance master with NBT," Chris whispered. "There was an article on him in *Dance News*. He's supposed to be a real terror."

He looked like a terror, Steph thought. He did not need to clap his hands or clear his throat for attention. His very posture, the energy focused through his narrow eyes, commanded silence; and the silence crushed the room. He introduced the judges, thanking McBride and Bonnefous for volunteering their time and expertise.

The candidates applauded. Steph felt odd, as though she were applauding her own executioner.

The candidates were divided into groups of fifteen. Those not auditioning sat against the walls, watching the routine and marking it. From the very first *plié* Steph could tell today was going to be tough.

"Jerry Zimmerman's a real pianist," Chris whispered. "He played *Other Dances* last night, with Baryshnikov and Makarova."

Steph had never seen *Other Dances*, but she knew it was one of Jerome Robbins' piano ballets, with the piano onstage. She daydreamed that someday she would call those people Misha and Natasha and Jerry. After all, ballet was a first-name world.

But then she saw how difficult the *tendu* combinations were, and she thought, with a pang of dispair, *Maybe they'll always be last names to me*.

The barre work was longer than before. The adagio had more

balances and turns. The *petit allegro* was quicker, with five and six beats of the feet during some of the jumps. The *grand allegro* called for full extensions in the air and feather-soft landings.

The judges took notes on large yellow note pads. From time to time one of them leaned to whisper something in another's ear. Steph could not tell from their eyes what they were thinking or even which dancers they were watching. Their eyes took everything in, let nothing out. They were experienced eyes, exacting eyes, and they frightened her.

Chris's group was called, and Steph whispered, *"Merde."*

Chris was nervous and it showed. She rushed combinations, finishing ahead of the music. The pirouettes were weak and twice she turned *en dedans* instead of *en dehors*.

Yet for all the nervousness, the basics were there. The movement of the arms was graceful. The feet stayed arched and the spine never stiffened. She moved lyrically, even in the mistakes. Steph envied her balance in arabesque: without the slightest hint of rush or unsteadiness, Chris extended fully, and it seemed she could have held the position for all eternity.

Marius Volmar motioned the dance master over and whispered to him.

"Girls, if you please," the dance master said, "we'll take that arabesque balance once again."

When Chris came back to sit Steph whispered, "Volmar likes you. I saw him whisper to Pat McBride."

Chris was fretful and fidgety. She pulled roughly at her laces. "I danced like an elephant."

"You were wonderful!" Steph cried.

"No. I was nervous."

What Steph felt was worse than nervousness. By the time her group was called her body was tense and her *développés* weren't anywhere near what they'd been in rehearsal and her balances wobbled like sick gyroscopes.

"I flunked," she whispered to Chris afterward.

"But you were beautiful!" Chris said.

Steph stared at the blue eyes, wide set in the pink-white face, and she saw the utter honesty of a child. They sat together against the wall and waited through the last groups and then they waited in throat-choking silence for the verdict.

Patricia McBride seemed to be totaling up points on her pad.

Marius Volmar sat with his arms crossed as though his mind was made up. Dorcas Amidon and Jean-Pierre Bonnefous conferred, whispering. Occasionally a glance or a pencil pointed. Heads nodded. Heads shook. Faces did not smile.

The room seemed very small and tight and hot. Watches could be heard ticking in pockets and bags.

The dancers' minds raced back through time, through the ten years of turned-out legs and arched feet and bent bodies, the ten years of class after school and class on Saturday, the ten years of never having time for parties or even for friends, the ten years of sweat and sacrifice and never giving up, the ten years' preparation for this moment.

And now they prayed.

Marius Volmar handed the dance master a piece of yellow paper. The dance master read off the numbers of the candidates who had won scholarships. There were ten. Of the three hundred ninety who had spent half their lives in preparation and hope, ten had made it.

Chris's number came third and she stifled back a yelp.

Steph's number came heart-poundingly, agonizingly last and she didn't bother to stifle back her yelp. She screamed with unbelieving happiness and hugged Chris and ran to tell her mother.

# three

Anna was sick with relief. She hugged Steph and whirled her around. "Didn't I tell you—didn't I *tell* you?"

"I couldn't have done it without you, Mom."

"Come off it. You did the footwork. All I did was the nagging."

A girl had stepped quietly out of the crowd and stood two feet from them. She held a fistful of five- and ten-dollar bills crunched in one hand. It took Anna an instant, and then she remembered. She had mistaken the girl for Steph. But that had been a trick of backlighting. Now she could see there was hardly any resemblance. The hair was dark blond, and without the barrette it hung straight to the shoulders. The eyes had a vacant, staring blue innocence and the nose was a little upturned thumb of a thing you'd see on a child's doll.

"Excuse me, Steph," the girl said. "I don't have a dime for the phone." The hand holding the money made a jerky movement as though to exchange it all for ten cents.

"Oh—sure." Steph stretched an arm into her shoulder bag, and after an instant's burrowing beneath the canvas out came a dime.

"Thanks. I have to tell my mother I passed."

Anna watched the girl edge her way across the crowded vestibule. "Steph," she said thoughtfully, "who is that girl?"

"Her name's Christine. She's nice."

"She passed?"

"She passed."

Anna watched the girl drop a dime into the pay phone. The lips were puckered in an odd pout and the chin was weaker than Steph's, tiny like a cat's. Anna wasn't sure a girl could get anywhere in dance with a chin like that. "Where's she from?"

"I don't know," Steph said.

Anna thought of all that money clenched in a nervous fist. Fifty dollars cash and the girl didn't have a dime. A dime meant a local call, so the mother had to live in New York. But she hadn't even come to her daughter's audition. Anna couldn't figure it.

"She talks nicely," Anna said. "Educated."

"I guess she's my first ballet friend."

Anna stared. Same height. A little bit the same build. Otherwise no resemblance between the two girls at all. Still she remembered that instant of confusion through the observation window and she couldn't shake a slightly eerie feeling.

"Go change, honey," she said. "Let's celebrate. I'll buy you a shrimp salad at the Theater Pub."

\* \* \*

When Steph went into the ladies' room Chris was standing with a handful of paper towel bunched to her face.

"Hurt your eye?" Steph asked.

"I can't join the school." Chris's voice was clogged and weeping and there was a pair of almost new ballet slippers in the trash basket.

Steph was stunned. "But why not?"

"My mother says I can't live in New York alone. She says there are plenty of ballet schools in Chicago."

"Schools, sure. But *ballet* is here."

"Oh, Steph, I was so sure—if I proved I was good—"

"And you *are* good," Steph said, "and you *did* prove it and your parents *have* to let you join the school. That's all there is to it."

Chris shook her head. Her eyes were red and swollen and miserable. "I can't force them."

"And they can't force *you*."

"They can, Steph. They can."

There was surrender in Chris and it made Steph angry. She had seen Chris dance and she knew Chris was strong and she knew Chris had it in her to fight these parents. All she needed was a little faith in herself.

"Are these your shoes?" Steph pulled the ballet slippers out of the trash.

"They were."

"They still are and there's still some dance left in them. Come on."

She took Chris to the vestibule where Anna was waiting. She explained the situation. Anna's eyes exploded in disbelief.

"Your mother *what*? She *what*? Does she know how many girls that school turns *down*?"

Chris shook her head. Anna stared at this child, timid and weeping and caved in. It wasn't her child but it was still a child and something in her bled for it.

"She doesn't come to your audition, she doesn't let you join the top ballet school *in the world*, you call that a *mother*?" And then a collision took place in Anna's head. Morality crashed headlong into practicality and practicality flicked out a spark of inspiration. Anna had an idea. Two birds with one stone. "Where is this mother of yours?"

"At the Hotel Pierre," Chris said.

"I want to talk to her."

\*    \*    \*

A tall swift woman with ash-blond hair headed them off at the entrance hall. "Christine, go put on a clean dress this minute."

Chris introduced Anna and Steph to her mother. "They gave me a lift from the audition."

Mrs. Avery wore a sapphire pendant and it matched the eyes that raked Anna up and down. "That was very kind of you. Christine, your father has guests. Now will you please get out of those filthy clothes before anyone sees you."

Anna spoke up. "Steph, go help Chris. I want to talk to Mrs. Avery."

"I'm sorry, Mrs.—I really don't have time." Mrs. Avery tossed a nod toward the drawing room. Guests stood about in groups with drinks and cigarettes in their hands, talking in voices that were still clipped, not yet drunk. Maids circulated with trays of tiny sandwiches. Anna smelled more money than she'd ever smelled in one place before.

"Do you know how unhappy you've made your daughter?" Anna said. "This could have been the happiest day of her life."

"I don't care to discuss it."

"If you'd seen her cry, believe me, you'd care."

"I've seen Christine cry, thank you."

"And so have I, Mrs. Avery. And so did half that school."

"You're very kind to concern yourself, but you don't understand the situation and you don't know Christine."

"I don't need to know Chris. I like her. And I want to help."

"There's no way you can help."

"My girl's a dancer, your girl's a dancer. I can help. Now let's go somewhere quiet and sit down for thirty seconds."

Mrs. Avery's silk print dress pulled itself taut across the narrow, almost visible bones of her shoulders and hips. There was no movement except the slow turning out of her lower lip. Anna felt a surge of impatience.

"Mrs. Avery, I'm not doing this for my own fun."

Mrs. Avery stared at her a very long moment. "I'm sorry. You're very kind and I'm not very polite, am I?" She took Anna through a doorway and into a bedroom. She closed the door. The words came in a tight rush. "My husband and I are at the ends of our ropes with that girl. We don't want Christine to be a dancer."

"So why did you let her get this far?"

"We never intended to. It happened so gradually. Day by day, year by year. We never imagined it would turn out this way." Her eyes met Anna's for one instant of naked pleading, then fell in embarrassment. "I haven't the right to bore you with all this."

"Bore me. Come on." Anna smoothed the already smooth corner of a twin bed and settled herself down for a good listen. She was interested. Other people's problems were never dull.

"It's strange," Mrs. Avery said. "You always hear of people having trouble with the adopted child."

"She's adopted?"

"No. She's our natural child—our only natural child. We had her first, and she was born sick, and the doctors said—don't have any more. So we adopted Sammy and Ruthie. They're wonderful children. They've never given us any trouble at all. But Christine—she's been an agony for us."

Somehow Anna couldn't feel sorry. This woman's dress and jewelry and this penthouse and those maids in the other room didn't look like agony to Anna. So Mrs. Avery had a little trouble with one kid; at least she called it trouble. So what? She sure wasn't having any trouble with her bank account.

"Christine's loved dance ever since she was a child. It was the only thing that seemed to bring her out of herself. She'd sit in a corner of her room—four years old—never moving, never talking. We weren't sure she even knew *how* to talk."

Mrs. Avery moved to the window and stood gazing down at the park.

"One day the radio was on—a concert of some sort, I forget. She began moving. The nurse called me—'Mrs. Avery, she's moving her feet!' Suddenly she was dancing. She was *alive*. I was so happy I wanted to cry."

Mrs. Avery's hands with their short gleaming nails clasped and unclasped. There was a gold rattle of bracelets.

"After that she asked for music. She actually said the words. 'Music, please, music.'"

"We gave her a phonograph. We gave her records. She laughed and she danced. Overnight she was a normal child. Almost normal. The doctors said, 'Put her in dance class. Keep her there. It will be therapy. It will help.' We were so relieved we didn't think."

Mrs. Avery's forehead wrinkled. Her voice shrank to a monotone.

"In kindergarten she did eurhythmics. In first grade we started her in elementary dance. By the time she was ten she was in the children's division of a professional ballet school. She kept moving up to the next level. Always the next level. 'The next will be the last,' we kept telling ourselves. But the teachers kept saying she had talent."

"Teachers always say that. They have to earn a living too."

Mrs. Avery looked at Anna. The eyes of a complete stranger were fixed on Anna Lang and spilling tears. Mrs. Avery blotted her cheeks with the back of her hand.

"But she *does* have talent. That's the terrible part of it."

"Mrs. Avery—what do you and your husband want out of that girl?"

"We want her to be well and happy."

"She can't be well and happy and dance?"

"Two miles from Evanston we have one of the best neurological institutes in the world." Mrs. Avery sank onto the edge of a chair. Her voice seemed to fight its way up through layers of time and sadness. "Christine goes once every twelve weeks for a complete examination. Twice a year doctors inject dye into an artery of her brain. They track it on an X-ray scanner. They test every reflex. They measure the level of every mineral in her blood."

"What's her problem?"

"It's called Petersen's syndrome. It happens mostly in people with Scandinavian backgrounds." Mrs. Avery exhaled. Her pendant caught the bright penthouse sunlight and sparkled. "They think it's genetic. She's had it since birth. When she was born—she didn't cry. Can you imagine a baby not crying?"

"You're complaining?"

"If a baby can't cry, it *dies*."

"All right, she needs medicine, she needs checkups. What's the hassle? She can get all that in New York."

"A professional dancer has to tour."

Anna hesitated a moment. "And who says she's a professional?"

"Why couldn't she have failed the audition?" Mrs. Avery's voice clenched. "Why does she have to be a dancer? Can't she just go to college like other girls? Can't she just marry and be happy? She doesn't even have boy friends!"

Anna frowned. "Can we keep this simple? We're talking about ballet school, period. And for every hundred girls that get as far as your daughter, not three make it any further."

"And if she's one of the three?"

Anna had listened closely, all eyes and nods. She had caught enough of Mrs. Avery's gist to know the direction her answer should take. "Look, Mrs. Avery—I saw your girl dance. Now it was only an audition, and probably she was nervous. But confidentially, I don't think you have much to worry about."

"I'm not sure I follow you."

"No flow. Your daughter doesn't flow."

Mrs. Avery sat suddenly very still in her chair. "What are you saying?"

"Okay. There's more to ballet than knowing the positions and the steps. Any idiot with a memory can do that. You have to make one step lead into the next. You have to phrase. Like music. You don't sing one note at a time. You put them together and you get a melody, right? Or talking. No one talks. Like. This. Well, your daughter breaks her phrases."

Mrs. Avery was squinting at Anna, squinting hard. Her plucked eyebrows came down in a wedge.

"I'm not criticizing," Anna said quickly. "Each individual step is great. Fantastic. A knockout. She has a beautiful body and she must have had terrific teachers. But she doesn't put it together. Looking at her is like flipping through snapshots in a how-to book."

"Christine is a bad dancer?"

"Not bad, I didn't say bad. Chris is good. And so are two thousand other girls that come crawling out of Kansas every year. Being good isn't good enough. To be a ballerina you have to be great."

"And I suppose your girl *is* great?"

"How do I know? I'm only her mother."

Mrs. Avery drew herself up sharply; and then the breath left her in a sigh. "But you *want* her to be a dancer. That's the difference."

"Put it this way. I'm not stopping her from trying. And I don't think you should try to stop Chris. Let her fall on her own face by herself."

"And if she doesn't?"

"She will."

"I wish I had your confidence, Mrs.—"

"Lang."

"Lang. But she didn't fall on anything today."

"Look, a puppet could do what she did today. So, she's better than four hundred other girls. You should have seen those other four hundred. Half of them couldn't hold an arabesque if you hoisted them in a sling."

Faint voices floated over the hum of the air conditioner. Somebody laughed in the other room. Mrs. Avery shook her head. She pursed her lips. The oval of her face came to a point.

"What's an arabesque?"

"Arabesque?" Anna said. "It's a pose. You balance on one leg and the other leg's out behind you."

Mrs. Avery nodded. "What do you suggest I do? She has no relatives here. I have a family in Evanston. I certainly can't move to New York to look after her."

"Board her," Anna said.

"She wouldn't take care of herself. She has no practicality."

"Board her with me." *Why not?* Anna thought. The responsibility didn't sound all that bad. This woman could pay two, three hundred a week. Anna and Steph could get a big apartment, something comfortable for a change. And Steph would have a friend; someone her own age to talk to.

"I'll see she takes her medicine and goes for her checkups. She'll eat the same food I give my own girl. Look, Mrs. Avery. Do it your way, she blames you all her life. Do it my way, she blames herself a year."

"I wish she didn't have to blame anyone."

"So? Life's hard. But dance is harder. Mrs. Avery, I was a dancer. I didn't make it. I've seen your girl. She's not going to make it. So relax."

Mrs. Avery's finger traced out a thread in the arm of the chair. She looked up. Her face seemed frightened and tiny.

"All right, Mrs. Lang. We'll try it your way."

# four

And so Anna Boborovsky Barlow Lang became the manager of a sunny five-room boarding establishment on West Seventy-ninth Street. There was an elevator and there was a doorman and the building had cable TV. It was more luxury than she had known in twenty years. Christine Avery's room and board almost covered rent and food for Anna and Steph. It was a happy period for Anna: every penny she earned was profit. She was able to do things she'd always dreamed of—buy a freezer, open a savings account, get pretty clothes for Steph.

The girls took three classes a day, six days a week: regular dance, *pointe*, partnering, Russian folk dance; plus three hours a week of solfège, de-re-mi and slapping out rhythms and sight singing. The first week they were dead tired. The second week they were just very tired. The third week they couldn't remember what it was like not to be dancing six hours six days a week.

The school allowed students to choose between Madame Lvovna's class and Madame Zhemkuzhnaya's. Steph asked her mother's advice.

"They're both nuts," Anna said. "You'll get better balance from Lvovna and Zhemkuzhnaya will give you strength."

"Which do I need more?"

"Both."

Steph went to both and Chris tagged along.

In her first class, Zhemkuzhnaya picked on a girl's pirouette. "What is that—pirouette or philosophy? If you want to be philosopher, go to Lvovna—if you want to learn dance from me, you learn how to *work!*"

In *her* first class, Lvovna picked on a girl's balance. "You will wind up with *muscles!* Look like one of Zhemkuzhnaya's little bulls! You'll be good for pulling plow or being prostitute!"

Steph compared rumors. She compared firsthand impressions.

Lvovna had trained at the Maryinsky—now the Kirov— where Pavlova, Karsavina, Nijinsky, Nureyev, Baryshnikov, and two million other legends had trained. She had danced with the original Ballet Russe. She was in her seventies now. Time had made her even tinier than the sylph suggested by her photographs. She walked with the help of a silver-knobbed stick. The turban, the dress that always came to mid-calf, the comfy unstylish shoes, the sweater she wore over her shoulders on cold days, were always black. If it hadn't been for the turquoise in the turban, you'd have thought she was in mourning.

Zhemkuzhnaya was in her fifties. She was built like an ox. She dressed in navy-blue pants suits and white turtlenecks. She wore her dyed red hair piled on her head and she clattered through the school on platform heels. She claimed to have danced with the Bolshoi, but not even the students believed her. "Look at her," they would whisper. "Tell me she danced with *anyone.*"

Steph and Chris went to see both women's dancers in performance.

Zhemkuzhnaya's dancers had strength; Lvovna's had lyricism. Zhemkuzhnaya's looked like gymnasts; Lvovna's looked like tuberculars. Zhemkuzhnaya's were bulky little machines who could do miracles on brute strength alone. They could pirouette any number of times, barrel turn, leap, get from any position to any other; the movement was choppy, but they got screams and applause. Lvovna's were gazelles who could balance and sustain and tie eighteen movements into a single flow. They got breath-held silence and applause.

It struck Steph as the difference between grabbing and sustaining, between filibustering and mesmerizing. She decided she wanted to sustain and mesmerize.

"I'm going to study with Lvovna," she told her mother.

"Why not?" Anna said. "Lvovna has good contacts."

Chris said, "Then I'll study with Lvovna too."

*    *    *

Lvovna had her own way of doing everything.

At the very first closed class, after it was too late for the students to transfer out, she rapped her cane on the floor. "Now you will unlearn all that you have learned—or what you have been pleased to call learning."

Madame was too old to demonstrate movements herself. She sat on a chair and watched, hawklike, while a professional student demonstrated. In ballet classes the world over you began with your left hand on the barre and exercised the right side of your body first. In Lvovna's, you began with your right hand on the barre.

Occasionally her cane would snap up at a girl. "You—turn your leg out more." Madame demanded a perfect turn-out. It struck Steph as too perfect, an exaggeration that ground your knees and hips to powder. But she wanted to please Madame and she did as told.

"Don't balance too long," Lvovna would say, pointing the cane. "You get ugly calves like Zhemkuzhnaya." Steph was careful not to balance too long.

Madame demanded impossible stretches at the barre that became less impossible with time. If you weren't extending far enough in balance she would grab you and yank you further. If you angered her she would chase you around the room and spank you with the cane.

There was an unwritten color code in class. Madame once sent a girl home for wearing a red blouse, and she made Steph leave her red plastic leg warmers in the corridor.

"Red is Soviet," she stated. "Not artistic."

All sorts of people came to Lvovna's class to be humiliated. Steph once found herself doing *tendus* next to Dame Margot

Fonteyn, and in February of her first year the dancers from a Broadway musical began showing up.

One day Madame covered the mirrors in black cloth. At first Steph thought it was because of a national hero who had died the day before. But that was not the case.

"A true dancer should not need to see himself," Madame said. "He should feel. A great dancer should be able to dance blind. And very soon I am going to blindfold all of you."

Madame never went that far, but she did things almost as bad.

She exploded at a girl who could not pronounce *port de bras*, the French term describing the movement of the arms in classical ballet.

"Where were you born?"

"Here, Madame."

"New York City? Bronx? Brooklyn?"

"Yes, Madame."

"I do not care that your English is vile—utterly vile. But for a dancer not to speak French is inexcusable! French is the language of dance! You will take French lessons if you expect to continue in this class!"

"Yes, Madame."

Another time she exploded at Chris, not for the way she pronounced *port de bras*, but for the way she executed it.

"What do you call that monstrous movement with those paws?"

"I was going into second position *en haut*, Madame."

"A wheat field in a hurricane has more grace. If you have not grace it means you have not control, which means you will never dance, never."

"I'm sorry, Madame."

"And I am sorry—for you."

Chris dragged herself home like a broken-backed kitten. "Is my *port de bras* that awful?"

"It's fine," Steph said.

"Then why does Madame pick on me?"

It seemed to Steph that every dancer had to have an inner preserve of serenity, some private space to escape the world. In some dancers it took the form of stupidity; in others, a sense of humor or an ability to drop off to sleep anywhere, any time. Chris did not seem to have any sort of serenity at all, and it worried Steph.

"Madame does it to everyone," Steph said. "She does it to make us strong."

"All it does is make me smoke more cigarettes. I've gone through a pack since she screamed at me."

Steph looked at Chris's pale skin that seemed to tremble with each heartbeat. "You can't take it personally," she said. "Madame was screaming at your body, not you."

But she knew exactly what Chris was going through.

Like most dancers, Steph herself was up to a pack of cigarettes and five cups of coffee a day. Ballet school was a nervous life, a constant war with your body. You looked in the mirror and you didn't see Stephanie Lang: you saw a foot that didn't arch far enough and a left turn-out that kept slipping and an ass with just a hint of jelly when you went into arabesque. You saw eyes that would *never* project to the back of a high school auditorium, let alone the Met, a mouth that needed a pout-transplant if you ever expected to dance a Black Swan, breasts that you'd just as soon give to the girl next door, because the one thing you didn't need in ballet was a bust.

When you looked at a boy, you didn't think, *He's nice* or *He's sexy*, you thought, *How would he look partnering me?* If he was broad-shouldered, which most were, and tall, which most weren't, and strong, which they all were, and had long muscles, not the knotty bulges half of them developed, and if he could dance, you said: "*That* is for me"—because that was all that mattered in the opposite sex.

When you weren't arguing with your body or inspecting your feet for fungus and bunions, you were washing leotards or slamming doors on *pointe* shoes to break them in or putting stitches in the toes to make them last longer. Everything became dance, and there were days when you didn't have time to read a newspaper or even the energy to turn on the TV. Some of the students didn't know or care who the Vice-President of the United States was, and Steph had stopped caring too.

Dance demanded everything and gave no guarantees, no refunds. There was nothing fair about it. Nothing predictable, either. Steph saw some girls work themselves to death and get nowhere. She saw others work half as hard and get twice as far.

Some dancers were disqualified by their own bodies. A girl over five foot seven might have the most beautiful form in the world, but she'd never get a job; the big companies were scaling themselves to their Russian defectors, hiring Munchkins only. Or you might be overextended, with joints too flexible. You could do every leap and turn and stretch in ballet, but your line was broken, not classical, and there wasn't a damned thing you could do to correct it.

Some dancers were disqualified by their own zeal. There was an exercise called "the frog" to help stretch the legs: you lay on your stomach, legs to the side, bent at the knees—and risked wrecking your hips for life. If turn-out was your obsession, you went to sleep with telephone books on your knees—and dislocated your kneecaps.

If you were worried about weight you wore plastic sweat pants and put Saran Wrap around your legs and tried one of the diet fads that swept the school like measles: water, or water and wheat germ, or a carrot, a stick of celery, and a carton of plain yogurt. The diets took their toll. In Steph's first term two girls came down with mononucleosis and a third developed myasthenia gravis.

Some girls took birth control pills to cut out their periods. The pain of menstruation wasn't a problem—dancers routinely put up with far worse discomforts in every class and performance—but the embarrassment of having your period come unexpectedly *was* a problem. Ballet folklore was full of horror stories of White Swans caught in the climactic *pas de deux* without a Tampax. One girl in Steph's class, Marie-Claude from Switzerland, took the pill *and* smoked two packs of cigarettes a day. She came down with severe blood clots, lost sensation in her right arm. She left school to go to the hospital for surgery and never returned.

The school warned you that three classes a day were enough, but there were girls who sneaked off and took extra classes outside school and wound up with tendonitis and arthritis at age nineteen.

Some students worked out on their own, unsupervised, and there were accidents. An Argentinian girl attempted a *tour jeté*, a leaping turn in the air, and her partner wasn't paying attention.

She landed on the floor and snapped her Achilles' tendon. A girl from Wisconsin did the same thing and broke her toe. Neither girl danced again.

Even in the supervised classes there were accidents, some of them crippling. One girl did a *tour* into a boy's testicles. He had forgotten to wear his guard. He had to give up dance. One warm April day when a window at barre level was open, a boy from Arizona did a *piqué arabesque* turn, lost his balance, and went into the courtyard. He tried to *plié*, but it didn't save his legs.

There were times when Steph was sick of the risks, sick of the aches, times when the smell of sweaty exercise clothes and the sound of a thumping practice piano filled her with an almost hysterical nausea.

*Is this what I've given my life to?* a voice within her screeched. *Where's the joy, where's the fulfillment?*

There were times when she wanted to eat a strawberry shortcake or get drunk or smoke pot or have a lover or go to the theater or read a book about people who *didn't* dance. There were times when it seemed she had nothing, no friends, no hobbies, no ideas she could call her own, nothing but bunions and a turn-out and a pirouette.

There was a time, when Madame stopped her in mid-pirouette, when it seemed that all she had was the bunions.

"But, my dear," Madame said softly, "you are not remembering."

They were in class, and if Madame had come stumbling at her, the sure tip-off of a spanking, Steph would have run. But Madame approached with almost even steps and Steph stood holding her breath. The cane struck her, almost gently, buttock and stomach.

"Balance," said Madame.

The cane struck Steph's left foot, not so gently.

"Keep from sickling." It was called "sickling" when the foot slid out of position. "Ribs *in!* Knee *out!* Drop your pelvis!"

The cane gave successive and successively less gentle taps on each part of Steph's body as Madame reeled off its particular crime.

"Weight *forward!* Head *up!* Shoulders *down!* Abdomen *in;* back *in;* chest *up!* Hold your turn-out; keep your legs straight; and spot *correctly!*"

Steph tried, but it was impossible to remember everything with Madame standing there shouting. For ten minutes Steph was the center of attention, class dunce, trying and failing time after time. Scorched with humiliation, she remained after the others had gone.

"Madame," she said, "is there such a thing as a perfect ballet body?"

Madame's eyebrows arched. "Is no one perfect ballet body, no. It helps if limbs are long, torso short. Like yours."

"If there's no perfect ballet body, how can there be a perfect pirouette?"

"Are many different perfections."

Steph felt cold and exhausted, beyond help. "And do you expect them all of me?"

Madame stared at her. "Of course. Don't you?"

"Sometimes Madame makes me think—I should have studied nursing."

"Why not? So long as you are perfect nurse."

"I've seen performances—I've seen ballerinas, Madame's own students—who weren't perfect. Why must *I* be perfect?"

A dark vertical line appeared between Madame's eyes. "But naturally you see imperfect performances. It takes fifty Giselles, three dozen Auroras, before dancer can begin to call herself ballerina."

"Then why can't I be imperfect?"

Madame closed her eyes. A sigh whispered out of her. Sometimes they forgot who and what she was. She was a grandmother, an artist who had trained artists who had gone on to train other artists. She had had her firsts: there was Tmouravaya, her first ballerina, and there was Windermere, who was Tmouravaya's first. There could be only one first child and one first grandchild, and yet the students still came to her, asking to be her children, asking to be first. She had no room for firsts any more.

However, there was something special about the Lang girl. Something that entitled her to an honest answer.

"Ten thousand girls are trying to be dancers. One hundred of them *are* dancers. There are positions for ten of them. I want you to have one of those positions. When you are with a company, on the stage of Lincoln Center, when you are dancing Aurora and Giselle, *then* you can cheat. But not in this classroom. My dear, I would not be hard on you if I did not think there was hope."

Steph bowed her head. There was shame in her but there was happiness too and together they hardened into a fierce determination.

"Thank you, Madame."

Madame stayed behind to stare out the window. Halfway through her mentholated cigarette she saw the Lang girl hurrying up Sixty-sixth Street. There was no question in Madame's mind. The Lang girl had every sign of talent. She did not need Madame constantly at her side to solve every difficulty and correct every error. Quite the opposite. The girl learned through her skin. She watched this one's mistake, that one's success. She listened to Madame's shrieks and—most important—to Madame's silences. It took but a hint, and the girl understood.

The most Madame could do with such a student was to direct her a little here and there, shout at her now and then to keep her from getting lazy.

The Avery girl was a different case. She had ability potentially as great as Lang's, but she learned unpredictably. She had areas of fantastic intuition, areas of breath-taking incompetence. The most Madame could do with a case like Avery was to knock her like a punching bag.

Madame sighed. Soon it would be spring recital time, and Avery and Lang would be ready.

*I shall lose them,* she thought. *I have come to know their bodies and, a little bit, their souls; and, a little bit, I love them. I have given them their style. Whether they dance in Buenos Aires or Moscow or Chicago, they are Lvovna dancers. There is no more I can do. I must hold them like prize horses at the starting gate and point them in the right direction.*

She wondered what the right direction would be for Lang; and for Avery.

\*          \*          \*

"For you," Madame told the Lang girl two months before the recital, "the *Don Quixote pas de deux*—simplified, I regret to say, but very worthy simplification—Marius Volmar did it for me."

Madame turned to the Avery girl, whose eyes were stretched with almost pained expectancy.

"And for you, Snow *pas de deux* from *Nutcracker*."

"But, Madame—" the Avery girl stammered. It sounded like a protest and Madame nipped it.

"You will have good partners—best I can steal from Zhemkuzhnaya. You will look extremely lyric. Companies are looking for extremely lyric girls. I will coach you myself. It will mean working evenings, but if company takes you, you will have to get used to that anyway."

"*Will* a company take us?" the Avery girl asked. She stared at Madame with eyes that were dark and starved and eager and Madame stared back at her indignantly.

"How do I know?"

The child's gaze sank slowly to a crouching position. "But don't you have any idea?"

A wind of annoyance gusted through Madame. She rewarded persistence at the barre, not in cross-examination. She arranged her reply carefully. "I suppose company might be persuaded to take one of you. It should not astonish me too greatly."

Madame turned her back, ending the absurd conversation. For a moment neither Chris nor Steph spoke.

"One of us..." Chris's voice was pale and her lips were trembling.

Something was still waiting to be said. The two girls could feel it, like a presence outside a door whose bell had just softly rung. For two bone-crunching years they had been allies. It had never occurred to either of them that the alliance might one day have to end.

"Maybe a company will take us both," Steph said hopefully.

Chris's head was lowered. In her face was a gentle determination that seemed to reach out and touch the world. "I won't join a company that doesn't."

*She'd give up her chance for me,* Steph thought. *How odd and wonderful and brave. And foolish. And I love her for it.*

Steph took Chris's hand. "Then I won't either."

\*     \*     \*

Steph told her mother about the promise the next day. They were sitting at breakfast. Steph was dribbling honey onto the health-food cereal that one of her friends in toe class had said was good for energy.

"We gave each other our word of honor."

The child's face was serious. Eighteen years old and grim as an old woman. A red stop sign went up in Anna's brain.

"Eat some cottage cheese. I don't trust the protein in that stuff."

Anna went to the refrigerator. She ripped the lid of a Tupperware bowl and dolloped six good tablespoons of cottage cheese onto a plate.

"Mom, she's my best friend."

"She's your only friend, which, please God, is a situation you'll wake up and change."

Steph gave her a questioning look. "Why don't you like Chris?"

"Chris is an angel. I just want you to have friends like any other adult eighteen-year-old girl. And you don't need to go around throwing away promises like autographs. What if you get an offer from a company and she doesn't? Where'll you be then?"

Anna watched Steph stir the honey into the health-food yuck. She didn't see how a human could eat such bird feed, let alone dance eight hours a day on it.

"We'll both get offers."

"That so. Well, Sleeping Beauty, you have a scholarship to the top ballet school in the world. Those people worked with Petipa. Cecchetti. Balanchine. And they're paying *you*. I don't see anyone paying your dear sweet friend to stitch ribbons on a *toe* shoe."

"She could have had a scholarship, but she wanted to pay her own way."

"Luckily."

"Mom, you're being unfair. She—" Steph put down her spoon and began crying.

"Aw, honey, why tie yourself down? I know it's only a promise—but why? In ballet you travel light or you never make it."

Steph turned away from Anna's kiss. "Sometimes you sound

so mean. You say you want me to have friends and then you won't let me."

Anna exhaled a long, deep, weary breath. "I've been through it, honey. I made promises all my life. Sickness and health. For richer, for poorer. I know how it starts. And ends. Now hurry up or you'll be late for class."

Anna scraped the cottage cheese back into its bowl. *Kids*, she thought. *You teach them to read, you teach them to make their beds, you can't teach them to eat.*

"And take your new shoes," she called. "You got a crack in the pair you're using. I swear they make those things out of paper nowadays."

# five

Anna got to the recital hall a half hour early.

So did everyone else.

A mob was pushing past the single ticket-taker, streaming up and down the aisles trying to locate their seats. Anna wedged her way past two gossiping women into row M. She found her seat, settled herself, looked around her.

The theater was packed fifteen minutes before curtain. She saw dancers, ex-dancers, dance hopefuls, dance nobodies. You could always spot the nobodies because they dressed for the event like opening night at the Metropolitan Opera. Floor-length gowns at 5 P.M. on some of them.

Balanchine was there, and Robbins, and Tetley and Tudor and Twyla Tharp, scattered like flecks of gold among chattering parents who didn't even know who they were. Anna saw Marius Volmar slip into a seat five rows away and a twitch of anxiety tugged at her. Heads turned like a field of wheat in the wind. Nora Kaye and Herbert Ross were negotiating the steeply declined aisle. They made movies nowadays, Anna had heard, and Nora was working her butt off trying to get American Ballet Theatre back in shape.

The house lights dimmed, hurrying stragglers to their seats.

The theater sank into expectant silence. Anna's stomach made a knot. The student conductor came into the pit and the curtain rose to good-humored, tolerant applause. Anna's hands stayed in her lap, trembling.

The stage lights came up, and a stageful of children broke into movement.

These recitals always followed the same pattern. First came the kiddies for openers, six-year-olds cutesying their way through the Stravinsky *Happy Birthday* or *Circus Polka* and wearing any critical edge off the audience. After a stageful of bumbling toddlers, anyone who could go on half *pointe* would look like Melissa Hayden taking a twenty-foot fish dive into Nicholas Magallanes' arms.

The kids looked like kids, no *port de bras*. But the bare cyclorama looked surprisingly professional. So did the neat, simple costumes. *I'll bet the parents pay the cleaning bills,* Anna thought.

She settled back for the agony of waiting.

*     *     *

Lvovna watched from the wings, and Zhemkuzhnaya, whom she detested, stood watching beside her. There were always surprises in the student recitals. Lvovna saw things she could not possibly see in the studio: she saw who had courage in front of an audience and who did not; she saw who could hold an audience and who could not.

Now her eyes were fixed on the Bailey girl. Bailey could throw off double *fouettés* in class but onstage she was freezing up. Because they both had shocks in store, because Zhemkuzhnaya could not help that God had made her a Marxist mediocrity, Lvovna was willing to whisper to her.

"Bailey will teach—nothing more."

Evans, who barely trusted herself to pirouette in class, was responding to the applause, taking risks, changing her solo: a triple unsupported pirouette—naughty; but good, very good.

"I think Evans will dance in Stuttgart."

Zhemkuzhnaya nodded, and Madame knew these opinions would be repeated as though they were Zhemkuzhnaya's own.

Madame squinted. Sanchez, who could hold a balance

forever, could not hold the stage. What was this mystery called
stage presence; why could it not be taught?

"Luckily Sanchez is beautiful. She will marry."

Madame's eyes were caught by another, Levine, forgetting
her *port de bras*, but smiling the only smile onstage. The
audience saw nothing else but that smile. Levine could stumble
and they would still love her.

"Such a little thing, a smile. And so important. We should
teach them to smile in class."

"Do you think so?" Zhemkuzhnaya said.

"And it's interesting how they take to the music. For many,
this is their first orchestra. But what an orchestra!"

"Students," Zhemkuzhnaya said coldly.

"Young and unpaid and on fire with music," Madame said.
"These thirty-two pieces are playing with the joy of ninety. They
are a symphony that has not yet fossilized into a union."

"I do not care to discuss your economic theories."

Zhemkuzhnaya turned one way and Madame turned the
other. Two questioning, anxious faces were watching the stage.
*This will be interesting*, Madame thought: *Christine is lyric and
Stephanie has brio and I don't know if either of them has
courage.*

They should not have been in the wings and Madame should
have scolded, but she decided instead to chat.

"You are scared, I hope?" she said pleasantly.

"Scared stiff," Stephanie said.

"Good. Body must have proper tension before performance.
And you, Christine?"

"I'm all right."

Not good. Either she was not telling the truth or she was not a
dancer. Nor was Madame pleased by Christine's appearance.
Before performance a dancer's body was normally glazed with
the fine mist of warming up. But Christine's face was in a sweat.
Her body too. Madame could see the blouse of her tutu stuck to
her back in clots. This sweat did not come from stretched
muscles. It came from stretched nerves.

"Christine dear, how soon before you go on?"

There were three numbers to go before Chris's *pas de deux*
but already her heart had started racing wildly. "I'm third from
now, Madame."

"Then there is time. Go fill sink with water. Very cold, otherwise make-up will run. Put face under water. Count ten. Pat face, make-up will not smear. You will feel wonderful."

"Yes, Madame."

Christine did not appear happy with the idea and it occurred to Madame that she might not obey.

"Stephanie, go help her."

*     *     *

The girls went downstairs to the shower room. Steph let the water run till it was ice cold to her fingers. She plugged the sink.

"Dive in."

She could see the gulp ride down Chris's throat and then Chris plunged her head into the water. It was no count ten, but when she came up she looked like a drowned cat, the edges of her hair dark and plastered down.

"I feel like an idiot," Chris said.

"You're afraid and you just don't know it." Steph helped Chris towel her hair dry.

They got as far as the bottom of the stairway. The allegro from the Bizet symphony came down, cascading and silver, from the stage. Chris stopped short.

"Steph, I—"

She turned and ran and when she came back Steph could tell she had thrown up; which was odd, since Chris hadn't eaten anything all day except a mouthful of bee pollen.

"Are my eyelashes still on?"

"On and beautiful. Come on, let's watch." Steph dragged her up the stairs and they stood in the wings, watching the lightning-fast finale of the Bizet.

Madame touched Chris's shoulder. "Much better, yes? Happened to me every night in Monte Carlo."

The dancers in the Bizet bowed and came streaming offstage. The sweat and exhaustion showed. "Very, very nice." Madame pushed them back, and they returned for second and third bows. Madame cocked an ear to the applause. She was able to detect condescension in the clap of a hand but she detected none now.

Her boys and girls were good. It was amazing to think that in her own day no one could have danced a Balanchine presto, not even Nijinsky. The technique had not existed. Nowadays students could do it.

*But is it progress?* she wondered.

The house grew silent again and the orchestra thundered out the opening chords of the *Don Quixote pas de deux. That's a good tempo*, Madame thought. She touched the red ruffle on Stephanie's shoulder.

"Remember, darling. Spanish. All chili powder and *olé*."

\*    \*    \*

Steph tested her *pointe*, up down, up down, stood braced. Her eyes met her partner's in the opposite wing. He mouthed a *merde*. She did not need to count. As she felt the music rushing headlong into her cue she leapt on stage.

*My God*, it dawned on her, *twelve hundred people are watching!*

Nicky Riveras' leap was late, but it didn't matter. His hand touched her waist and it was far firmer than in rehearsal. The audience, the pulsing reality of the orchestra, seemed to drive all hesitation out of him. Suddenly he was *partnering*.

Suddenly Steph trusted him.

She threw herself into balances and turns and there was none of the awkwardness of the studio run-throughs. She went on *pointe* for her series of hops and there was a sudden silence in the house and then an explosion of applause. It was the first time she had ever heard an audience applaud her dancing.

*They like me*, she thought. *Twelve hundred people like me!*

The applause went into her blood like adrenalin. Nicky's hands were around her waist, assisting her *soutenu*. But she didn't need the assistance and because she didn't need it the step was higher and lighter than ever before, with an instant's weightlessness at the top of the movement that she had never felt before. She drew her right foot, then her left up beneath her, came down lightly in fifth, *bourrée*'d forward for her pirouette.

She heard the murmur in the house and felt energy flowing from the audience into her. There was too much energy in her now. It had to be released.

Without thinking, without effort, a single pirouette came out double.

*    *    *

For several seconds Anna floated on a sea of uncertainty. She'd never been so afraid in her life. This was it. The moment. She'd staked everything on the next thirty seconds.

She sat very still, eyes pinned to the girl onstage.

Steph looked pretty as a Spanish doll in her black skirt and red blouse. Yeah, but could she handle the pirouettes in the variation—and what about that stinking *passé* balance in the coda? Anna's fingernails dug into the flesh of her palms.

Coming out of a turn, Steph arched her wrist and fingers over her head, as though she were holding castanets. *Why didn't someone tell me to do that when I was dancing* Don Q. *with Bobby Baylor in '55?* Anna wondered. Her head bobbed, marking the familiar movements: *plié, plié,* breakaway, pirouette—who was that zombie they'd given her for a partner?

Nice pirouette.

Anna sat up straighter. She squinted. Was Steph going up onto full *pointe* for those *pas de bourrée?* Most dancers only went to half toe for them.

And then out of nowhere Steph shot into a double turn that hit Anna like a shaft of sunlight. She wanted to jump up applauding in her seat.

And another double turn!

And *another!*

Anna didn't believe it. Where did the girl get the speed from? Anna saw it happening in front of her but she didn't believe it. No preparation—just blinding speed.

She sensed a fever of whispers sweeping the audience. The lump of fear in her chest began going down.

She hated to take her eyes off the stage, but she couldn't resist peering around to see how the audience was taking it. Her eyes groped through the darkness to Marius Volmar's seat.

*    *    *

*Of all the cheek,* Marius Volmar was thinking: *that girl is changing the choreography!*

Eighteen years ago Lvovna had asked him to simplify the *Don Q. pas de deux* for two of her "very talented students." And now this girl was throwing out the Volmar simplifications, restoring Petipa's original double pirouettes and *fouetté* combinations and a dozen other details.

Fascinated, Volmar leaned forward in his seat.

The girl came *bourrée*'ing forward, a wonderful springiness to the steps. She whipped into a double turn that was not even in the original. The footlights caught her blond hair and for one emerald instant he saw the color of her eyes. She held one spectacularly long balance and he jotted rapidly in his program: *excellent legs; fluidity; extremely strong; places weight well; adjusts to partner's deficiencies.*

The adjustment had to be instinctive, not conscious, and it meant she was a professional.

Volmar felt strangely exhilarated watching her. He couldn't be angry at such a dancer. Not even when she held a balance and, instead of bringing her arms into fourth position sharp and Spanish, she brought them in slowly, romantically.

It was not the choreography at all. But the balance was astonishing and there was something true and appropriate about the movement. The music was not sharp, not Spanish: it was pure Minkus drivel, the same throbbing strings and harp that the composer used for the kingdom of the shades in *Bayadère*. The girl was dancing the music, and she had instinctively altered the one movement that flatly contradicted it.

In very large capitals Volmar scrawled across his program VERY MUSICAL.

He drew two lines under the words.

\*      \*      \*

Chris stood listening to the applause. Steph's *pas de deux* had been a success. Chris was relieved. Now she had only herself to worry about.

She watched Steph and Nicky Riveras take their bows, and then Nicky swept past her, ignoring her, as though he were a star and the applause had been all for him.

Steph whispered, *"Merde",* and hugged her. There was another kind of applause and Chris knew the conductor had come back to the pit. She felt a wave of unfriendliness sweep in from the dark house. She knew she had no one out there.

At first she had taken it philosophically that her parents hadn't come to the recital: after all, as they explained, her brother's graduation was just as important. But suddenly she wished she had a pair of hands applauding for her.

Just one pair.

The orchestra began the introduction to the Snow *pas de deux* from *Nutcracker*. The music had always seemed soft and unhurried as snowflakes but now it seemed a torrent of icicles.

Eight counts before her cue Chris felt a savage need to turn and run from the stage. But Lvovna was beside her, gentle and nudging.

*"Allez, mon petit."*

There was a push and she sprang, landing onstage with a muffled thud. Something felt undefinably wrong. She was aware of a silence in the audience that drowned out the music.

*It would be a different silence,* she thought, *if I had someone out there. Just one person rooting for me.*

Her partner was nervous. As he was lifting her his hands slipped and she had to touch down very lightly to keep from looking as though he'd dropped her. Suddenly she overshot a *piqué*—a stiff-legged step directly onto half toe—and almost lost her balance.

She stopped dead in her tracks. Panic struck her across the chest. For a terrifying instant she lost her count. Her center of gravity rose into her throat and she couldn't adjust. She managed her *développé* but her leg wasn't nearly as straight or slow or high as she wanted.

The music wasn't giving her time.

She had three pirouettes coming up and she had to step into arabesque but the music was rushing her. Her hand went up and her partner's fist closed around her finger to guide her in the finger pirouette.

*How damp and cold his hand is,* she thought.

She brought her leg up and around for momentum to make the turn but she didn't have time to pull in. Her knee bumped into her partner. Suddenly there was no momentum, no movement, no memory of what next.

Her back was to the audience and humiliation paralyzed her.

She stood alone, stranded in the moment, the music by-passing her, and then she felt a tug and her partner was pulling her into *penché arabesque.*

He was pulling a corpse and the corpse was Christine Avery and she didn't know how to come to life again.

\*    \*    \*

Applause was polite, nothing more.

Chris and her partner took one curtain call and then she made her way miserably into the wings. She was glad her parents hadn't been able to come, glad they hadn't seen her disgrace. Her eyes and forehead were burning with anger and failure and hopelessness.

Steph had seen. "Chris," she said softly. "It could have happened to anyone." She reached to wipe Chris's face with the clean edge of a tissue.

"It was my fault," Chris said tonelessly. "I'm not a dancer."

A panic rose in Steph. *What's going to happen to Chris?* she wondered. Chris was injured and she didn't know how to pick herself up or keep going.

"You *are* a dancer. One of the best."

"I'm good in class," Chris said. "You're good in class and you're good onstage too. That's the difference between us."

Steph looked at the huge wounded eyes. The idea took hold of her that it was her fault for having danced first. Chris had been standing there watching and everything she should have been saving for herself she had used up being scared for Steph.

*I've got to bring her back,* Steph realized. *I owe it to her.*

"Shower and change and we'll talk, okay?" Steph said.

Chris forced a smile and nodded and went down the stairs to the dressing room.

Madame Lvovna intercepted Steph at the water cooler. Her face was rigid and disapproving, as though she had caught Steph cheating on a turn.

"You are no longer girl, Stephanie. I am not one hundred per cent certain, but I think you are dancer."

"Thank you, Madame."

"I know you are friends with Christine. But you cannot give someone else courage. You can lose your own trying. Be selfish,

Stephanie. A dancer needs all her courage. God gave you yours for you, not for anyone else."

\*   \*   \*

The audience came streaming and chattering up the aisle. Anna pried her way to the stage entrance, bucking the tide. She whooshed past the guard, waded into a flock of little girls still in their *Circus Polka* costumes, pushed open a door.

Wrong shower. Boys.

The next door opened onto giggles and sweat, girls sprawled in chairs unlacing slippers and peeling off tights. Anna's eye traveled down the row of dressing tables. There was Steph, cold-creaming her face.

"Hurry up and take your shower, honey. There's someone I want you to meet."

"Does it have to be now? I'm pooped."

Anna made a mental note: calf's liver for supper, twice a week. She held out the box of Kleenex. "It'll take five minutes."

Steph sighed. "Who?"

"Only the director of Empire State Ballet, that's who."

The girl at the next mirror stopped brushing her hair and stared.

Steph's face colored. "I promised Chris I'd—"

"Honey, this is important."

"Mom, her *parents* didn't even show up. She's heartbroken."

"So? It's your fault the Averys are dizzy socialites? You can leave her a note."

Lester Croyden was waiting by the fountain in Lincoln Plaza, a short plump man leaning on an ebony cane. One hand fidgeted with a pocket watch as though it were a yoyo on a gold chain.

Anna yoo-hooed, made introductions. Lester Croyden steered them across Broadway toward a table at the back of Fiorello's.

"What will you two ladies have to drink?"

"Ginger ale for both of us will be terrific," Anna said.

Lester Croyden shuddered. "You have stronger nerves than I do, dearie." He ordered two ginger ales and a double Tanqueray martini with a twist straight up.

Anna's eyes adjusted to the dimness. Three tables away she

saw Heidi Mayerhoff, who did publicity for Volmar and dyed her hair red and was the biggest gossip in the business. Anna shifted on the bench so Heidi could get a good view of Steph and Lester. She wished Steph would try to look a little perkier.

"It's a shame Cynthia couldn't have seen your performance," Lester was saying to Steph. "She was supposed to come with me tonight."

Cynthia *Gregory?* Anna wondered. Who did he think he was kidding?

"But I'm meeting her for dinner and I'm going to tell her all about you." Lester Croyden drained his drink like ice water and called for another. "You gave a wonderful performance, dearie. Star caliber."

"Thank you," Steph said softly.

"I haven't enjoyed a performance so much since Nora's first *Pillar* in '42."

Anna couldn't even smile, it was so pathetic. Nora *Kaye, Pillar of Fire?* How could he even compare it to a student production of *Don Q.?* Then he got on to Hugh Laing and Maria Tallchief as if he'd given them their first chance. And Magallanes, who'd never danced for him. And Robbins! Anna was speechless. Jerry had already choreographed *Cage* when Lester got his big break booking pickup bands for Hurok. If his dad hadn't left him twenty million from that chain of clothing stores he'd still be booking schlock.

"I'll be talking with Erik," Lester Croyden was saying. "He's anchoring that series on modern dance for educational television? They're looking for a young, unknown dancer to—"

Erik Bruhn, Anna supposed. And then he mentioned Rudy, and Anna had a hunch he didn't mean the red-nosed reindeer; and then Eddy and Patricia. *All right, she wanted to scream, so Villella and McBride say hello to you in the hallway, so what?*

Steph sat twisting the stem of her maraschino cherry.

Lester Croyden ordered another round and inched his way to the point. "The long and short of it is, Empire has room for you, dearie."

Anna was proud of Steph. No yelp, no reaction. Just a nod.

"There are two superb *coryphées* we'll give you in *Swan Lake* and *Fille* and there's no question you'll be dancing solos within the year. Elizabeth is leaving us, which leaves us without a

Princess in *Bluebird* or a Prayer in *Coppélia or* a younger sister in *Pillar*. So you can see, you'd have plenty to do. You don't have to answer right away but I do hope you'll consider the offer."

"What about Christine Avery?" Steph said.

Anna winced.

"Who?" Lester Croyden said. "Christine who?"

"She danced the Snow *pas de deux*," Steph said.

Lester Croyden frowned. "The girl who couldn't hold her arabesque?"

"Anyone can stumble," Steph said. "I almost slipped too."

"I didn't notice," Lester Croyden said. "Sorry, dearie."

He wanted Steph badly. Anna could smell it. The teachers must have put out word on the grapevine: *Watch Stephanie Lang—she's going places.* Lester Croyden's eyes were tiny and black as two raisins in a lump of raw dough and they watered as he looked at the girl. He ran the third-best ballet company in the United States. He pulled down federal grants of a million, two million a year. If he wanted a dancer, then every company from fourth best on down would be after her too.

Anna exhaled. She'd been holding that breath for the last ten years.

"Steph and Chris are best friends," Anna said. "They'd like to go to the same company."

"I understand, dearie, and when Stephanie's friend is ready, we'll be glad to take another look at her." Lester Croyden jiggled the ice in his glass. Anna could tell he wanted to order another. After Marty, she had no trouble spotting a lush. "Maybe next year."

Anna arched her eyebrows, shot Steph a look that said, *I tried.* She raised a hand to her mouth, forced a yawn, and patted it back. "Gee, that program must have run an hour overtime. Steph's too tired to make any decisions tonight."

"Naturally you'll want time to consider other offers," Lester Croyden said.

Anna couldn't tell if he'd heard something she hadn't or if he was just fishing. He was watching her closely now.

"NBT is scouting six girls for the corps," he said.

Anna's heart gave a kick in her rib cage but she managed a noncommittal grimace as though she'd heard it all before. "Volmar keeps those girls in the corps till they're grandmothers." She plunked her purse onto the table. "C'mon, Steph. Bottoms up."

"I can promise you—Empire wouldn't make that mistake with Stephanie." Lester Croyden pulled a business card from his billfold. He carefully wrote a number across the back. "One little favor: this is my home phone. Give me twenty-four hours to match Stephanie's best offer."

Anna took the card. "Sure, Lester. We'll keep in touch."

\*        \*        \*

As she slipped out onto Sixty-sixth Street, wincing away from the sting of sunlight and traffic, a voice called out to her.

"Chris—Christine!"

She turned, squinting. The sun was in her eyes.

"Have I changed that much? Don't you recognize me?"

She did not want to be rude but at the same time she did not want to stand by the stage entrance with pitying smug eyes gliding past.

"Good lord, Chris—its Ray, Ray Lockwood from Evanston—remember?"

When he said it, of course she remembered. It had been two years ago, and he seemed a little taller and more broad-shouldered now, but he still had the same alert gray eyes in a sensitive face. She shook hands with this stranger from the past and they stood on the sidewalk, talking and trading news of old friends.

Ray Lockwood said he'd seen an announcement in the paper; he'd remembered his mother's saying Chris was studying at the school. "So I cut afternoon classes, and here I am. My God, Chris—I don't know anything about ballet, but you were terrific."

"You—saw?"

She felt a bell clap of terror as his glance met hers. But there was no smugness, no pity in it—just a healthy, cheerful ignorance.

"Wouldn't have missed it for the world. Look, you must be worn out. Can I take you some place quiet for a drink, or a cup of coffee? I mean, if you have a moment?"

She didn't feel up to play-acting or asking about people she didn't remember and had never cared about. She didn't feel up to pretending her life wasn't a wreck. "I'm sorry, Ray—I don't."

"Okay. Some other day. Now that we're fellow New Yorkers, we're bound to bump into one another." There was a flicker of blue-webbed pulse just above her collarbone, and he thought, *How delicate she is.*

"You're living here?" she said.

"Have been for almost two years. I'm up at Columbia Law."

"I didn't know you were interested in law."

"I wasn't when we last met. Two years ago I didn't know what the hell interested me. And I don't remember you as much of a dancer."

"I've always been a dancer," she said.

"Not with me you weren't."

She remembered now. "It was my sister's coming-out and you were wearing a madras jacket and a little bow tie that matched . . ." *And you were drunk and you terrified me*, but she didn't say that.

"And I kept asking you for the next dance and you kept saying yes and then disappearing. I got the idea either you were scared of dancing or you were scared of me. And since there's nothing scary about me, obviously it had to be the dancing."

"But that's not dancing—that's not even music!"

The simple vehemence of her reaction startled him. And instructed him. It was as though she had thrown open a window and let him glimpse the mechanism of her thinking. He was a practical young man, and he did not have time or talent for art. But it hinted to him of the magical and the miraculous, of all sorts of music and dance and poetry his own life lacked, and he would have liked to be at ease with artists. He would have liked to be at ease with this frail young girl.

"Anyway," he smiled, "I looked for you all night. I even wrote you letters. I don't suppose any ever got forwarded?"

"I sort of remember a postcard from Europe."

"From me a postcard's a letter."

She felt awkward. She wondered why Ray Lockwood wanted to talk to her. She had never been comfortable with lawyers and businessmen. They seemed a foreign race who owned large cars and large houses and played golf at country clubs and drank cocktails at noon and only went to the ballet to fall asleep. She had never spoken their language and yet she sensed Ray Lockwood, in a stumbling way, trying to speak hers.

*I've got to make a good impression*, she thought, *and I'll say good-by as quickly as possible.*

She'd forgotten how you made a good impression on people like Ray Lockwood: there was a pattern to it, like ballroom dancing. She'd forgotten how to say good-by to them. There was a pattern to that too. She began edging back toward the crowd, taking up a good-by distance, but he edged right alongside her, not about to let her slip away.

"I hope you won't think I'm still trying to pressure you into that waltz—but I'd like to see you, Chris. For dinner or a movie. Or maybe dinner *and* a movie. If dancers like dinner and movies."

She didn't answer. If he hadn't been a link to her family, if she hadn't disgraced herself, she would have said yes.

"Can I phone you?" he said.

She hesitated. "You can phone the place where I'm staying." She gave him the number and he wrote his down for her.

"Thank you, Ray. Thank you for coming today. That was kind of you."

"It wasn't kind at all. You were beautiful—really beautiful."

He sensed an odd vulnerability in her and it made him hesitate, debating whether an old, not very good friend had the right to kiss her. By the time he had made up his mind to risk it she had slipped into the crowd and was waving good-by. He waved, disappointed, and then thought, *At least I've got her phone.*

But he hadn't.

The woman who answered didn't speak English, and he wondered if Chris had given him the wrong number on purpose.

# six

Marius Volmar hurried across Lincoln Center Plaza back to his office. The memory of the girl stayed with him like the afterimage of a blinding flash. He saw her pale face with its firm white curves and loose blond hair. The eyes were huge and green. There was a hint of smile in the narrowly parted lips.

His throat pounded. His heart felt tight. He did not want to lose the image. His mind played over the extended neck, the soft shoulders, the long lovely arms, the singing movement, the pliancy and balance and serenity, the unbroken flow of line from fingertip to toe, the body so perfectly mastered that it could perfectly serve the music.

Well, perhaps not quite perfectly: her footwork was slow. But all girls were slow till they came to Volmar. He would tap the speed in her.

He locked the office door behind him. From the safe he took the sketches of *The Sleeping Beauty*. They were almost forty years old and he had to be careful of the paper turned brittle. He spread them across the already littered desk. He had looked at them only five times in all those years. But without hesitation he took up his pen, began notating, amending where he had left off.

The past came back effortlessly across the forty-year abyss.

Faster than his hand could move the dance rushed past his eyes, the music past his ears. An explosion of memory filled him like a hot wind gusting through a tunnel.

He was twenty years old again, already a principal with the Royal Danish Ballet, the youngest choreographer ever to have six works in the international repertory. He was mounting a *Sleeping Beauty* that season: coaxing long-lost material out of Copenhagen's tsarist refugees, he had restored most of the original Petipa choreography and Tchaikovsky score. The ballet starred his first teacher—his mother. At thirty-eight, she was at the height of her powers. But the year was 1940 and the Nazis ran Denmark.

The Nazis had laws, Nuremberg laws, and his mother had had a Jewish grandfather. She was famous, she had enemies within the ballet, she could be made an example. Opening night the occupation police came to the theater, told her to put on a coat over her tights, and took her away.

The ballet was never danced. Marius Volmar never saw his mother again.

Nuremberg laws did not care about Jewish great-grandfathers. Volmar was allowed to live and to work. But there was a bitterness in him, a freezing contempt for humans and their laws and their nationalisms and socialisms.

He never choreographed again.

He directed, he mounted, he improved other men's work. He staged productions in London and Paris, Buenos Aires and New York. He made American ballet and he made New York a capital of world ballet.

But the dance that was in him, the dance that was his, stayed frozen up.

Until now.

When he laid down his pen to take a breath, his shirt was drenched in sweat. His watch told him he had been at his desk three feverish hours.

He knew creativity. It had its seasons and they were different from the earth's. For half a man's life the soul could be blanketed in ice till spring came with its slow gentle thaw. Or there could be a rush of summer, unexpected as an ambush, when the spirit burst violently into bloom—and just as quickly died.

He knew what was happening to him. This was summer,

short and savage, and it gave him very little time.

According to the recital program, the girl's name was Stephanie Lang. Her teacher was Vera Alexeyevna Lvovna.

Marius Volmar reached a hand for the telephone.

\*       \*       \*

"Who is she?" he asked. They were speaking Russian.

"She is a girl," Lvovna said tartly. "A girl who wants to dance."

The narrowness of the room, made narrower by bookcases, the tiny space of shawled tables and hideaway bed, heightened Volmar's awareness of her mood. It was not co-operative. "You must know more about her than that."

"What is there to know about her? She is learning. So long as she learns, she is in my class. When she stops learning..."

Madame Lvovna shrugged. She admitted to seventy years, which meant she was eighty, but it was an energetic shrug. Her eyes, always made up, always expressive, traveled the wall. Everything that was not a book or an autographed ballet shoe was a photograph, signed with love or esteem or respect. Some who had signed were great. All had been her pupils. Her eyes seemed to say, *That is what happens when they stop learning: they become photographs.*

"She has great promise," Volmar prodded.

"Acorns have promise."

"She knows a good deal more than she shows."

"So do acorns."

Ballerinas would do better not to get old, Volmar reflected. But then, he thought, so would human beings.

"You've taught her well," he said.

"I've taught her nothing. What she took from me I took from Galinova, who took it from Krasnova, who took it from Petipa... Dance is a language. No one teaches a language. Except to foreigners, and then it's always too late. All we can do is speak the language distinctly for our children and let them imitate.... Later they'll invent.... They'll change things.... Look how they've changed Russian, dropped three letters from the alphabet."

She sank more deeply into the cushions with which she had

stuffed her chair. She sighed heavily, as though the Bolsheviks had eliminated the three most beautiful letters in the language.

"There are girls in my class who can do combinations for which there are not even names. Pavlova could not do an *entrechat huit*. My girls are required to. Is that progress? No. It's just change."

Volmar sensed Madame drifting from the subject he had come to discuss. "This Lang girl seems advanced for her age."

"Advanced? Bournonville created *La Vestale* for Lucile Grahn when she was fourteen years old. *That* was her debut. One hundred forty years ago. Do you know a fourteen-year-old today who could dance *La Vestale?*"

"How old is the Lang girl?"

"Seventeen, eighteen—I am not the Bureau of Records."

"She could dance *La Vestale*."

"But why? It would prove she could do it, nothing else."

You had to be cautious with Lvovna. She was like one of those maddening boxes in which you try to tip the tiny metal ball into the tiny hole without reaching under the glass. One false tilt and she could escape you.

"What would you have her dance then?" Volmar asked.

"In time, when she has suffered, Odile/Odette; Giselle—stop making faces; *Fille Mal Gardée;* any of Tudor's neurotics; she could do Baryshnikov's *Nutcracker*. I don't like it, but she could do it."

"Then you see her as a ballerina."

"All my girls are ballerinas. I do not train corps."

"You mention two Tchaikovsky heroines. You think she has the affinity?"

"I mention a Baryshnikov-Minz heroine," Madame corrected. "I mention a Petipa-Ivanov heroine."

"Petipa did some wonderful choreography for *Sleeping Beauty*."

"Everything he did was wonderful. Without Petipa there would be no reason for Tchaikovsky."

She was an impossible woman with impossible opinions, but Volmar was not going to be goaded. Since his heart attack eight months ago he had had to ration his anger. "The Lang girl has an affinity for Petipa, perhaps? Watching her balances and arabesques, I thought of the Rose Adagio."

"I have eight girls who could do Rose Adagios. But where do you find the princes?"

At last the little ball was circling the hole. Just one careful little tilt . . . "Why not a Rose Adagio without the prince?"

"Why not a Beethoven violin concerto without the orchestra?"

"There are Bach unaccompanied sonatas," Volmar said. "And there is a Petipa adagio without the prince."

Her eyes darted an alert glance at him through the heavily blacked eyelashes.

"The *pas seul*," he said. "The solo. *Sleeping Beauty*. Act One."

"But that is an exception. It's an experiment. Besides, no one knows about it."

"You know about it. You could teach it to the Lang girl," he suggested softly.

Madame gave a shrug as instant and instinctive as a horse's tail flicking off a fly. "She is too young. She is not an artist yet."

"She's too young to understand it—but if someone were to show her the steps—very distinctly—she could imitate it."

Madame stared down into her *stakanchi chai*, the hot tea in a glass that she drank at all hours and which, he knew, after 7 P.M. had vodka in it. "Always you want to chop people and twist them and rearrange them. Why not let her finish growing?"

"It wouldn't stunt her growth."

"There is an impossible *penché*—very deep—unassisted—do you know what that does to the calves?"

"She'll do extra exercises to warm up the calves."

"But what is the point? Even Petipa had to withdraw the dance. Besides, she won't be a ballerina for two, three years."

"If she can do the *pas seul*," Volmar said, "I'll restore *The Sleeping Beauty*. Miss Lang will be a ballerina next year."

The silence thickened and shimmered.

"The complete *Sleeping Beauty?*" Lvovna said.

"Complete."

"But Tamarova is sitting in Copenhagen with two of the numbers in a bank vault."

"If Tamarova sees the Lang girl dance the *pas seul*, she'll give me the missing numbers. I can guarantee it."

Volmar could not read Madame's expression. It seemed

resentful and kind, smiling and sad, all at the same time. When she spoke he realized there was nothing kind in it at all.

"Tamarova gives nothing. One day she will go to hell for her selfishness."

"My dear," Volmar said, "you hate her. But I *know* her. Teach Miss Lang—and we will have our *Sleeping Beauty*."

For a long while Lvovna sat shaking her head. So long that her head seemed to be shaking her. *She must have something left*, Volmar thought. *Vanity, at least.*

"You don't recall the *pas seul* any more?" he said.

"Of course I recall it," she bridled. "I saw Petipa himself teach Tamarova's mother. *She* was a dancer. If she hadn't died . . . it would still be part of the ballet."

Volmar heard the sadness in Madame's voice as her mind roamed that fairyland of tsars and tutus that she called Russian history. He paused, settled back in his chair, and let slip the cruelest temptation of all.

"And of course, the program will say that Vera Alexeyevna Lvovna reconstructed the choreography from memory."

\*     \*     \*

Madame Lvovna asked Steph to remain a moment after class. "Stephanie, you have been good student."

Madame had never told her that before. Steph's heart gave a tiny leap of joy. She bowed her head. "Thank you, Madame. Thank you very much."

"You have earned reward. Come to studio 4, three o'clock this afternoon. Wear rehearsal clothes and be warmed up."

Steph was warmed up and hardly able to control her excitement when Madame limped into the room on the dot of three. In one hand Madame clutched her silver-knobbed cane and a manila folder of music manuscript. In the other she clutched the rehearsal pianist's shirt sleeve.

"Izzy, this tempo, please."

Madame counted two measures. Izzy crouched forward on the piano stool. He squinted a long moment at the spider-scrawl notation. Finally he played, hands scrambling to catch sheets that fluttered loose at the turn of a page.

Steph had never heard the music before, and obviously Izzy

had never seen it before. It sounded like Tchaikovsky, but
several of the chords were peculiar. Madame interrupted.

"Something wrong—that *poco accelerando* is too *poco*. Izzy,
I think it is you."

"I'm only playing what's written."

"I don't believe you. Play it again."

He played, and she listened critically.

"Ah, you see? This time was much better."

"I didn't change a thing, Madame."

"No? Then leave it alone more and maybe it will be perfect."

The lyrical, flowing *adage* ended in a very fast coda. Madame
let the last notes die away. Her eyes rested on Steph and there
was stoicism in them. *Madame is risking something*, Steph
realized. *She is taking a chance on me.*

Madame inhaled deeply, as though preparing to dive from a
very high board. "We start *piqué*, *chassé*, *piqué*, *chassé*—very
precise, very delicate—feet pointed, high. You are dancing on
bells."

Steph tried to dance on bells.

Madame frowned but let it pass. She let the *jetés croisés* and
the *cabrioles* pass. But when it came to the first balance she
clapped her hands for silence.

"You call that balance? Who taught you that?"

"You taught me, Madame."

"I never taught you balance like that. You went to
Zhemkuzhnaya when I had grippe?"

"Never, Madame."

"You are using muscle. Zhemkuzhnaya trick. Is ugly. Pony
balances like that and that is why pony has pony derrière.
Balance with your center, everything from the center."

Steph had no idea what Madame wanted of her but she knew
it was a reward and an honor and she wanted desperately to
show respect. On the other hand Madame was being unfair.
Madame was asking the impossible.

"But, Madame," Steph pleaded, "there's a retard, and I'm
leaping into a balance."

Madame stared at her as though nothing ought to be
impossible for an artist. The voice dripped patience. "Darling, I
do not ask God to retard gravity, I do not ask you. Come down
light, deep slow *plié*, do not be afraid, all of foot on floor. You

are not using whole foot. That is problem. Why God give you foot? There are seven places you can balance on that foot. When foot says *this* is right—not before—come up very slow. Let balance rise from center. Always trusting foot. Foot never lies."

Madame's hands shaped a balance, materializing like a spirit at a séance.

"Do not stretch balance, balance stretch you. When balance reaches fingers and toes, let it go one inch further—into space—and you have your retard."

They took the leap and the balance eight times. On the ninth attempt Madame sighed and said it would have to do for now. Madame was not pleased.

"Tomorrow, here, three o'clock."

She went to collect her music, muttering Russian. Izzy asked to study the score overnight.

"Is my only copy," Madame snapped, and took it with her.

The next day's rehearsal was even worse.

"No, no, no, no, no!" Madame cried. "If I want girl running backward I get eight-year-old."

"But you told me *pas de bourrée* backward on the third diagonal."

"Stop counting diagonals, what do I care diagonals? You are young girl, princess, you do not even know diagonals, you know only you yearn for love, you yearn for love so strong your love is there with you."

Beneath her white face powder, Madame's face showed traces of red. Steph felt stupid and clumsy, a pig in toe shoes. She had betrayed Madame's faith.

Madame placed a hand on Steph's cheek, provisionally forgiving. "He touches you—we see him touch because you shiver like girl always shivers when love touches her first time. Stephanie—for this you are virgin. I do not know if you are virgin; is better you remember virgin than be. You are thinking this love and because you are thinking so strong, yearning so strong, he is there. He seizes you—first time man ever seize you, is delicious, is awful—lifts you—you resist but not resist. He carries you backward. You scared, you happy. Everything is yes, no. Your toe drags. Toe very important, tells whole story. And *then pas de bourrée* backward!"

"But how does he lift me if he's not there?"

"That is the point!" Madame exploded. "That is why the dance!"

Steph's eyelids clenched, stung and mute and hurt. She realized she was not an artist, never would be. Madame would not shout this way if there were any hope at all.

"You *show* us how!" Madame cried. "Your *center* goes up, it is all in the center! Your shoulders relax, your center goes backward, far far far. Eyes very important, here eyes must steal from feet. You must be silent movie, head back, mouth almost open, wanting him to kiss."

"But if I fall—"

"Of course you fall, but you *bourrée* faster than you fall and everyone watch your eyes and no one know how you do it. Now that is what I want and if you are dancer and not elephant you give it to me!"

Steph tried.

Madame watched. Madame breathed deeply.

"Darling," she said, more softly now, "enough groaning cat in heat. This is not *Fire Pillar*. Not Bronx girl. This is princess."

Steph shook her head. She felt tears threatening. "I'll never do it."

"You will do it because I tell you to. Tomorrow, three o'clock."

*   *   *

At the third rehearsal Madame blocked out the coda. It was a fiendish whirl of jumps and turns, with leaps becoming faster and longer, stopping dead in a *penché*.

"A true *penché*, Stephanie. Leg well extended up behind you, head and throat lifted. It must be absolutely secure, absolutely beautiful. You are leaning on *his* shoulder."

He, of course, was not there, though Madame said Steph must imagine him, a prince kneeling in extended fifth. Imagining did not make the dead stop or the *penché* or the one-legged balance any easier.

"Madame," Steph pleaded, "how long do I hold the *penché*?"

"Forever."

The dreadful fact was that Madame sometimes meant what she said. Steph felt her bones caving in to despair.

"Izzy," Madame commanded, "play her the re-mi-fa, re-mi-fa."

Izzy played the soft, tinkling, next-to-last phrase.

"That is your *penché*, my dear. Two counts, over and over as long as you wish. And when you no longer wish, you look the conductor straight in eye, *boom*. Give him one count warning. He will follow."

Uncertainty still gnawed. "But, Madame, how long do dancers usually hold the *penché?*"

Madame stared at her. "Why should you care about usually? For this you create your own usually. Is great opportunity, my dear."

"But, Madame—" Steph swallowed. "What would you recommend?"

Madame snorted. "Am I couturier? Am I dressing you? Have you no taste of your own?"

"Madame, if you could suggest a length—it would give me courage."

Madame sighed deeply. "If I give you courage now, next week you ask me more courage and maybe next week I am dead. No. The courage comes from you." And then Madame smiled mischievously. "But I would not mind eight counts. And I would not mind eighteen. Try to surprise me. Tomorrow, three o'clock."

Turning to go, Madame stopped, remembering something Petipa had told Tamarova's mother, the most important thing of all.

"And, my dear, as you lean into the *penché*—kiss him."

## seven

Anna got home from work to find the refrigerator door open half an inch. Chilled air was steaming into the kitchen. No wonder the Con Ed bill had been sixty dollars last month! She knew Steph was working late with Lvovna, so it had to be Chris's fault. She shut the door, made sure it was sealed, and marched to Chris's room.

She knocked.

The shades were drawn and at first she could see nothing. The air hummed softly. Her nose caught the cool chemical smell of air conditioning, a faint sweet jab of cologne. The room felt eerie and deserted but Anna sensed she was being watched.

Her eye picked out a movement on the bed. A hand gripped the post, a figure slowly sat up. Anna felt her way through shadowy obstacles, raised the window shade with a snap that sent dust spinning in the evening light. A canvas tote bag lay agape on the floor, spilling toe shoes and make-up and money.

"What's the matter with you?" Anna said. "This place is a pigsty."

Chris sat at the foot of the bed, half clothed. One hand pressed a pillow to her stomach and she seemed to be holding her head up with great difficulty. "I'm sorry. I'll clean it up."

"How long have you been sitting here?"

"Just a while."

"Have you been out of the house at all today?" One glance at the gray circles under her eyes and Anna knew she hadn't. "What about toe class? What about interpretation class? Do you know how many girls would die just to get *into* that school?"

"It's no use."

"What's no use?"

"Me—dancing..."

Anna bent, scooped junk back into the tote bag, slammed it onto the rocker. "It's no use paying good money for lessons and not going."

"A scout from Delaware Ballet came to class yesterday. He offered contracts to Sandy Stone and Ginny Webster. Last week a man from Santa Fe Opera signed Margie MacInness."

"And maybe a man from the Kirov was there today and where were you?"

"Nobody wants me."

Anna wheeled. She wasn't going to put up with whining, not in her house. "Look in that mirror. Do you see a dancer? Do dancers slouch? Do dancers mope? Brush your hair. Put on a pretty blouse. Hold your chin up. Smile. Dancers are supposed to be beautiful. You're a mess."

Chris rocked slightly, as though the words had hit her with physical force. Her gaze came up, slow and scared. "Mrs. Lang, you know ballet. Tell me honestly. Am I any good?"

Anna hesitated. She was furious enough to tell the truth, but she didn't want to lose a boarder. Even if they accepted the Empire State Ballet offer, Steph wouldn't be getting principal's pay for a year at least.

"From what I can see, you're better than some, you're worse than some."

"They're better than me. All of them."

Anna stared at the soft questioning face poised on the brink of tears. Slowly, surfacing through the angry stream of her thought, came the realization that the girl meant it. Anna forgot about the refrigerator door.

"Now wait one minute. Lili Swinburne—prima ballerina with National. No ankles. Miss Wobble. Lara Collins—ten years she's been a principal with Empire State. Can't count beats so she dances modern and her feet stink. Nora Parsons—hasn't danced with her own company in eight years, but they print her name in the program and she pulls down three thousand a shot doing guest appearances. Her waist is up around her neck, who can partner her? They have to import six-foot Danes. How do you think those girls got to the top—because they were good? Because they didn't give up. They didn't cut classes. They didn't sit with the shades pulled down feeling sorry for themselves."

"They had talent," Chris said quietly.

"They covered the roles, *period*," Anna shot back. "They learned the repertory, *period*. They were there when Allegra pulled a tendon or Gelsey caught flu. *Period*. And if that's talent, you got it coming out of your ears. Start using it."

Anna sat down on the bed. She reached a hand to smooth Chris's tangled hair. With those huge blue eyes and the droopy bee-stung mouth, the girl looked like a broken-hearted doll.

Chris took a long, deep breath. "You're right. I've got to keep trying." She stood. She picked up a pair of blue jeans from the floor, folded them, and laid them neatly in a drawer. "Please don't tell my mother I don't have a job."

"Look, Steph doesn't have a job either. It doesn't happen overnight. We're all in the same boat."

\*　　\*　　\*

Before the demonstration, Lvovna, whispered to Marius Volmar outside the rehearsal studio. "I have been cruel to this girl."

Volmar smiled. "You're learning, Verushka."

"Don't joke. She is not yet artist. Someday she will be. But you gave me no time. No choice. For today, I have been Gestapo KGB. I do not approve. Fear is worst teacher."

"You show strength."

"Cruelty is not strength. Now promise: do not smile when you say hello, do not smile when she dances, above all do not smile in the final *penché*. Do not let her know you like anything about her. What you will see this girl do is beyond my understanding and very far beyond her ability. You must keep her terrified or she will never get through it."

"I will be as quiet as an acorn."

Madame had an inspiration. "And pretend to take notes."

Lvovna took Volmar into the studio. "Marius, this is Stephanie Lang."

The girl was stretching at the barre. She turned and saw Marius Volmar and her face went white.

"I have asked Mr. Volmar to look at your solo, Stephanie. He can tell us what you are doing wrong. Izzy, when you are ready."

Lvovna and Volmar took seats at the side of the room. Volmar set his face in a scowl. The girl walked quickly to the center and waited. Volmar could see she was biting her lower lip.

The music began. He took a note pad from his pocket and laid it on his knees. His ear winced. The melody was undeniably Tchaikovsky, but the harmony had to be Lvovna's reconstruction. It didn't matter.

The girl's balances were perfect. Volmar almost forgot to keep scowling. She had no trouble sustaining movements to retards in the music. Most surprising of all, she managed to suggest the presence of the invisible prince. There was a clear distinction between assisted pirouettes and unassisted, assisted balances and unassisted. At one point the prince seemed to lift her onto his shoulder, and it was clearly his left shoulder. At another she was dragged backward, just a beat, but definitely dragged with one toe trailing.

*Skillful*, Volmar thought. More than skillful. Convincing. He was reminded that dance is, after all, theater.

As the music approached the coda he heard Lvovna suck in a whispered *"Bozhe moi."*

Now the girl's movements came in dizzying fours: *pas de cheval, pas de bourrée, piqué* turns *en dedans*, each leap faster and longer and more daring than the preceding, ending with a leap into a perfect *plié* in arabesque, an instant of inmobility that rose with absolute control into *relevé en pointe*; and then, right foot holding the *pointe*, and the left leg extended up behind, the torso curved slowly down, supporting itself on shoulders that were not there.

One seamless movement.

The head and throat lifted, arching smoothly from bust up. She turned her head to the right, kissed a mouth that was not there. And held the *penché*.

And held it.

Eight counts. Twelve counts. Fourteen. Sixteen. On seventeen her eyes flicked sideways toward the piano.

That was the only movement.

On eighteen it was over.

"May I clap?" Volmar whispered.

"No. I have told her she is bad. Do not contradict."

"Very nice," Volmar said in a grudging voice.

The girl's gaze brushed his and scurried away.

"Go dress," Lvovna said. "Then come back and Mr. Volmar will give you his notes."

The girl went.

"Well, Marius—was she perfect little Sleeping Beauty?"

Already Volmar was planning. He would give her token corps work and start her in solos. Prayer in *Coppélia* and American Beauty Rose in Waltz of the Flowers and a wonderful little presto in the *Enesco Rhapsody*. In three seasons, perhaps two, she would be ready for *Sleeping Beauty*.

'She was."

He kissed her and there was sadness in her smile.

"She is yours, Marius. Take her. Make her grow. Perhaps you will grow too. It will hurt, but if that is what you want..."

"I'd rather be hurt than dead."

She angled her head as though she saw him more clearly from the side.

"Do you love this girl?"

"Verushka, I love dance, I love music, and sometimes I love you."

"At least you put me in good company."

When the girl returned her eyes seemed near exhaustion. Her blond hair was wavy now from the shower and Volmar felt a pressure in his chest that was like a young man's remembering.

"You show promise," he said.

He saw her tremble under his eyes. He would have liked to emphasize the remark by laying a hand on her shoulder but he did not.

"Your footwork is slow, and you must space your fingers evenly. I know it sounds like a small detail, but there are no small details in ballet."

She lowered her eyes, acknowledging guilt. He noticed the

neatness of her dress, the faint scar of darning thread on the collar of the blouse. He saw there was a mother in her life, and economy. He wanted her to know he could be kind.

"I think we can make room for you at National Ballet Theatre."

Lvovna stood back, nodding, and Volmar explained the contract. He made it clear he was giving the girl an opportunity. He made it clear that many girls were waiting for this chance. He made it clear that, despite what he had seen today in this rehearsal room, he had confidence in her talent.

She was silent and seemed embarrassed.

He had not expected the silence.

"Stephanie," Lvovna said, "Mr. Volmar's time is precious. He has already been kind. Tell him yes, tell him no, tell him one thing or the other."

Her voice was pale and tiny. "I have to ask my mother."

Volmar was annoyed but not disappointed. A mother who darned collars could not object to a daughter's earning money.

"I'll be at the theater," he said. "Let me know before curtain time."

She promised.

When she had gone, Volmar asked about this mother who darned collars.

"A workhorse," Lvovna said. "But you know her—the woman danced for you."

"Lang? I never had a woman called Lang."

"Anna Barlow."

"Oh yes," Volmar said. "I remember Anna Barlow. Long ago."

"Nowadays," Lvovna said, "everything seems long ago."

\* \* \*

When Steph told her mother the news a gust of triumph blew through Anna like the spark from a pilot light rushing to all four burners at once. "Honey, you made it!"

"Thanks to you."

They were in the kitchen drinking coffee, Anna's late afternoon pick-me-up. She almost knocked over the sugar bowl jumping from her chair to hug her little girl. "Thanks to no one.

You're a born dancer. And don't think Marius Volmar doesn't see it. He saw it at your recital. He saw it at your audition. He's been wanting you two years."

"I can't believe it. Marius Volmar—wants—*me*."

"Believe it." The news, Anna decided, called for a celebration, and not just warmed-up coffee left over from breakfast. She pried a box of Bavarian-cream-filled chocolate éclairs from the freezer. Supper wasn't for two hours, and Steph loved sweets—what dancer didn't?

"How did he look?" Anna asked.

"All right."

The éclairs felt hard as popsicles. Anna read the directions to see if there was any mention of quick defrosting in the oven. Nothing. She set the oven to 450 and laid the pastries on a cookie sheet on the top rack.

"Did he ask about me?"

"No."

"He didn't say, 'Hello, how is she?'"

Steph shook her head. "No."

"Doesn't he know you're my kid?"

"There wasn't time for small talk."

"Small talk? Who does he think you are, anyway?"

"Somebody he wants in his company."

Anna stared at Steph and saw a child happy as a Christmas tree. *Kids*, she thought. They were all rush and clatter, never any time to think things through. "Well, he's not doing you any favors. Get that idea out of your head."

"Mom, I'm a nobody. He could have anyone."

"He'd be lucky to have twelve nobodies like you. And he knows it."

"He's invited me to company class day after tomorrow."

"Invited you? What's he got now, spectator seats?"

"No, he wants me to start taking his class."

Anna's mind fumbled with a suspicion. "He's had his look. He doesn't need to check you out twice."

"He wants to put me into the company right away."

"You mean he wants to put you into the corps right away."

"It's a good corps—and it's a good contract. Fifty-two weeks *paid*. And during the season it's two-fifty a week."

"If it's such a good contract, where is it?" Anna held out her hand. She knew Steph didn't have the contract on her. She knew, too, that, like a baby in a carriage, Steph needed someone else's hand on the bar and someone else's foot on the brake.

"Oh, Mom, stop being so suspicious. It's only one or two classes. I'd have to go to class anyway, and at least his are free."

"I'm not talking about classes. I'm talking about that role he made on you—without telling you. Without permission. Without pay. Do you know what you just did? He's seen how the role dances, and now he'll hand it to one of his ballerinas and you won't dance a step of it or see a penny."

For Steph, it was as though a hand had nudged her out of a dream. She tried to delay the moment of reality. "You're wrong, Mom."

An instinct as sudden as the drop of a guillotine made Anna say, "Turn him down."

*"What?"*

"You heard. He hasn't signed you yet, it's his own fault. Don't join NBT."

The kitchen was hospital-quiet. You could hear the throb of the freezer pump, the labored sigh of gas in the coils. Anna's instinct took on the hard certainty of ice. She realized she'd been dealt a hand with an unexpected wild card, and for Steph that card could mean all the difference between getting to the top and getting to the top fast.

"Are you serious? Mom, he's the top man in ballet. He runs the best company in the country. I couldn't do better anywhere else."

"Yes, you could. Take Lester Croyden's offer. Go to Empire."

There was shock on Steph's face. "Empire's dancers are on unemployment eight weeks a year. And the pay's less."

"Go to Empire."

"They're a museum. They're still dancing Fokine's *Firebird.* They only do one Balanchine, and the only choreographer they have is—"

"I don't care. Go to Empire."

"Mom, they dance *junk!*"

"And you can dance that junk in your sleep. Which is why you'll move up fast. You'll make soloist in six months. With Volmar, you don't advance. Believe me, I know. He stockpiles talent. He's got dancers buried at Fort Knox and he's got them in holding patterns at JFK and the only place he doesn't have them is on the stage. At Empire you'll be seen. You'll be reviewed. And when Marius Volmar comes crawling back to you, you'll have leverage."

"Marius Volmar isn't going to come crawling back to anyone."

"And you're not crawling to him either."

"I'm *not* crawling."

"You are if you take that contract! You're crawling and he'll bury you!"

Steph sat staring, mouth open. She had the tangled look of someone trying to fend off two conversations at once. "Why would he do that?"

"To get back at me. To get back at your father. Because we stood up to him."

"Oh, Mom—a man like Marius Volmar's too important to hold grudges."

"A man like that is never important enough." Anna's mind skimmed the past, counted the years that had turned to powder like rosin on a dance floor. "Honey, I know. I've been through it. This is your mother talking. I've made mistakes, I'm the first to admit it. My whole life has been nothing but, and if you don't learn from my mistakes, then what's the point? Honey, I know the business. I know him. I know *you*. Trust me. Just this once, *trust* me."

Anna lifted the telephone from its wall cradle. She placed it in Steph's hand, underbelly up with plastic pushbuttons twinkling.

"Call him."

\*　　\*　　\*

Marius Volmar was in his office, frowning at sketches for the new mounting of *Alborado*—too much pink—when the telephone buzzed. Stephanie Lang began talking in a soft, uneasy voice.

"I've talked your offer over with my mother, and the problem is, it's not my only offer."

"Naturally not. But that shouldn't be a problem."

"Empire has made me an offer, and Lester Croyden is a good friend of my mother's . . ."

"I'm glad your mother has good friends."

"She doesn't think I should join NBT."

The words cut with gentle unexpectedness, like a blade of grass. Pride was stronger than disappointment, even this disappointment. Volmar allowed himself not a sigh. But his heart clutched painfully. For an instant he thought he would have to take a pill. And then his breath returned.

"May I ask you a personal question, Miss Lang? What do *you* think you ought to do?"

"Mr. Volmar, my mother was a dancer and she knows the dance world much better than I do, and she's never given me bad advice."

His reply was that of a man absolutely in control: of others, of his art, of himself. "You do realize it's a question of your future, my dear, not your mother's."

"I'm very sorry, Mr. Volmar. I'm really very sorry."

She was making a mistake, a serious one, but there was nothing he could do to stop her.

"In that case, my dear, I can only wish you all good luck with Empire."

"Thank you, Mr. Volmar."

And then the voice was gone. Something had died. He had experienced a loss so personal, so unexpected, that he could not at first make out exactly what it was.

He felt helpless, strange to himself. There were vestigial stirrings beneath the pain that blanketed him. Memory flashes of Denmark, winter, his mother waving for the last time from the window of a moving police car. He sat adrift in a sudden emptiness, drowning in a *now* that had no shore. The future receded into the fog like the light of a departing ferry.

A ferry that he had missed.

He stared at his left hand and then his right hand. They were shaking. He thought: *What am I doing? Why am I letting this happen? This is absurd. This is not real. This is not Marius Volmar.*

He made fists of his hands. His mind clenched, secreting the fluids of thought. Finally he picked up the telephone receiver again and dialed.

Lvovna's voice came on the line, bad-tempered. He was interrupting her dinner or her television. With Lvovna everything was an interruption.

"Vera Alexeyevna? Am I calling at a convenient time?"

He spoke Russian because she was pleasanter in her own language; and, since her vocabulary was larger, she could be made to gossip more easily.

"Marius—it is you? Let me turn down the news."

The shouting in the background stopped. He recognized the clink of spoon against glass. She had brought her *stakanchi chai*, her excuse for vodka, to the phone.

"Now we can hear each other. What do you want?"

"I was thinking of you, Verushka. That is all. I called to chat."

"Very well. Chat."

"I need to know more about the Lang girl."

# eight

The blow fell the next evening. Anna had fixed a supper of cold cuts and soup. Steph had seen the movie *Stars of the Royal Ballet* that afternoon and she was trying to cheer Chris up with a description of Fonteyn's arabesques.

The telephone rang. Anna answered. A man asked for Miss Avery. The voice disturbed Anna; she wasn't sure why.

"Chris," she said. "For you."

Chris walked slowly to the phone, munching a raw carrot stick. She stood listening for two minutes. There was an expressionless "Thank you." She fumbled the receiver back into the cradle. When she came back to the table Anna could see there was trouble.

"Who was that, Chris?"

Chris hesitated. A look of something like panic passed across her face. "That was Marius Volmar's secretary."

Anna was silent. She stared at Chris, her mind refusing to believe what she had just heard. Finally she picked up her soup spoon and said, "What did Mr. Volmar's secretary want?"

Chris pushed her soup plate away. Her voice was very slow and even and faint. "He wants me . . . to join . . . National Ballet Theatre."

Steph squealed and jumped up from her chair and ran to hug Chris. They were laughing and kissing like two kindergarten playmates and then they were dancing in circles around the table.

Anna's mind moved swiftly, sorting one buzzing suspicion from another. Volmar couldn't want Chris—she wasn't nearly ready for NBT. The man was a gambler, with a gambler's larger-than-life vanity. Dancers were dice to him. He had a scheme, Anna was certain of it, something to do with Steph. And he was working it out as cunningly and elaborately as he did the steps in a ballet.

Chris kissed Anna. Her eyes were sparkling. "You were right, Mrs. Lang! You were right! How can I ever thank you?"

"You're going to take the job?" Anna said.

Chris stiffened. The laughter was erased.

"Take it," Steph cried. "Please take it."

"But we promised—"

"What does that matter? We'll be working in different companies, but we'll both be *working* and that's what counts!"

"Steph is right." Anna began clearing dishes. Her hands were shaking and she needed to keep them busy. "It's a good company. Take the job."

*       *       *

Chris telephoned Marius Volmar's secretary and then she telephoned her parents. "Mother, I made it!"

"Made what, dear?"

"National Ballet Theatre has given me a job!"

"Oh—are they good?"

"They're the best."

"And you're happy?"

"Happier than I've ever been in my life."

"Then we're happy, dear. I'll tell your father."

"Could I tell him myself?"

"We have dinner guests. I'll tell him later."

Anna had been able to overhear only half the conversation. She asked Chris, "What did they say?"

"Nothing, really. I guess they're pleased."

Chris looked let down. Anna felt sorry for the girl and

wondered what the hell kind of idiots she had for parents. *Nothing, really,* when their kid landed a job with the top outfit in the U.S.A.

*Nothing, really!*

\*     \*     \*

Steph and Chris both had jobs. They were eighteen and supporting themselves. It seemed silly not to have their own apartment.

"So long as you're not living alone," Mrs. Avery said when Chris phoned.

"I'll be living with Steph."

"Then I suppose it's all right. You have to be grown up sometime."

Anna didn't agree. "What do you two need your own apartment for? You'll never find an apartment. Not in this town."

They found one.

It was on the fourteenth floor of a post-World War II high-rise—thirteenth if you counted the fact that there was no 13 in the building, but Steph didn't bother mentioning that to Chris.

The super called it four rooms. Steph counted a bedroom and a living room, plus kitchen and bath and the hook of an L. Chris had her heart set on a fireplace, but Steph pointed out the huge bathtub and the needlepoint shower and the dishwasher and the air conditioning.

"Besides, the building pays for gas and it's a ten-minute walk from Lincoln Center."

They debated and finally signed a joint lease and handed over a certified check. They packed their possessions into a chaos of suitcases and mover's cartons and two dozen overstuffed paper bags.

"How the dickens are we going to move it all?" Steph said.

An idea came to Chris. "I have a friend." *Even though he's never phoned.* "Maybe he'd help."

Steph was surprised. Chris had never mentioned a friend. But Ray Lockwood was glad to help.

He rented a van and said it belonged to a friend. He drove the girls to the thrift shop where they had made down payments on a dining table and a rocking chair. He lugged and twisted and managed to get the disassembled twin beds up the service elevator and into 14-K. He carried heavy packages cheerfully, set them down carefully, didn't break a single dish.

And he watched Chris.

There was a beauty and delicacy about her that seemed to reflect all the beauty and delicacy that were ruled out of his own world. He tried to gather all his feelings into a smile and smile it so clearly Chris couldn't help but understand.

From time to time, as they shifted cartons and furniture, she brushed the hair out of her eyes and saw him smiling and smiled back at him.

"He's working like a demon," Steph whispered. "You two must be best friends—or something."

"He's just someone from my home town," Chris said. "He's a lawyer. And very smart."

"And very nice."

When Chris was in another room, a loose lid fell off a box. "Whose are these?" Ray asked.

"They're Chris's," Steph said.

Because they were Chris's, the simple, senseless knickknacks moved him with an involuntary power. They looked like charms for bracelets and party favors for eight-year-olds. There were tiny violets in glass and butterflies in plastic and cloth animals. He tried to construct Chris from the jumble of her possessions.

"Chris collects things," Steph said. "That doll comes from the St. Anthony fair down in Little Italy. She won it shooting out candles with a water pistol."

He lifted the small stuffed doll, looked at it, wondered why she kept it. Then he laid it down gently without disturbing the other trinkets in the box.

The moving was almost done when finally he was alone with Chris.

"It's good to see you again," he said.

"It's good to see you." She shifted. Packing cartons pressed in around them, making the space tiny. She let his glance hold hers for a long moment, till she began to feel nervous. "This will be the bedroom," she said.

They stared at each other. There was a gravity in his eyes and she tried to oppose her smile to it.

"I tried to phone you," he said.

"Oh?"

"I even wrote a letter." He had written three letters and he had thought about writing a dozen.

"I never got a letter," she said.

"I never mailed it. I didn't know your address."

She laughed and the laugh felt uneasy in her throat. "You know it now."

"I intend to remember it." He had a young face, a Midwestern face, and there was something open and honest in his gaze. It made her feel she was standing in a too bright light.

She smiled faintly and then looked away from him.

"I'd like to see you again, Chris."

"I'd like to," she said.

"I'd like to see you some evening in the not too distant future."

Her eyes hesitated and then her gaze lay still on the neutrality of a stack of records. She struggled to say yes. But something frightened her.

"The corps dances every performance," she said.

"But you have a night off."

She didn't want him to expect too much of her. He was used to debutantes and bright girls with bright laughter. "I'm pretty tired my night off."

"I understand that. We can have a restful evening together."

"I wouldn't be much of a date. Maybe after I'm more at home in the company..."

"You talk as though it'll be years before you can go out for a cup of coffee."

"You don't know a dancer's life. It's physical work."

"I've done physical work."

"But dancers are...different."

"Are they?"

A change had come into his voice. She looked up at him and saw him take the look for some kind of reply. She pulled away from his gaze, pushed open the window, let in a cone of air. Her eye took refuge in the view: a sliver of New York sky, trapped chemical and shimmering between two high-rises.

"Chris, can I ask you something?"

She leaned on the window sill, feeling safer at a distance, however slight.

"When you told me your telephone—did you mean to give me a wrong number?"

She flushed. "I don't remember doing that. I'm sorry. I'm not good with numbers."

"But you remembered mine."

*But yours was written down*, she wanted to say. But she sensed the lawyer in him, trapping her into something.

"Chris, will you be honest with me? Does it bother you to see me?"

The question surprised her and it stung like a slap.

"I'd rather know straight out than waste my time."

*Maybe I would be wasting his time*, she thought. A warm, damp breeze blew through the open window. She didn't know what to answer. She was overwhelmed by a shaming sense of her utter incompetence.

"You saved our lives today," she said. "We would have been lost without you."

"Then will you phone me in a few weeks?"

He was leaving it up to her and that frightened her, but he had been kind. "All right," she said. "In a few weeks."

*        *        *

The days that followed were lucky and crowded. Steph was busy discovering a hardware shop that cut window shades to order and a Shop-Rite supermarket two blocks away and best of all a health store around the corner with year-round specials on bee pollen.

Chris found a brass lamp in a junk shop, perfect for the bedside table. There was a white sale at Bloomingdale's, and they bought linen. Mrs. Avery insisted on giving them silver from Altman's, but they were able to exchange it for a handsome set of Danish stainless steel, plates for eight, glasses, and five beautiful copper-bottomed pots.

Steph cut company class Tuesday and stayed home waiting for the telephone man. Her very first call was to her mother, to give her the number. She could tell that Anna was in one of her moods, resentful that the girls had moved out, annoyed at having to find a smaller apartment. But Steph felt happy and busy and invulnerable and invited her mother to supper the following night. "It'll just be hamburger and frozen vegetable."

"Not spinach," Anna said. "Frozen spinach has twice as much folic acid as fresh. That's the last thing a dancer needs."

"String beans," Steph promised.

Anna arrived a half hour early. She inspected the bathtub and the kitchen faucets and asked about cockroaches. She wanted to know about the lease.

*"Two years!"* she gasped.

She peeked in the corners of closets and found a window that didn't slide open all the way. She wouldn't sit in the rocker.

"Where'd you get that? It'll break if you look at it."

She spent ten minutes tapping on walls. She criticized a loose inch of baseboard that someone was going to break their neck tripping over. She didn't see why the girls had to fry their hamburger when gas was included and grilling produced less saturated animal fat.

"I just don't understand," she sighed. "I hope you two know what you're up to, because I sure don't."

At nine-fifteen she gathered up her cigarettes and her purse. She waved a glum good-by from the elevator.

Steph felt a little sorry, but more than that, she felt relieved. She sat rocking in the rocker and tried to decide—when they could afford it—what color the living-room rug should be.

# nine

From the very first Steph loved Empire State Ballet. It was a huge family. Within two weeks she was calling the kids in the corps by their first names, within a month the whole company.

Jan-Pieter de Jong, who was Dutch and six foot two and blond and a superstar, was Pete. His cocker spaniel, who for some reason was allowed to run loose backstage, was Max. What a mess when Max took a crap in a box of *Petrouchka* prop rubles thirty seconds before performance! Ilona Banska, who had defected from Hungary and drew huge audiences and three-thousand-dollar fees for every performance, was said to be a standoffish bitch, but everyone called her Ilonka, because in Hungary that was short for Ilona. Lester Croyden, who directed the company, was Lester. Hannah Meredith, who was society and had money and *thought* she directed the company, was Hannah—always bumbling around with a notebook, spending her life and the company's patience making sure who was substituting for whom.

"Sally, you're substituting for Amy? Who's Amy doing?"

"I think she's doing Clara."

"Well, I have Millicent down for Clara . . ."

Steph had never seen so many substitutions in her life. One

evening the principal dancing Firebird was out with food poisoning, so the girl dancing Aurora in *Aurora's Wedding* had to be put into *Firebird*, and the younger sister from *Pillar of Fire* had to dance Aurora; and the substitute younger sister was thrown into the role so late her name wasn't even in the insert in the program, and Hagar, the older sister, had to whisper the steps to her. Two minutes before curtain Phyllis, who did lighting design, was stomping across the stage yelling at an electrician to re-angle number 35 because Suzie, in tears that her variation hadn't been getting applause, had decided that it was all the lighting's fault and wanted her exit to be *visible*.

Everything at Empire struck Steph as helter-skelter and wonderfully haywire and it seemed a miracle that the show ever went on.

Company class was obligatory. Scheduled for 11 A.M., it was a hit-or-miss affair—on good days. Bad days it was indescribable. Steph was always on time, warming up by eleven-five, and she was usually the first.

The studio was three stories below ground level, as big and brightly lit as the main stage. One wall was mirrored floor to ceiling and the wall opposite was a great blue-red splash of a Dufy mural of ballerinas and butterflies. The dancers generally started fluttering in around eleven-fifteen.

"How *are* you?" Steph called to Daphne, one of the soloists.

"Great—I had a *nap* yesterday!"

By eleven-twenty bodies were writhing on the floor, stretching legs at the barres, wiggling toes one-at-a-time. The air began to thicken with cigarette smoke and talk and the first hint of sweat. The boys did deep knee bends at the barre, down and down further and rotate the ass, stretch each knee like a slow-motion Russian dance. The girls did splits, and Andrea, who'd just been made a principal, did splits with a Virginia Slim dangling from the corner of her mouth.

Lit cigarettes and rumors and half-drunk Styrofoam cups of coffee were passed till eleven twenty-five, when Heinrich Sanders, the dance master, made his entrance wearing a polka-dot babushka. A great laughter went up. From neck down Heinrich was a natty dresser, but his hair transplant was still growing in, and it was a great joke that every day he wore something different to cover his head.

At eleven-thirty Tommy the pianist arrived, without his

music as usual, and began improvising an oompahing 2/4 to the melody of "Baby Face, You've Got the Sweetest Little Baby Face." Plastic and Saran Wrap leg warmers were shed like used cocoons and Heinrich called the movements in time to the music:

"*Pli-é*—stretch—two *demi-pliés*, one *grand plié*, first position..."

At the first break in the music the dancers rushed from the barres to twist their toes in the rosin box in the corner, like cats stampeding to a litter box.

Heinrich called out the *ronds de jambe*, faster tempo, and sixty slippers whispered in perfectly synchronized circles, leaving the floor as chalky white as a used blackboard. Combinations next; "*Rond*—arabesque—*plié*—and close!" After that, "*Effacez!*" which was French for "Turn around." The dancers turned, left hand on the barre now, and went through the whole mess again, only this time the right side ached. "Do your own treatment, please."

The piano rippled a slow 3/4 and the dancers stretched and improvised. Heinrich went to the phone and for three minutes had a loud conversation in Russian.

Synchronization began to break down. The dancers shoved the barres to the side of the room and boys and girls alternated in center work. Half the dancers were standing, half lying on the floor. One girl was tying her laces and three were doing slow backward somersaults. The piano honky-tonked a tango. Hands arced overhead. Up on one foot. Leg out, slow slow slow till the slowness screamed. Leg down, remember to keep the foot turned out.

"One and two and NOT so fast!"

*Développés*—vertical leg stretches. *Grand tour à la seconde;* men's hair whipped out in the pirouettes; women's hair, fastened with barrettes and rubber bands, stayed as calm as a hair spray commercial.

Sally, one of the soloists, left the room and came back with a handful of paper towels that she distributed to needy friends. Dancers' metabolisms varied, and one girl could get bone dry through a combination that would leave another dripping wet; but by the end of Heinrich's *petit allegro* everyone was in a running sweat.

"Two groups, girls. Two groups, boys. First group girls start from behind, diagonal." Heinrich reeled off steps like a shopping list and the piano improvised a wild Cossack dance on "Baby Face." The room erupted in leaps and spins and collisions.

"And, boys, I asked you for *two* groups!"

By twelve-thirty towels and sweat shirts were draped over the barres. Boys were dancing bare-chested; girls had unbuttoned their blouses to ventilate glistening upper bosoms. Sylvia and Victoria simply gave up and stood chattering Portuguese. Two of the boy principals waved to the dance master and walked out.

Though there were ninety dancers in the company, only fifty came to company class. The rest, Steph had heard, went to class outside. They paid $2.50, but at least they *learned* and didn't waste their time. Eventually she might do the same, but instinct told her that for the moment she'd do better to prove her team spirit and stick with the company.

"And we stretch the *feet* and *cabriole!*"

At the end of the class, "Thank you, girls." The girls clapped and disbanded. One more exercise for the boys, and "Thank you, boys," and the boys applauded.

After class you took your cigarette and coffee break, or if you'd taken it during class, you took another. Steph took most of her breaks with Linda—a lanky, dark-haired girl, a half inch too tall, they said, who might make it to soloist but never to principal.

Linda was inseparable from Al, a blond farm-boy type who could hold a balance till the cows came home and always had the latest, gamiest gossip. Steph quickly learned which corps girl was sleeping with which principal, who was gay but not letting on, who was straight but pretending to be bi to get ahead—"And either way," Al roared, "he's still a lousy lay!"

Steph knew she shouldn't enjoy that kind of talk, but it fascinated her. This one was a vegetarian—*and* an alcoholic ("vodka in the carrot juice"); that one was on health food for her (hush-hush) ulcer; he was on cortisone for his (hush-hush-hush) fractured arch; she had *two* doctors because she couldn't get enough Valium from one; *he* was going to an analyst because his umpteenth lover had dropped him; *she* was thirty-eight and lying about her age and losing her turn-out, and *he* had made a pass at Hannah (ugh!) at President Carter's Kennedy Center party and *still* didn't get to dance Bluebird (ha!).

Steph counted three types of kids in the corps. Some were killing time till they married or gave in to their parents and got a job with money and security. Others weren't certain of their own ambition or ability: they'd smoke pot one week and cut class, and the next they'd crash-diet and take two classes a day. Then there were the determined ones, who never touched drugs or alcohol, didn't waste time partying or sleeping around, never missed a class or rehearsal or performance even if they'd mangled a foot.

Steph ranked Al type two, unsure and covering up with a lot of camp. Linda was type three, determined. It struck Steph as odd that Linda and Al were pals; it struck her as even odder, one day after class, when Linda suggested, "Hey, a bunch of us are goofing off this afternoon—you're invited."

"I can't—I've got rehearsal."

"I didn't know you were in *Fille.*"

"I'm understudying Vicki."

Linda made a face. "Oh, Christ, the *Ribbon* Dance." It was a number in Act One of *Fille Mal Gardée.* Linda was understudying it too, but she'd been with the company two years and knew the repertory. "You could walk through that blindfolded."

"I've never danced it. I'd better stay and watch Vicki."

"Follow the girl on your right. Come on." Linda looped an arm through Steph's. "Danny and Al are waiting."

"Danny?" Steph was surprised. And interested. There was only one Danny in the company. Danny Gillette. A tall, dark boy with moody eyes. Rumor had it he was going to be made a principal that spring. Steph had admired his Cowboy in *Billy the Kid.* It seemed peculiar that he hung out with kids from the corps like Linda and Al.

"He wants to stop at Liberty's," Linda said. "They've got some kind of special on earphones."

*Why not?* Steph decided. She vowed she wouldn't feel guilty.

The two boys were waiting at the elevator. "Danny, you know Steph, don't you?" Linda said.

Danny was staring straight at Steph. His eyes were brown. "Sure. I knocked into you in *Arcade.*"

Steph was amazed he remembered. And pleased. A lot of the

male soloists in the company acted as though they had it made, especially if they were tall. Danny was different. She'd seen him in class and he was a perfectionist. Onstage he was that rare thing, a partner who knew exactly how to show a woman off.

And his eyes had beautiful gold flecks.

They went laughing and chattering out to Ninth Avenue. They were waiting to cross when Steph noticed people watching them. She'd been aware of it before: the Lincoln Center area was a dancers' ghetto, and non-dancers were always staring.

"Why are they looking at us?" she said. "What's so odd about four dancers?"

"We've got great bodies," Al said, loud enough to be overheard, "and we're dressed like bag ladies—right down to the tote bags."

Steph supposed it was true: blue jeans, tie-dyed shirts, sneakers, weird jewelry.

"Bull," Danny said. "It's your feet. We're like swans out of water—they can spot us two blocks away. Look at Linda. What human being waits for a light like that? She's in fifth position. Feet turned out, right foot in front of left."

"Sloppy fifth," Al said.

"What about you?" Linda shot back. "What's that supposed to be, fourth position *croisé?*" It was an exaggeration but only a slight one: Al's right foot was turned completely out and he was tapping the curb with the toe of his left.

"Okay, schmucks." Al arced his left arm up, hand overhead; he smoothly extended his right arm and his tote bag slid to the sidewalk. His left leg came up, knee bent, at a ninety-degree angle behind the right, into a classic *attitude*.

An old man gave him a terrified glance and hurried across the street mumbling and they all burst out laughing.

They took a bus to the Liberty Music Shop just across from St. Pat's and Danny tried out a half dozen stereo earphones.

"That one," Al said. "It's absolutely *you*."

Steph noticed that Danny's checks were printed *Daniel Gillette aka Goldberg* and she asked what kind of name *aka* was.

"*Aka* is Japanese for *also known as*, and *Goldberg* is Jewish for *Gillette*. A dancer might sneak by with *Gold* or *Berg*, but *Goldberg*, forget it."

"That's why they call it the *Gillette Variations?*" Al said.

A lot of dancers took stage names, and Steph had suspected Danny's Gillette hid something Greek or Italian. She'd never thought of Jewish. Now she'd learned something. There were Jews with beautiful Mediterranean eyes.

They went to Burger King and ordered burgers with all the weird combinations of extras they could think of, just like the Burger King commercials on TV. The girl taking orders gave them terrible looks and dumped mustard and onion on everything but the milk shakes. They laughed and burped all the way to Fifth Avenue, where Al and Linda wanted to buy dog collars in a Sixty Nine Cents shop.

"They come in brass and stainless steel and they make terrific necklaces," Al said.

"For a dog?" Danny said. He had thick dark eyebrows and when they arched he looked very skeptical.

"For us, stupid," Linda laughed.

Danny and Steph were alone. A Con Ed drill team was ripping up Forty-seventh Street and there was no sense trying to talk. The sidewalk crowd kept jostling them. Three or four times Steph felt the pressure of Danny's body grazing hers, light and accidental. She moved away a little but only a little, and the pressure followed, just a little. She felt his glance keep skimming over her.

"Steph," he shouted, "do you know how you look when you dance?"

"How?" she shouted.

"Like you're asleep."

She was silent a moment. A long speechless moment. The remark felt like an insult but his eyes weren't insulting at all. They were soft as a baby's fingertips exploring her face.

"That's the way a dancer should look," he shouted. "You're a wonderful sleeper."

Al and Linda came out of the store, giggling and arf-arfing with matching brass dog collars around their necks. Al struck a high-fashion pose with one wrist dangling and shouted, "Chic, hey? The Countess in *Giselle*?" and Linda shouted that they'd better hurry if they wanted to make the special on women's lounging pajamas at Lord and Taylor.

All the way down to Thirty-eighth Street (they could have taken a bus but it was a crisp glowing fall day and they voted unanimously to walk) Danny kept looking at Steph's hands. She wasn't wearing any rings and her hands weren't doing anything and she couldn't understand the reason. It was as though he was measuring her.

Al tried to gross out the saleswoman at the store by asking to try on a size eight. In a very grandmotherly way, she explained that he could change in the employees' men's room, but a guard would have to stand in the stall with him.

Linda broke down laughing and said *she* was the gentleman's size, she would try on the clothes. Danny looked uncomfortable and Linda and Steph went into one of the women's changing rooms.

"What's the matter?" Linda said. Steph was staring at her.

"You and Al—are you—"

"Are we what?"

"Are you lovers?"

"Oh, Christ, everyone asks that. We just happen to like each other."

"And you sleep together?"

"Why not? His roommate threw him out, he needs a place to crash."

"But isn't he—"

Linda gave her a look edged in amazement. "Gay? Are you kidding? He's gay and a mess and he's hung up on some student at ASB who's straight."

"Then what do you see in him?"

"Beggars can't be choosers, and if you're a girl in the corps, you're begging. Besides, he can talk about dance and he gives a hell of a massage; he's got a great body and he makes me *laugh*. And frankly, he listens to *my* problems the way no man would."

"And is Danny—gay?"

"Half the boys in the corps *and* Lester Croyden have tried and I've never heard a whisper. Believe me, if there was anything to whisper about, I'd hear." Linda twirled and made a face. "Tell me the mirror's lying. I *haven't* got hips like that."

"It's the pajamas that are lying," Steph said. "They make you look pregnant. And the color—"

"Yeah, I know. Something Al would wear to a Halloween ball." Linda stepped out of the pants.

"Does Danny have a girl?" Steph asked.

"A lot of girls have tried."

"If he's not gay, why haven't any succeeded?"

"Okay, let me give you the Danny Gillette story, capsule form. He's a sweet kid from Scarsdale and he's breaking his parents' hearts. *They* want him in law school or pre-med, *he* wants to mess around with tutus and toe shoes. *He* knows he's going to make it, the company knows he's going to make it, the parents don't know a pirouette from a pecan and they're petrified."

"But what does that have to do with girls?"

"Look, if on top of everything else he got serious about a girl in the company—and he could—his mother would throw herself off the Bronx-Whitestone Bridge."

"Why?"

"Because it's got to be a nice Jewish girl. That much he owes the folks."

"But there must be some Jewish girls in the corps."

"Bess and Lizzie. And they lasted a week each."

Steph's mind explored the puzzle. It was like a trick box. There had to be a hidden spring somewhere that would snap it open. She wondered if she should spread a rumor that her name was really something Jewish beginning with an L.

Stephanie Liebowitz.

Linda was staring at her. "Hey, he's a nice guy. But aren't you making a production out of it?"

"I think he's nice, that's all."

"I'll tell you something. He thinks you're nice."

"Did he say so?"

"Not exactly."

"Then how do you know? Don't tease me, Linda."

"Because he asked me to ask you to come shopping. Danny Gillette doesn't give a damn about shopping and he hates Al's camping. And I've seen the way he watches you in class."

"You're making that up. He doesn't watch me."

"Then he's incredibly interested in who cuts your hair. Who does, by the way? I'm sick of mine."

For the rest of the afternoon Steph couldn't be sure: from the corner of her eye she tried to keep track of Danny and he did seem to stare at her hair and her hands a lot. Once or twice their eyes met but she lost her nerve and let her glance slide away.

When they got back to the theater Vicki had tripped on the hood of the prompter's box, which some fool had left up. She'd twisted an ankle, so Steph had to go on in the Ribbon Dance after all.

She was petrified. It didn't help that Al was standing in the wings mugging, trying to break her up. Danny, who was playing the foolish suitor, swatted her with his butterfly net on one of his leaps and she knew he'd done it on purpose. But she kept her eyes on the girl on her right and never let herself so much as smile. Amazingly enough, she got through the steps and the turns and the audience went politely wild and called the girls back for two bows.

"You weren't sleepy tonight," Danny whispered afterward in the wings, grinning.

Steph went home feeling happy and high, thinking: *This is too easy, this is too much fun, this couldn't be ballet.* And when she fell asleep she saw Danny Gillette aka Goldberg's gold-flecked eyes smiling at her.

# ten

With Chris it was different.

For the first several weeks she was thrilled to be part of National Ballet Theatre. Then she was puzzled; and then, she realized, sad. She was lonely and it baffled her.

She had known the solitude of doctors and nurses and doting parents, but now she was learning the solitude of being shut out. There was talk and there was laughter at NBT, but they were always around a corner and she was never part of them.

The other girls had friends to help them practice. They had friends to gossip with and have coffee with. They had friends to cry with. Chris didn't have anyone. She warmed up by herself, practiced by herself, ate by herself. Half the time she couldn't get the food down.

She came to dread company class. The music was fast, and the dancers muttered about "concert tempo." It seemed there was a separate step for every note in every trill. Volmar thought nothing of throwing an *entrechat huit* at the company—one tiny jump and you had to beat your feet eight times before you landed. The best Chris could manage was six beats, and even those weren't clean.

The other dancers saw she was sloppy and they saw Volmar

come and explain to her and put his arm around her and she
heard them whispering.

Even as she came to master the unfamiliar footwork she felt
no sense of accomplishment: she learned to move faster—that
was all. She felt betrayed. She had expected ballet to light up her
life and instead there was a darkness growing around her.

She pulled herself from company class to rehearsal, from
dressing room to performance. The corridors of the State
Theater were industrial gray and they seemed to suck the
strength out of her. Some days she had time to go home for a
nap. But when she was cast in a new production there was no
time; she had to go to the women's lounge and pray there'd be a
free couch or space on the floor to lie down.

The worst evenings were *Köchel Listing 312*. She heard
dancers say there were more steps in the allegro of *Köchel* than
in all of *Giselle*. She believed it.

The company took their places on stage at eight-five and the
curtain rose at eight-seven sharp. There was always applause for
the bare stage and the sky-blue cyclorama and the corps lined up
dramatically along the diagonal. The conductor gave the brisk
downbeat. The corps linked themselves quickly, orange and
black. The music kept them blurred and bouncing, like a giant
hand slapping thirty basketballs. By eight-fourteen Chris was
dead tired, could hardly see clearly.

A wedge of purple sent green spinning away from it. A
fluttering V of gray entwined with a stripe of yellow. Streaks of
white streamed past, tilted way off the vertical. Rosin squeaked
like a massacre of cats. The chirping Mozart music went on and
on, repeat after repeat. The dance mirrored the music: repeat,
repeat, repeat. Hot needles went through Chris's calves. Red
male rectangles hoisted whirling blue female hoops. At last the
retard: preparation, *plié*, leap into the wings.

Chris's hand found the honey that she had hidden in the
electrician's box. She gulped.

Energy. A thick sweet taste blotted out the rhythms and the
colors. Five counts till her cue. Her toes were squashed and
screaming in their slippers. Four three two NOW—

She was one of eight spinning skirts. The lights slapped her
eyes. She leapt. Was caught. Was thrown. Was caught again.
Her lungs were burning. She couldn't catch her breath and her
breath couldn't catch up with the music and the music never

stopped screaming orders, like a mad general in a battle that had no victory, no defeat, no truce or finish.

At the end of the evening Chris sat in the wings on an electrician's stool, crumpled over as far as a human body could crumple. It seemed she was the only one in the company who ever sprained an ankle or tore a toenail halfway off or was exhausted all the time. It took her an eternity just to get her breath back.

The dancers streamed past. She didn't know where they got their strength from. They laughed, and cursed their slips, made dates for nightcaps at favorite bars, dates for the night.

"Did you see Pierre cheat on that double turn?"

"And the idiots *applauded!*"

"I hear his wife hires them."

Not one of the dancers glanced at Chris. In stage make-up their eyes were cruel and catlike and the not-glancing was a trick, because dancers missed nothing and she knew they saw her seated on the stool in the dimmed stage lights, not moving.

"Little Miss Muffet sitting on her toosh again."

"Does she *know* how to talk?"

"Why should she talk to any of *us?* She has Volmar teaching her finger pirouettes *personally.*"

She glanced up and caught the eye of a female soloist flicking something mean and crafty at her.

*They're laughing at me.* The realization hit her like a slap on the cheek. Panic held her nailed to the stool. She closed her eyes, tried to ignore her thumping heart, tried to blink the theater away.

She waited till the sounds of hurry dimmed, till the stage lights clicked off and there was only the naked bulb on a poke stage center and a stagehand looking at her oddly.

She crept back to the dressing room on tiptoe. She was the only person there. Something cold and wet crawled over her skin.

Fear.

                    *       *       *

"Why so glum?" Steph said.

They were standing in the kitchen. It was Chris's turn to fix dinner and she was snipping the ends of string beans. She'd discovered that fresh beans were cheaper than frozen, cooked faster, tasted better, and had more vitamins.

"I don't know," Chris said. "Hard class, maybe."

Steph gave her an odd look. Chris knew it wasn't much of an excuse: class had been more than eight hours ago.

Suddenly Chris decided to let everything out. A little. "Steph, do you have friends at Empire?"

"Sure—it's a friendly company."

"But do you have *friends?*"

"Friends to joke with, to have coffee with—that kind of friend."

*And I don't*, Chris thought. *What's wrong with me?*

Steph bit down on a carrot stick. "Why, don't you have friends at NBT?"

*I'm not going to let Steph see. It's not fair heaping my problems on her.* "Oh sure, friends to joke with and take coffee break with. But there's no one I can really talk to."

Steph laughed. "By the time I'm through with class and rehearsal it's all I can do to pant—let alone talk." She glanced up at Chris and her expression turned serious. "Look, expecting to find a best friend in the corps is like—its like expecting to find the love of your life there."

Chris was silent. She'd always believed that somehow she'd wind up in the arms of a prince, not just during *Sleeping Beauty*, but after the curtain came down. "But some girls—*do* fall in love with men in the corps."

"*If* they're men," Steph said. "No, I take that back. Some of the girls at Empire sleep with gay boys. Linda says they're good lovers."

Chris made a face. "That's just—sex. If I slept with someone, I'd want it to be love."

Steph smiled. "Everyone wants that. I guess either you settle for less or you grow old waiting for Mr. Right to join the corps." She shrugged. "Or you shop around outside of ballet."

*I wouldn't know what to do outside of ballet*, Chris thought. But she tried to sound flip and confident. "Who has the time? Or the energy?"

"Then you have to choose. Dance—or a man."

*No*, Chris thought, *there's some other way, I know there's some other way.*

* * *

"Tell me, Christine, how have you been feeling?

The doctor's voice was professional cheerful, almost chatty. But his eye took in the flushed patches of skin, the abnormally small pupils, all the evidence of undernourishment and overwork and self-destruction.

"Just fine," Chris said. She had learned it was the only safe answer. She didn't want to be imprisoned in a hospital for days and days of tests. She didn't want to miss class. She was far enough behind already. She buttressed her lie with a wavering smile.

"Unbutton, please," the doctor said.

She unbuttoned. Her hand trembled and her fingers were clumsy.

The doctor reached a stethoscope beneath her hospital smock. He bent his head slightly and he listened to her breathing. The instrument left an icy track along her ribs. She hated stethoscopes. They were lie detectors that always found her out. When she was a child doctors had come and listened to her breathing and she'd had to go to the hospital.

The doctor's face showed no reaction to the rapid, uneven beating of her heart. She was relieved when he said she could button up again.

"Young lady, you need a lot more sleep, a lot more food, and a lot less coffee."

"I'll be all right. It goes away after a while."

"What goes away?" he asked, alert.

Her eyes darted in confusion. "What you were just talking about."

His eyes changed depth of focus. There was sympathy in them, but criticism too. "Are you taking anything to rev up your energy?"

"Don't all dancers?"

"I want to know what you're taking. Diet pills? Ginseng?"

She shook her head. He didn't seem to know much about dancers. "I don't take drugs. Just honey."

"For you, honey's a drug. Lay off it, will you?"

The hell she'd lay off honey. She'd never get through

company class, let alone a performance, without half a jar of it.

"Okay," she lied.

The doctor nodded and went into the next room. Concern rimmed his eyes as he hunched over Christine Avery's records. Pen in hand, he skimmed the medical history: blood pressure, pulmonary function, weight, blood sugar, urine. He paused and added a notation.

\* \* \*

Chris remained alone in the examining room, legs swinging impatiently off the edge of the table. She hated hospitals. They were jails where doctors locked you up and probed you and pulled blood and marrow out of you and then told you there was nothing wrong. Doctors had once kept her four days in Evanston General and she'd missed the school recital.

She would have danced Ondine.

She had a vague impression of time drifting by, of voices whispering. A knock interrupted her thoughts and the door opened and the doctor stood gazing at her.

He added what he saw to what he had read in the records and he felt he had been staring at her for many, many years. She looked very small and delicate. There was a fragile grace to the way she held herself and her face was fulfilled and luminous, like a martyr's.

"You're doing fine, Christine, just fine."

His face was friendly and wise and false, like all doctors' faces she had known.

"But remember. Never go two months without a complete checkup."

In Evanston they had said three months. He couldn't be a very good doctor.

"And if you ever black our or feel faint or the least bit dizzy—see me immediately."

The doctor patted her shoulder and made a gesture for her to dress. She could tell he didn't understand. To him, health was an end in itself. To her, it was a ladder to something higher.

"And no more than one cup of coffee a day. Decaffeinated if you can stomach it."

She nodded. Give up *coffee?* The man had to be crazy.

# eleven

---

"Hey—aren't you Avery?"

Chris whirled, tried to locate the voice and stave off its hinted threat. Just inside the stage door, a dozen girls clustered chattering around the bulletin board where the day's schedule was posted. Chris had skirted them and gone straight to the elevator. She already had her schedule memorized: company class at eleven, rehearsal of the new choreography for *Köchel Listing* at twelve-thirty, lunch break (yogurt and an apple), and stage rehearsal at three of Tchaikovsky's *Serenade*. With luck she'd squeeze in a quick nap (God, how she'd been needing those quick naps!) and a bite at home, then hurry back to the theater at six-thirty to change and warm up for the 8 P.M. curtain.

And now, just as the elevator doors whooshed open, one of the girls at the bulletin board called over, "Hey—aren't you Avery?"

It was Madeline Robbins, the redhead who danced Tulip in *Waltz of the Flowers*. She'd never said so much as a hello before.

"You'd better take a look at this."

Chris hesitated, then crossed warily to the board. The girls backed off. She could feel their eyes encircling her. A last-minute change had been penciled onto the schedule: *12:30,*

*Studio 3: New Work; Avery and Collins.*

She recognized the thick, slashing capitals. So did every other girl there. The handwriting was Marius Volmar's.

Her mind lurched. A new work for Avery—Christine Avery? It had to be a mistake. But she knew Marius Volmar didn't make mistakes. Ever.

A dozen silent stares tracked her to the elevator.

In the dressing room, flutters of panic began in her stomach. Wally Collins was a principal, one of the top male dancers in the company. In the country.

By the time she got to class she felt she was going to throw up. The ballet master yelled at her twice about her turn-out. The girls kept throwing her ricochet glances in the mirrors, eyes hard as sharpened rocks.

Wally Collins, two positions down from her on the barre, went through the movements flawlessly, tall and blond, fluid and untroubled as wheat bending in the wind. He didn't look at her once. The whole company saw him not looking at her and the corps began smirking.

Chris excused herself after the *petit allegro*.

She locked herself into a toilet stall and put a finger down her throat. Breakfast—half a doughnut and black coffee—came up.

After that she was able to control the trembling. She gargled and showered. At twelve-thirty she tiptoed to the door of Studio 3, braced for humiliation.

Marius Volmar, elbows propped on the top of the upright piano, was nodding a tempo to the pianist. He turned as Chris slipped through the door. His eyes acknowledged her. There was no frown, no smile, nothing. He gestured to the pianist to keep playing.

"It's the Andante Cantabile. You know it, of course."

"I've heard it." Chris felt the floor sway. She steadied her knees. "It's very pretty."

"It's trash, but it's Tchaikovsky—and Tchaikovsky is always genius."

Wally Collins came shoulder-swinging through the studio door, crisp and bright-faced as a mountain climber setting out before sunrise. He had changed into fresh green tights and a loose moss-green shirt. Chris felt herself grow small in her rumpled, dirty leotard.

Volmar stretched a hand. "Wally—come help us. You know Christine?"

Wally smiled. He had healthy, meat-murdering teeth. "Hi."

"Sit." Volmar patted the wood floor. The three of them sat. Volmar nodded and the pianist began to play again. Volmar shut his eyes. The music flowed with the melancholy asymmetry of a sigh. At a quickening in the tempo Volmar raised his hand. "Sammy—if you please—a little more pizzicato in the left hand."

Chris stole a glance at Wally Collins. He was winding his wristwatch.

Volmar let the music continue to the end. He thanked the pianist, got to his feet, and began pacing, waving his arms.

"Music is our staircase. This is simple music; it makes a simple staircase. No spirals, no zigzags, no drooping over the bannister. We go up, we come down again. We have two tempos: the *andante*, the *più mosso*. They are repeated. Same stairs up, same stairs down. Wally—where is our emotional climax? Where are the stairs steepest?"

"The last *allegro*."

"Christine?"

She hesitated to disagree with her partner, but... "The second *andante*."

"What phrase in the second *andante*?"

"The two silences."

Volmar's gaze probed hers, lingered. "And which silence is steeper?"

"The second."

A soundlessness expanded through the studio. "Correct. We are aiming at the second silence."

Volmar rubbed his hands briskly together, like a baker preparing to pummel a wad of dough into strudel.

"All right. Christine, you lie down on the floor. You're a dead princess, dead swan, any dead beautiful thing you like. Wally, you enter from that diagonal. You're going to bring Christine back to life."

Throughout the music's first *andante*, Chris lay on her side on the floor. Volmar took enormous pains positioning both her arms behind her head.

"A swan, Christine—not a chicken. Your neck *extended*.

Wally is moving, you are not moving. The audience is watching you because you are *beautiful* not moving."

Fingers marking rapidly, Volmar gave Wally his steps. The music picked up from the *più mosso*.

"When Wally touches you, open your eyes. *Not* like that. There's no alarm clock. Slowly. *Andante*. Do you know what *cantabile* means? Singing. Your eyes sing."

Chris opened her eyes, and opened them *and* opened them, till on the umpteenth opening Volmar said that would have to do for the time being. Her hip was howling from digging into the floor.

"He kisses your fingers—your fingers move. Look. Look at my fingers. The fingers *sing*. Your hand comes to life—always *cantabile*.... All right, we'll work on that. Your arm rises—singing..."

Through the first *andante*, Volmar limited Chris's movements to eyes, hands, arms, and—finally—shoulders.

"Use no strength, Christine. Wally is supporting you."

At the *più mosso*, with an assist from Wally, she rose—"flowed uphill," in Volmar's phrase—to her feet. Her legs were numb from pressing into the floor and she promptly wobbled off her balance. Oddly enough, Volmar didn't seem to mind in the least.

"Let's change that. Wally, can you step in closer? She has a turn, so don't get in the way of her knee. Extend your right hand, let your finger touch hers. Give her enough support to hold the balance. Christine, you're not falling off a cliff. Stop grabbing."

Volmar came and took her hand.

"One finger. *This* finger. It's lovely, use it. Wally is there, he is rock. Your finger touches his very lightly—only the tip—and the rock flows into you. All right." Volmar hummed a phrase for the pianist. "Let's take it from the turn—*and!*"

Wally pulled her into a turn. She unspooled, bent her legs in preparation. He lifted her, and her arms and legs floated in momentary arabesque. The hand that supported her crotch was strong, secure, but suddenly she was not sure of its sexlessness. She felt herself blushing as Wally lowered her.

The crease in Volmar's forehead deepened.

"Christine, you're still working too hard. Can't you let the pirouettes just happen?"

"Mr. Volmar, I don't *have* multiple pirouettes."

"Go on *pointe* and Wally will spin you. *And!*"

Volmar snapped his fingers. The girl went up on the point of her right foot, pushing off with her left. The rest was Wally's hands, strongly deft knots of muscle and nerve, almost invisibly kneading the spin into her waist.

The girl gave no feeling of lift or lightness: that would have to be worked on, and Volmar knew it would come. There was a trick of spotting—whipping the head around before the body, keeping the eyes fixed on a point stage front—that would increase the girl's momentum, give the turn snap, and make it seem more her and less Wally's doing. She hadn't yet mastered her spotting.

But for the moment there were five pirouettes, not badly faked. It was a start.

Volmar was not entirely dissatisfied.

\*     \*     \*

When Chris got home after rehearsal she found Steph and Ray Lockwood sitting in the living room. Ray said he'd happened to be in the neighborhood, just stopped by, and Chris was horribly aware that she was dirty and sweaty and the rug hadn't been vacuumed.

"I brought some ginger ale." Ray gestured with his glass. "Since you dancers don't drink on duty. Care to join us?"

"And he brought those." Steph nodded toward a decanter of roses on the table. Ray was smiling and Chris thought, *He's spent his money on roses and we don't even have a pretzel to offer him.* She felt dirty and sweaty and the sort of person her mother called "ungracious."

"I'll have a little ginger ale," she said.

"I'll get it," Steph said quickly, and Chris was alone with Ray Lockwood.

"Aren't you going to sit?" he said. "It *is* your home."

There was room on the sofa beside him but she sat in the rocker so he wouldn't get too close a look at how messy she was. He swallowed and sat a little straighter.

"They're beautiful roses," she said. "Thank you."

"You're welcome."

They were silent and then he cleared his throat and said he was having a bitch of a time with international sea law. Chris wished she could get the new ballet and all its worries out of her head. She wished she could say something about sea law.

"That sounds complicated," she said in a soft voice that was hardly there at all.

Steph brought the ginger ale and Ray asked how life had been treating Chris. She couldn't think of anything intelligent to answer. There was Volmar's new ballet, but she didn't see how a lawyer could be interested in that. She shrugged her shoulders and the blue cotton of her dress bunched up.

Ray's eyes stuck on the tiny crescent of freckles at the collar. *He's in love with her*, Steph thought. *He'd better learn to lie a little better with those eyes if he expects to go anywhere in law.* They were attractive eyes, gray and shining and warm. *Why doesn't she look at him?* Steph wondered. *Doesn't she know?*

"I thought you dancers were supposed to lead exciting lives," Ray said. "Not like the rest of us mortals." His glass was nervous in his fingers. "Always getting your pictures in the papers and dancing premieres and going to penthouse pot parties."

*He's joking*, Steph realized, *but not really: he wants to know if Chris goes out.* Chris was biting her lower lip and Steph could see something was bothering her.

"Dancers go out maybe once or twice a month," Steph said. "And we're not all that exciting. We can't get drunk, we can't take drugs, we can't stay up late, and our best conversation is who did what in class and how's your triple *fouetté*."

Ray nodded, eyes fixed on Chris. "Law's a little like that. You have to narrow your focus."

"Mr. Volmar's doing a *pas de deux* on Wally Collins and me," Chris blurted.

Steph stared one slack-jawed moment. "Chris, that's wonderful!" *Open up*, she wanted to say, *sparkle—you've got an admirer hanging on your every word—impress him!* "Come on," she prodded. "Tell us about it."

Chris explained as much as she'd been able to understand, glancing now and then at Ray to see if she was boring him: the choreography was Volmar's, more or less, a dead swan coming back to life. The music was Tchaikovsky, the Andante Cantabile. Her partner, Mr. Super-Prince of NBT himself, turned out to be completely un-stuck-up and surprisingly helpful.

Ray Lockwood listened, interested and wanting very much to grasp whatever it was that so excited Chris. He had trouble following what the girls were saying: much of it seemed to be communicated in telepathic shrugs and glances; the fingers had something to do with it too, and there was a great deal of technical French.

*I'll get better at it*, he thought. *All it takes is time and exposure—like international sea law.*

For the moment he was able to take an almost parental pleasure in watching Chris and noting the ways she had changed. Before, she had been strange and sweet and out of place, a pocket of quiet in a whirling debutante brawl. Now, with her own apartment and life, she was animated and alive and eager.

Steph listened too, nodding, trying her damndest not to feel envious. But in a corner of her mind she wondered if her mother's advice had been all that shrewd: if she'd taken the NBT offer, maybe she'd be doing solos now, just like Chris. And Wally Collins—my God, he was the best American male in the business.

"Your own *pas de deux!*" Steph said. "You've sure come up fast."

"But I . . ." Chris glanced at Ray. His eyes were clouded by something undefinable. *I'm boring him*, she thought, and suddenly she couldn't go on. "Excuse me."

She got up and left the room and a moment later the bathroom door shut and clicked. Steph and Ray sat staring at one another.

"Is something wrong?" he asked.

"Let me go see." Steph went and rapped on the bathroom door. "Chris," she said softly, "anything the matter?"

The door opened. Chris's eyes were red and she spoke in a whisper. "He can't hear, can he?"

Steph closed the door. "Now what's the trouble?"

"I don't know. I think maybe too much is happening at once."

"Stop talking like that. You should be happy, you should be celebrating!"

"Steph, I'm scared."

"Why in the world?"

"I've been in the corps three months and suddenly Marius Volmar gives me a premiere. Why me?"

Which was exactly what Steph was wondering. "Because you're good."

"There are principals at NBT who've been waiting three *years* for a premiere!"

"And you're better for the role than they are."

"I don't have ankles, I don't have any strength in my turns, I don't have balance. Wally's carrying me through half the ballet and pulling me through the rest."

"Stop putting yourself down. You're the best one for this role and Volmar sees it."

"Every girl in that company's going to hate me. They're whispering already."

Steph had heard about the NBT corps with its gossip and backbiting. It wouldn't be at all odd if one or two of the older girls picked on a promising newcomer. "Chris, what does it matter? It's not your job to listen to whispers and you're not running for most popular girl in the class. Just stick to your dancing and learn your role. And if you can do that, every girl in that corps is going to worship you."

"I wish . . ." Chris's voice trailed off. Something whisped across her face.

"What?"

"I wish we were in the same company."

Steph smiled. "And *I* wish I was getting a solo premiere. Now you've got a visitor out there, so fix your eyes and come on out and sparkle."

Chris clutched Steph's sleeve. "I can't."

"What's wrong with you, Chris?"

"I just can't go out there and face him."

"You're not scared of Ray Lockwood!"

"I don't know what I'm scared of. But I don't want him to see me like this."

"Use Lvovna's trick. Splash some cold water on your face and you'll be fine."

"Not tonight. Please. I can't make chitchat and smile. I just want to lie down."

Chris was begging with a child's urgency and it baffled Steph and alarmed her. But instinct told her not to push. "Okay, Chris, You lie down and rest."

Steph went back to the living room.

"Everything under control?" Ray asked.

"Chris feels a little nervous about that new role and she's substituting tonight, so she's resting."

Ray was watching her carefully and she couldn't tell if he believed her. She felt like a louse and a liar.

"She's very sorry."

Ray set down his glass and stood. He had hoped Steph might in some way help link him to Chris. But he saw it was pointless. And cowardly. People had to do their own linking.

"I shouldn't have come barging in," he said.

"You didn't barge in. Really you didn't."

"Tell Chris I hope she feels better."

They went to the door and he seemed thoughtful and hurt and Steph said, "Ray—you *will* phone, won't you?"

"Sure. I'll phone."

# twelve

With each rehearsal of the *pas de deux* Chris found herself
trusting Wally Collins, physically trusting him, in ways she had
never before trusted another human being. She relied on him to
catch her and to hold her and to lift her and to shape her every
move. The more completely she opened herself to him, the more
pleased Volmar became. After one of Chris's not bad multiple
turns he even muttered, "Good. You're beginning to learn, my
child. Beginning to learn."

After rehearsal Wally kept inviting her to lunch, and she was
afraid and kept saying no. The fourth time he wouldn't even
listen to her excuse. He looped an arm through hers and dragged
her across Columbus Avenue to O'Neals' Baloon.

It was Philharmonic matinee day. The restaurant was awash
with ash-blond and blue-haired grandmothers, oozing jewels.
Wally must have made a reservation, because the waiter led
them straight to a table in a corner of the rear room and asked
what they would drink.

Wally looked at his watch—a cracked Timex. "Just enough
time to metabolize a white wine spritzer before rehearsal. What
about you?"

Chris shook her head. "I'd better not. Alcohol knocks me out."

"One spritzer, two straws."

The drink came with two candy-striped straws. Wally set it midway between them and hunched forward, elbows on the table, to stare at her. "Whose life story first—yours or mine?"

"I don't have a life story."

He had beautiful dark dancer's eyebrows that could have projected emotion to the top balcony of the Met. They arched. Almost to his hairline. He leaned back in his chair and lit a cigarette. After a while he exhaled a neat ribbon of smoke.

"Evanston, Illinois. Posh Chicago suburb. Father on board of General Motors, Exxon, Anaconda. Finishing school. Studied with Magallanes and Eglevsky. Competed for scholarship to school, won scholarship, renounced it, signed on as paying student. That's not a life story?"

Chris looked down at the napkin writhing in her lap. "Who told you that?"

"Spies. Any of it true?"

She decided to trust him. "My parents didn't want me to dance. They still don't. I tried for the scholarship to see if I could make it on my own."

"And you found out you can. Congratulations."

His stare was warm and persistent and she felt her shyness beginning to melt. "What's your life story?" she asked.

"Ever heard of Hamtramck—a little slum three feet west of Grosse Pointe? Dad runs a thriving business there—undertaker. My little sister saw *Red Shoes* on TV and decided to be Moira Shearer. It was a rough neighborhood. I walked her to ballet school. I was bored, I worked out with the girls, I got better than the girls. I wound up with a scholarship. I also wound up not talking to my dad."

"Why not?"

"He wanted an all-American quarterback for a son. Instead he's got Prince Siegfried from *Swan Lake*. That doesn't go down too well in Hamtramck."

Even though he was smiling she sensed that she had tiptoed near the edge of some hidden hurt. She did not step back. It was his turn to trust her. "Don't you ever hear from your family?"

"Mom phones now and then—collect. So it won't show up on the bill."

"They never help you or send you money?"

"I don't need it. I make more than Dad."

"But before you were a principal?"

"Not two cents."

"Then how did you live?"

He tossed a shrug off his right shoulder. The flesh on his collarbone glinted smooth and ivory. "Tended bar; pushed pot; made porn films. Your jaw just dropped into your butter plate. I like your tonsils."

"You're joking. About pot and porn."

"Just trying to bulldoze through a few defenses. You're supposed to trust me, remember? Orders from Volmar. How am I doing?" His smile glowed like a match held near a candle.

"You're making me laugh."

"We're getting somewhere. Want to hear about my prison record?"

"You don't have a prison record."

"I used a slug in the IRT subway. They caught me, put me in the Tombs overnight. I'm still on probation."

"You really have an imagination."

"I don't imagine a thing. It's total recall. How else do you think I get through all those steps?"

She felt bathed in sunlight. She couldn't believe anyone could be this kind to her, this interested. She clutched for words to cover the commotion of her feelings. "I feel badly—that you're doing all the work."

"*Andante Cantabile?* You call that work?"

"It certainly is for you."

"I could do it in my sleep. In fact, I *have* done it in my sleep." He saw the bafflement in her eyes. "You know what Volmar's done, don't you?"

"He's made a ballet with an easy part for me and a hard part for you."

"The opening *andante*—that solo adagio business I go through—it's the crypt scene from *Romeo.* Where you wake up—the bit with the hands—*Harlequinade.* The *pas de deux* is *Jason and Medea.*"

She searched his gaze. This time there was no mischief

bubbling from the green depth. He was telling the truth. Her voice felt crushed and small in her throat. "He stole it?"

"In ballet never say 'steal.' He borrowed. A little Ashton, some Petipa, a bit of Martha Graham. That whole thing with your eyes is Twyla Tharp. The assisted stuff is Jerry Robbins."

"But—that's not right," she said softly.

"Who's going to put him in jail—you? Ninety per cent of the critics can't tell the difference between an *entrechat* and an entr'acte. Half your choreographers borrow anyway. Someone's going to scream that Volmar pinched a *pas de deux* from them that they took from MacMillan?"

Her heart knocked at her ribs. She swayed forward, managed to anchor herself to the arms of the chair. Wally didn't seem to notice. It was as though his great shoulders and smile held him high above such shocks.

"Look," he said, "if I hadn't danced the roles, *I* wouldn't know. You think the audience will know? They're too busy timing balances and counting barrel turns."

"But somebody will know."

"Who?"

"Somebody who—somebody who loves ballet. There's bound to be somebody who loves ballet enough to *know*." If there weren't somebody, if ballet were just a trick and a rip-off, then there might as well be no God. Maybe someday she would be able to tell Wally that.

Maybe he understood it already.

His hand closed on hers, in full view of the restaurant. She didn't care. She didn't see anyone else caring either.

Suddenly, she was happy.

"You know what you are?" Wally said. "You're an optimist. I hope you stay that way."

After lunch Wally wouldn't hear of their going Dutch but insisted on paying the whole bill himself. In the theater, when they were alone in the elevator, he kissed her on the cheek.

*    *    *

Chris caught some of Wally's ebullience and energy. All afternoon her nerves and muscles were vibrating. The 3 P.M. stage rehearsal didn't tire her in the least. She didn't need to go home for a nap, and all it took to get through the evening performance (she danced Prayer in *Coppélia*) was three tablespoons of honey on half a container of cottage cheese.

Afterward, changing back into street clothes, she stopped humming long enough to hear half-muted voices from another aisle in the dressing room.

"I hear she can't even hold a balance. Wally's pulling her through everything."

"Wouldn't surprise me if Georgette commits *murder*. Volmar's been promising her that premiere for three years; along comes Miss Muffet and grabs it."

"What do you expect? Her family's got eight zillion dollars—they probably endowed the season."

Chris fought to keep the day's glow from going out. *They're not talking about me.*

As she left the dressing room she had to cross the two girls' sight line. The gossip stopped in mid-sentence, sliced off, and mascara'd eyes darted guiltily to cold cream jars.

*They weren't talking about me they weren't they weren't they weren't!*

In the elevator, she remembered Wally's kiss, and the lump in her stomach dissolved.

*        *        *

When Chris said she'd invited Wally Collins to dinner, Steph almost dropped the entire blender full of Adelle Davis high-protein pep-up drink.

"For dinner? Here? What'll he sit on, the thrift shop chair or the Salvation Army rocker?"

"He's the most unsnobbish person in the world. He doesn't give a damn about furniture. All he's got are two orange crates and a mattress and a Honda."

For a moment Steph was speechless. It didn't seem possible that Chris and Wally could have been having an affair. "Oh, you've seen his place?" Steph said, trying to sound very matter-of-fact.

Chris's gaze met her with seamless innocence. "No. But he tells me about it."

It wasn't a particle of Steph's business, but she was relieved. "What night is he coming?"

"Next Sunday. That gives me all day to clean and cook."

"I suppose I can go to a movie that evening. Maybe Al and Linda are free."

"Oh no—you have to be here too. Wally's bringing a friend. It's going to be a real sit-down dinner party. With cloth napkins and wine and something very, very delicious for the main course."

Steph had not seen Chris so happy since the night NBT took her. It was better than the funk she'd been going through. But there was something feverish and unreal about the glow. Steph was bothered. Life seemed to be all ups and downs for Chris, all hurt and happiness, with no safe middles.

"But, Chris—you don't know how to cook."

"I'll buy a cookbook." Chris squeezed Steph's hand excitedly. "Steph, he's helping me so much—I *have* to do something special for him."

In that phrase "something special" Steph detected something extra-special. "Chris, how well do you know him?"

"That's the whole point. I want to *get* to know him."

"And who's this friend he's bringing?"

"Ellis Watkins." Chris added quickly, much too quickly, "He's with the company. He's not a very good dancer but Wally says he's an awful lot of fun at a party."

Steph had heard of Ellis Watkins. So had everyone else in New York ballet except—apparently—Chris. He was the sort of gay boy who made it into the corps on height alone. He couldn't partner worth a damn because he wanted the audience to look at him, not the girl, and worst of all, he never looked at the girl himself. He'd be lucky to make it to soloist by age thirty, and without a gonad transplant, he'd never make it beyond. He was a nobody; yet somehow he'd latched on to one of the top American-born principals in the business.

An alarm rang in the back of Steph's head.

"Chris, as long as you're going to so much trouble, why not pay off a few obligations? How about inviting Ray instead of Ellis? He did help us move. And we haven't done a thing for him."

Chris hesitated, and then she shook her head. "Ray wouldn't enjoy an evening of dance talk."

"If he came it wouldn't have to be dance talk."

"But he's . . . he's a lawyer."

"What does that have to do with it? He eats, he talks, he's nice."

"With him I have to . . . measure up. With dancers I can burn the spaghetti."

"I think you're wrong. I bet he'd love your burnt spaghetti."

"It's too late. I've invited Wally and Ellis and they've accepted."

Steph couldn't shake her misgivings. "You've got a tough solo to learn. I wish you'd put this dinner off till after the premiere."

"Don't you worry about a thing. I'll handle it. In fact I wish you'd go to a museum or something that afternoon."

Reluctantly, Steph agreed.

# thirteen

The day of the big dinner, Steph got back to the apartment just before six. She sniffed. A yumminess hovered in the air, tantalizing and unidentifiable. She peeked in the kitchen.

With the grim concentration of a child at finger paints, Chris was slicing handfuls of leeks and onions and potatoes on the butcher board.

Steph peeked through the oven window. A huge shoulder of boned meat had been tied and latticed with garlic- and anchovy-stuffed incisions.

"Say—what's cooking?" Steph asked.

"James Beard says it's braised shoulder of lamb with ratatouille. He'd better be right."

"I saw that dress you've laid out on the bed," Steph said. "Wow, you're going to look terrific. Who else did you invite—Rudolf Nureyev?"

"I just felt like wearing something nice," Chris said.

"Nice and *new*," Steph teased.

Chris blushed.

"Sure I can't help with anything?" Steph asked.

"Thanks, it's all under control."

As seven-thirty approached Steph heard Chris making

panicky last-minute noises with the plumbing in the bathroom. The kitchen was a maelstrom of ticking timers and half-washed pots and grocery-store litter that needed to be thrown out. Steph rinsed and hid, neatened and sponged, faked an orderly look.

At seven-thirty Chris was still in the bathroom.

Steph sat down with last month's *Dancemagazine*, tried to be interested in the Atlanta Civic Ballet, and was furious at her heart for beating so fast, as though she gave a *damn* that the top American-born *danseur noble* was coming to dinner and was already two and a half minutes late.

The doorbell ding-donged at twenty minutes to eight.

"I'll get it," Steph shouted, hurrying to answer. She felt a disconcertingly teen-aged tingle at the back of her neck as she pulled open the door.

A tall young man stood grinning at her. He wore a white shirt of stretch cotton with an Adidas trade mark on the chest muscle, immaculately faded farmer's overalls, and jogging sneakers. He was crisp and light-haired, well built—and alone.

"Hello," Steph said. Despite her misgivings about the evening she put on her best smile. After all, this was her first guest; her first party. Well, maybe not exactly *hers;* the apartment's.

"Hi. I'm Wally." The tall man thrust out a hand and Steph shook it. His grip was gentle in a way that suggested he was a strong dancer. "Sorry I'm late."

"Not at all. Chris isn't even ready yet. Come on in."

"Ellis was held up," he said. "I don't mean mugged or anything—just held up."

It was hard for Steph to believe: when she'd seen him onstage, he'd been a man, a prince. Here in her living room he was an awkward, speechless farm boy, shifting weight from one foot to the other. She wondered what the hell to say: *I loved your* pas de deux *from* Voluntaries, *I hope I can catch your next* Giselle, *if you dare hurt my roommate I'll wring your Achilles' tendon?*

At that moment there was a rustling sound, and Chris stepped into the living room, ballerina-pale in her vin rosé lounging pajamas.

She froze, staring.

It wasn't so much a rude stare as a childish one, as though she'd never imagined that sneakers and overalls and a cotton shirt could be put together in quite that combination.

It was Wally who spoke first. "Ellis was held up."

"Oh no."

"I don't mean mugged or anything. Just held up."

"Oh."

"But he'll be along, just as soon as he can make it. Ellis is a real laugh. You'll like him." Wally brought his left arm out from behind his back. He handed Chris a bulging three-foot cone of florist's paper. "Happy house warming, Chris. And you too, Steph. From Ellis and me."

Chris unrolled the paper, careful not to rip. It held a dozen roses, six red, six white. "Oh my gosh."

The paleness drained from Chris's face, leaving only gray shock.

"They're beautiful..."

Steph waited for Chris to kiss him, or at least to thank him. Not a move. Not a word.

"I never know the names of flowers," Wally said. Suddenly he was a gangly, apologetic twenty-year-old and Steph couldn't help liking him. "So I always get roses. Hope you don't mind."

"Mind?" Steph lifted the flowers from Chris's immobilized hands. "Look at that, Chris—twelve hothouse roses! Wally, you *are* a prince. Let me put these in water."

As she hurried into the kitchen she heard Chris blurt something about the third lift in the *più mosso*. She hoped it wasn't going to be an evening of braised lamb and shop talk.

"Damn," she said, thinking out loud. Vases were among the umpteen less-than-necessities they hadn't yet bought for the apartment.

She stood on a stool and reached to the top of the cabinet for the white wine decanter. Tonight it would just have to double.

When she came back into the living room no one was talking. Wally had settled on the sofa and Chris was rocking in the rocker, ten feet across the room.

Steph cleared her throat and said, "There we are!" and set her work of art down on the coffee table. Not bad.

She turned brightly to Wally. "How about a drink?"

Chris jumped to her feet. "I'll do that."

"You two just relax. What'll you have, Wally?"

"Vodka tonic if you have any."

"And you, Chris?"

"I'll have a—" Chris hesitated. "Vodka tonic too."

Steph translated the hesitation with no difficulty: easy on the vodka.

Like hell.

She half shut the louvered kitchen door and did her dirty work in secret: double shots of vodka for Wally and Chris, a half shot for herself. She angled an ear to the other room. The silence screamed. She switched on the radio, station WPAT in one of its syrupy moods, and turned it just loud enough to work subliminally.

"Here we are." Steph set Wally's vodka tonic on a coaster on the coffee table. "Chris, you don't have a table—why don't you come over here?" She plunked Chris's down next to Wally's.

Chris came across the room and sat on the edge of the sofa, one cushion away from Wally.

"To your very good health, ma'am." Wally lifted his glass to toast Steph, then clinked with Chris and took a long swallow. He didn't seem to mind the alcoholic strength at all. Steph wondered if he even noticed. She went and sat in the rocker and set her glass on the floor.

The conversation felt like a clamshell. They exhausted the weather, the high cost of ballet shoes, the impossibility of finding really good leg warmers except the kind you knitted yourself.

Steph made a second round of vodka tonics and the laughter got louder and the talk faster. By the time she made a third round of drinks the kitchen was sending out unmistakable messages of basil and garlic and young, crisp lamb.

Chris glanced for what seemed the fortieth time at her watch. She could no longer ignore the panic wriggling like worms in her stomach. Partly it was nerves, the nearness of Wally with his laughter and his handsomeness and the hope/terror that he would accidentally stretch out a hand or knee and touch her.

Partly it was the knowledge that dinner was peaking: in another five minutes it would be ruined.

She put down her glass and left Wally and Steph debating science fiction movies and went to peek through the oven window. She thanked God that Steph was a talker. The lamb was coming up blisters and the ratatouille at the bottom of the pan was black and thick-bubbling like a tropical swamp.

Steph came rushing into the kitchen. "You get right back out there and entertain your guest."

"But the meat is scorching and the ratatouille—"

Steph pried the wooden spoon from Chris's grip. "I'll take care of it. You take care of *him*. He's too damned sweet to leave sitting out there alone."

Steph did a rapid check. *Well*, she figured, *what's sauce for the lamb had better be sauce for the ratatouille.*

She wrestled the cork out of a bottle of Macon and dumped a half cup of the wine into the vegetables and stirred. She lowered the heat in the oven till it was barely a flicker. Just as she was sliding the pan back in, the front doorbell gave two ding-dongs.

She rushed to answer, throwing a wave at Chris to stay on the sofa with Wally. They weren't necking, but at least they had progressed to neighboring cushions.

The boy in the corridor was wearing army fatigue overalls. Period.

Correction.

Rope sandals and a five o'clock shadow, yesterday's time.

"Hello there," he said. "You don't look a thing like the up-and-coming Miss Christine Avery."

Steph sniffed and the sniff drove her back a step. *You*, she thought, *are late and you're rude and you're marinated in banana daiquiris.* "That's because I'm Chris's roommate, Stephanie Lang. And I'll bet anything you're Ellis Watkins. Won't you come in? We've been waiting for you."

"Sorry about that. I had to walk the whole fucking way."

She led Ellis into the living room and let Wally stumble to his feet and stutter an introduction. Chris's smile blanked out.

"We'll be eating in a minute," Steph said.

Ellis made a pout. "Suppose it'd be too much trouble to rustle up a godmother?"

Steph stared at him. He wasn't joking. "If that's a drink, I'll try. If it's something out of *Sleeping Beauty*, you're out of luck."

"It's a drink, honey. You take a glass yea tall and three ice cubes—can you manage three ice cubes?"

"For you, four."

"Vodka to the top of the ice cubes and a half jigger of Amaretto—if you haven't got a shaker, just stir."

Steph had been in ballet long enough to tag the new arrival: a corps-boy brat and a week-end lush; beautiful build, no brains, and in two years he'd be running an antique shop some old man had treated him to. Every company had a couple of Ellises. She saw a choice: she could pretend Ellis wasn't there, which would upset Chris. Or she could pretend he was human, male, and adult—which would upset Ellis.

She decided it would be kinder to upset Ellis. "I'll shake *and* stir."

She had a hunch that in his condition Ellis Watkins wouldn't know the difference between Amaretto and arsenic, and unfortunately she'd forgotten to stock either. She dropped three ice cubes into a tumbler, splashed in enough vodka for authenticity, enough water to slow him down, and enough sherry to color the concoction. It looked like something a goldfish had had the trots in.

When she came back into the living room Ellis was sitting on the sofa next to Wally. Chris had moved back to the rocking chair. She gazed at the two young men with subdued eyes, coddling her drink in both hands while Ellis sketched NBT disasters in the air and chattered about missed pirouettes in the week's rehearsals.

Steph stopped Ellis' hand in mid-gesture and deposited the drink in it.

He shot her a smile and took a kissing sip from the rim. Obviously his taste buds had been dry-iced some time ago, because all he said was, "Next time a little easier on the Amaretto, okay?"

Steph looked at him. His knee was extended across the middle cushion toward Wally's, not quite touching.

"I've never been inside a girls' dormitory before," Ellis was saying. "It's interesting to see how the other half sleeps."

Chris laughed nervously. "Sleeping's about all we have time to do around here."

"Yeah—the place looks it."

Steph thought for one moment that he was trying to be clever. She searched his baby face for some hint that the rudeness was a joke, but his lips were unsmiling as a straight razor and his bloodshot eyes nailed hers.

"Do you two have twin beds?"

"The store calls them twins," Chris said. "It's a fancy word for narrow."

"Siamese?"

Steph could see that Chris wasn't quite sure what he was getting at. "Just identical," Chris said.

"With pretty Yves St. Laurent sheets from Bloomy's last white sale?"

"We're saving for those," Steph said coolly.

"Shouldn't take too long on soloists' pay. Unless they're soaking you on the rent. What does one of these boxes go for nowadays?"

"We don't get soloists' pay," Steph said.

"You mean you're both common corps members, like me? From what Wally's been saying about that *pas de deux*, I thought Volmar had at least sneaked Chris up a notch."

Steph held her best stage smile, wondering how Wally had gotten hooked up with a beaut like Ellis.

"Excuse me." Chris rose from her chair and went into the kitchen to check the lamb. The overhead fluorescent lights dimmed. *What's happening to the electricity*, she wondered, *another blackout?*

Suddenly she was overpoweringly aware of garlic and oil and cooked fat. She felt a rushing stab of nausea and the room grew so bright she had to shut her eyes. *Not Con Ed*, she realized; *me—something's wrong with me*.

She managed to grip the edge of the sink, sweating, fighting a dizziness that wanted to suck her down to the floor.

Steph's voice came to her, concerned and close. "Are you okay?"

"I just slipped. Guess I put too much wax on that linoleum."

"How well do you know Ellis?" Steph asked. "Ever talk to him at work?"

"He runs with his own bunch. He doesn't have time for me. His friends are all very bright and giggly and up on everything. I always feel like a dope when I'm with them."

"Maybe they're the dopes." Steph took the garlic bread from the oven and wrapped it in a napkin and couldn't find a plate long enough. She glanced up and saw Chris staring at her.

"What's wrong with me?" Chris whispered suddenly.

"What in the world are you talking about?"

"Why does Ellis hate me?"

"He's drunk. He doesn't hate anyone but his own sweet little self."

"When he stares at me I feel the whole corps is there, whispering and hating me. Steph, I haven't done a *thing* to him—ever."

"Maybe you ought to. Something good and swift where it hurts." Steph thought of saying more but she stopped herself. When they returned to their guests Ellis was talking about Bobby Baylor, one of the older principals with the company.

"He's gone back to his wife—can you *believe?*"

"I'm glad," Chris said.

"*You're* glad! What about the kids at the school? It's safe to take a shower again!"

"Why do you always have to exaggerate?" Wally said.

"Me? Exaggerate? The freak practically stood sentry in those showers. Every time a new kid came in he stared—and stared—and stared. Remember that seventeen-year-old from Colorado—terrific body—the kid went to take a shower after class and there was *the* Robert Baylor, *danseur noble* of the decade, staring. *Well.* Bobby's got thinning hair. He uses that spray paint, Nestlé's Streaks 'n' Tips, to cover the bald spot. He was standing under that shower for so long, staring at this kid, the Nestlé's started streaking and tipping *down his face.*"

Ellis took a huge swallow of his drink.

"Bobby looked like the Black Swan on the hundred twentieth *fouetté.* I mean *evil,* mascara to the jowls. The kid was scared stiff. Here was the big star of the company coming on to him like tea for two with Jack the Ripper. Well, the kid got out of that shower and ran for his life and never showed up at another class. Any other dancer but Bobby would know you don't screw around with the students. The corps boys, okay. They're adults."

"Are they?" Steph said.

Ellis shot her a glance. "They're as adult as the girls, honey."

Chris fought to keep her head clear. She felt Ellis was laying a lasso of chatter around the evening, waiting for the moment to jerk it tight.

Ellis got up. Swaying, he leaned over Wally and began massaging his shoulders. "Why so tense, sweetheart?"

"Why don't you just relax?" Wally said.

"I'll do that little thing."

Ellis walked unsteadily into the kitchen. Chris heard a cabinet door being tugged open and then the freezer door slamming and Ellis came wobbling back with what looked like a fresh tumbler of vodka. He dropped onto the sofa.

"So tell me, Chris—what's the story about this *pas de deux?*"

"It's a sort of Sleeping Beauty," she said. His eyes made her uncomfortable. "I spend four minutes on the floor and then Wally wakes me up."

"I hope he's gentler with you than he is with me. But what's the *story?*"

"That *is* the story."

"Three weeks ago you were in the corps. Three weeks from now you're dancing a premiere. *That's* the story I want to hear. Are you and Volmar having a thing?"

"Ellis, will you lay off?" Wally said.

"I'm only asking what everyone else is wondering. How did you swing it, Chris?"

"You have to excuse Ellis," Wally said. "He doesn't usually drink this much."

"I *always* drink this much," Ellis shot back.

"And after twelve drinks," Wally said, "he starts saying stupid things he doesn't mean."

"I'm saying stupid things I *do* mean. I want to know what Chris did to get that role."

"Maybe Chris didn't do anything," Steph said. "Maybe Volmar likes her work. He did hire her for the corps after all." Steph couldn't stand ballet losers. They were always whining that everything depended on your connections. It wasn't so. Everything depended on work.

"And he *did* hire sixty other girls after all," Ellis said, "but when he wants to demonstrate a finger pirouette whose finger is in his hand? Little Chrissie's. And when he demonstrates a lift, whose little waist is in his trembling paws? Little Chrissie's little waist. Some of those girls have been with NBT twelve years and they say never, but never, has Volmar come on to anyone, male, female, or poodle—and now he's making an ass out of himself—over little Miss Chris."

"He's not making an ass of himself," Wally said. "It's a damned good *pas de deux.*"

"Thank you, Prince Charming, for making the ballerina look pretty as usual. But now that we're all offstage, lets hear the unpretty facts. Tell me, Chris—what does Volmar do in the sack? Is he freaky? Can he get it up?"

"I don't know what you're talking about."

"Honey, you can ease up on the innocence. I'm not an idiot."

"Yes, you are," Wally said, "and a damned rude one."

"Emily Post, why don't you go shove it?"

"We're guests, Ellis, and you're drunk."

"Okay, I'm high. But I'm not a moron and I'm not a patsy. I've been working my balls off in that company for three years, and little Miss Chris *jetés* her way into a starring role in three months—not even a season, three fucking *months*. I want to know how." He gave Chris a long stare. "Tell me, honey, when did you start studying ballet?"

"Oh—around seven."

"One class a week?"

She sensed a shift in his malice: it was blowing from a different direction. "One or two, I don't remember."

"And by the time you were twelve, a class every day after school, right? And in high school two classes a day after school, and week ends doing homework, right?"

She couldn't understand what he was trying to trap her into. She threw pleading glances at Steph and Wally, wishing they would say something to deflect him.

"You never had time to date, and even if you *were* invited to a prom you didn't go. And of course there was never any time for anything extracurricular like the Student Council or the high school paper, and you were never a cheerleader for the football team. Right? Right."

She set down her glass firmly. "Look, Ellis. I didn't go to high school. My parents sent me to a private school for girls. There was no football team, no proms, we didn't have a Student Council and we didn't have a school paper."

She mentioned the private school only as a last resort. She knew he would use it against her, spread word through the corps that Christine Avery was a stuck-up finishing-school snob. But it was the one thing that would shut him up.

Only it didn't.

"Oh, in that case your first crush was on—let me

guess—Eddy Villella. You took his master class. He was courteous, he was gentlemanly, he knew all about ballet and art and music, he wasn't like those pimply seventeen-year-old boys that tried to drag you out to football games and grope you under the blanket. Am I warm?"

Chris drew herself up stiff in her chair. She felt a premonition as unmistakable as the glint of a steel blade in a dark alley. Before tonight she had never spoken a word to this baby-faced stranger, never exchanged more than two nods with him at rehearsal. Yet here he was in her home, trying methodically, smilingly, to annihilate her.

*Why?*

"I never took a master class with Villella," Chris said.

"Well then, your first big heterosexual experience was—let's see—Ballet Theatre was touring and you got a backstage pass and Ivan Nagy bumped into you and said, 'Excuse me.' Am I getting warmer?"

"Why are you picking on my friend?" Steph cut in.

Ellis' gaze swiveled. "Picking on her? *Warning* her, honey. She's spent her life commuting from Miss La-de-da's School to toe class. To her the whole world is *Swan Lake* and *Raymonda* and *Giselle.* Some gay boy from the corps invites her home for Christmas to prove he's straight, and she thinks it's the big love, the White Prince. As soon as she's recovered from *that* shock, *if* she recovers, some principal with a wife stashed in Scarsdale invites her to a hotel room and it's the big love, the White Prince all over again. Between gay dancers using her for a front and straight dancers tearing off a piece between rehearsals she's going to be a ping-pong ball with one raging case of clap."

Steph was angry now, ready to attack. To hell with being a hostess, this tarantula needed squashing. But the puzzled hurt in Chris's eyes warned her to hold off.

And then it dawned on her: Chris still didn't understand about Wally and Ellis. She didn't see that Ellis was defending his property. *Oh, Jesus,* Steph thought. And then Ellis said it.

"Look, Chris, I'm gay."

The room was silent. WPAT was playing "Smoke Gets in Your Eyes."

"Now tell me honestly. Is that news to you or not?"

Chris stared at him. Cold panic began creeping up from her

legs. *Why?* The word screamed in her head. *Why does he hate me? Is it the gay thing?*

"I—hadn't thought about it." Her tongue felt heavy, a sour dead weight in her mouth. "It doesn't make any difference. Not to me. Should it?"

"Well, that's white of you, but it's pretty damned stupid. Don't you realize that Wally and I are lovers? No, you don't."

"You stupid lush!" Wally's face was red and the arteries stood out rigid and pulsing in his neck. "Just shut the hell up!"

"Blew your cover, did I? So sorry."

"The last thing you blew was this afternoon in a Christopher Street bar and I wish to hell you'd stayed there."

"And missed your balancing act? You're the only player who can cover first and third bases in one stretch. I love watching it."

"I never lied to Chris."

"You never spelled it out in skywriting either."

"The skywriting's your specialty, is it, Ellis?" Steph said.

"Hold it," Ellis said. "She's in love with him. He's gay. She's going to find out. It'll hurt."

"So you dropped by to do a little mercy killing?" Steph said.

"Now I get it," Ellis said. "*I'm* the villain, *I'm* making Bo-Peep cry. Well, let me tell you something, St. Joan, and you too, Mr. Prince Macho. She may be a ninety-two-pound nit with a strangle hold on Marius Volmar, and she may be nine tenths of the rent on this pretzel box. But to me she's Miss Horner sitting in a corner stitching elastics onto her toe shoes. And, unlike either of you vampires, I don't need a drop or ounce or penny of her. I don't need to pretend to like her. I can look her in those big cistern eyes and tell her straight out: 'Honey, you are a ballet classic, virgin at eighteen, victim at nineteen. You are a sitting duck soon to be a roast sitting duck, you are a one-girl slaughter of the innocents, unless you wake up and jump into your magic *pointe* shoes and *bourrée* away from these two users as fast as your underdeveloped little ankles can take you.'"

"Ellis," Steph cried, "you're a jealous, vicious wrecker."

"What am I wrecking, Wally's and your plans for carving up Chris?"

"She has the most important debut of her career coming up and you're systematically destroying her confidence in her partner and in herself."

"Can I help it if she's got a low tolerance for truth?"

"If you have a fight to pick with me," Wally said, "save it for home."

"And *that*," Ellis said, "sounds like the best suggestion of the evening." He got to his feet, tapped Wally on the shoulder. "Let's go, lover."

"Ellis," Wally pleaded.

"Home, baby. *Ahorita*." Ellis snapped a finger.

Wally rose slowly, as though he'd been sandbagged.

"Do you have to?" Chris blurted.

"He has to," Ellis said, "if he expects to have an apartment left in one piece." He tilted a grin at Wally. "You have two minutes to *faire* your *adieux*. I'll hold the elevator." Now the grin included the girls. "*Ciao*, ladies."

The door slammed behind him.

"I'm sorry," Wally stammered. "He's not usually that way."

"Guess we just hit an off night," Steph said coldly.

"He doesn't mean it, it's just the liquor.... He's got a lot on his mind.... I'd better go, he might get in some kind of trouble by himself. I'm really sorry, I..."

"I understand." Chris's voice was bled of all expression. "Anyone can get drunk."

Wally darted a kiss on her cheek and then very quickly he squeezed Steph's hand.

Chris turned away. She began picking up glasses to take into the kitchen. She stood at the counter a long time, staring at cups and plates and saucers stacked in unleaning towers, awaiting a dinner that would never be. She heard the door shut. A stillness seeped into the apartment.

Steph came up soft-voiced behind her. "Chris—I'm sorry. You did your best and you did a wonderful job. If it hadn't been for that little rat Ellis—"

Chris turned slowly. They looked at one another. For a moment neither spoke. Chris tried very hard not to sob.

"No," she said. "If it wasn't Ellis it would be someone else. But it wouldn't be me." Her eyelashes flickered, little and golden without their stage make-up. "Wally doesn't want me. He just doesn't want to hurt my feelings."

"It's not your fault."

"I made a fool of myself and that is my fault."

"You didn't make a fool of yourself. You were perfect. No one could have handled it better."

"I was a perfect ass. Everything Ellis said about me was true."

"Everything he said was vicious and twisted and he was only trying to hurt you."

"He succeeded." Tears moved down Chris's face, inching along faint lines that Steph had never seen there before.

*Good lord*, Steph wondered, *is she in love with Wally?*

"I wanted everything to be perfect," Chris whispered. "I tried so hard."

"And everything *is* perfect," Steph said. She brought the lamb out of the oven and set it on the butcher block. "Come on—we're going to have dinner."

"I couldn't."

"You go sit at the table and relax. And have a big glass of wine. You've earned it. I'll take care of everything."

"Steph, I'm not hungry."

"We're not going to let a gourmet dinner go to waste. It smells terrific and I *am* hungry."

Chris went to the table with a big glass of red wine and Steph served dinner and they ate in silence. Two years ago they had been children and tonight they sat alone at their first party in their first apartment with two empty places at the table and dying memories of garlic and lamb.

Steph insisted on doing the dishes and later, as she got ready for bed, she heard the muffled clatter of Chris cleaning and recleaning the apartment. It was one-thirty when Chris finally came into the dark bedroom and lay down on her bed. Steph could not see her, but long into the night she heard the faint sound of tears being crushed into a pillow.

# fourteen

"You paid *money* for these seats?"

"Mom, it's Chris's solo debut."

"I could've gotten us walked in." Anna slung her wool coat over her arm. It looked less woolen that way. She ignored the stares and pushed through a row jammed with knees and minks and umbrellas.

The seats weren't bad: Row R, dead center. Anna looked around. *Full house—how come?* She leafed through the program, frowning. *Must be a subscription night.* She stared at a full-color photo of Catherine Deneuve modeling Chanel Number Five. Who cared any more? She found the program notes.

"We have to sit through *Firebird?*"

"Mom, please."

They had to sit through *Firebird*. Anna squinted. Same mess it always was. "Whose dancing Firebird—Volmar's new girl friend?"

Anna could sense Steph cringing into a corner of her seat. What the hell was she nervous about, her friend wasn't even dancing yet.

"She's never going to get through the *pas de deux*," Anna

whispered. "Look at those feathers, who did that costume? The Prince will pull her through one pirouette and the stage will look like a henhouse."

And it did.

Anna sat back, satisfied, waiting for the princesses to come on and form their little circle and toss golden balls back and forth. Anna had been a little princess in *Firebird* once. No one had taught her how to catch ball. No one had taught these kids either. One gold ball rolled into the footlights and another bobbed into the orchestra pit. Same as in the old days.

Anna couldn't help smiling. A little of the tension floated out of her. The Infernal Dance was sluggish, but wasn't it always, and the Berceuse looked like a pajama party.

"Looks like a pajama party," Anna whispered.

Steph put a finger to her lips and Anna shrugged. The lights came up for intermission and she crumpled a dollar into Steph's hand.

"Go get yourself an orangeade."

Anna stayed behind and studied the program notes. *At curtain's rise the Girl is onstage. The Boy approaches.* One of those, Anna thought: The Girl, the Boy. Real abstract. *At first the Girl does not respond to his advances, but as his ardor increases . . .*

Anna patted back a yawn, flipped to Catherine Deneuve. *Someday this Girl is going to buy herself a bottle of Chanel Number Five.*

Steph slid back into the row and Anna could see she was edgy.

"Don't you worry." Anna squeezed her hand. "Your friend'll do just fine."

The lights dimmed. Anna sat straight in her seat. This she didn't want to miss one second of.

The conductor hurried into the pit and the audience clapped. Anna's hands stayed in her lap. She didn't believe in payment in advance. The conductor raised his baton, waited for some idiot in the third ring to stop coughing, gave the downbeat.

The music came sobbing out of the strings, familiar but not exactly familiar, like an old friend who'd had a face lift. Anna clenched her memory. The program said *Andante Cantabile from the String Quartet*, but this was a sixty-man quartet. Since when?

The curtain rose. You-know-who was sprawled on the floor. A spot came up, haloing her.

"Mattress commercial," Anna muttered, just soft enough so Steph couldn't shush her.

Wally Collins tiptoed onstage. Good dancer, but he'd look better partnering Steph. Same old schmaltz. The Boy, lonely and heartbroken and aching, was looking around everywhere for Miss Right, except under his nose where she happened to be dozing. Beautiful arms, that Wally had; knew how to use them.

But wait one minute.

Anna craned forward. Either *he* was wearing gloves that matched the mid-section of Chris's tutu, or that mid-section really *was* skin, in which case his hands and her belly had both been under the same sun lamp. And since when did anyone wear gloves onstage except magicians and the Merry Widow?

It took two minutes before Chris even lifted an arm, and that was the good part. Anna stared in disbelief. The girl had no ankles, no pirouette, no balance. Her *port de bras* had improved; so who couldn't wave her arms? She looked like a cheerleader on downs.

The whole damned ballet was the male. Chris didn't use her legs *once!* Never even went higher than half *pointe* without help. Wally partnered her so-called balances, steadied every wobbly extension. He stood her up for her pirouettes, gave her a push to start her, kept her spinning, clamped a hand on her waist to stop her. He molded her through her variation like a lump of Silly Putty.

Those gloves almost worked.

Almost.

A little nugget of anger began radiating in the pit of Anna's stomach. "I—don't—*believe*—it," she muttered, one hand cupping her eyebrow and miming a very loud *ouch*.

Wally propped her up for her *développés,* let her go long enough for a *piqué* turn, caught her before she fell—and she would have. He backed off, presenting her—Jesus, what was that she was doing, a *curtsy?* Now the male knelt in extended fourth. Very pretty, like a bookend waiting for the Encyclopaedia Britannica.

Chris *pas de bourrée*'d over, if you could call it a *pas de bourrée*, pulled alongside, backed up a little like a truck that had overshot the gas pump. She went up on *pointe*, no help this

time—how come?—*développé*'d into third arabesque and held
the balance—

Wait a minute.

That was no balance. His left hand was on her waist and he'd
raised his right arm so it looked like third position *en haut*.

"He's *holding* her!" Anna hissed.

But Chris's body was in the way and you couldn't exactly *see*
him holding her, and then the lights dimmed, and now Anna
understood why the male was wearing a dark long-sleeved
shirt—it looked like Chris was floating over him, unsupported,
balancing on that wobble she called an ankle.

The audience started clapping.

Anna couldn't believe it. Didn't they have *eyes?* She wanted
to stand up and shout, *Fraud!*

Not that anyone would have heard her. The so-called string
quartet swelled into a fat brass fortissimo and—Jesus!—a
cymbal crash, and smack on the crash Chris let her head and her
wrist jerk down and some idiot screamed, "Brava!"

Anna grabbed her coat. She wasn't going to stay and clap for
*that*.

"Come on." She grabbed Steph too. "Buy you a ginger ale."

*       *       *

Chris's parents had promised to fly East for her première and
she had left a pair of tickets at the box office. But when she got
back to the dressing room she found a florist's bouquet with an
envelope addressed to her in a strange handwriting: *Christine
Avery, deliver after performance.*

The note was in the same unfamiliar hand.

*Heartbroken we could not make it. Dad was called suddenly
to Anaconda board meeting. Know you did brilliant job. Love,
Mother and Dad.*

*       *       *

"You're better than her."

"Mom, that isn't true."

They were sitting at a corner table nursing ginger ales. The
lights had been turned down and the Theater Pub was almost
dark. A waiter went from table to table blowing out bottled

candles. A drunken clarinetist from one of the ballet orchestras slapped a tip down on the bar and struggled to his feet.

"We're completely different dancers," Steph said. "You can't compare us."

"Amen," Anna said. "You're twice as good as she is, that's how different you are. Should have been you on that stage tonight, not her."

Steph's eyes jerked up, green and surprised. "How can you say that? After all the work Chris has put in—?"

"Has she put in more work than you? Or me? She zooms ahead and you're stuck in the back line of the corps—like your father."

"You're not being fair to Chris."

"That's just beautiful. She grabs the job that could have made your career and you stand up for her."

"She didn't grab anything."

"Oh, didn't she now? Volmar would have taken *you* if it hadn't been for her sneaking around."

Steph sighed, wishing her mother wouldn't rewrite history. "She didn't sneak around."

"He just phoned a perfect stranger out of the blue? *You* saw her Snow *pas de deux*—pas de klutz!"

Steph was silent.

"Volmar would have taken you *and* given you a good contract *and* he would have given you that role! They would have been clapping for Stephanie Lang tonight and you would have deserved it because you're a dancer, not some duck with a waddle and eight million dollars!"

A questioning crease furrowed Steph's forehead. "How can you talk like that?"

"Because I'm sick and tired, that's how. Twenty years I've scrimped and slaved. Twenty years I've fought your battles. What for, for her? Tell me what for!"

"I don't know what for. I just wish you'd stop fighting. *Please.* I don't want fights. I don't want battles. I can't stand it when you're like this."

"And I can't stand the idea of your winding up like your dad! *Nowhere!* He put in twenty-six years and *he got nowhere!*"

*And what about you, Mom*, Steph wondered: *where did you get?* She squirmed into a corner of the bench. "Can't we just relax and be happy for Chris? Tonight's her night. Truce."

"*Someone* has to stick up for you. You don't know how to fight for yourself." Anna laid her hands on the table, palms up, empty, showing she had nothing hidden, no weapons, no motives. "Oh, honey, you have the sweetest face in the company and no one has better feet and your top's terrific and everyone says you have a memory like Einstein—but it's not enough."

"Tell me what is enough then."

"People have to like you."

"I thought some people did."

"Forget some people, I'm talking about the people who count."

"And who are they?"

"Come on, use your head. Your director. Your board. Your choreographers. Your dance masters. Your conductor. Your rehearsal pianists. Sure, go ahead and smile. It may sound funny but think about it. If they notice you—and like you—and go out of their way for you—you're home free."

"And how do I arrange all that?"

Anna jabbed finger number one in the air, ticking off her catechism. "First off, company class. Get there early. Get a good position at the barre so the dance master can see you. Center of the room. If you can manage, get a position between two boys. That way even if you make a mistake you'll look more fluid, more feminine. *And* your extension will look higher because you'll be between two lower extensions. Watch what the principals do wrong and *you* do it right; if it kills you, you still do it right. And make sure the dance master *sees* you do it right! Stay after class and ask questions. Even if you don't have any questions, ask them. The dance master will remember you: *she's the kid with a better lower back than Martine!* He'll have you covering roles and one night you'll go on and you'll be good and you'll start getting write-ups and the directors will notice you."

Finger number two shot up.

"Secondly: shyness has to go. A dancer can afford cigarettes, coffee, lousy marriages, but shyness will sink you. Cozy up to the boy soloists. Tell them you're having trouble with your finger pirouettes, can they help you. Don't bother with the boys in the corps, they're nowhere; and the principals will know what you're up to. But latch on to the right soloist now, and you'll have a principal on your side in two years, and he'll ask to partner *you*."

Steph was staring at her blankly, uncomprehendingly. Anna didn't see how she could lay it out much plainer, but she kept trying.

"When you're not rehearsing, don't just sit and stretch, go sit and stretch by the piano. Talk to the pianist. Turn his pages for him. Compliment him. *Wow, what a sight reader! Did you ever do concert work? Do you compose?* Get the pianist on your side and he'll make you look good even when you stink; and he may make someone else look bad just to make you look a little better."

All the while Anna talked, Steph continued to stare. There was something removed and defiant about her; she could have been a conscientious objector waiting out a war.

"And don't be shy with the conductor either. Say hello when you pass him in the corridor. His *Pillar of Fire* may sound like *Til Eulenspiegel;* tell him it made you *swoon.* He'll give you time to prepare, he'll slow down when you're out of breath, he'll watch out for you. Believe me, it can make a difference."

The color had bled from Steph's face. When she finally spoke, the words came out edged and hoarse. "You mean I should lie and make a fool of myself."

"I mean you should do what your dear friend Christine Avery did."

"How can you be so sure what she did?"

Anna looked at the ceiling as though it could offer help or succor. "Because I *saw* her dance. Because I heard three thousand idiots go crazy over a no-talent."

"You happen to be dead wrong. Chris is one of the most honest and hard-working people I know."

"Look, you idiot," Anna shouted, "I'm on *your* side! And the sooner *you're* on your side the sooner we'll see some results!"

Steph did not move. Anna pulled herself up short.

"What are you staring at?"

"You," Steph said.

"What have I got, two noses all of a sudden?"

"I never realized how you felt about me."

"I love you, that's how I feel about you."

Steph turned her face down toward the table. Her shoulders began shaking. Anna realized her little girl was crying. The tears made no sound but they were tears all the same. Anna wondered if she had pushed too hard. The shaking went on a long time, too long. Ashamed, Anna touched a hand shyly to Steph's face.

"I'm sorry if I sounded off. But, honey, you're every bit as good as she is, don't try to tell me you're not, I won't listen."

The evening had ended and ended badly. Neither of them could finish her ginger ale.

"I wouldn't try to tell you anything," Steph said softly.

Anna inspected her little girl's face. She reached a finger and adjusted a curl of hair and then she kissed Steph on the cheek. "Come on. You'll tell me when I'm a nag and I'll tell you when you're an idiot, is it a deal?"

"It's a deal. You're a nag and I'm tired."

"You're an idiot and I'll give you a lift home."

\*     \*     \*

Ray Lockwood went backstage after the performance. He knocked at the door that the guard said was Chris's, and a Chinese woman who must have been her dresser let him in. Chris was standing, still in costume, staring at a bouquet of red roses.

When she looked up at him he felt a soft footfall of fear. The body that had looked so strong onstage seemed fragile and undernourished now.

"You must be very happy," he said.

"Relieved. I never thought I'd get through it."

She came to him and held both his hands for just an instant. Behind that smooth forehead he sensed the gray chambers of her mind twisted in a fierce and unhealthy concentration.

"You did a hell of a lot more than get through it. Tonight calls for a celebration."

She smiled weakly. "Thanks, Ray. But tonight calls for a good sleep."

He felt like an idiot who didn't understand dancers and their needs. He tried to think of something to keep the conversation going. There were flowers on the dressing table, and a little cloth panda was propped against the mirror. The layout of the dressing room reminded him of a tourist cabin on a steamer.

"Do you always have this dressing room?"

"They let me have it tonight."

The dresser, firm as a nurse, sat Chris down in a chair and helped her out of her slippers and then stood behind her and

daubed the sweat from her neck and shoulders with a virgin
Kotex. The Kotex embarrassed Ray, and he said without
thinking, "Chris, don't you *ever* relax?"

She smiled up at him. "I sleep eight hours a day."

"I mean *relax*. Let yourself go. Reward yourself a little."

She looked at him with wondering blue eyes. "Reward for
what?"

"For tonight. It was the most beautiful thing I've ever seen."

She saw the sincerity and ignorance in his face and thought
how sweet he was, how well meaning. A vague sort of animal
gratitude lit her. "Thank you, Ray. I'm glad I make somebody
happy."

"You know you do. I just wish to hell I could do something to
make you happy." He stared at her. "I'm a great cook, you
know."

"I didn't know lawyers cooked."

"This lawyer cooks a terrific beef bourguignon. Interested?"

"I like beef bourguignon."

"What night are you off?"

"Monday."

His mind skimmed upcoming tests and papers due. "Next
month? The twelfth?"

"Every Monday."

"Eight o'clock? My place?"

*He's kind*, she thought, and she smiled at the notion of this
lawyer who was willing to cook beef bourguignon for her. She
remembered her sister's parties and all the college boys who
never gave her a glance. She remembered her parents' dinners
and the men in three-piece suits who tried to talk golf and travel
with her and then gave up. She wasn't glamorous and she wasn't
a hostess and most men who were serious about what her
parents called the serious things in life didn't waste their time on
her.

She didn't know what Ray Lockwood saw in her, but she was
afraid it was something that wasn't there.

"You were sweet to come by, Ray. Thanks. I appreciate it."

The dresser had turned on the shower and stood holding a
bath towel. Chris pushed up from her chair.

"Sorry I'm such a wet blanket. It's the post-performance
blahs."

"I understand." Ray put his hand gently under Chris's chin

and turned her face toward his. His finger traced the line of her cheekbone and touched the tininess of her ear. There was no movement, no objection. He bent to brush his lips very lightly against hers.

As he left the dressing room he felt giddy and weightless and off balance and happy. On his fingers he counted the weeks till the twelfth.

# fifteen

The corps rehearsed onstage the next day. Heinrich was tidying up the *Nutcracker* waltzes for tomorrow night's benefit. "Hold it!" he screamed. "Stephanie, you're one measure ahead of everyone!"

The rehearsal pianist, bent like a coal miner over the little upright, went back eight measures. Again Heinrich shouted the music to a halt.

"Stephanie, your *hands!*"

Steph felt sweaty and dirt-streaked and tired of being singled out. Everyone was off today, not just her. "Where *are* my hands?"

"Here." Heinrich demonstrated, cupping an imaginary beer belly. *"En baisse!"* He was wearing a purple beret and Steph wondered if his transplant was hurting, because he was in one of his picky, tyrannical moods. Over and over, he made the kids hone their turns and arabesques. They danced full out, on *pointe* and not marking, till their calves screamed.

"Central couple!" Heinrich waved furiously. "Somebody have wrong runs—red couple, ask it another couple. Downstage, all of you—absolutely move! Almost in orchestra, please!"

The company dragged through the waltz formation like smashed, earthbound butterflies. Their circles grew lopsided, wheels pressured out of shape. One boy's hand got too sweaty to grip and a girl went spinning into a canvas *Giselle* tree that had no business being there.

More and more dancers gave up, dropped to the floor. With the unspoken understanding of cats huddling together for comfort, couples massaged one another's muscles.

Heinrich grimaced at his watch. Five o'clock.

"We have just tomorrow, last rehearsal. We have to figure out right tempo for this. We have to do it, kids. Tonight, early to bed. Every one of you."

He stamped offstage. A spattering of applause followed him, grudging and perfunctory. Dancers gathered up their bodies and their tote bags and straggled toward the dressing rooms.

"What's wrong?" a fading voice complained. "The more we rehearse it, the worse it gets."

Steph stayed behind. There was no sense rushing to line up for a shower. She shut her eyes, stretched on the floor. She liked to smell the desertedness of the house. It reminded her of long ago when she had dreamed of being a real dancer, privileged to wander the wings and backstage of a real theater.

In the orchestra pit a pianist was playing a Chopin nocturne for the evening's *Dances at a Gathering*. He sounded like a real pianist, not one of the rehearsal trolls. She let the music fill her, lullaby her. She was almost able to forget the toe shoes blistered to her feet, the aching weight of her muscles.

She must have dozed.

When she opened her eyes again the fire curtain was half lowered. The lights were dimmed. A solitary electrician adjusted a gel on a spot in the wings. He used one of those poles that grocers use to get at faraway shelves. And then he was gone, pole and all, and the stage was peaceful as a country road at night.

Steph stood up. She walked to stage center. She planted herself firmly on one foot, tucked the other up, went on *pointe* and did a double turn.

Not bad. Amazing what was possible when you didn't have an itchy-scalped ballet master yelling at you.

She tried it again.

Better.

And again.

She smiled at herself. *Steph, it may take a decade or two, but you'll make it to* prima ballerina assoluta *yet*.

She realized the piano had stopped, but she could not remember the exact moment of its stopping. The darkness of the house stared at her, tempting her, telling her she was alone.

She walked to the stage apron, stood at the dark footlights, gazing over the tide of empty seats. She lowered her eyes and on a sudden impulse she curtseyed: Makarova's solo curtsy, the little-girl "Who, me?" that brought bouquets and bravas showering to the stage.

Her heart was beating very fast. The blood was applause in her ears. She raised her eyes, smiling her Makarova smile, and the darkness winked back at her.

She began another curtsy.

And stopped.

Her muscles stiffened. She sniffed some warning, some chemical change in the air. She took a step back from the darkness. This wasn't the first time: she'd felt it before at stage rehearsals, something out there, observing, invading.

Her eyes flicked across the blackness. Not a shadow twitched. She scanned the orchestra seats, each layer of boxes.

Then she caught something. The shift of a barely visible bulk. Her eyes jerked back to the source of movement.

There.

The grand tier box on the left, nearest the stage. A ringed knuckle glinted on the railing. Something was tilting out of one of the chairs.

She squinted. Her eye groped out dim contrasts. A head—a bald head. A body straining forward, wrapped in dark cloth. A bald man in a dark suit, unmoving as a painted shadow.

She held her breath and when she could hold it no longer she took a quick little suck through her nostrils. Fear shot through her, electric and stinging. She backed away, eyes on the box where something had shifted. She slid one foot carefully behind the other, aiming toward the light in the wings.

And then she turned and ran. And felt a hand.

And screamed.

"Hey!"

It was Danny Gillette, standing in the half shadow of a wing,

watching her with a smile that was ever so slightly off center.
"Long rehearsal?"

She managed, barely, to pull herself together and say,
"Killing."

"Why'd you scream?" He asked offhandedly, as though it had
been a very offhanded scream.

"I—didn't expect to see you." She felt warmed by the
cloudless spread of his good humor, protected by it. She moved
near to it. "You're not in *Nutcracker*, are you?"

"Lester wouldn't even let me dance Candy Cane. Not that I
didn't try."

"Then why were you in the wings? You weren't *watching* that
mess, were you?"

"Just waiting."

"What for?" That smile again. Was it for her, or was it the
face he kept turned toward the world?

"You."

"Me?" The disbelief must have been audible in her voice.

"Haven't seen you in a while."

"I've been here. I guess I'm pretty hard to spot in tutu."

They walked, not quite touching, through dark wings where
the season's props were stored in bins the size of garbage trucks.
Canvas-covered planking whispered under their feet. They
passed through a security door and came blinking into the bright
fluorescence of a corridor.

"I thought of putting a note in your box," he said, "but I'd
rather talk to you. If you have a minute."

"Now?"

"If you have a minute."

She stared at him. His blue shirt was open at the neck. The
taut unassuming dancer's muscles of his chest rose and fell.

"Just let me shower and change."

"Meet you at the stage door."

Steph practically broke her neck showering and changing.
She rushed to the stage entrance foyer.

A great lump of disappointment thunked inside her.

Dancers scurried past, some just arriving, some just leaving,
a few stopping to trade pellets of gossip. The switchboard
operator, with her frizzy hair that had to be a wig, was busily
fending off phone calls, and the uniformed guard, tipped back in

his chair, was calmly fending off crashers.

Everything was movement and voices and nattering fluorescence: but no Danny.

And then he stepped out of a phone booth.

She saw him before he saw her, and there was a soft sweet strength about him that awakened something in her. He waved and came toward her with the cool, gliding strut of the offstage male dancer. He was sexy. She had a feeling he knew it. The funny thing was, he didn't need to act sexy to be sexy and she had a feeling he didn't know that.

"If you ever need an answering service," he said, "*don't* use mine."

He reached an arm to hold the door for her. She saw a shape flick across the corridor behind him—a bald man in a dark suit. Her heart thumped.

"Danny, wasn't that Marius Volmar?"

Danny glanced over his shoulder. "Didn't see. Not much hair and a teeny-weeny Legion of Honor red thread in the lapel?"

"I didn't notice the lapel. Would he be hanging around Empire?"

They took the escalator up to ground level.

"Who knows?" Danny said. "He could be comparison shopping for dancers—stealing company secrets—maybe he needs some pointers on how to screw up a *Nutcracker*."

"Seems funny."

"He is said to be an extremely funny man with no sense of humor."

They cut across a corner of Lincoln Center Plaza. The sun had dropped below the skyscraper tops and the air was cool and blue now, shadowed and soft like a forest. Children were jaywalking, arms outstretched, along the edge of the fountain.

Danny touched her arm lightly, steering her. It seemed a very natural thing to do. The stage of the Metropolitan Opera felt far away. They strolled past the Vivian Beaumont Theater and stopped to stare at the reflecting pool with its huge, tranquil Henry Moore sculptures.

"Steph—the reason I want to talk to you—I got a grant yesterday, from the Harkness Foundation. They're giving me five hundred dollars to do a ballet."

"That's wonderful!"

"It'll be small—four dancers, taped music—part of the series at the Damrosch shell."

She gripped his arm. "Danny, I'm so happy for you."

"I have an idea—two women, two men. My own twisted version of a Greek myth." His face was tensed in some hidden pocket of thought. "Steph, will you dance it?"

"Me?" She felt Manhattan tremble beneath her.

"I've seen you dance, Steph, and I saw you tonight. You do a very good Makarova, by the way, but don't let Natasha see it." Something changed. The brown of his eyes deepened. "I've made the part on you, Steph. I mean, on my idea of you. It uses your extension and you'd look great and *it* would look great. I can't pay you, but—"

"Pay me!" It was honor enough, nowadays, for a dancer to have any sort of part made on her at all. But there were problems, and her mind sifted them. She was under contract and she'd need permission to work outside the company. And then there was her mother.

They were standing on the bridge over Sixty-fifth Street and his hands were on her shoulders in a good-by way. He was looking into her eyes asking, "Yes?"

"Danny, I—oh, I want to so much."

"Then it's yes, yes? Yes."

"Yes. Don't you dare offer it to anyone else. Yes."

He kissed her. On the lips. Very fast, very soft, but on the lips.

"We start rehearsal Sunday."

"Sunday?" Her one day off, the day of apartment chores and visiting her mother.

But Danny's ballet was more important.

"It's a date. Sunday!"

*     *     *

"Mom, I'll be leaving early today."

They were sitting in the breakfast nook of Anna's apartment. Anna had missed her daughter in little ways since they'd moved to separate apartments and she was grateful for the weekly coffee and muffins and gossip, the chance to listen and advise and remember she was needed.

"And would you mind if we didn't see one another for a few Sundays?"

Anna couldn't have been more surprised if her daughter had slapped her. "Of course I'd mind—unless there's a damned good reason."

Steph talked excitedly about the project. Anna listened quietly. Steph hadn't even asked about her week at Arden's, which had been hell. At the mention of Danny's name Anna laid a silencing hand on Steph's shoulder.

"Who? Who did you say?"

"Danny Gillette. He's been with Empire three years and he was one of Lvovna's star pupils. He's a soloist now but they're going to make him a principal next year."

"I know who he is. I just didn't know you were involved with him."

"I'm not involved with anyone. He asked me to help out, that's all."

"*He* must think you're friends. He wouldn't ask a perfect stranger, would he?"

"He's asked me and two other dancers to contribute time."

Anna watched her daughter's eyes. They were butterflies, never stopping anywhere. "How much time?"

"A couple of Sunday afternoons till he works out the choreography. Mom, he's good. You wanted me to make contacts in the company. Danny's a contact."

For some time Anna had been aware of a certain loneliness in her daughter. "He could be—someday. Where does he want to rehearse?"

"He's borrowed a loft down in SoHo."

"Where they have all the muggings?"

"I'll share a taxi with Linda."

"Linda's in on this too? Danny sure gets around." Anna spread corn-oil margarine on a muffin, thinking. Danny Gillette was a good-looking boy. It was no secret he had caught Lester Croyden's eye. He was bound to climb in the company, and if he wanted to take Steph along for the climb, why not? Anna saw only one objection.

"I've heard rumors about that Danny."

Steph's glance tipped up at her, green and fragile. The girl was braced as though Anna might purposely say something to wound her.

"He's not gay," Anna said.

"What does that matter?"

"What does it *matter!*" Anna could not help feeling shock.
What surprised her was not the girl's innocence but her own lack
of a ready answer. She realized that her daughter did not think
the way she did. There were assumptions they did not share. A
terrible sadness hovered near. She raised her voice, as though a
shout could bat it away.

"I can't run your life for you. Go. Work." She was talking
through a mouthful of muffin. "I'll find something else to do
Sundays."

                    *        *        *

Steph didn't share a taxi, and she arrived for rehearsal, and
there was no one in the loft but Danny. He was sitting
cross-legged on the floor, turning through the pages of an
orchestra score.

"Do you read music?" Steph asked, surprised. Most dancers
that she knew couldn't manage anything more than a one-finger
lead sheet.

"A little." He showed her the cover. "Benjamin Britten—
Sinfonia da Requiem. Do you know it?"

"No," she admitted, wishing she did, wishing she could say
something to impress him.

"I first heard it when I was a child. And I knew one day I'd
choreograph it. Would you like to hear it?"

"Very much," she said. She felt the music would tell her
something about him. She wanted to know about Danny
Gillette aka Goldberg.

He went to the tape recorder that had been rigged to the
stereo. At the touch of a button, music—wrenching,
lamenting—leapt out of the speakers. The loft was an artist's
floor-through on Grand Street. The windows had been flung
open and the sounds and fumes of traffic drifted up from the
street, mixing strangely with the orchestra.

Steph watched Danny, absorbed in his score. She wished she
could read music, wished she had an excuse to sit near him and
lean close. She tried to fathom what this tragic outpouring of
notes meant to him.

She had never seen a monk at prayer, but she had an idea he
would have Danny's face, all life and movement concentrated in

the eyes. He was ignoring her and yet she felt comfortable, like a cat in front of a warm stove.

It was almost an annoyance when Linda and Al came thumping in with their tote bags and wisecracks. Danny switched off the tape recorder, went to the stove, and poured coffee for everyone. There was three minutes' small talk and then he explained the ballet.

"We're dealing with two Greek myths. Cupid and Psyche; Diana and Endymion. Does everyone know the stories?"

Silence.

"Does anyone know them?"

Silence. Al lit a cigarette.

"All right. All you need are the basics. Cupid was a god; Psyche was a mortal. He made love to her while she was asleep."

"Mixed marriage." Al drew a long puff and exhaled.

Danny gave him a glance and went on. "Diana was a goddess; Endymion was a mortal. She made love to him while *he* was asleep."

"Who plays who?" Linda asked.

"You and Al are Diana and Endymion. Steph and I are Psyche and Cupid."

*He's made us partners*, Steph thought. *He's made us lovers.*

# sixteen

Sundays were full of Danny's ballet; and sweat. He laid the broad frame, then added the small strokes. He showed how Endymion turned in his sleep, how Psyche awoke, he even demonstrated the look he wanted on Diana's face when she discovered her shepherd love.

The dancers made mistakes. Sometimes Danny would stop the tape recorder and cry, "No! No!" Other times he would take his notebook and write in it. "I like that—it's better your way—let's keep it."

Steph listened and observed and tried to bend her body to Danny's choreography. Her nerves and muscles protested some of the movements, sending out waves of discomfort that she had to fight back. *I will do it*, she told herself, *and I won't let him see it's hard for me!*

The dancers grew tired quickly and every half hour or so Linda and Al would have to sit down. But Steph never sat. She was afraid that if she once relaxed her determination she might lose it.

Danny watched her during breaks. She wasn't certain whether he was scowling or just appraising, but she sensed he wasn't pleased.

"Can you stay a minute afterward?" he asked. "There's something I'd like to work out with you. Alone."

She stayed, heart pounding. Linda and Al showered and left with a pointed-sounding "Good night, you two—see you in class tomorrow."

The loft was hot. The street suddenly was quiet. Danny's hair lay flattened to his head like a skullcap. His face glistened with sweat. Silence widened in ripples around them.

He stared at her, not talking, eyes calculating, and he reminded her of an animal trainer.

"I'm going to ask you to do something very funny," he said softly.

"I promise not to laugh."

"You don't have to dance. Mark the part, walk through it, whatever you feel comfortable doing. But sing the music."

"Sing—I can't sing!"

"Then hum. Or growl. Just mark the music while you mark the movements."

"I'm not a musician."

"Every dancer's a musician."

"Danny, I don't *know* the music. I have to hear it. It's not in me."

"Yes, it is. But you're not letting it out. And that's the trouble." He waited. "Any time you're ready. Your own tempo. Take as long as you need. We have all the time in the world."

He didn't move. Only his eyes touched her. She got down onto the floor, into the sleeping position that opened the ballet. She waited, obedient and stupid and six years old.

"I'm not cuing you, Steph."

"But I need the cue—I don't even know how many counts I have."

"Yes, you do. The music will tell you. Just sing it."

She felt foolish but she swallowed back her humiliation and did what he wanted. She thumped her fist on the floor, marking the two deep chords that opened the score. She began humming, sketching what she could remember of the music's highs and lows, the louds and softs, the swifts and slows.

And something amazing began to happen.

The music spun itself out of her, like a strand of web, and gradually the web lifted her and she was standing, letting it guide her through her embarrassment and fear, beyond them, out into open space.

"That's it, Steph. You're getting it. Hold on to it—hold on—"

Now his voice was humming alongside hers. He guided her, twisting her leg in, her arm out. He smelled of the day's work. His hands coaxed her body into a dream. She began dancing full out again. She had no breath to hum: the music was inside her head, silent and all the more audible for its silence.

Her body felt different. It did not complain. There was no pain, no fatigue, no uncertainty. It dawned on her what was happening: her body was beginning to understand.

To sing.

She felt her bones shifting like the changing shapes of a melody.

"What did I tell you?" he said. "It was in you all the time."

Steph smiled. They were standing alone, not touching. She knew he was going to kiss her.

But he didn't. "Why don't you shower and change?" he said. "I'll walk you to the subway."

They walked to the subway, not talking. Her pulse raced.

"Which train do you take?" he asked.

"The A."

"Here we are then."

He left her at the token booth: not a kiss, not a touch. Disappointment turned over inside her.

\*      \*      \*

The night of Danny's premiere they warmed up at the theater. They were all jittery.

Steph managed to pull a blanket of willed calm over herself. Linda and Al cracked jokes. Danny chain-smoked. Steph tried to catch his eye to reassure him. He flashed a rugged smile, but she could see he preferred to stay locked up within himself.

They left the theater a little before eight. Steph missed her mother: not so much the nagging as the comfort of the familiar. Anna had begged and threatened, but it was her late night at work, and Arden's had refused to let her off.

They crossed Damrosch Park with jackets and jeans over their leotards, hurrying before the summer air could chill the muscles they had so carefully readied.

The evening light caught the rows of wooden seats, thickened the boxed trees and bushes with broad strokes of shadow. An early sprinkling of spectators had staked out positions among the free seats. There was something amiable and makeshift about tonight—dancers about to dance their own dances, dance lovers waiting to watch, a hovering awareness that legends were born on nights like this.

Other dancers taking part in the program stood in the band shell doorway, talking and joking. Several were helping with sound equipment and props. The musicians' and stagehands' unions, who had strangle holds on New York's performing arts, had consented to the dancers' using taped music and non-shop props. As Al had remarked, "Fucking gracious of them."

Steph lingered at the band shell door, watching the daylight dim down from amber to blue. For one dying moment, as audiences poured into the Met and the State Theater and Avery Fisher Hall, a wind of human voices blew over from the plaza.

An instant later an eerie silence fell, as though an iron door had shut out most of humanity. All that were left were a few dancers, a few spectators, and Danny at Steph's shoulder, looking out into the park, brow furrowed.

They went downstairs to wait.

The dressing rooms—if you could call them that—were a string of open-ended cubicles crowded beneath the band shell, like toilet stalls without doors. Cleaner, but no more private. Two dozen dancers paced, smoked, whispered; executed nervous little bends and *penchés*, holding onto chairs, table edges, each other—anything to keep from tightening up.

The program began at eight-thirty.

Applause and taped music filtered down. Danny's ballet came third. Steph felt her heart thumping. She was afraid. Muscles in Danny's face stood out where she had never seen muscles before. Al and Linda passed their last cigarette back and forth.

With each wave of applause there were fewer dancers left pacing. The fear climbed from Steph's heart to her throat. Al was peeling paper from the butts in an ash tray, trying to roll a cigarette in a piece of Linda's Kleenex.

Up in the band shell, the p.a. was blasting Moog-synthesizer

Bach. Danny shook his head in rhythm, not smiling.

Applause.

Silence.

Footsteps on stone.

The volunteer stage manager, a former dancer from Balanchine's company, poked his head around the corner. "Places, please."

The girls led the way. They stood in the wing. No turning back now. Danny was sweating badly. A look of panic passed across his face. They whispered and kissed.

"*Merde... Merde... Merde*, honey."

Steph waited for the stage manager's signal. She stiffened her courage into a stubborn line. A thought flashed through her head.

*Icarus.*

Everything before had been preparation and sweat and everything afterward might be disaster and broken bones. But this was take-off.

The stage manager's handkerchief flashed white against the dark wing. *All right, Icarus*, she told herself, *fly.*

She stepped out onto the dark stage to take her sleeping position. The music let out its two monster heartbeat thumps. The light came up in a pool around her. There was no fear now, only the voice of the music filling her and driving out every doubt.

\*       \*       \*

Chris was late.

At first Ray tried to deny the fact: *She couldn't be late; I must have told her eight-thirty, not eight o'clock. Maybe she took a subway. Maybe the train broke down.*

He told himself he was lucky to have the extra minutes. He filled the wait with tiny last-minute adjustments: the beef bourguignon simmering in the oven needed a splash more wine, another half bay leaf; the gladioluses on the dining table were irksomely symmetrical, and so he rearranged them; his fingers found a patch of stubble on his chin and he shaved for the second time in two hours, leaving the bathroom door open in case the doorbell rang.

It didn't.

At eight forty-five Ray Lockwood was still alone in the little studio apartment that he had tried to make festive with candles and a new tablecloth. He rinsed wineglasses that were already clean and then he dried them to a second shine. He checked tops of picture frames for dust. He restacked lawbooks on his desk so it looked less legal, less cluttered.

He went into the kitchen five times to check his wristwatch against the electric clock.

At nine he telephoned. There was no answer at Chris's apartment.

*She's on her way*, he told himself.

At nine-fifteen he ran out of chores. He sat on the edge of the neatly made daybed, hands dangling between his knees. His heartbeat felt thick and tight against the side of his chest. He loosened his tie.

*If she'd been going to that festival at the band shell she'd have told me, wouldn't she?*

The walls of the room pressed in on him, buzzing dully with her absence. He stared at the sudden blank space of the evening and the vaster blankness it implied.

At nine-thirty he could stand it no longer. He got to his feet and put on his jacket.

*     *     *

Long after the last bell, Ivor Noble, dance critic, emerged from the grand tier men's room. He stood a moment, swaying, unable to place himself among marble dunes and red velvet plains.

He made an eye-catching figure.

His hair was oily black, his face at the moment bright red. He wore a gray suit, broadly pin-striped; a trendy op-art shirt (he still thought in words like "trendy"); and, capping it off like the candy rose on a cake, an explosion of striped bow tie that had somehow, his hand told him, wriggled half loose. Not trendy, that.

He'd correct it in his seat.

Where *was* his seat?

His ear clutched at a ribbon of sound: thin violins, unsteady flute, not quite making their unison. He took one-eyed aim and veered toward the door to aisle 3. It was shut. And blocked.

"I'm sorry, sir. You can't go in."

He noted the usher's glance directed at his hand. The hand still held an eight-ounce translucent plastic cup. From the jiggle and slosh he judged the cup still held a good four swallows of scotch on ice. He wasn't about to let good Johnnie Walker go to waste, not at the prices the Opera Bar charged this season; not with all of *Les Sylphides* still to get through.

He took his four swallows in one, crumpled the cup, and dropped it at a standing ash tray. His aim was good. The cup landed in white sand studded with cigarette butts. Management forbade drinking in the house; management forbade smoking in the house. *Damn*, he thought, *they should forbid* Les Sylphides *while they're at it*.

"All right—*now* may I go in?"

"I'm sorry, sir. The performance has already begun."

"Look here, my wife's in there waiting for me. We've got aisle seats, I'm not going to be disturbing anyone."

"If you'd care to go to the lounge, you may see the performance on closed circuit—"

"I don't care to go to your damned lounge!" When he lost his temper his voice reverted to his native Australia. "I'm Ivor Noble, ballet critic, and I'm reviewing this disaster. Now will you let me in or do I have to call the manager?"

"No late seating allowed." No *sorry* this time. No *sir* either.

The usher was a nobody and Ivor Noble was a somebody. But the usher was tall and Ivor Noble was not. The usher was lean and Ivor Noble was not.

The usher was sober.

Ivor Noble glared at the uniformed nobody forbidding him entry: young, vain, cocky—probably some kind of aspiring dancer. Ivor Noble would be damned if he'd argue with an aspiring anything.

Damned if he'd subject himself to another *Sylphides*, either.

He grunted, went back to the bar, and armed himself with another scotch, retreated through glass doors to the balcony. It was twilight. The evening was warm. He was alone. And angry.

The State Theater and Avery Fisher Hall faced one another across the deserted plaza, gigantic parody Parthenons. Between them somebody-or-other's memorial fountain disturbed the darkening air with computerized, illuminated towers of water, white and milky as the sheathed finger of a proctologist.

Ivor Noble pondered American vulgarity, American audacity, the audacity of the management of Lincoln Center to deny entrance to the most influential critic in the city; damn it, the most influential in the nation. . . . Face it, damn it, the most influential critic *in the world*. . . .

Music buzzed at his ear.

He flicked it away, taking it for *Les Sylphides*, that awful corn-syrup Chopin. But it wasn't Chopin. It came from another direction, sinewy and strong and astringent. He turned his head, tracking it to the right, to the grove of trees at Damrosch Park.

A recollection tugged at him.

Wasn't there some sort of festival at the Damrosch Park band shell tonight? Aspiring would-be's dancing free? Hadn't he tossed the mailing into his wastebasket only last week?

A notion zipped over his mind.

Why not take his scotch—no, finish this and take a fresh one—over to Damrosch Park? Why not ignore *Les Sylphides*, ignore Lincoln Center and its preening ushers, why not review the free festival instead?

He stared at the fountain giving him the finger. He gave it the finger right back.

He picked up another scotch on his way out of the Met and made for Damrosch Park. Programs were stuck like bird feed in baskets on the trees. He whisked one loose, stumbled into a chair, and tried to focus.

The stage: pools of light, four figures.

The program: eight ballets, which the hell one was he watching?

His drink: half empty.

With effort, he lifted his eyes back to the band shell, to what appeared to be—odd—two *pas de deux*. Interesting.

Why two?

Ivor Noble braced his elbows on his knees, belched, and leaned forward.

*     *     *

Chris watched from the fifth row.

Psyche stood tree-still among the lengthening shadows of dying music. Downstage from her, Endymion—asleep—was kneeling in extended fourth.

Abruptly, movement shattered the frieze.

Diana, the goddess, raised one leg in a long, effortless, breathtakingly straight *développé*. In a sudden swoop of black and white unitard, she *tombé*'d onto Endymion's shoulder in a split *jeté*. Endymion lifted her. Sleepwalking, moving backward, he carried her to the front of the stage. Still sleeping, he set her down.

Now it was Psyche's turn. A trembling shook her. Chris sensed it was not fear but effort. Psyche had to resist the instinct of her muscles, the hurrying pull of gravity. Keeping her movements slow, long, sleeping, she *développé*'d—stretched—held. Chris could see it was harder for Psyche than for Diana: every movement was twice as slow, twice as long, twice as painful.

Psyche's *cinq* looked soft. Her fall onto Cupid's shoulder wasn't slow enough and Chris could see she was early.

But Cupid the god was ready for her. He covered. His arm arced, filling the gap she had left in time.

The light tightened in a circle around them. He lifted her. She let herself float up through the dusk. He held her aloft five beats.

Then, gently, not waking her, he set her down again.

A moment of fading music.

The gods regarded the slumbering mortals, then turned, drifted in separate directions into the dark. The pools of light dimmed and died.

\* \* \*

Out of breath, chest thumping, Ray passed the Lincoln Plaza fountain and the blare of lights at the Metropolitan Opera. As he neared the band shell he saw heads turn and he realized he was running.

He slowed to a tiptoe, moved along the path behind the audience. He stood tall, adjusting his eyes to the layers of light and dark. Anxiously, he searched.

The air was warm and drum-taut and it beat like a heart to the amplified music. The band shell threw a fan of light across the first two rows of spectators. After that they were shadows, each of them caught in shared, secret communion that somehow excluded him.

And none of them was Chris.

After a long, aching moment he gave up hope. She wasn't there. He pressed a hand to the sudden cold hole in his chest. Flashes of mugging and rape and subway murder went off in his head.

*Why did I invite her to my place? Why didn't I pick her up at hers?*

On the band shell stage Chris's roommate turned and leaped and balanced. The skin-tight black and white costume emphasized the terrifying perfection of her movements. He was struck by the arrogance of dancers' beauty, by the poignance of its perishability.

*Where's Chris? If she's not here, where is she?*

The stage lighting changed and the spill-over thrust deeper into the audience. Suddenly he thought he saw her. It *was* Chris, sitting at the far end of the fifth row, a motionless profile with hair that glowed like moonlight.

*Thank God*, he thought, *she's all right*, and then a fog of anger closed in on him and he thought, *God damn her*, and he wanted to take her in his hands like a tiny white bird and crush her into a fistful of broken bones. Then in a wave of repentance he wanted to gather her up in his arms and beg forgiveness.

He began working his way around the back of the audience to where she was sitting. The stage lights went down and the applause caught him by surprise. When the lights came up again he shouted, "Chris!"

She was standing now and she looked in his direction. He grinned and waved.

He could have sworn she saw him. She *must* have seen him.

But there was no reaction. She stared blankly for a moment and then she turned away, as though he weren't there at all, and he felt a part of him die.

\*     \*     \*

At first there was only a murmuring of applause. The dancers sprang into position for bows.

Lights up.

Applause up.

The dancers held hands, stepped forward, bowed.

Lights down. The applause stayed up. Way, way up. Bravos. Lights up. Another bow. Lights down.

The applause followed them all the way down to the dressing room. Steph could still hear it, like wind in a forest, as she sat in front of her mirror. Her body was drained even of exhaustion. She heard voices in the corridor. She heard laughter, relief, congratulations.

Chris was at her shoulder, bending to hug her.

"My God, it was fantastic. How can you pirouette that *slowly?*"

"Liar," Steph smiled. "But thanks. It should have been slower."

And then she recognized Danny's voice, fending off congratulations with modest little self-deprecations.

Her heart gave a little sideways leap. She knew she'd done a good job and she knew he was waiting for her. At that moment she wished she were the worst dancer in the world. She wished she could know for sure it was Stephanie Lang he wanted, not her turn-out or her *développé* or her placement.

Or was it all the same thing?

Her glance flicked up, caught his in the mirror. Neither spoke. Neither looked away.

There was a fresh burst of laughter and Linda and Al came crowding into the cubicle. After a round of kissing and hugging Danny said, "Anyone for supper? I know a terrific place."

Silence. Steph could feel Al and Linda and Chris exchanging glances.

"Great food," Danny said. "My treat."

"I've eaten," Chris said.

"Al and I have plans," Linda said. Firmly.

After a pause Danny's gaze flitted down to where Steph sat Kleenexing cold cream from her face.

"Steph?"

"Sure," she said, and his face went wide with smile.

# seventeen

---

They walked to Seventieth Street, just off Broadway. There were trees and a churchyard and townhouses with neat stone steps and it didn't feel like New York City at all. They went into a little place that Danny knew. The Frenchwoman at the cash register waved a hello, and Danny led Steph to a quiet table in a corner.

"There are two types of dancers," he said. "Type A are so tired after a performance they have to go straight to bed. Type B are so excited they can't get to sleep for four hours. Which type are you?"

Steph suddenly felt she was not going to be able to manage small talk. She would have been happy just to sit there in silence, happy just to be with Danny sharing the excitement of his success. But people didn't go to restaurants to sit silently, and tonight she wanted very much to be a person, not just a dancer.

She tried to think of something clever to say. "Type C. I can't get to sleep for six hours."

"That must be a hell of a nuisance."

"With a glass of hot milk and a soak in a tub, I can usually get it down to three hours. And what type are you?"

"Type D."

"What's D's pattern?"

"Sometimes D goes straight to bed, sleeps for days. Sometimes he can't get to sleep for a week. With Type D it all depends."

"On what?"

"I've never found out. Right now I have a feeling I'm going to be up for a week."

"Oh, Danny, if I were you, I'd be up for the rest of my life. It went so beautifully."

"Thanks to Benjamin Britten. And most of all thanks to you."

"No thanks to me. I just did what I was told. And I loved doing it."

"And I loved telling you. And I hope we'll be doing it again one of these days."

A waitress handed them menus. She was a large, cheerful woman and she seemed to regard Danny as a son. *"Bonjour, mon petit, ça va?"*

*"Ça va* just fine," Danny said. "Estelle, this is Stephanie—Steph, Estelle."

"So you have a friend at last." The waitress smiled at Steph. The smile was long, examining, and—finally—approving. "Always he eats alone, always I say, 'Daniel, you kill your digestion eating alone.' Tonight, mademoiselle, you make sure he chews his chicken, not just swallow?"

"And how do you know I'm having chicken?" Danny said.

"Because it is the specialty. Chicken with tarragon. And for you, mademoiselle? The same?"

"Spaghetti," Steph said. "With lots of sauce."

"Spaghetti! Daniel, what kind of friend is this?"

"A very good friend and a very hungry one and she needs her carbohydrates."

The waitress eyed Steph. "You are dancer too, mademoiselle?"

Steph nodded.

"I can tell dancers. Always they want the crazy food. Pasta, cakes, Coca-Cola, cigarettes. It has taken me three years to make this boy eat meat."

"And maybe in another three you'll persuade Steph."

The waitress considered Steph, as though calculating the years required. "And to drink? Half carafe red for you, mademoiselle?"

"No, thanks. I don't drink wine."

"Come on," Danny coaxed. "It's a celebration. And I'm drinking."

"All right," Steph yielded. "A glass."

"Half carafe," the waitress corrected. "It's cheaper."

Danny explained that he ate here two or three times a week after performances. "There's always plenty of special left over, and Estelle would just as soon give it to me as dump it in the stew."

"Don't you ever cook for yourself?"

"Anything you can make with boiled water I'm a master of. Soft-boiled eggs, instant coffee, frozen dinner baggies, you name it."

Steph thought: *He lives by himself.*

They chatted till the chicken and the spaghetti came, and the half carafe of red and the half of white, and then they were alone. Danny filled Steph's glass, filled his own, and proposed a toast.

"To the future."

They clinked glasses. Steph couldn't help wondering whether he'd meant two separate futures or one combined future. She tried to imagine her future combined with his: soft-boiling his eggs, unfreezing his dinner baggies, dancing his ballets. His hands guiding her through steps. His hands guiding her through love-making. The fantasy appealed to her.

Maybe it didn't have to be a fantasy. He lived alone. Apparently she was the first girl he'd brought to his favorite restaurant. That had to mean something.

She sipped. The wine stung agreeably, like a finger probing some unsuspected pleasure zone.

"No one in the company seems to know very much about you," she said.

"You've been asking?"

"No. But I've been listening."

"What do you hear?"

"He's a nice guy, he works very hard, he's very quiet."

"Me in a nutshell."

"No one's ever seen your apartment."

"No one would want to. It's buried under three years of silt and New York *Times*."

"No one knows your phone number. Including directory assistance."

"My phone number's a secret. I pay New York Telephone a dollar a month to keep it that way."

"You don't like to get phone calls?"

"Only the anonymous raunchy variety."

"Does that mean you live alone?"

"Not necessarily."

"Do you?"

"Do *you?*" he said.

"I have a roommate."

"Male or female?"

"Female. What about you?"

"Geoffrey. Definitely male."

Disappointment stirred in her. *Well*, she thought, *it's better than if he were living with a girl. I guess.* "Does Geoffrey dance too?"

"Geoffrey's specialty is clawing the upholstery and peeing in the wrong place when I forget to empty his litter pan. With him, peeing is constitutionally protected symbolic speech."

"I like cats," Steph said. It wasn't exactly a lie. She'd never met a cat she *hated.* Anyway she loved Geoffrey for being a cat and not a gay boy.

She was aware of tiny disorders on Danny's side of the table. He lifted his glass and the wine made waves. He set it down and the wine splashed. When he reached for his fork he picked up his spoon instead. When he tried to slice his chicken the chicken dodged the knife. He was like a jittery smoker lighting the filter end.

"Do you have pets?" he asked.

*Oh, God*, she thought. *We're going to get bogged in pet talk. Damn you, Geoffrey.* "No. My roommate's allergic, and when I was a child we moved around too much." Steph twirled a forkful of spaghetti into her spoon. It glopped back onto the plate. "I wouldn't mind having a dog someday. Maybe a little highland terrier."

She tried again, glopped again. She smiled to hide her embarrassment. *I couldn't be drunk from half a glass of wine*, she told herself. *Or could I?*

Danny was talking about the cruelty of keeping a dog in the city.

She made a third attempt, turned half a forkful of spaghetti very slowly in the spoon till it made a nice manageable mouthful, lifted the fork very carefully, opened her mouth . . . and wound up with a beard of damp pasta straggling down her chin.

She covered with her napkin, glanced at Danny to see the verdict in his eyes on her terrible table manners.

She couldn't believe it: Danny Gillette, who could orchestrate the movements of human bodies, who could wring poetry from the sweating limbs of scared kids, who could hold a balance for eighteen counts—still couldn't get his fork into a dead piece of chicken.

"But it's hard," she said, trying to keep conversation going and running out of things to say about pets. "A dancer's on tour half the year. You can't pack an animal in your suitcase. You can't leave it alone. Boarding it costs money. Maybe house plants are safer."

He was blushing. Not at her, but at his lap. A trail of sauce led from his empty plate to the edge of the table, like a track of a skier gone off a cliff. With both trembling hands he lifted his napkin to table level. A hammock of tarragon chicken moved cautiously back toward his plate.

She studied the mural behind him, an out-of-perspective Eiffel Tower, as though it were the most fascinating thing since Rouault's sets for *Prodigal Son*.

He filched a napkin from the deserted table next to them and daubed at his trousers. He tried to smile. "Close call."

She tried to think of something pleasant to say; something to ease his embarrassment. "According to the *Guinness Book of Records*, the leading cause of accidents in French restaurants is chicken."

His blush deepened.

"Second leading cause is spaghetti," she said, and his blush deepened more.

And then it dawned on her. *She* was causing his nervousness.

Stephanie Lang, so used to being confused and uncertain, was causing confusion in someone else; and not just any old someone else, but Danny Gillette.

She sat back. Astonishment glowed in her. She had power over him. She couldn't believe it. But the proof was written all over the tablecloth: spilled sauce, spilled wine, spilled salt.

It was the first time in her life she'd ever done this to a boy.

And she enjoyed it. Suddenly she felt strong: not bossy-strong or gloating-strong, but gentle-strong. Pleased. Alive. Stephanie Lang had the power to move another human being. To move Danny Gillette!

*He likes me*, she realized.

She stared at the wine spots on her side of the tablecloth and something else dawned on her.

*I like him just as much.*

"Do you suppose the laundry bill is included," she said, "or do we add it to the tip?"

He smiled and she could see the tension beginning to trickle out of him. "Steph?"

"Yes, Danny?"

"Here I am, big choreographer taking rising ballerina out to chic but little-known *boîte*, trying to impress hell out of her, and all I've accomplished is a tablecloth full of tarragon-flavored goo."

"But you have impressed me."

"As a klutz."

"See my side of the tablecloth? Spaghetti-flavored goo. That's because you impress the hell out of me, Danny."

"Funny. You impress the hell out of me."

"Well, now that we're both impressed, maybe we can take the tablecloth home in a doggy bag."

He burst out laughing and reached across the table and gave her hand a squeeze.

And suddenly everything changed. Chicken stopped skidding. Spaghetti stopped dripping. Wine stopped spilling. Talk and laughter flowed. Even when he asked about her family she managed to keep her smile up. The best evasion, she decided, was the truth.

"I have a mother. My father died when I was a baby."

"Do you remember him at all?"

"Once somebody held me against his face and it was very rough. Mom says that was my father. That's my only memory of him."

"I'm sorry."

"It's better than bad memories, I suppose. At least I never had any traumas with squabbling parents or sibling rivalry."

"It was just your mother?"

"Sometimes just a mother is enough."

He was smiling at her almost sadly. "How well I know."

"Your parents are both alive, aren't they?"

"They're kicking."

"Are you close?"

"I try to keep out of kicking range."

She sensed in him a hurt that was still living, a wound edged in anger and best avoided. But there was one thing she had to know, even if it hurt them both. "Linda says you only like Jewish girls."

He hesitated just an instant. "Are you Jewish?"

"No."

"Then I guess Linda doesn't know everything, does she?"

She was relieved. So relieved that she didn't object when Danny ordered more wine, so relieved that she drank two more glasses. When she glanced at her watch and saw the time, she was shocked.

"It's almost one!" she cried. "I'll never make class tomorrow!"

He fixed a gentle stare on her. "Do you have to?"

She could feel wine and blood drumming in her cheeks, warning her. "We *both* have to."

His stare lingered one questioning moment and then he turned and signaled the waitress. When the check came Steph opened her purse.

"Oh no, you don't," Danny said.

"At least let me pay my share."

"This is your choreographer talking. Keep those hands in your lap." He added a tip, signed the check, and announced he was taking her home in a taxi.

She knew he earned a soloist's pay, a hundred fifty more than she did, but still he lived alone and had rent to pay, and if he ate out all the time he was probably just as broke as she was.

"I only live a couple of blocks away," she said. When you had two half liters of red wine in you, when you'd just danced a successful world premiere and spent one of the nicest evenings of your life with someone you really liked, there was no difference between twelve blocks and a couple.

"Then I'll walk you."

He waved good night to the waitress and good night to the

woman at the cash register. He reached to open the restaurant door. Steph brushed past him. For an instant his arm was very near her waist, almost touching. The night was cool.

"Which way?" he asked.

"East."

He took her arm and they walked slowly. There was no traffic but they stopped at a red light anyway.

"Danny?"

"Steph?"

"I think I'm drunk."

"You seem to be walking pretty straight to me."

"I'm not walking, I'm standing."

"You seem to be standing pretty straight."

"That's because I've had twelve years' training, Danny?"

"Steph?"

"I've changed my mind. I don't want to walk."

"Do you want a taxi?"

"I want to stand here. Just like this. Right here. I want to go to sleep standing up." *Leaning on you.* But she didn't say that.

The light changed to green. His hand became firm on her arm; managerial. He was walking her. As though she were a child. Or a ballerina.

The streets rolled gently, like waves. She liked Danny's arm around her, steering. It kindled a feeling of security in her. She could feel her heart beating as though her chest were made of paper.

They reached the building.

"This is it," she said. "Home."

The night doorman was watching them from his chair, over the top of his early bird *Daily News*. She debated whether or not to ask Danny up. She thought of Chris awake and it seemed like an awkward idea and she thought of Chris asleep and it seemed just as awkward.

"Danny, thank you for a beautiful evening and I'm sorry I'm drunk."

His hands were on her shoulders. "You're not drunk, so don't be sorry and thank *you* for a beautiful evening. See you in class tomorrow, okay?"

"If I can see straight."

His hands slid off her shoulders. He was smiling at her, but she sensed she'd put him off not asking him up, and she sensed it was one of those instead-of-a-kiss smiles. She felt heavier without the weight of his touch. Something in her sagged.

"Good night, Steph."

"Good night, Danny."

She turned to go into the building. He stopped her.

"Wait a minute, Steph."

And kissed her.

A very quick, soft kiss. Shy. His lips not quite centered on hers. It was so last-minute, so all-of-a-sudden, she didn't have time to respond. She opened her eyes and Danny was gone. And the doorman was smiling. Let him smile. She was smiling too.

All the way up in the elevator, all through the fumbling with the door key, the realization sang in her: Danny Gillette aka Goldberg liked her!

*Wanted* her!

*       *       *

As she let herself into the apartment her mother rose from the sofa and advanced on her. "Congratulations. And where—have—you—*been?*"

"Mom—what are you doing here? Where's Chris?"

"In there asleep—like you should have been two hours ago. I've been worried sick. Chris didn't know where you were. Lester Croyden didn't know where you were, your friend Linda didn't know where you were, so don't try to tell me you were with her."

Suddenly Steph was sober. All the giddiness in her evaporated. And with it the happiness.

"You didn't *phone* all those people!"

"Damned right I phoned them. You expect me to sit home chewing my nails, wondering whether you're dead or alive or spending the night with God knows who?"

"I wish you wouldn't pester all my friends. It makes me look like a fool."

"And you are a fool. A full day's work tomorrow and you're out all night."

"Which is why I'm going to sleep right now. Good night, Mom." Steph put down her bag, stepped out of her shoes.

"Just a minute. I want to know where you were, who you

were with, what you were doing."

"I was with Danny. We were celebrating."

"Celebrating how?"

Her mother had no right to cross-examine her, not now when Steph lived in her own apartment and paid her own way. She was tempted to lie and cut the discussion short. But something told her that to lie now would be to give in forever. Besides, she hadn't the strength to lie or the imagination. All she wanted was sleep.

"We had dinner."

"You've been drinking."

"Mom, it was a *celebration*. We had a little wine and we laughed and we talked and we forgot what time it was."

"I'm very happy for Danny. And I'm very worried about you."

"Mom, I'm tired. I'm not up to an argument."

"Who's arguing?"

"You're arguing. Chris is in there trying to sleep and the walls are very thin."

"So lower your voice and sit down and talk to your mother for one minute. I haven't seen you in five Sundays, you know."

They sat on the sofa, side by side. Anna angled to face her daughter, Steph angled so as not to have to face her mother.

"Are you in love with this Danny kid?" Anna asked.

"He's not a kid and I'm not a kid."

"Are you in love?"

"I like him."

"And he likes you?"

"I hope so."

"I *knew* it."

"Do you expect me to be a nun all my life?"

"I expect you to be a dancer. And once you're a dancer you can fool around with all the Dannys you want."

"Mom, I've got to have *some* friends!"

"So they can keep you out all night? So they can wreck your career?"

"It's my life! Let me live it!"

"Twenty years I put into you. Half my life."

Abruptly, Anna had become pathetic. Steph did not need to look or even to listen. She had seen and heard it all before, the hurt tone, the bent posture, the eyes shimmering on the brink of tears, the voice that suddenly dropped to a pleading whisper. She had heard of attack wolves, cornered, baring their jugulars. Her mother, now, reminded her of that bared jugular.

The words flowed over her, familiarly.

"I scrubbed floors and I ironed shirts and every penny I made I spent on you. So you wouldn't have to go through what I had to. So you could *have* something in life. So you could *dance*. And now you're telling me no thanks!"

"What can I say, Mom? What can I do that'll satisfy you?"

"You could show some gratitude, that's what you could do!"

"I *am* grateful. You know I'm grateful."

"No, I don't. I don't know anything. I don't know *you* any more."

"Please, Mom. I'm tired."

"All I want is what's good for you. That's all I'm asking. Is that so much?"

Anna took Steph's hands. Steph could feel the old knives twisting in her.

"I *know*," Anna said. "I *did* it. I fell in love. I threw everything away. I couldn't take it if you did the same. Honey, sometimes I'm so scared. I have nightmares. I wake up shaking. I see you making the same mistakes I did. Honey, these are the make or break years of your *career!* A dancer's got five, ten years—that's *all!* Every day, every night, every hour *counts!* After all we've been through, please—*please—*"

Steph couldn't bear it.

She pulled away from her mother. She opened her purse and then she held the front door open.

Anna's eyes followed her. "What are you doing? What's that?"

"It's five dollars, Mom."

"What for?"

"I love you and I'm dead tired. Take a taxi home."

# eighteen

Anna grabbed a cab on the corner of Central Park West and dumped herself into the back seat. All the way home terror and impotence gnawed at her.

*Steph's making the same mistake I did. She's so close to the top it's got her dizzy and she's going to throw her career away for a guy.*

Anna's hands balled into angry little fists. Even though she'd cut her nails short they found flesh to dig into. Her head throbbed and she tried to fit the problem into some kind of context where she could cope with it.

*Why the hell can't Steph learn from what happened to me? Twenty years ago I was exactly where she is...almost.*

Anna sighed, and the cab driver's eyes flicked up in the mirror.

*Who can reason with kids? If anyone had told me my career was about to blow up, I'd have said just what Steph said to me: "Drop dead."*

If Anna had only known that that season twenty years ago was to be her farewell, she might have handled everything differently. It might all be different today. She might still be a dancer.

*Instead of a pushy mother....*

She clenched her eyes shut, squinting back what felt like tears.

*If only if only if only...*

It seemed to Anna Lang that *if only* was the story of her life.

\* \* \*

The company played at City Center in those days. There was no overtime pay and there was no air conditioning and it was hard to say which hurt more. A boy called Bobby Baylor was partnering Anna in *Moonflower*. He was scheduled to dance the spring gala. For two weeks Anna had racked her brain debating the best way to get him out of the role. It was one of those muggy New York afternoons when she finally hit upon a plan.

The door to the director's office had been left open a crack. Anna could see him at his desk in shirt sleeves. He kept jabbing a hand to blot the sweat from the neat black line of his goatee. Without the goatee, he would have been handsome.

Anna made a fist and gave a single rap. "Got a minute, Mr. Volmar?"

He was marking cues in an orchestral score and he didn't look up. "Not now, my dear."

Anna saw that he wasn't alone. Dorcas Amidon, crisp as a Waldorf salad in her money-green dress, stood arranging set sketches on an easel. Dorcas served on the board and she had millions and Volmar let her help him in harmless ways.

Anna hesitated. She hadn't calculated on an audience. On the other hand, if she was going to make her move, she had to do it today, before the programs went to press. She stepped quickly into the office and eased the door shut behind her.

"It's about the gala," she said.

Volmar's glance flicked up. "Well, what about it?"

"Those turns in *Moonflower* bother me."

"Your turns are fine."

"Today I almost stumbled."

"Then forget the last *piqué* and take a half-beat preparation. Do whatever you have to. I trust you." Volmar gave a wave, like a magician telling her to vanish.

But Anna didn't vanish. She placed her hands firmly on the

edge of his desk. "It's not the preparation, Mr. Volmar. It's Bobby. He's pointing me wrong."

"I didn't notice. Well, tell him to point you right."

Anna was prepared for stubbornness. Volmar had stood up to the Nazis in Denmark and he stood up to his board of directors every spring. She wasn't foolish enough to expect him to back down right away.

"It's not *just* the pointing. He's catching me high. He lowers me too fast. I'm not comfortable with him."

"Comfortable? You're in ballet, my dear—not a suite at the Ritz."

Anna was prepared for rudeness. Ash Wednesday, when she'd come to rehearsal with ash on her forehead, Volmar had shouted at her to wash her face. People said he was an atheist and she'd heard he was half Jewish and nothing he did surprised her.

"He almost dropped me twice in rehearsal today. Mr. Volmar, I need a partner I can trust. That adagio's murder."

A sigh came out of him, grudging as a surrender. Most people said Volmar was a woman-hater, but most people weren't as observant as Anna Lang. She'd seen his eyes sweep the curve of her hip, linger on the auburn of her hair, just as they were doing now.

"Very well, Anna—whom *would* you trust?"

She knew she couldn't just push Marty at him. Volmar was foxy as a landlord. She'd have to work him around to the idea. So she named a dancer she knew he disliked. "Somebody taller. Like Alfie. He's good at catching."

Dorcas Amidon made a snorting sound. "Alfie has no elevation. He couldn't handle the variation."

"And who's going to teach him? Who has time?" Volmar gestured impatiently toward the sketches and scores and unopened letters piled on his desk.

"Martin Lang's a good partner," Anna said quietly. He was good in other departments too, but for the time being she was keeping that to herself. Instinct told her Volmar wouldn't like her auburn hair quite so much if he knew she'd married Marty five days ago.

"Marty?" Dorcas Amidon's voice was incredulous. "For *Moonflower?*"

"He's covered the role," Anna said. "He knows it by heart."

"Anna, my darling." Volmar spoke gently now, as though to a child. "Leave the casting to me."

He'd never been this difficult before. She supposed he had to put on a show for Dorcas Amidon. He wanted Anna to beg? Okay, she'd beg.

"Come on, Mr. Volmar. I *can't* do that adagio with Bobby."

"Don't be so modest. You do it beautifully."

The words shot out of her before she had time to think. "I won't do it with that idiot!"

The air in the room seemed to darken. Dorcas Amidon's head came around sharply and Volmar's eyes were slivers of Baltic gray.

"You're refusing the part?" he said.

It wasn't going the way Anna had planned. She was flailing. "Look, just give me Martin Lang. He knows how to partner. He makes me look good. He'd make *Moonflower* look wonderful."

"*Moonflower is* wonderful," Volmar said. "And you'll dance it with Bobby."

"Not on your life."

"Then you're fired."

Anna couldn't have been more surprised if a jar of pickles had exploded in her hand. She hadn't foreseen this. If only they'd been alone she could have kneaded Volmar like dough. She saw there was nothing left now but to play her trump. Volmar could fire a woman in a fit of pique but he'd never fire a top male dancer—there weren't enough of them.

"If I go," Anna said, "Marty goes with me."

She had him. She knew she had him. Dorcas Amidon stopped shifting sketches and the room was so quiet you could hear Volmar's watch ticking in the jacket slung over the chair.

"Then both of you go," Volmar spat. "And don't waste any more of my time."

For one split second Anna couldn't believe she'd heard right. She didn't believe any man, not even Marius Volmar, could be so stupid.

\*     \*     \*

The bus was jammed, wouldn't you know. Anna fumed all the way across town.

There wasn't a straight man in the company who could

partner better than Marty. No one else could lift Hildie Cavanaugh now that she'd put on ten pounds. Sandy Marco's right foot was zilch since he'd fallen in *Black Swan*, so who did that leave for *Spectre de la Rose* and *Filling Station?* Marty Lang, that was who.

Anna stopped at Tenth Avenue to pick up two mocha éclairs from the French bakery. Her hips didn't need them but Marty loved éclairs. She got a bottle of California chianti from the liquor store and the butcher let her have credit for two rib pork chops. Meat prices in this town were murder, but Marty loved her baked pork chops with onions and sour cream.

Balancing packages, she let herself into the run-down brownstone and began the five-story climb. Anger drummed in her.

Did Volmar actually think audiences were going to pay three ninety-five to see a gay boy twirl Lena MacDowell or watch Galina Nurevna grope her way through another *Giselle?* Nurevna was so blind they had to put red runway lights in the wings and half the Wilis crossed themselves before her turns. Without Marty, Nurevna would be doing Act Two on her *knees*.

The apartment smelled of gas. The pilot light was out again, wouldn't you know. Anna sliced up an onion and wished it was Marius Volmar and slapped the chops into a pie plate.

Who the *hell* did Volmar think he was?

Without Marty Lang, National Ballet Theatre would collapse faster than a tent without a pole. Volmar would have to come crawling to get Anna and Marty Lang back. And Anna would make him pay twenty bucks over scale, the same as he gave Hildie Cavanaugh.

\*     \*     \*

Anna broke the news to Marty over supper.

"We're wasting our time with NBT. Volmar's never going to give you a role."

Marty's spoon stopped and fell back into the plate of cream of tomato soup. "What are you talking about? He's given me plenty of roles."

"Sure—eight hundred Albrechts. You're the only one who can lift Nurevna—or steer her to her lights. That's not a role.

That's a seeing-eye dog with muscle."

"I'm already the lover in *Lilac Garden*."

"Then how come you've never done a Siegfried? Volmar doesn't think you can handle prince roles, that's why."

"I've done three Franzes in *Coppélia*."

"*Coppélia* doesn't even have a male variation."

"He put one in for me."

"Are you kidding? A thirty-second *petit allegro* lifted from *Sylvia*? I'm telling you, Marty, you're not a principal with NBT and you never will be. Look who's getting the roles: Bobby Baylor does umpteen Prodigal Sons, Sandy Harris is forty and can't even pirouette and *he* gets all the Apollos. Volmar may *tell* you you're a principal, he may pat your ass and make you *feel* like a principal, but where are your premieres? Where are your galas? When did he ever make a new role on you?"

Marty's eyes were green and thoughtful. The skin around them crinkled. "He never has made a new role on me. Not yet."

"And he's never going to. He's got you typed as a nobody."

Marty smiled and his face was strong and handsome, like the rest of him. "Come on. We've only been in the company two years."

Anna looked away. She could not cope with his good looks. They lit things up. She wanted to see the apartment as it was: stained wallpaper, cracked moldings, worn linoleum. A trap.

"How many years does a dancer have? It's fine to schlep around in the corps at nineteen. But you're twenty-four. Think of the future, Marty. Where are we going?"

She went to the oven. The gas made a thin flickering line around the door. She put the pork chops on plates. Down in the street a fire engine was screaming. Marty was staring at her with that baffled look of his.

"I'm not in the corps any more," he said.

"You might as well be."

"We're getting good pay. We have security."

"Eight crummy solos in two years, you call that security?"

"I sure do. Most dancers don't even know where their next cup of coffee's coming from."

"You're not most dancers. You're one of the best. You could dance anything, anywhere. Beats me why you have to stay tied to that man's apron."

"Honey, I'm at the breakthrough point." Marty's voice was gentle and pleading. "He's building me. You have to understand the way he works."

Anna was sorry for him. She wanted to handle this so as not to hurt him. It was like tearing the bandage off a child's cut: a little ouch and the quicker the better.

"I know exactly how he works," she said. "Just two hours ago he tried to get me to go to bed with him."

"He tried to *what?*"

Anna could see the sudden anger choking him. She let him be miserable a moment and then she went to him and kissed his forehead. "And it wasn't the first time either. But he never ripped my blouse before."

"You're kidding. You must be kidding."

"Kidding, am I? And why the hell do you think I quit?"

She saw the shock building in his eyes. "Quit the *company?*"

"Makes me want to throw up every time he paws me. 'Let me show you that lift, dear.' 'Put your weight against my hand, dear.' I'm not staying in NBT and that's that."

"Anna, are you sure you—"

"Okay, stand up for your dear friend Marius Volmar. I'm sick and tired of fending him off. I'm clearing out." She gave the words a minute to sink in. "Are you coming with me or staying with him?"

Marty scowled and shook his head. "Let me think. Give me a minute."

"You'll be thinking a year. I haven't got a year, Marty. I'm pregnant."

"Jesus, Jesus . . ." He stared at her with panicky eyes. He drew in a breath and his head sank down on the table. Thick dark hair tumbled over his fists. There was a retching sound in his throat and his body twitched like an old man's.

She stood looking at him a moment, wondering if she had gone too far. She told herself he'd be all right; he'd get over it in an hour. "Look, it's up to you. Him or me. I don't mind getting a divorce."

He raised his eyes to hers. It was as though, for the very first time, she was seeing the man she had married. He could lift a hundred-twenty-pound woman one-armed yet his hands were gripping the table as though to borrow its strength. He stood six foot two and his stomach was lean but here he was bent like a fat man over a pain in his belly. She saw something in him stretch out and die.

"All right," he said. "All right. We'll join another company."

\* \* \*

But it wasn't that easy.

The major companies acted scared, wouldn't touch Anna and Marty Lang. They did guest stints with old friends like Eglevsky and Magallanes, and when they'd used up their contacts they hired an agent. For thirty per cent he got them three minutes on Ed Sullivan and seven weeks in Radio City Music Hall. Those were the high points.

Then came summer tents in Westchester and Chautauqua, guest shots in Wyoming and Delaware, recitals in high school auditoriums. Anna's hands were raw from washing the grime out of Marty's Dacron shirts, wringing the filth out of four pairs of tights. Her rear end ached from bus rides. For three months she couldn't afford to buy herself a new pair of nylons.

Through the grapevine, they heard of teaching jobs. Marty did a term of master classes at Chapel Hill, hating it, and Anna taught toe till it turned out she really *was* pregnant. After the baby came, Marty's drinking began to show. His face got red and he thickened around the middle. He spoke in a constant whining slur and most of the time Anna couldn't understand a word he said, not that she cared any more.

Amazingly, he could still dance. But he was a fat man doing pirouettes, and not even TV wanted him, not even for laughs. So he taught exercise at the Y and started staying out nights. The baby kept him awake, he said—all that screaming.

Once, in a rooming house in Oklahoma City when Marty had run out on her for the hundredth time, Anna put her hands on the back of a chair and extended her leg. She tried to do a *rond de jambe à terre*—a circling motion of the foot on the floor. She couldn't keep her hips square; they tilted. She couldn't do a *rond de jambe* in the air. She couldn't *développé*—raise her leg and hold it straight. She had no turn-out for second position.

Everything was gone: the balance, the strength, the toes—all that she'd worked for since she was seven years old.

She sat down and cried. It wasn't fair. Fat, drunk Marty still had his feet and she didn't have anything.

Except smarts. Overnight, Anna Lang got smart.

She learned not to wait up for her husband and she learned how to get down a fire escape with a baby in one arm and not wake the landlord. She learned how to switch price stickers in supermarkets, how to lie to collection agencies. Most important of all, she learned there were three things in life not worth the time of day: idleness, regret, and Marty Lang.

She couldn't afford a baby sitter so she worked at home. She ironed other people's shirts, baked pies, licked envelopes. She boarded cats and she boarded house plants. She opened a mail forwarding service. She knitted tea cozies and afghans and she dunned boutiques into selling them. She pinched pennies till there was blood on Abe Lincoln's face. She made enough to feed the baby and when Marty was there she managed to feed him too.

She wasn't happy, but she wasn't ashamed either.

Sometimes at the end of a day she'd sit down by the window, too exhausted to keep her thoughts from drifting. She'd remember her photograph on the cover of *Dancemagazine*. She'd remember evenings of curtain calls and bouquets and applause and an ache would rise in her chest.

She'd wonder what would have happened if only Volmar hadn't been such a bastard, if only Marty hadn't been such a weakling.

"If only," she would sigh.

*If only* was the story of Anna Lang's life.

\* \* \*

The marriage came to an end in Cleveland.

Anna had managed to find them a furnished room over a tobacco shop. One Saturday morning Marty went out for a drink. Monday morning the ballet school where he taught ten-year-olds phoned asking for him. Tuesday afternoon two cops knocked on the door.

"Mrs. Lang?" the tall one said. "Mrs. Martin Lang?"

"Yes?"

"Do you recognize this wallet?"

The wallet was stained three different shades of sweat, curved to the hip pocket Marty had carried it in. She knew at a glance there was no money left in it.

"Where'd he lose it this time?"

"It might be better if we came in."

She took the door off the chain. The chain was for bill collectors.

The two cops came in. They held their hats in their hands. She'd never seen a cop with his hat in his hands and it seemed odd to her. They didn't react to the mess but she felt she had to explain it anyway.

"Been busy all morning—selling magazine subscriptions on the phone. *Reader's Digest, Time*—either of you interested?"

"Not for us, thanks." The cops stood looking at her. She didn't see how they could be comfortable, jackets buttoned on a hot day. She saw they were wearing wedding rings.

"Maybe your wives could use *Good Housekeeping?* Fifty per cent off newsstand price."

"It's about the owner of this wallet."

Anna wasn't certain she was ready to hear about the owner of that wallet, not if there were cops involved. "Say, would you fellas like some iced tea? I got a whole pitcher in the icebox."

"Not right now, thanks."

It was the tall one who did all the talking. The fat one kept sneaking looks over at the crib where the baby was sleeping.

"Marty's got a bottle of gin," Anna said. "I could flavor it."

"No, thanks."

"At least I could offer you a seat, right?"

The two cops sat on the sofa. A spring squeaked. Anna hated that spring. She went back to the card table and picked up licking envelopes where she'd left off.

"Don't mind me, I'm listening. Gotta have these envelopes stuffed by five." A mail-order house paid her a third of a cent per envelope. She could do six a minute. And she was nervous—she needed something to hide the twitch in her hand. "So tell me about Marty. Where is he? Jail? Hospital?" Not that she cared any more.

The two cops sitting on her landlord's sofa had tight lips. "Not exactly."

"If you're looking for him, you're not going to find him

around here. I keep a cold meal in the icebox for him and that's all."

"This wallet was found in a dead man's pocket, early this morning." The cop wasn't looking at Anna. He was looking at the brown spot that Marty had burned in the lampshade.

Anna's fingers stopped. "Marty's *dead?*" She stood. She felt stronger standing. She wiped her hands on her apron. "What are you telling me? What happened?"

"It's being investigated."

"Where'd you get the wallet?"

"It was found in a hotel in a dead man's pocket."

"So where'd you find him? Where's Marty? What hotel? Where's my husband?"

The fat cop nodded toward the crib. "Is that your kid?"

"That's my daughter. Marty's and mine. Stephanie."

"Maybe you could ask a neighbor to watch Stephanie. We'll have you back in an hour or so. It won't take long to identify him. If it's him."

Anna untied her apron and carefully folded it over the back of the rocking chair. "He was gone four days this time. Never told me anything."

"I'll get the neighbor," the tall cop said.

"Meat loaf." Anna didn't know why it popped into her head. "I got meat loaf in the icebox for him. He hated meat loaf."

She bent down to check the baby's diaper. The fat cop watched.

"Maybe you could use a little of your husband's gin, ma'am."

"I don't touch that stuff."

The tall cop came back with Mrs. McElheny. He must have told her. Her face had gone white and her hands kept fluttering around Anna.

"The milk's in the icebox," Anna said. "Warm it in the saucepan, give her half a bottle when she starts crying."

They took Anna to the morgue. The right side of Marty's face was one fat purple bruise. She looked away. She didn't want to remember him like that.

"We're sorry, ma'am."

"It's not your fault. It's not anyone's fault but his."

They took her home in the squad car. Mrs. McElheny said

Stephanie had been a darling, hadn't cried once. Anna could tell the old woman was dying to pump her. Anna didn't feel like being pumped. She sent Mrs. McElheny away.

She sat staring at the empty wall, not crying, not feeling anything. She wondered what she'd tell Stephanie when the time came.

She tried to remember Marty's face and instead she saw the bruise. She thought of all the fights when he'd slapped her, all the nights she'd waited up for him, all the debts she'd inherited now that he was gone. She took Marty's supper from the icebox and scraped the plate into the garbage can. The last food she'd ever waste, so help her God.

The baby was jingling the bells in the crib.

"Be quiet, Steph. Momma's gotta think."

It turned dark outside. The blinking *Pabst Blue Ribbon* sign came on across the way.

The baby was standing, holding on to the edge of the crib. Her fists were tiny and pink and her eyes were a soft wondering blue and she hadn't made a sound for forty-five minutes. Anna jumped up.

"What are you trying to do—wreck your feet?"

She snatched the baby into her arms.

"When you're twelve you'll stand on your toes—and you'll do it right—five minutes a day after class. Now you go to sleep, understand?"

She checked the diaper and kissed Stephanie and laid her in the crib. Then she sat in the rocking chair and went on thinking till dawn.

$$* \quad * \quad *$$

It took some looking, but Anna found a priest who was willing to give Marty a Catholic burial. She moved to Kansas City, where she'd heard a waitress could make eighty dollars a week. She used her maiden name, Boborovsky, so the bill collectors couldn't track her, and she used her professional name, Barlow, to talk her way into a job teaching exercise at the women's Y.

Between waiting tables and teaching fatties to slim down she made enough to pay the neighbor to baby-sit. Some weeks the tips were so good she even had a couple of extra dollars to put away for Stephanie's future.

Steph was a good girl—a pleasure to come home to. Her blue eyes turned green, which almost broke Anna's heart, but her hair stayed blond. She had a dancer's high arches. Anna limbered her in the crib—rotated her feet and calves, taught her to stretch and contract. She bought a secondhand phonograph and got records of *Swan Lake* and *Petrouchka* so Steph could grow up hearing good music, not that Elvis Presley junk.

When Steph was old enough to take her first steps Anna showed her how to put her feet in first and second position and how to keep them there. The hardest part of dance, starting out, was just learning how to stand still and stand straight. Steph was a dream at it.

Old Mrs. Epstein, the widow from next door who baby-sat, was always saying how quiet Steph was, how gracefully she moved, never bawling or bumping into things or losing her balance like most kids her age.

Anna would smile a smile of secret pride.

For Steph's birthday Anna had a carpenter make an adjustable barre—nothing fancy, a broomstick and two supports—but solid. She hung a fourteen-dollar mirror low on the kitchen wall. She chose the kitchen because it was the biggest room and she wanted to be able to watch Steph practice while she cooked and washed dishes.

She showed Steph the basic movements, the bends and leg raises.

"I wish I'd had your advantages," she said. "If only *my* mom had started me out when I was five."

*If only . . .*

One afternoon over coffee Mrs. Epstein asked about the mirror. "Don't you have to bend down awful far to see yourself?"

Anna laughed. "It's not my mirror—it's Steph's."

"But what does a little girl need with a mirror that big?"

"A mirror is a dancer's best friend."

Mrs. Epstein's eyes bulged behind their bifocals. "Is little Steph going to be a dancer?"

*Going to be?* Anna thought. *If only you knew!* "Anything's possible if you work for it. And Steph's a born worker."

Mrs. Epstein tipped the coffee that had spilled into her saucer back into the cup. "When I was a girl in Milwaukee I saw Pavlova dance the *Dead Swan*. I cried. It was the prettiest thing I ever saw."

Anna's teacher had studied with Pavlova in St. Petersburg. Wow. How time flew. *"Dying Swan,"* Anna said. "Wasn't her best."

For her daughter's sake, Anna got back in touch with dance. When a company came to town, she took Steph. She subscribed to the magazines, kept track of who was still at the top and who was up and coming. She got out her old address book and sent birthday cards and Christmas greetings to dancers and stagehands and musicians she had known. A few of them replied. It made her happy to know that Anna Barlow wasn't completely forgotten.

For Steph's eighth birthday, Anna wrote to *Dancemagazine* to get the name of a good, reasonable school in the area.

*       *       *

Anna pulled Steph up the dingy stairs.

"Come on, stop being scared!"

The chipped gold lettering on the frosted glass door was barely legible: *Elise Meyer, formerly of the Atlantic Civic Ballet, Academy of Classical Dance*. Class had already begun. Nineteen little girls in pink leotards and pink shoes were lined up at the barre. They all had identical pink flowers in their hair. The air had the faint, rancid smell of sweat. Reminded Anna of her own student days.

A tall, middle-aged woman was barking at the kids in time to the music: "*Pli-é*, three four ... *Pli-é*, three four ..." She was dressed exactly the same as the students, with a few extra ruffles on the skirt to show her rank. Her face was set in a bored scowl that deepened when she saw Anna and Steph. "Keep going, three four ..."

She came across the room, flexing a four-foot switch as skinny as she was. "Help you?"

Anna hadn't heard a voice like that since she'd left New York. She'd been out of touch too long, much too long.

"I want you to teach my little girl," Anna said.

Steph hid her face in her mother's skirt. Anna had to tug her by the ear. It was ridiculous for the girl to be shy: she was eight years old, the teachers at public school loved her, they were always saying how pretty and well behaved she was.

"We'll have a look at her after class," Elise Meyer said. "Why don't you just take a seat and watch how we do things?"

She nodded toward a row of wooden slat chairs. Two women sat knitting. Mothers. An Indian war whoop came up through the floor. The academy was smack over a movie theater.

"Why not have a look at her now?" Anna said. "You got room at the barre. Steph, go change into your dance clothes."

Elise Meyer gave Anna a look and then she turned and went back to her students. The phonograph was scratching out the Pizzicato Polka from *Sylvia*. Elise Meyer patrolled up and down the barre. She touched the tip of her switch to a girl's calf.

"Foot out straight, Cleo. Point those toes."

Anna sat down to watch. Half the kids didn't know the difference between a *plié* and a deep knee bend. La Meyer had to keep switching at them like ponies. And that girl in the torn leotard! Who but a mother would have put such a fatty into ballet school? Ten years old if she was a day and still had pig's knuckles for feet; forget it.

Steph came back, trim and graceful in her clean pink leotard, and took her place at the end of the barre. Anna winked. She caught the other mothers stealing glances in the long mirrored wall. She knew all about mothers. They were jealous because Steph moved like a ballerina—kept her back straight and turned her leg out correctly and held her chin up. True, one other girl did turn her leg out nicely, but she had no chin and you couldn't make it in ballet without a chin.

Class lasted an hour and forty-five minutes. It was baby stuff: *relevés, battements, tendus*. Steph handled everything except one *rond de jambe*. La Meyer had to correct the position of her supporting leg. Anna grimaced. How many times had she nagged Steph about that supporting leg?

Discipline in class was good. There was no giggling, no horse play between exercises. La Meyer was an okay teacher. At this stage of Steph's career, she'd do.

At the end of class the kids clapped. Reminded Anna of her

own dancing days, when you clapped to thank the teacher. The two mothers gathered up their knitting and their daughters and Elise Meyer collapsed into the chair beside Anna. She wiped the sweat from her face. Her handkerchief smelled of Lanvin and it was losing its monogram.

"I don't see why we can't make an opening for your daughter, Mrs.—"

"Lang. Anna Barlow Lang."

There was not even a twitch of recognition. She couldn't believe Elise Meyer didn't remember Anna Barlow and Marty Lang and the cover of *Dancemagazine*. She had half a mind to say something, but instinct told her to forget it. Let La Meyer think Stephanie was a no-talent like the rest of her students. She'd find out soon enough.

"Now you understand, Mrs. Lang, we make no promises. But ballet *is* very useful in developing co-ordination, balance, poise. Far better than sports and a lot safer."

What the hell was she trying to do—sell Anna on *dance?*

"Your daughter obviously has a feel for music, and she's lyric. If you like, I could teach her *pointe.*"

And wreck her feet? "She doesn't go on toe till she's twelve," Anna said. "She needs four years' training still."

La Meyer sighed. "She needs everything. Strength, balance, feet, arch, *développé*. A lot of work."

*How the hell would you know, you con artist?* Anna thought. *Steph's not even grown yet*. La Meyer obviously took Anna for a dance ignoramus.

"I'll tell you what's really bothering me about Steph. After she passes sixteen counts in *passé* balance she doesn't hold her turnout."

La Meyer's expression narrowed and Anna knew she had hit home. No one that young could hold a balance that long, let alone a turn-out, and none of the mothers around this town could pronounce the words.

Anna motioned Steph over. "Steph, Madame Meyer is going to teach you. Say 'Bonjour, Madame.'"

Steph curtsied the way her mother had taught her. It was the same deep curtsy Anna had used for the last curtain call of her *Lizzie Borden*, and to see an eight-year-old do it was a knockout.

"You can go change, honey." Anna took the checkbook from

her purse. "How do I make it out, to you or the academy?" First academy she'd ever seen with laths showing through the plaster.

"Academy will be fine," La Meyer said. If she'd said "cash," Anna would have worried.

"Look, I know the kind of guff those mothers give you. I'm not one of them, and I'm not paying for Steph to take naps. Don't be afraid to be hard on her."

La Meyer tucked the check for the term into her skirt without even looking at it. Some businesswoman, Anna thought. No wonder she was operating out of a fleabag movie house.

Steph clung tight to Anna's hand all the way down the stairs. "Is Madame Meyer a dancer, Mommy?"

"She used to be, honey."

"Like you?"

"More used to be than that, honey. But you don't have to be a dancer to be a teacher. Me, I was a terrific dancer but I can't teach worth a damn. So you listen to everything Madame says. It's costing money."

\*       \*       \*

Anna wasn't one of those mothers who have to supervise their daughters' every leap and *tendu*, but now and then she did look in on the Elise Meyer Academy of Classical Dance.

Within three months Steph's *pliés* were *liquid* and she had no trouble at all keeping her heels down in fourth. At age nine she had the best pirouette in the class, and at ten the best *fouetté*, and Elise Meyer suggested that Steph might care to dance a featured solo at the annual recital.

"Naturally," La Meyer said, "she'll need a special costume, and I'd suggest getting a record to practice to at home, but you can buy those through me."

"Naturally," Anna said. "How much?"

Naturally it was too much, but it was also Steph's chance to appear in public, and the sooner a dancer got used to that, the better. Anna paid the thirty-two dollars and made a face. Not at the money, but at the record: "Waltzing Cat." And at the costume: "Waltzing Cat."

The recital was a madhouse. Reminded Anna of her own student recital.

Most of the little girls had never worn make-up or costumes before and they were crying their eyes out, scared stiff at the idea of standing up in front of strangers. Their moms were going crazy trying to get them to sit still long enough to take the rollers out of their hair.

Not Steph. Steph was an angel. Not a tear, not a whimper.

When it came time to perform one little girl forgot her steps entirely and just stood on the stage peeing in her pink leotards. Anna could see the dark spot. The kid just wasn't a pro.

It was a typical schlock recital. The music was on tape and only one of the speakers worked; the other kind of hummed along. The footlights had two levels, on and off, and that was it. La Meyer danced *Dying Swan* herself and four of her older students flapped through the *Dance of the Little Swans.*

The corps was hopelessly out of sync, a bunch of frightened little girls watching one another to see who'd have the nerve to move first. Steph had the nerve. She was always right there on the beat, always first. Half the girls watched their feet. Steph never even glanced at her feet: her eyes were on that make-believe horizon right above the audience's head, just as Anna had taught her. Most of the girls were too busy trying to remember steps to smile. Steph never stopped smiling.

She was a pro.

And even in that ridiculous *Waltzing Cat*, with the corps meowing and waving tails, she was a knockout. The little extra unsupported pirouette that Anna had had her sneak in brought the house down. Three curtain calls.

There would have been more if La Meyer hadn't gotten jealous and cut them short. "I'm sorry, ladies and gentlemen, but we really must get on with the baton twirling."

\*       \*       \*

At eleven, Steph joined toe class. She had fabulous turns and a balance on *pointe* she could hold forever without a hint of a wobble. *What a pro*, Anna thought: *pro, pro, pro!*

When Steph was thirteen Elise Meyer said there was nothing more she could teach the girl. If she hadn't said it, Anna would have.

"I'd like her to study with Buddy McKay in Chicago." La

Meyer looked sad. "He'll help her footwork."

"Can she get a scholarship?" Anna said.

"I'm afraid he doesn't give them. You could try applying to the National Federation of Dance or the Harkness Foundation."

Anna applied. They turned Steph down. What did they know?

She took Steph to Chicago anyway. She waved her photo on the cover of *Dancemagazine* and talked her way into a job teaching calisthenics at a department store. The pay was enough to send Steph to the École McKay for ten hours a week.

Steph's body developed. Her placement got even better. She was doing triple unsupported pirouettes by the time she was fifteen. Her *jetés* were as high as a boy's and her *fouettés* were fantastic.

By the time Steph was sixteen, Anna knew her little girl was ready. She cashed in her savings and bought two one-way plane tickets to New York. She groveled in front of Dorcas Amidon and she groveled in front of Christine Avery's mother and she groveled in front of anyone else who could help.

She wangled a scholarship for Steph. She wangled a decent home for Steph. She wangled a career for Steph. She realized now she'd spent half her life groveling and wangling for that kid.

*And what for,* Anna wondered, *what for?*

She paid the cab driver and let herself into the empty lobby and stood with a finger jammed against the elevator button.

*I'm not going to let her throw it away,* Anna vowed. *I'm not going to let her.*

\*        \*        \*

Steph awakened to the sound of a phone. It seemed to have begun ringing a thousand years ago in a dream she could no longer remember. She heard a mattress squeak and Chris's shadow moved toward the door.

"If that's my mother," Steph said, "tell her I'm in coma. No, don't. That'll just bring her over again."

"We don't have to answer," Chris said.

Steph shook the sleep out of her head and turned on the light. "I'd better talk to her." She sighed, thinking what nuisances mothers could be, and Chris stood watching her.

"You know, Steph, you're lucky to have her."

"Lucky?"

"I wouldn't mind having someone who cared . . . even if they cared too much."

"Too much is putting it mildly." The phone was still ringing and Steph sensed it wasn't going to give up easily. "I'd better answer before she sends the fire department."

She stumbled into the living room and groped in the dark for the receiver. A man said, "Chris—is that you?"

Steph didn't recognize the voice. It was slurred, with an edge of hostility. "Who is this?"

"It's Ray. Is Chris awake?"

*Something's wrong,* Steph thought. "Just a sec."

She went and told Chris and Chris made a curious face.

"At this hour?" Chris pulled herself back out of bed and went to answer. "Yes, Ray?"

"Why didn't you phone? I had dinner ready and wine and flowers—"

She could tell he was angry, angry at her, and it frightened her. "Dinner ready for what?"

"For us. We had a date, remember?"

"Ray, it was Steph's premiere tonight."

"As you conveniently forgot to tell me. Damn it, Chris, I was worried about you. I thought you'd had an accident. I even went looking for you."

"I'm sorry you worried, Ray, but I didn't have an accident and we couldn't have had a date."

*But he cooked dinner for me,* she thought. Not once in her life had a man cooked dinner for her.

"I told you I was cooking beef bourguignon and you said okay."

Vaguely, she remembered the beef bourguignon.

"What is it about you dancers, you think nobody else matters?"

"Ray, I honestly—"

"Well, you can just go to hell for all I care!"

The receiver went dead in Chris's hand. She jiggled the cradle and got a dial tone. Her heart was thumping. She dialed three digits of Ray's number and the next three and then her finger lost its courage.

After an aching moment she hung up.

As she came back into the bedroom Steph was staring, a faint wrinkle of perplexity between her eyes. "What was that all about?"

"He says I broke a date without telling him."

"Did you?"

"We didn't have a date. We couldn't have." She slipped back into bed and turned off the light. "He shouted at me."

"Don't let it worry you. You'll make it up to him. Chris, he really likes you. You know that, don't you?"

"Does he?" Chris pulled the covers up to her chin. She didn't think Ray Lockwood liked her at all. You couldn't like a person and shout that way.

*I've lost a friend,* she thought. *I have so few, and now I've lost one.*

# nineteen

---

Lester Croyden heard the telephone ring.

He was still in his bathrobe, watering geraniums on the terrace of his Central Park West penthouse. He glanced at his watch. Curious, he went indoors to the library. He dropped two tabs of saccharin into his *café au lait*, stirred, and made himself comfortable on the Mies leather lounging chair.

When the ringing stopped he quietly picked up the receiver. Hannah Meredith, his co-director at Empire, was arguing with the answering service.

"I know he's there, I just heard him pick up."

"I'm sorry, ma'am, if you'd care to leave your—"

"That's all right, dearie," Lester Croyden cut in. He called his answering service *dearie*. "How are you, Hannah? Why so bright and early?"

"Have you seen the paper?" She sounded as though she'd ripped her dentures on the late city edition.

"Why should I spoil my coffee, dearie? We both know that, of two decades of *slovenly Sylphides*, last night was the all-time *slut*. Who needs to see it in print?"

Hannah's silence was ferocious.

Lester Croyden reviewed the links in last night's chain of

disasters. Ilonka had been partying, though she denied it. As a result she arrived late, rushed her warm-up, sprained her Achilles' tendon. Sylvia Farnum, her cover, had to substitute. Naturally Sylvia couldn't do Ilonka's *fouettés* to tempo in the *Grande Valse Brillante*—who could? So naturally Teiji Yushima, the conductor, took the *Grande Valse* at a slower tempo; and naturally, being an idiot, he took the entire score slower, dragging the Nocturne at such a funeral trot that the corps couldn't hold their balances. You could hear heels thumping like storm troopers as the girls tried to sneak down ahead of the beat.

Laughable.

Disaster.

So what?

"You did or did you not consult Ivor Noble on the casting?"

"Dearie, I suffered through three drunken lunches with Ivor. He thinks it was *his* idea to put Victor into *Sylphides*. I also paid him three thousand from contingency—once again."

It was standard operating procedure for Lester Croyden to "consult," unofficially of course, with Ivor Noble. Ivor felt flattered to be asked his opinion—which was worthless—and, more important, he felt obligated to give good reviews. Empire was pegging half its spring gala on Victor Topacio. Lester Croyden had gone all out—three drunkathon lunches with Ivor at the Century Club—to guarantee Victor six months of good personal notices.

"If this is the review Ivor gave Victor," Hannah said, "you damned well get that three thousand back."

"Dearie, I haven't read the review. Now remember, the corps was *not* their twinkle-toed best and Sylvia *did* fall and she *did* leave out her variation without telling anyone. Ivor has every right to be mean. But surely he did manage to say something glowing about Victor?"

"Why don't I read you the glowing something he said about Victor?"

"Gladly, dearie. All ears."

Hannah put on her "I quote" tone of voice. "'We are in the presence of a great contemporary choreographer.'"

Lester Croyden coughed up *café au lait*. "Contemporary? That rehash of Fokine? How many scotches did Ivor have last night?"

"The bartender says he had eight Ivor Noble specials. '...great contemporary choreographer, probing the interworkings of fantasy and reality, passion and purity, death and immortality.'"

"That's the trouble with Ivor's reviews. He doesn't know the names of any of the steps. Could you skim a little, dearie, and cut to the hard-core quotables?"

"Very well. I skim. 'This was, by in large'—whatever 'by in large' means—"

"Typo."

"No, that's the way he talks too.... 'by in large a dazzling achievement, deft, fitful, beyond measure brilliant. Mr. Gillette promises to be—'"

"Gillette?"

"'...promises to be—nay, on the evidence vouched safe by *Lacrymosa*—'"

"'*Lacrymosa*'?"

"'...safe by *Lacrymosa* there can be no doubt is—one of our best choreographers for women, certainly the best presently under the aegis of Empire Ballet, though interestingly this work was presented at the independent Pepsi-Cola-sponsored Damrosch Festival.'"

Lester Croyden dropped another saccharin tablet into his *café au lait*.

"'Mr. Gillette's females are fascinating chiaroscuros of the psychological layers that lie betwixt public patina and private persona. What he has accomplished here in one bold stroke is altogether remarkable, the first work of rank since Antony Tudor's *Pillar of Fire* worthy of being mentioned in that breath. All concerned for the future of dance in his country owe it to themselves to attend the next performance of this unforgettable, staggering, seminal work, which we hope and are confident will soon be seen in circumstances more deserving of its stature.' End of review. *Voilà* Victor's rave."

Lester Croyden watched a spume of saccharin fizz to the shoreline of his cup. "Gillette? *Danny* Gillette? *Our* Danny Gillette?"

"As you well know. You gave him and three of our dancers permission to perform at that band shell pass-the-hat business."

Lester Croyden's mind slipped into a higher gear. "Dearie, did you happen to see this *Lacrymosa* yourself?"

Hannah drew out a long arc of "Noooooooooooo."

"Who saw it besides Ivor?"

"Every hobo in Needle Park, I suppose."

"Did anyone *qualified* see it? Anyone in the company?"

"Heinrich saw it."

"And?"

"He says the review is idiotic."

"Dearie, what did he say about the *ballet?*"

Her "I quote" tone again. "Brilliant."

"You'll have to excuse me."

"You're phoning Heinrich?"

"I'm phoning Danny Gillette."

"Not listed."

"Oh, you tried? Well, where there's a will, dearie. Talk to you later."

* * *

It was five-thirty that evening when the doorbell rang.

The houseboy let Danny Gillette into the penthouse, murmured that Mr. Croyden would be with him "directly," and vanished into the pantry, where Lester Croyden had nearly finished a small Finlandia vodka on the rocks.

The houseboy nodded, and Lester Croyden understood that his guest was on time and waiting. The wait was strategy. Danny Gillette had to be given time to marvel at the high-ceilinged living room that had been expanded by a knocked-down wall, at the meticulous furnishings reflecting the distinction and taste of Empire's top designer and no little cash from Empire's contingency fund.

Danny Gillette had to be given time to get the message: *Play the game Lester Croyden's way and you too may wind up with a pot of gold, a view, and an étagère full of Sèvres.*

At five thirty-five Lester Croyden buttoned his burgundy smoking jacket and made his entrance.

Danny was standing at the northernmost of the three double windows, staring down at Central Park. From twenty-three stories you couldn't see details, and the park looked almost clean.

"Excuse the *pied-à-terre*," Lester Croyden said breezily. "It's a mess."

Danny turned. "If this is a mess, it must be blinding when it's neat."

"Just wear your dark glasses when you come to dinner. How goes, my boy, how goes?"

"Fine, and you, sir?"

"Dandy, but let's skip the trivia. Your ballet"—Lester Croyden was about to say "I hear," but he decided to omit those two little words—"was wonderful."

Astonishment flashed over Danny's face. "You saw it?"

An important point to glide over. "Enchanting. I can't find words. Something to drink?"

"Thank you."

They moved to the bar, a lovely eighteenth-century Île de France cherrywood peasant's chest that Empire's top designer had converted into a home for bottles, glasses, and ice cubes.

"I'm flattered you had the time to come to the recital," Danny said.

"It's important to know what my boys are up to." Lester Croyden arranged glasses, napkins, tongs, a bowl of nibblies: a priest setting up his altar. "What's your poison?"

"Vodka tonic?"

"Can do, can do."

Lester Croyden stooped and pulled out two splits of Schweppes tonic. One, half full, had been recapped. "Wonder if there's any fizz left in this?" He shook, detected life, and pried the cap up. Quinine geysered over cherrywood. Lester Croyden grabbed an LC-embossed paper napkin and sopped. *Croyden, get ahold of yourself.* He fixed two vodka tonics, not scorchers but strong enough to get things moving, and led the way to the sofa grouping at the south end of the room.

They settled themselves. Lester Croyden stared dreamily at a Chagall.

"In a curious way it reminded me of Nora's first *Pillar.* You're too young to have seen that, of course, but did I detect a Tudor influence? The blend of psychology and myth and dancing that has to be unique."

Danny hesitated. He dressed abominably, Lester Croyden reflected, but in the proper light he really was a handsome boy.

"Aren't we all influenced by Tudor?" Danny said.

"Very apt observation. Aren't we all influenced by Tudor." Lester Croyden jiggled his glass. There was a certain tinkle to ice on chilled crystal that nothing else quite equaled. The sound was Mozartean, when you thought of it. "Aren't we all indeed. Danny, I would like you to do something for me."

"Sure."

"I would like you to stage your work for the company."

What Lester Croyden detected gushing from his guest was not so much silence as speechlessness.

"Could you do that for me?"

Danny Gillette tried to answer but his thoughts were reeling. His head felt weightless and his heartbeat raced. From a great distance he heard himself say, "I most certainly could."

"With the right lighting and a touch of scenery it should make a very interesting premiere. I see something abstract. Pools of white on black. And you might consider which of our principals you'd care to use."

Danny hesitated. "Do you feel it needs principals?"

"Your work is perfection, Danny. And you've done wonders with your dancers." Lester Croyden leaned toward Danny. His hand touched the boy's knee but quickly returned to its owner's lap. This was, after all, business and not fun and games. Lester Croyden wanted Danny Gillette to understand that. "But you might think of someone along the lines of—oh—Victor Topacio. A premiere needs principals. After all, over at the Met, it *is* a paying audience."

\*   \*   \*

Danny walked back to the theater. Walking helped him think.

Here was his chance, his breakthrough as a choreographer. And there was the price tag: Victor Topacio.

Three years ago Victor had won the Varna competition, the second Westerner ever to do so. He ought to have made headlines and his career ought to have soared. But two days after Victor's gold medal, one of the Kirov's *danseurs nobles* had defected to the West. All the headlines, all the career, had gone to the new Soviet sensation. And Victor Topacio had lingered, like a beautiful, embarrassing third leg, at Empire.

Topacio was a fine dancer. Danny had no objection to using him. The question was, how?

Danny weighed alternatives.

He could drop out and give Cupid to Victor. That would leave Al, who was corps—not Victor's league. It would show.

Or Danny could drop Al and let Victor dance Endymion. That would be unfair to Al. Worse, it would be discouraging, cruel. Endymion was Al's best dancing in three years.

Danny thought the problem through—deliberately, slowly, over and over. Each time he kept finding himself boxed in.

There was only one solution.

\*     \*     \*

Danny took Al to coffee the next day after company class. Al was all bubbles and smiles as they slid into their booth and he asked, "So how does it feel to be an overnight smash?"

*To hell with the rituals of conversation,* Danny decided. "Lester wants to put the ballet in repertory next season."

"Beautiful. Hey. Wow. Then what's the matter? Why so cheerful?"

"He wants to use a male principal."

"You'll be a male principal next season."

"He wants to use Victor."

Al didn't exactly lose his smile, but it thinned. "Which means you're dropping—eenie, meenie, minie—me?"

"I'm dropping both of us," Danny said.

Al put down his coffee cup. He fixed a disbelieving gaze on Danny, then leaned back against the bench as though to get a clearer view. "Can I ask you a personal question? Why both?"

"Because I want to do the best possible job choreographing and I can't if I'm dancing."

"Then let me rephrase. Why me?"

"Because you're a good dancer, Al, but Victor's a Varna gold medalist."

"And you're afraid I couldn't stand up to him?"

"Would you want to try?"

"Frankly, yes."

"It wouldn't work. You're not ready."

"I can get ready. Fuck it, Danny, give me a chance. I worked my ass off on that role. And part of that review, whether you want to admit it or not, was *me*—silly flitty little Al from the corps, yeah, *me*. I gave you a break. Now it's your turn."

"I can't do it. David Cummings is dancing the role."

"Man, you sure move fast."

"It's nothing personal, Al."

"Obviously not to you."

"Look, do you think for one moment Lester and Hannah would let a boy from the corps dance that role?"

"Maybe if *this* boy from the corps danced *that* role he wouldn't be a boy from the corps any more."

Danny had the impression of something yanked up by the roots, helpless, dying in his hand.

"Why didn't you at least *ask* Lester and Hannah? Why didn't you tell them you *want* me. Hell, I've *proven* I can dance it."

Al drew close to the table, staring into Danny's eyes. Danny fought the urge to look away.

"Danny, you're breath-taking." There were tears in Al's eyes as he shoved up from the bench. "It's been an education knowing you."

# twenty

Anna tried the door of one of the side boxes. It was unlocked. She opened it just wide enough to slip inside and closed it quickly behind her.

From far across the emptiness of the Metropolitan Opera House came voices and light and laughing, shushing movement. The gold house curtain and the asbestos fire curtain had been raised. There was no set: only a black velvet backdrop and black wings. The girls' corps was filtering offstage. They must have just finished the run-through of *Bayadère*.

Anna felt her way cautiously to the front of the box. The floor took a two-inch dip that she hadn't seen in the dark. She almost tripped. She caught the railing in time to break her fall. Keeping a tight grip, she lowered herself into a chair and sat rigid, tense, half expecting heads to turn and fingers to point accusations from the stage.

The orchestra pit was dark. The upright piano stage right with a lamp burning looked like an intruder from a saloon. The pianist—a heavy-set woman wearing a spotted babushka—sat arranging her score on the rack.

Danny Gillette came springily onstage carrying a director's chair. He looked trim and lithe in his black leotards and black

T-shirt. He set the chair up beside the prompter's box, made himself comfortable, called, "Places!"

Steph came onstage. She looked small and frail, like a lost little girl who had wandered there by mistake. She sat on the floor, peeled off her pink plastic leg warmers. She did a stretch and a bend, then moved to the center of the stage. She faced the house, feet turned out in second, arms slightly bowed, fingertips grazing her thighs.

*Now that's a dancer!* Anna blew a kiss, then waited, holding her breath.

Danny shot Steph a questioning nod. She nodded back, lay down on the floor. "Curtain!" Danny called.

Anna waited for the first sound, the first movement.

Nothing.

Suddenly it hit her: Steph had the stage alone—no motion, no music to distract from her. Anna measured the silence. She counted six adagio beats. *Six!*

Two men came on, leading a girl between them. Must be Steph's friend Linda. Anna wondered if this was a black-leotard ballet or if the men would have costumes. Above all she wondered what Linda would be wearing.

The pianist struck a chord.

*Ouch!*

Was that a mistake or did Benjamin Britten *mean* it? No matter. The ballet began allegro—high solo leaps along the diagonals with complicated foot- and legbeats—too complicated, Steph's feet weren't quite catching the beats. Anna relaxed a little when she saw Linda was no better. Danny would simplify those foot-beats—he'd have to.

In the assisted lifts Steph pulled ahead. Linda prepared badly, her partner had to work to get her up and it showed.

Anna couldn't help feeling excitement. The movements seemed to express an absolute stillness; the sudden long-held freezes screamed with tension and energy. The gimmick was so simple, so direct that even a *critic* would get it, and what's more he'd congratulate himself for getting it.

Anna foresaw good reviews: and the praise was bound to splash over onto Steph. She relaxed in her chair.

There was a series of alternating balances where the boys assisted and the girls mirrored each other. Anna frowned. She didn't see why Danny had to have the girls doing the same steps and stretches. It looked cheap, like a contest.

But in the supported adagio things got better.

Steph's line flowed. She looked soft, romantic. Linda looked lanky and staccato by contrast and she didn't quite feel the music: her movements began slow—which was lovely in itself—and she had to rush every one of them to catch up with the beat. The effect was flow, jerk, flow, jerk, and the jerks killed the flow—which left Steph holding the stage.

By the time the dancers separated into couples Anna knew that Steph was home free.

Steph's couple was downstage, nearer the audience. Good.

The couples alternated a series of killingly slow, ever higher lifts. Anna's arms ached just thinking of what those boys were going through. With decent music, strings instead of the barrel-organing piano, the lifts would soar.

Now Steph's partner prepared. Anna could see this was the big lift, the topper. She squinted critically.

*Trouble.*

Steph's *plié* was shallow, she didn't bend her knees far enough to help her partner. The lift came out sharp and ragged and *wrong*. The boy had to shift weight and his foot came out of position. Of course it didn't *look* like Steph's fault but it still looked like shit.

Once Steph was up, it was beautiful. She leaned out into space and slowly, effortlessly, she dipped—eight sustained beats of slow motion, with never a break. Her head arced down and her feet arced up till her partner was holding her almost upside down.

Then, with a movement so swift Anna couldn't believe it had even happened, he was holding her in arabesque. Her position was sharp as etched crystal. The house would go crazy, they'd *have* to go crazy!

Now he was bringing her down in a slow sliding movement and just as her toes touched and she found her balance she whipped into a turn—out of nowhere, a turn!

And then, to top *that*, a sudden stop motion and there she was in *attitude*—cool and still and not even out of breath—as though she hadn't taken a step in the last three minutes!

Anna almost broke into applause on the spot.

She checked herself, gripped the railing, leaned forward. *What next?*

Her heart sank as she saw what was coming next: the other couple, who'd been standing upstage in absolute stillness, began executing exactly the same sequence of movements.

Helplessly, Anna watched her little girl standing downstage, motionless, while Linda went up into the same lift, Steph's lift, and the same arabesque, Steph's arabesque, and then came down into a—

Anna couldn't believe it, she didn't *want* to believe it.

*A double turn!*

Danny had given that girl a *double* turn! Why? To make Steph look like some kind of dumdum who could barely creak out a single?

Anna's eyes stung and her heart hammered.

She could barely focus on the four-dancer clover-leaf patterns that followed or the two women alone on the stage, slowly backbending toward one another. The question stabbed at her: why *two*, why the hell did Danny Gillette need two women? He could as well have used Steph and a mirror for all that second girl added.

Anna blinked away the sting and when she opened her eyes Danny was standing close to Steph, an arm around her waist, giving the dancers his notes.

That was it. That was the ballet.

Well, at least Danny seemed pleased with it.

Anna gripped the railing and got to her feet. She found her way out of the box and went home. Her resolve was gathered into a painful little nut in the pit of her stomach.

She told Directory Assistance she was Danny Gillette's doctor's nurse and she wrung the unlisted number from them.

She began phoning at four-thirty. At five-thirty he answered.

\*   \*   \*

"I did something I shouldn't have. Steph will murder me if she finds out."

They were sitting at a back table in the Theater Pub. It was four o'clock, not yet cocktail hour. The neighboring tables were still vacant and there was no one near enough to overhear.

"I peeked at a *Lacrymosa* rehearsal last Thursday."

Danny Gillette took a deep breath and his black T-shirt became too tight for his torso. The collar exposed a tensed, pulsing crescent of skin. He reminded Anna of a dancer trying to relax before a difficult entrance.

"That rehearsal was pretty ragged," he said.

"You're telling me? But the way Steph's been talking about it, I couldn't stay away. I even sneaked off work early."

She made a pretense of sipping her ginger ale, of enjoying it, of inspecting the customers huddled at the shadowy little tables. She sensed Danny waiting for her to go on but she dawdled, smiling and stirring her ice cubes with her swizzle stick.

"Did you like the ballet?" he asked.

"I was curious about one thing. Is Linda covering for someone else?"

"No, she's dancing."

"The way she handled that half turn in mid-air where Victor catches her?"

"It's a whole turn."

"Oh, that explains. I couldn't figure it out. That was the only thing that bothered me."

"You liked the rest?"

He looked at her, eager and worried and young, just as Marty Lang had once looked at her. She felt a desire she had not known in years, an impulse to make her hand soft, to reach out and touch a man's face. She had to remind herself, firmly, that Steph was her concern, not this boy.

"Well, I could see it was rough—there's so much going on. But it's all brilliant. You know, it reminded me of Jerry's first version of *Cage*." So far as she knew, Jerome Robbins had done only one *Cage*, but Danny Gillette was too young to know the difference. "There were so many soloists, so many bits—but he realized that at the dress. He ripped it apart, he simplified, he had a hit."

Anna let the word "hit" sink in. She sipped her ginger ale, giving Danny the chance to speak. If he'd said she was full of horse manure or defended his ballet or even changed the subject she would have backed off.

But he chose to remain silent, and that choice told Anna everything she needed to know about Daniel Gillette.

"I danced in *Cage*," Anna lied. "Nora Kaye knocked me down the second night—everyone thought Jerry had changed the steps again. What a perfectionist that man is. Never satisfied till he has a hit."

"I like *Cage*," Danny said. "I never thought of the resemblance."

"No big deal. Jerry's brilliant his way, you'll be brilliant your way. I agree with Steph. She has great respect for you. Great respect."

"Thank you."

"And she's fond of you, which I'm sure you don't need me to tell you, and she trusts you, and she doesn't trust just anyone. Which is why I feel I can trust you too. I hope you won't mind if I'm very, very open with you."

"Of course not."

Anna stared down at her hands and her eye caught the troubled angle of his face. She felt an instant's guilt. She fought it back but could not keep a slight quiver from her voice.

"It's Steph. She's very depressed."

"She seemed okay last week."

"She'd die before she'd let anyone know. Especially you. But between you and me, she's very discouraged with the company."

The bar light struck a soft glow from the boy's hair. It seemed to Anna in that instant that if he looked at her or touched her a sudden pity would go out from her, paralyzing her.

Instead he frowned.

"What's the trouble?"

"Empire's not giving her roles. Oh, I know, *coryphée* here, thirty-second solo there—but she's better than that. You've seen her, you know. You chose her for *Lacrymosa* after all. *You* know she's good."

"Yes, she's good."

"I probably sound like a ballet mother, and God knows I am. The trouble is—Now don't tell anyone, don't you dare tell her I told you, can I trust you?"

"You can trust me."

"She's had an offer from another company—I'm sure you know the company I mean, frankly it's the only one she'd consider, and she has an in because—not many people know it—but we happen to be very close to the director and he's her godfather. Now she wants to make it on her own, and she hates to use a contact like that. But this director means business. Solos, principal roles—it's all spelled out in the contract. And the pay's higher and it's a full year's employment."

It was all a lie, but all that concerned Anna at the moment was whether or not the lie was believable. Yvette Blanchard had walked out of NBT two days ago, leaving a hole at the top. Even if Volmar moved all the girls up a notch, there was still a gap to fill. This was public knowledge, and it fitted with her invention, and she waited to see if it would convince Danny Gillette.

"Is she going to accept?"

"Could you blame her? I'm staying out of it, I'm not advising her yes or no. She's grown up, she runs her own life. But I'd hate to see her give up Empire after all the work she's put in—just because they won't give her a solo."

Danny kept his eyes lowered and his shoulders hunched. He kept them that way a long time before he spoke. "She has a solo in my ballet."

"And your ballet's going to be a knockout." Anna placed her hand over his and it lay there, firm and steady, as though she were guiding him in a finger pirouette. "But that's like a featured solo. I'm talking about a principal. There's no real female principal in *Lacrymosa*. It's really an étude for two women. You handle them beautifully, but it's a duet—you know what I mean?"

"I hadn't thought of it like that."

"She needs a principal role, even if it's in a small ballet. She needs the exposure, and she needs it now. Dancers don't keep forever."

"When does the other company want her?"

Anna did not answer. She wasn't certain, afterward, what warned her not to look away from him. Some instinct flashed that this was the win-or-lose instant. The instinct told her to fasten her eyes on his and not let go. It was Danny whose eyes dropped, whose fingers twisted the peppermint-striped straw in his vodka tonic.

"Oh, Danny, I *want* her to dance your ballet, I'm praying she'll dance it. It's such a sweet little role, and you understand her body. Frankly, whatever happens, I hope someday you'll do a major role on her."

"Would she leave before we premiere?"

"From the look of things—the way the other company's pressuring—who knows? Danny, she's going through hell. She doesn't want to let you down. But he *is* her godfather and he's offering a terrific chance. Maybe if she had something at Empire, a real principal role . . . I'll bet she'd stay."

A mother has an intuition about certain things. If there had been anything more Anna could have done for her little girl, she wouldn't have hesitated. But in her heart she knew she'd done enough, exactly and precisely enough.

"Don't tell her I told you any of this. She'd hate me."

"I won't," Danny said dully.

"You'll think of something. You're a bright boy and she really likes you."

Anna kissed him on the cheek and she felt she was kissing a mannikin through a pane of glass.

"Sure," he said. "I'll think of something."

*     *     *

Afterward Danny walked.

The air smelled of traffic. It was loud with the anger of brakes and horns but it was free of her voice, that terrible voice that had twisted him like a stick of licorice. At least he could breathe again.

His thoughts were an agony, an undigested lump bursting against his skull.

He walked across Broadway and then over to Central Park West.

He didn't cross to the park side. He walked north past co-ops with names like "Majestic" on their awnings and uniformed doormen scowling in the doorways. His parents had friends in those buildings. Lester Croyden lived in one of those buildings. He thought of those friends, successful lawyers and doctors; he thought of Lester Croyden, of the dictatorship that old people wielded over young people in ballet, and his heels were snappy and irritable against the pavement.

He wanted to scream. He exhaled, let the scream out silently, a bit at a time.

The pressure in his head eased a little.

Gradually it came to him that he was being a child, acting as though he were about to lose his life or his career or someone he loved. In fact he wasn't going to lose any of those things.

The air awakened him. He began to think logically.

Sometimes, he saw, you couldn't expect everything at once. Sometimes you had to make a choice.

*So be practical,* he told himself. *What do you lose if you change the ballet a little, make the female role a solo?*

*You lose part of your ballet, you give up a little of the truth that went into it.*

*Is that so bad?*

*It hurts.*

*What do you lose if you don't change the ballet?*

*You lose Steph. And if you lose her you lose the ballet anyway because you made it on her. That hurts worse. That hurts more than anything.*

The more he walked and thought the more clearly he saw the choice. Lose the whole ballet or lose part of it. Lose her completely or keep her completely.

At the corner of Central Park West and Seventy-second Street he stopped and turned abruptly around.

*Keep her, you nut. Most definitely emphatically no-question-about-it keep her. Because she happens to be exactly right.*

*And besides you're in love with her.*

# twenty-one

Danny kept phoning, but he couldn't reach Linda over the week end. At rehearsal Monday he tried to let the guillotine down gently.

"Linda, you don't have to bother with that *relevé*."

"All I need's a half-beat preparation."

"Please. Don't bother."

"I'll get it. I just have to find my center coming out of that turn."

"Linda, I'm cutting the part. There's not going to be any Diana in the ballet."

Her face went white.

He explained that he felt like an idiot. He should have seen his mistake at the very first run-through. He'd been bothered by the band shell performance but he hadn't understood what the matter was. Then, in rehearsals, able to stand back and watch, he'd understood: the ballet had to be a *pas de trois*, not a *pas de quatre*. The focus had to be Psyche or there was no unity.

"Damn it, Danny, you're wrong. It would have made a damned good *pas de quatre*." Deep breath; shoulders back. "Well, no sense holding up your rehearsal."

She grabbed her tote bag and tossed her toe shoes into it and left the studio without a wave or even a glance at the other dancers.

Danny clapped his hands for attention. Carefully, with no emotion at all, he explained the changes.

* * *

Linda was still in the dressing room when Steph went back to change.

"Hats off. You've got yourself a beautiful little role."

"The ballet was perfect the way it was," Steph said. "I don't see why he had to change everything around. Linda, I'm sorry."

"Why be sorry? Go celebrate."

"If he was going to cut someone, it should have been me—not you."

"That's a matter of opinion. And obviously it's not Danny's opinion."

"I'll never be able to do those balances the way you do."

"Cut them."

"I can't cut Danny's choreography."

"You seem to be managing so far."

Steph stared at her, amazed. "You don't think I *asked* him to cut your role!"

"Want to know what I think? I think you're a really fast learner."

"That's not fair."

"Don't tell me about not fair. Yesterday I had a role. Today I don't. Yesterday I thought I had friends. Today I know I don't."

"I never asked him to change a step! Linda—please—believe me!"

"Believe you? No. Trust you? Never again. Hate you? With pleasure."

* * *

At the next *Lacrymosa* rehearsal Lester Croyden opened the studio door and stood looking in. A wordless moment of observation and then he was gone.

The next day Ilonka Banska appeared in the doorway beside him. They came quietly into the studio, threw Danny don't-mind-us-we're-not-even-here glances, and took seats on wooden chairs against the mirror.

Danny was directing Victor and Steph in their allegro. The floor beat with the rhythm of leaping feet.

Ilonka sat motionless as a passenger braced against the swaying of a ship. She was diet-pale, exercise-thin, her hair a cropped spill of Magyar gold. Her violet eyes loomed wide and wet as two hungry mouths. She watched for several minutes, then turned quickly and whispered something to Lester Croyden. She kissed him, tiptoed with elaborate silence from the studio, and let the door slam.

Lester waited till the end of the rehearsal. "I see you dropped one of your girls," he said.

"It seemed to focus much better as a *pas de trois*," Danny said.

"Much better. More dramatic. You've made a real starring role there. Reminds me of one of Tudor's heroines. . . ."

"Thank you."

"I keep thinking of Nora's first *Pillar*. Too bad we haven't got someone of Nora's caliber to dance it."

"As far as I'm concerned, Steph's perfect."

"She's promising, yes."

"She *is* the role. I made it on her."

"Still, there's something not quite right. Victor and David are such powerful performers. Stephanie's soft by comparison." Lester Croyden's eyes seemed to retract slightly in their sockets. "Ilonka thought her technique was weak. If anyone could handle this role, Ilonka could. And she hasn't had a new vehicle in three seasons."

"Ilonka isn't at all what I had in mind. It isn't a display piece."

"I wonder . . ." Lester Croyden spoke with maddening slowness, a man pretending to be in the grip of a sudden and new idea that was clearly a thought-out intention. "I wonder if we could persuade her to dance the premiere . . ."

"That's not fair," Danny said quietly, firmly. "Steph's done all the work."

"With Ilonka dancing we could schedule it six or seven times—give Stephanie a matinee or two."

"Isn't it time an American dancer had a premiere in this company?"

Like all the major companies, Empire received federal funds. Like all except Balanchine's, it consistently threw lead roles to expensive imported stars. Danny would have expected Lester Croyden at least to pause and rebut the accusation.

But he did not. His eyes were dreaming. His hand was on Danny's elbow, congratulatory and conspiratorial. "I'll talk to Ilonka. And, Danny—you're lucky that an international star wants the role. You've proven that you're talented. Now let's see if you're practical."

*    *    *

The next evening, backstage after performance, Danny asked Steph if she'd like to have a steak at his place—nothing fancy. It sounded very spur-of-the-moment and she tried not to let her acceptance seem too eager.

She phoned the State Theater, left a message for Chris canceling dinner, and took a taxi with Danny to an old converted brownstone practically at Riverside Drive.

He led her into the apartment. A marmalade cat came running to greet them.

"The roommate," Danny said.

"Hi, Geof." Steph crouched and petted the animal and it purred.

"Want the grand tour?"

"Sure."

Danny showed her two rooms and an efficiency kitchen. The kitchen fixtures were turn-of-the-century, age-spotted, otherwise immaculate. The rooms were cluttered, but the clutter was clean and cozy. She liked the place right away. She could see Danny was comfortable in it.

She could see, too, that the invitation had been no spur-of-the-moment impulse. Before leaving for the theater he had prepared a table: place settings for two, wineglasses, paper napkins furled in Japanese napkin rings, candles.

He lit the candles. "Hungry?"

"Starved."

"You relax. This takes two minutes."

He poured wine and put music on the phonograph: a piano concerto, Mozart or Haydn, her ear wasn't sharp enough to tell the difference and probably never would be.

He went through astonishingly few movements in the kitchen and produced two steaks, steamed green beans, rice with herbs that she suspected came prepackaged but was delicious anyway.

They had dancers' appetites and were so busy eating that she didn't at first notice how little he was saying. When she glanced at him, upright and rigid in his chair, she sensed something wrong. She was aware of a clock ticking somewhere, a falsetto Big Ben chiming the quarter hour and then the half hour, and she began to feel uneasy.

"Something the matter, Danny?"

His eyes rested on her for a moment. "No, no. Everything's fine. Just a little tired."

He had obviously thought the meal out, and she felt flattered. There were two cheeses at room temperature, delicious and runny, and fresh fruit, and thick black coffee from the Chemex.

But no conversation.

Afterward he stood up, tall and white, and went to the sofa and lay down. She followed quickly and sat on the floor beside him.

"Come on, Danny, what's the big secret?" She held her hand against his cheek, trying to get him to talk. "You cooked me a beautiful dinner. You acted like it was all very last-minute but you obviously planned it, so there must have been a reason."

"I just wanted to see you."

"You see me at work every day."

"That's not the same. Work's work."

"Is work bothering you?"

"Maybe."

"But why? You're happy with the company. And God knows, they're happy with you."

"God knows."

"Is it something to do with your ballet?"

And the truth began trickling out.

"They want to change it," he said.

"Change it how?"

"Ilonka wants to dance your role."

She ought to have foreseen this. She tried to pretend it was all quite expected, which it wasn't, and quite wonderful, which it was. "Danny—that's terrific! She'll be brilliant!"

"No. I did the ballet for you. It *is* you. It *has* to be you."

"But with Ilonka the ballet will go on tour. You'll get reviews—international reviews—you'll go into the international repertory. Danny, people will *know* about you! It's a break for you!"

He was silent. She couldn't fathom his reaction to Ilonka's wanting the role. She felt happy for him and proud; he seemed angry, almost insulted.

She said, "Oh, Danny, I'm touched you'd even think of me—but this is important, this is your career. You've *got* to let her dance it."

She waited for an answer and finally he said, "I can't compromise any more. I've already compromised too much. There won't be anything left if she gets her toe shoes around it."

But Steph wouldn't let go. "There are compromises down and there are compromises up. You don't need to be ashamed of a compromise up. Ever. Ilonka is the best."

He laughed a soft, strangely calm laugh. His hand slid across the purring cat. He closed his eyes and asked how old she was.

Steph didn't see what that had to do with anything. "Nineteen. Why?"

He looked at her in astonishment and envy, thinking: *Time hasn't started for her yet, she doesn't know she's finite. She probably doesn't know anything is finite.*

"You have so much to learn."

"Not so much as you think, Danny. And maybe I know one or two things you don't."

She knew dance meant more to him than she or any person could. She knew this from legends and rumors of the great choreographers. She knew it too by intuition. It was the way artists had to be and there was nothing wrong with it. The only wrong thing was when an artist put a person ahead of his art. She didn't want Danny to have to blame her as her mother blamed her father. She wished she knew a way to tell him this.

"Danny, if you give up Ilonka because you're trying to prove something to me—there's no point. There's nothing you need to prove. You proved it all, just telling me. And that means more to me than starring in nine zillion premieres."

"I don't want to lose you, Steph."

"You're not going to lose anything."

He smiled and they huddled, his arm around her shoulder, and there was a strangely truthful moment when neither of them said a word.

The cat hopped nimbly across cantilevered stacks of books and magazines. A candle sputtered out and the light in the room was halved.

They became lovers that night.

\*      \*      \*

Chris couldn't sleep all night.

A dozen times she almost phoned the police and another dozen times she almost phoned Steph's mother, and when finally at eight-thirty in the morning she heard a key in the lock she felt sick with relief.

Steph bounced into the apartment, full of sun and bustle, cheeks flushed and eyes emerald-bright.

"I spent the night with Danny," she said.

Chris was too surprised to answer.

"I'm sorry, I should have phoned. I will next time."

*So there'll be a next time,* Chris thought, and something turned to ice deep in her stomach. She set out a second coffee cup and watched Steph butter a piece of toast. There was a long silence and finally Chris said, "What was it like?"

"Gentle—beautiful—exactly the way he is."

Chris had had sex education in school and she'd heard the fables girls tell one another. She knew the facts of love between a man and a woman but she did not know the touch of skin on skin or the taste of a man's tongue and these things filled her with vague and paralyzing premonitions.

"Were you scared?"

Steph looked at her with a kindly sort of astonishment. "How could I be scared of Danny?"

"Did it—hurt?"

"Hurt?" Steph was thoughtful and then she laughed. "I don't remember." In her own excitement, in the newness of her feelings, she forgot to take the pulse of Chris's mood. She described the evening and she described Danny.

But for Chris the description was useless: she needed a map and Steph gave her an out-of-focus photograph.

"Oh, Chris." Steph sighed. "I'm in love."

Chris knew Steph. She heard the question mark beneath her friend's euphoria. There was more here than excitement and discovery. There was nervousness and uncertainty. Faintly but unmistakably, there was a shadow of moral doubt. For all the spillover of happiness, Steph was looking to Chris for support.

And Chris tried.

She made approving faces, approving squeals. She asked questions, gasped with delight at each answer. She made coffee and clattered dishes in the sink. She listened to Steph rave about Danny's humor and intelligence and sensitivity and—though this was only a hint—his skill as a lover.

She tried to be happy for Steph, as she knew Steph would be happy for her if she came running home one morning and announced she'd found the perfect love. But she could muster only a thin topsoil of deception. She held her lips in a smile so tense they ached.

"And on top of all that," Steph cried, "you'll never guess—he *cooks!*"

"What did he cook?" Chris said softly. And every word that Steph uttered was a wrecking ball hammering the walls of her safety.

*It's over,* Chris thought. *We're not little girls huddling together in our high-rise make-believe home any more. Steph has found a man.*

Chris knew that sex had to be faced, like swimming or riding a bicycle or saying hello to strangers. She had hoped for more time and more moral support, but now she was without an ally. Steph had jumped safely to the other side of the ravine, leaving Chris alone and scared and staring down at the drop.

"Oh, Chris, I wish you—"

Steph stopped and Chris knew exactly what she'd been on the verge of saying: *you should do it too.*

"I know," Chris said. "I will. . . ."

After that Chris grew to hate the apartment at night. Even with the television turned up, the silence deafened her and loneliness pressed in on her. She lay awake till dawn waiting for the scrape of Steph's key in the lock and the jar of the door slamming.

Every morning she saw something new and rich and alive in

Steph's eyes and she wondered, *Why won't she help me?*

In the days that followed Chris felt more and more of Steph draining out of the apartment. A toothbrush and bathrobe disappeared from the bathroom. Fewer dresses were hanging on Steph's side of the closet. A raincoat and umbrella vanished.

Chris felt deserted.

One thing Chris feared more than any other: that Steph would leave and move in with Danny. Steph never brought the subject up and her silence was like a shriek ripping at the last shred of Chris's security.

\*   \*   \*

"Chris, would you mind very much if..."

They were sitting at the little ritual of breakfast that their friendship had shrunk to, and from the way Steph hesitated Chris knew: *This is it, she's leaving.*

"If what?" Chris said, braced and smiling.

"I've invited Danny for dinner next Monday."

Chris took a deep breath. She felt reprieved. "Am I included?"

"I'm counting on you. And I invited Ray too. That's all right, isn't it?" Steph knew she was meddling but it was for Chris's sake and she felt no shame at using strategy. "He phoned, and he sounded so damned lonely."

Chris sat staring at her coffee. Her mind winced at the idea of another dinner with all its tensions and silences and the ugliness that could spring like a tiger out of nowhere. "Fine," she said softly.

"I'll do the cooking," Steph said. "You did it last time."

\*   \*   \*

It rained the night of the dinner and Chris and Danny didn't warm to one another as easily as Steph had hoped. Chris answered attempts at conversation with monosyllables and nods, and when the doorbell rang Steph felt a surge of relief.

"What weather!" Steph closed the door behind Ray.

He shifted nervously on the balls of his feet, like a boxer about to enter the ring.

"Did you get rained on?" she said, taking his coat.

"Nope. I splurged on a cab."

She drew him forward into the room. "Ray, this is Danny Gillette. Ray Lockwood." The men exchanged how-do-you-do's, and Steph said, "Let me get you a drink. We have real liquor tonight."

"Vodka and anything," Ray said. "If you have it."

"Coming up."

He tried not to let his gaze fasten too obviously on Chris. She was sitting at the far end of the sofa. She seemed soft and tiny in blue lounging pajamas that brought out the pale blue of her eyes. He realized she was watching him. After his drunken behavior the night of *Lacrymosa* he wanted his movements to be graceful and careful. He stood perfectly still and looked around the apartment.

"You two have made this a real home since I saw it last."

"We're trying," Chris said, and she smiled in a way that made him hope she'd forgiven him for that phone call.

Steph put a drink in his hand and said, "Come on in and sit down."

The others were sitting in a triangle in the living room. He took the rocker. He sipped and rocked and the vodka began to reach soothing fingers into him.

They were talking about dance. He listened and caught a familiar phrase here and there. He was happy they took him for granted. It made him almost an insider. Steph mentioned that she was covering for one of the soloists and Ray said, "You know, audiences always groan when the understudy goes on. But Lupe Serrano got her big break substituting for Melissa Hayden in Washington—and the audience gave her an ovation."

He'd spent the afternoon at the library at Lincoln Center preparing for tonight.

"When Sadler's Wells came to New York after World War II," he said, "everyone had seen Moira Shearer in *The Red Shoes*. They expected her to dance opening night. Instead they got a nobody called Margot Fonteyn. They went in angry and came out cheering."

Steph smiled and shrugged. "It's only Prelude in *Les Sylphides*. Even if I did go on, no one's going to make a fuss. Besides, I doubt I'll get a chance."

"The law of averages is on your side," Ray said. "If you go outside of ballet, there are a hundred instances. Leonard Bernstein went on instead of Bruno Walter and it made his career as a conductor. Or look at Alexandra Hunt—she went on as Lulu at the last moment, one of the toughest roles in the soprano repertory, and she had to warm up on the stage of the Met, in Act One! The performing arts are full of substitutes pulling off last-minute miracles. Look at Roberta Peters or Martina Arroyo—from substitute to superstar in one performance."

"But that's opera," Steph said.

"It happens in ballet too. There are rumors of stars purposely calling in sick to give their covers a break."

Steph shook her head. "Not in ballet. Maybe in *books* about ballet, or movies. But after all the work it takes to learn a role and become a ballerina, I can't imagine a dancer giving up a performance. I know I wouldn't."

"Thumb through one of the dance encyclopedias," Ray said. "There's a lot of jealousy between ballerinas but there's a lot of friendship too."

Chris stared at Ray. *He's handsome, he's kind, he's smart,* she thought. *And he's trying to impress Steph.* She felt ignored and small.

They drifted into the area that was the dining room and sat down at the table. There were appetizers of avocado stuffed with shrimp. Steph called from the kitchen, "Don't wait for me!"

Ray told Danny how much he'd enjoyed *Lacrymosa*—though he didn't remember an instant or a step of it—and Danny thanked him.

"And what do you do for a living?" Danny asked. "Something saner than dance, I take it?"

Ray glanced at Chris. She was studying her plate gravely. "I don't know how sane," he said, "but it's a little safer and a lot duller." He described his law courses and he saw just the faintest flicker of a smile on Danny's lips.

"Wouldn't it be easier to shoot the Supreme Court?" Danny said.

Ray felt he'd been flicked aside with a joke but he laughed. Steph brought a huge pot of coq au vin to the table. Everyone was talking dance again. Ray looked down at his hands. He wanted to say something intelligent and relevant but he felt like a doorbell trying to be heard at a noisy celebration.

After dinner Steph made coffee and they all took their cups back to the living room. Ray sat in his rocker listening to dance talk, trying to understand the mysterious center of these people's lives.

Steph noticed how his glance kept creeping, secret and shining, toward Chris, and how Chris never returned it.

When the guests had gone, Steph said, "I like Ray."

"He hardly said a word to me," Chris said. She wasn't hurt, because she knew lawyers and she knew what to expect. Her father was a lawyer.

"Maybe you should have said a few words to him." Steph didn't want to push, but she had an intuition that Ray would be the best thing in the world that could happen to Chris.

"I tried," Chris said.

*If that was trying,* Steph thought, *I'm a ballet superstar calling in sick to give my understudy a break.* "Well, keep trying. He's worth a little effort."

\*      \*      \*

At the very first rehearsal with Ilonka, Danny realized he had a serious problem: the woman wasn't simply *good,* she was the best.

"How do you want this?" she asked at one point. "Bolshoi or Kirov?"

The choreography called for three leaps in rapid succession: the first moderate, the second higher and longer, the third—highest and longest of all—ending in a fish dive into Victor's arms. Danny had never thought of the sequence as Bolshoi *or* Kirov, but he saw from her face that the offer was serious.

Ilonka threw a nod to the accompanist. A furious dissonant allegro came crashing from the piano.

She demonstrated Bolshoi: She kept the first jump low and short, ending it a fraction of a beat early. That gave her extra time and strength for the second jump, which seemed explosive compared to the first. On the third jump she overextended her arms, turning the dive into a suicide leap that ended with her head two inches and a tenth of a second from the floor.

It was a stunning acrobatic illusion, it was cheap, and it would bring down the house. And Danny hated it.

Ilonka shook her hair out of her face, backed off on the diagonal, and demonstrated Kirov: The jumps came effortlessly, evenly, equal arcs of time filling ever larger arcs of space. The final dive came not as a leap into destruction but as an effortless fall into safety.

Without hesitation Danny said, "Kirov."

"Good," Ilonka said. "Is nicer. Better not to scare people too early."

The woman's memory astounded Danny.

Time and time again she picked up the most complex phrases—intricate *chaînés*, sudden reversals, syncopations—after a single demonstration. Once or twice she even anticipated movements before Danny showed them. He found this so baffling that he mentioned it to Victor after rehearsal.

"Memory, shit." Victor pointed to the observation window. "Didn't you see her sitting up there with the choreologist? They've been taking notes for three weeks."

The incredulity must have shown on Danny's face, because Victor guffawed.

"Come on, man, you *know* she's been hot for this ballet ever since you dropped the second female."

Which, if it was true, explained another oddity about Ilonka Banska. Her bad temper never surfaced once. The woman had argued with Balanchine and Robbins and called Tudor a twerp and thrown speghetti at John Cranko, yet she cheerfully took direction from an unknown soloist ten years her junior.

She even tried to be charming.

She began kissing Danny hello and good-by, calling him "Darling." She gave him a yellow rose after every rehearsal. She spread word that his work was "lovely." She told her dresser, and her dresser told the world, "That boy could teach Grigorovich."

Danny tried in small persistent ways to insult her, praying he could goad her into walking out.

He never returned her kisses or compliments. He worked her overtime, called Sunday rehearsals, never once thanked her. He insisted on Steph's covering the role. He shouted "Stop!" in the middle of Ilonka's most difficult steps.

"You're doing that wrong, Ilonka. Steph, would you show her?"

Steph would demonstrate, uneasily, and Ilonka would copy, perfectly, like a human Xerox.

Danny altered steps, devised impossible combinations. But nothing was beyond the woman. She could hop from Bolshoi gymnastics to Kirov schmaltz to Danish Royal elegance. She could handle presto footwork à la Balanchine and jazzy distortions à la Twyla Tharp. Her range was phenomenal. If Steph was one octave of the piano, Ilonka was the entire keyboard.

But Danny didn't want the keyboard: he wanted Steph's octave.

He wanted Steph.

It wasn't till they began rehearsing onstage again that he saw how to get rid of Ilonka.

\* \* \*

Like many East-bloc defectors, Ilonka Banska was a dancer of strong theatrical instinct. In a rehearsal studio, the instinct might slumber. On a stage, it took over completely.

Just before the climax of the ballet, there was a passage where Ilonka tore herself from David's arms and *bourrée*'d upstage. She stopped short, did a triple unsupported pirouette, and fell into Victor's arms.

At least that was what was supposed to happen.

The music for the *bourrées* was a series of rapid rising scales; for the triple pirouette, a tremendous fortissimo dissonance. Onstage, Ilonka *bourrée*'d forward exactly as she had done in the studio. But instead of a triple she did four. Probably she wasn't even aware of it. Her timing was flawless. It worked. It was far more theatrical. It ought to have stayed.

But it wasn't Danny's choreography.

"Ilonka," he said, "triple, please."

"Triple?" She had the face of an accused innocent. "But I *did* triple."

"You did four. I want a triple. Can we take that again, please? *And*."

The piano hammered out its scales. Ilonka came *bourrée*'ing forward once more. At the dissonance she whipped out another four.

"Ilonka—can you count? I want a triple."

Now the accused became the accuser. "A triple? How can I do a triple when the music—" Her English began failing. Her hands made rapid circles in the air.

Danny lit the fuse.

"In Hungary don't they teach you the difference between three and four?"

"Is not my fault!" she shrieked. "Is four-pirouette music, don't tell me triple turn, tell music triple turn!"

"The music stays."

"Music too loud. Too something. Wrong."

"*You* are wrong." Danny beckoned into the wings. "Steph—come show Ilonka how to do a triple turn."

Steph came hesitantly onto the stage. Ilonka's stare wheeled unbelievingly from Danny to Steph and back again. She ripped the kerchief from her head and flung it to the floor.

"Idiots! Not work with idiots!" She whipped around, cropped hair flying, and stomped into the wings.

It was the famous Banska exit, Danny's cue to go begging after her.

But he stayed put. He waited a moment, making sure she wasn't going to come stomping back. He clapped his hands twice.

"Okay, fellows, Steph. Why don't we take it from the very top?"

# twenty-two

It was one of the best orchestra seats in the Metropolitan Opera House, Row S three in from the center aisle, $22.50; but to Anna it felt like an electric chair. Steph's ballet didn't come on till after the first intermission. There was all of *Petrouchka* to get through. Anna shifted weight, opened and closed her purse a hundred times, fingers scavenging in the dark to make sure the aspirin bottle was still there.

Her knees kept bumping the press agent's and she kept whispering, "Sorry." When he patted her on the thigh she finally forced herself to stop squirming. She'd hired the man on the suggestion of one of her exercise students, a Mrs. Greenspan whose husband ran one of the TV networks. He was getting $300, which hurt, but he was supposed to be good and how else could she make sure Steph got exposure?

All through *Petrouchka* he kept covering yawns and looking at his watch. Anna couldn't blame him: it was a pageant, not a ballet. The girl dancing the role of the Ballerina didn't even bother to tap her triangle in time to the triangle in the orchestra. It was all careless and flat and the best Anna could think of it was that even if Steph fell on her ass she'd look good by comparison.

The lights came halfway up for curtain calls. Anna's eye

skimmed the grand tier boxes, stopping at the end of the row, the box that her friend in the ticket office had said was reserved for Marius Volmar. She knew he'd gone to Brussels the week before, but she'd been certain she'd see him tonight.

Disappointment dragged at her.

"Care for a drinkie?" the press agent shouted over the applause. "On me."

"Sure," Anna said. Why not? A ginger ale to wash down an aspirin. She didn't see how else she would survive the intermission.

They joined the tide streaming up the stairs: Hampton-tanned women glittering with Tiffany gold and diamonds; sleek men in high-fashion suits strutting with plastic champagne glasses; young people in denim and rolled-up shirt sleeves, all shouting their shrill ignorance. She side-stepped a pack of children in $300 outfits scampering down the stairway as though it were a jungle gym. The bar was crowded with noisy, chattering people: the same mob of ballet phonies she'd known all her life.

Tonight she was scared of them. No matter how hard she worked, no matter how hard she encouraged her little girl, in the end it was up to these yammering, preening balletomanes. They had the power.

The press agent kept jabbing her with his elbow, aiming low and secret, pointing out people: "Molly Weatherbee, *Women's Wear Daily* . . . Paul Schoff, *Cue* magazine . . . They're all here, the word's out, Stephanie is *hot*."

He even introduced her to a sad little woman from Associated Press who, so far as Anna could gather, had nothing at all to do with dance.

The lights stung her eyes and the shouting deafened her and the air rippled with $100-an-ounce French perfume. She saw a second-string dance critic at a table in the restaurant, hunched over what looked like a double scotch.

"I'm going to get a little air," she told the press agent. She edged out onto the balcony and stared at Lincoln Center Plaza and the computerized fountain shooting forty-foot jets up into the night:

She saw Lvovna, sipping champagne and laughing with two ballet masters from NBT. She nodded to Abe Greenfield from ICM and said hello to Mack Evarts from Columbia Artists. At least the pros were here. She didn't fool herself that they'd come for Steph. They were here for Danny. But they'd notice Steph. They'd have to.

She still didn't see Volmar. She hadn't expected him, but she'd hoped.

At the first bell she went back to her seat. Musicians were tuning their instruments in the pit. They were better dressed than half the audience, and no wonder—who was as rich as a union musician these days?

The final bell sounded. The house slowly filled up as the last barflies straggled to their seats.

Anna turned in her seat. The lights in the boxes blinked out one by one as ushers closed doors.

Volmar's box was dark and empty.

The press agent squeezed into the seat beside her, breathless and smelling faintly of bourbon. "Got stuck with Jack Sayre; you know what a talker *he* is. They're doing a spread on new dancers and he wants to use Stephanie..."

Anna heard and nodded, but she felt cheated. All the photographers and agents and ballet hangers-on in the world didn't add up to Marius Volmar.

The one man in all ballet who mattered wasn't here.

A follow-spot trailed the conductor through the orchestra pit to the podium. A sprinkle of clapping began in the family circle, spilled down through the balconies, built to respectable applause. He bowed to the house, gestured the musicians to their feet.

After ten seconds' applause there was silence. The conductor waited, arms folded. The house was hushed, holding its breath.

Anna fidgeted irritably. What the hell was holding them up?

*       *       *

Thirty-five minutes into *Petrouchka*, Steph's costume still had not arrived. She waited in the corps dressing room. Because of the dancers' superstition that it was bad luck to put on tights or toe shoes before the costume, she sat barefoot in her terry-cloth robe.

She played solitaire.

She cheated.

She tried to ignore the herds of butterflies building up to a stampede in her stomach.

The last ballet on the evening's program was *"Bizet,"* and

most of the other girls had already put on their white tutus. They played cards, turned pages of magazines, chain-smoked, sipped Styrofoam cups of four-hour-old coffee. Boredom hung in the air.

A few of the girls nodded at Steph or said hello. Most avoided her. They were Linda's friends, and company gossip had it she'd stabbed Linda in the back.

The loudspeaker on the wall, wired live to the stage, sent out the last measures of *Petrouchka*. The sound was tinny, like a paging box at an airport. Applause came in staticky, unreal waves as the dancers took bows, and then the box sent out a deadening silence.

Still no costume.

Steph dealt herself another hand of solitaire, couldn't concentrate. On the box a man's voice said, "Fifteen minutes."

She was aware of eyes grazing her, probing for panic. The voice said, "Ten minutes."

And then two men and a woman came bustling into the dressing room. The guard tried to stop them. "Hey, mister, you can't go in there."

"That's all right, we're expected. Has anyone seen Miss Lang?"

Steph recognized the costume designer, a young-looking blond man who wore tinted aviator glasses and a high-fashion suit and a great deal of confidence.

He saw her. "Ah, there you are!"

He came striding down the aisle, made a great show of not noticing the stares of the entire corps. His male assistant took the lid off a striped dress box. The female assistant lifted a shimmering bundle of moss-green satin from a cradle of tissue paper.

"And how are you feeling this night of nights?" the designer asked.

"Nervous," Steph said.

"Is that why you've lost weight?"

Steph wriggled carefully into the dress. Hands pulled at her waist.

"Harry, needle and thread."

The voice on the box said, "Five minutes."

"Is that for *us?*" the designer said. "Well, give me a pin."

"Please don't use a pin there—my partners have to catch me."

"Whoopsy. Harry, stitch. Frieda, can you baste that hem a little higher in back? Stand still, darling, leave the driving to us."

Hands kept tugging at her, adjusting. The voice on the box said, "Places, please. Curtain in three minutes."

"Will someone tell that bionic yenta to shut up?" The designer smoothed the dress down and frowned. "Harry, take this in an inch. My dear, have you been on a hunger strike or just jogging?"

Another voice said, "It makes a lump," and the designer asked for scissors. There was a snipping sound, a light sensation of pull and release. Steph felt oddly uninvolved, like an anesthetized patient in an emergency room.

"Frieda, stitch this and this." Hands patted at each *this*. "Darling, give us a little three-hundred-sixty-degree twirl."

Steph twirled. The designer, bent down on one knee, arched back to evaluate.

"Well, that should hold up, God willing. Just don't go near any magnets." He rose, touched her shoulder, kissed her on the cheek. "They're paging your flight—*bon voyage*."

Steph felt something more than hostility in the eyes that followed her. She felt forty girls in identical pink tights and twenty-year-old tutus envying a girl in a designer's green satin dress. She hurried from the dressing room, closed the door on the envy, ran to put the length of a corridor between herself and it.

The dress felt strange on her skin, like the hands of a last-minute partner who didn't know the role. Just as she reached to open the soundproof door that led to the wings, she heard something drop. It made a tiny, tinkling sound, clear as the fall of a penny.

She stopped.

A *pin*, she realized. One of the pins holding her together. "Oh, God . . ."

She crouched, eyes combing the gray concrete floor.

"Lose something?" Danny stood smiling down at her.

"I just lost my nerve and my memory and one pin."

He bent, picked up a pin, and held it out. "Here's your nerve. Where does it go?"

"Do you see anything loose or flapping?"

"Looks fine to me."

Steph peered down at her skirt, then over her shoulder at her moss-green fanny. "To hell with it. I'll just fly apart at the first pirouette."

Danny took both her hands. Steph wondered if he was at all aware of the crazy beating of her heart. She was very aware of his.

"*Merde*, Steph."

"*Merde*, Danny."

Their lips brushed. They pulled apart, saving the kiss for afterward, and Steph slipped into the wings. She picked her way through a twilight clutter of props: Giselle's cottage, Sleeping Beauty's pillared staircase, the puppet theater from *Nutcracker*, all canvas and flimsiness and broad paint strokes.

Dancers were warming up singly and in couples. Several sat in yoga posture on the floor, eyes shut. Frank Vandenburg, who was Ilonka's partner in the *Corsaire pas de deux* tonight, leaned against Petrouchka's bedroom, chewing a Milky Way candy bar.

Steph nodded a hello.

He didn't acknowledge her. She supposed Ilonka's friends were her enemies too, now.

She passed the control panel just off stage right. The chief electrician sat meticulously adjusting switches that seemed more complicated than anything on a jet plane. There were two black and white TV screens built into the console: one showed the stage with its curtain lowered, the other the conductor's podium, still empty. Just beyond the console Steph glimpsed a small room where stagehands sat around a table and slapped down playing cards and beer cans. They were shouting and they had a transistor radio blasting disco music.

David and Victor were standing in the front wing, limbering. She recognized them by their op-art unitards. She fixed a smile, prepared a hello. It froze on her lips.

"Will you shut up about the fifty fucking dollars?" David screamed, veins standing out taut in his throat.

The stage lights were blinking in some last-minute disorder. An electrician came scurrying across the stage, shoved Steph aside. Applause crescendoed in the house, welcoming the conductor. Victor shouted over it.

"What do you need it for tonight? Going to get laid?"

"I've had it with you." David touched his palms to the floor. He straightened. The make-up exaggerated his eyes to red coals of anger. "You're a pathological borrower. I'm telling every dancer in this company. You won't be able to borrow thirty-five cents for a Diet Pepsi."

A deep, dissonant chord thumped out of the orchestra pit. The curtain hissed up. David turned, arched his right foot, made his entrance.

"Watch out for that one," Victor whispered. "He's a real cunt tonight. *Merde*, sweetheart."

                    *   *   *

An uneasiness washed over Anna. Black remembered dread began pushing out from the back of her mind. She recalled a winter evening in Chicago when the sun set and Stephanie still had not come home; a morning pacing the corridor of a Minneapolis hospital while a surgeon operated on Steph's tonsils. She had felt helpless then and she felt just as helpless now.

There was nothing more she could do. No phone call, no argument, no begging or subtly dropped hint could alter what was about to happen on that stage. It was up to Steph now.

Anna sat exhausted and alone, unneeded, tensed forward in her seat, slightly out of line with the rows of profiles tipped with the faint glow from the orchestra pit.

The curtain whooshed up in darkness.

Anna waited, counting heartbeats, squinting, seeing nothing, hearing vague backstage murmurs.

Somewhere in the electrician's booth a switch was pushed. Light crashed onto the stage.

Anna lowered her fist from her mouth.

A tooth had drawn blood from her ring finger.

                    *   *   *

Victor kissed Steph, prepared with a deep *plié* and *jeté*'d smoothly onto the stage. The conductor was taking the score at a faster tempo than he had at rehearsal. The musical landmarks that she had fixed for herself, so clear and distinct on the piano, were barely recognizable in the still new and still confusing flow of orchestra color.

As a precaution she began counting the bars till her entrance: *eighteen, seventeen*...

"Well, well, big night for you," a voice cut in.

Steph whirled. It was Ilonka, sparkling in her *Le Corsaire* white and silver. She had drawn herself black tigress eyebrows that arched to her hairline. "I have a feeling you going to do well."

"Thank you," Steph stammered.

"Music is good, choreography is good, Victor and David are good—so, should be good."

Steph fought to keep her mind on the count (...*thirteen, twelve*...), fought to keep smiling, wished Ilonka hadn't picked this moment of all moments to be nice; or *was* she being nice?

"One thing—may I make suggestion? You don't mind?"

"No, no—please." (...*ten, nine*...)

"*Grand jeté*—before David catches you—you know the place?"

"Not exactly." (...*seven, six*...damn, had she missed a count or not?)

"It would work better if you—" Ilonka stopped short. "Ah! Better start listening to music, darling, or you will be late. *Merde!*"

Ilonka's eyes twinkled slyly behind an upraised hand and twinkling fingers. Steph's mind scrambled to remember whether she had four counts to go or three. Onstage, Victor and David were poised in one instant of symmetry to be broken by her entering *jeté*.

Three counts now or two?

A flute sparked up, four darting notes edged in harp, almost like the piane cue for three counts.

She trusted her instinct, *plié*'d, and on *three* she leapt.

The minute the light hit her eyes she felt she had missed something. It was like jumping into a safety net only to realize the firemen had whisked it away. She went through her *chaînés*, but something had been transposed. She was either wrong with the music or wrong with the stage. But which?

Her ears groped. She was aware of something more than the orchestra. At first it sounded like a scattered herd of cows. Then she realized the sound was booing. Faint, but still boos. Dimly, it occurred to her that Ilonka's fans were out there.

*My God, do they think I stole her role?*

She wrenched her mind back to the stage, back to the steps. David was passing her to Victor, gritting a smile. She slowed for her first retard.

The music didn't slow with her.

What was wrong with that conductor? The music was moving away from her, like a ferry slipping from the shore. She rushed her *bourrées*, trying to catch up, but the ferry wouldn't wait.

She was going to have to cut her pirouette—but would that throw Victor off when he caught her?

There was no choice. She tried to get his eye and warn him, but he was mouthing profanity at David. She fell toward him. His arms were there, waiting, not caring or even surprised. He didn't even look at her, he was too busy saying "Shit" to David.

The music surged forward and the conductor left out the second retard. Why the hell hadn't he come to rehearsal and learned the tempos? She realized she was going to have to follow the conductor. She squinted, trying to make out the blinking tip of the baton beyond the blinding arc of footlights. A firefly winked into visibility, swooped down and vanished.

She felt David's hands on her wrists, pulling her. This wasn't in the choreography! Then she realized he was pulling her into her *piqué en arabesque*, holding her, lifting her—moving her in a slow curve toward Victor. David set her down and she recognized the skittering figure in the strings. Her arm moved out toward Victor, her weight bent toward him, just as it should. His hands clasped her waist, just as they should.

She bent her legs, *plié*'d to lighten herself for the lift. But something was wrong, unfamiliar, she wasn't as light as she should have been. Victor was off balance and struggling, the lift was tilting—

It hit her that David was still holding on to her, not letting go.

"Bastard!" she heard Victor hiss and the answering hiss flew past her, "You started this war, you call it off."

She recentered her weight, trying to save the lift, but the movement was labored and unsteady and Victor set her down early.

"Will you two *stop* it?" she whispered.

David's head was tilted back, eyes half shut, lips slightly parted—the classic *danseur noble* in ecstasy. He turned and, perfectly on the beat, half lifted her.

"Sweetheart," he whispered, "Keep out of it. Two bitches are enough for this number." He set her down.

Now Victor half lifted her and she felt a pinch on her ass. "Don't worry," he whispered, "we'll get you through it."

David and Victor were pros, and they did just that.

\*    \*    \*

Anna's fingers relaxed their grip on the seat cushion. The ordeal of helpless watching was over. The gold curtain fell. The audience was applauding and the applause was building.

Some schmucks in the rear of the orchestra were booing. What did they know?

There were bravos in the family circle, bravos in the dress circle, bravos all around her. Anna let herself go quietly limp with relief.

The curtain rose again and Steph and her two partners came forward to take their bows. This was real applause, not just polite. The bravos were coming in avalanches. Anna settled back in her chair, smiling and weeping and too exhausted even to clap.

She waited, dazed, for the usher to bring out the bouquet. She'd bought an arrangement of red roses and lilies, thirty-five dollars' worth, and marked it *Deliver on stage*.

But what the usher brought out was not a bouquet and it was not red and white. It was a basket of black roses, so large he had to carry it in both arms and almost stumbled setting it down.

Black roses—perfect with Steph's moss-green dress. Now why hadn't Anna thought of that?

The press agent said, "Wow."

Anna craned forward in her seat. That basket had to hold a hundred dollars' worth of roses easily. Danny Gillette didn't have that kind of money. Who could have—?

A suspicion tugged at her.

She turned in her seat, eyes tracking the line of grand tier boxes.

The house lights were still down and the last box in the row was dark. Anna squinted and in the effort of her squinting a shadow seemed to shape itself in the rich, vibrating gloom, some crouching shape bent toward the railing.

She wondered if it could be her imagination. But the curtain lifted for another call and this time, in the reflected light, her eye picked out two hands clasping the rail, not applauding. Dimly she made out a jagged, high-beaked profile, a bald head.

The house lights came halfway up and the face turned suddenly toward her. A jolt went through her. This was not her imagination. Marius Volmar was here, here in the Metropolitan Opera House, staring down at her for one diamond-hard instant.

The gaze traveled back to the stage, to the little girl in moss green who curtsied and smiled and plucked from her bouquet two black roses and handed one to each of her partners.

Anna couldn't believe it. Her blood was singing like a victorious army. Marius Volmar had come back after all.

He had come back for her little girl.

* * *

The tickets cost a week's food budget, but Ray knew it was an important evening for Chris and he wanted to share it with her, so they sat in the grand tier for Steph's performance.

When the curtain fell Chris applauded wildly. Ray had not understood the ballet, but he wanted to make an informed comment. "Her arms," he said. "What do you call that movement—*port de bras*?"

Chris nodded, still clapping.

"Her *port de bras* was fantastic," Ray said.

"Her everything's fantastic," Chris said.

There was an avalanche of drinkers at the bar. It took Ray five minutes to get a ginger ale for Chris and a vodka for himself and when he turned around Chris was talking to a stranger. The young man was well built and handsome and he had the smile of a self-appointed god.

Ray's lips tightened. He didn't want strangers. Not tonight.

Chris reached out a hand to take her drink. "Ray, I'd like you meet a friend of mine—Wally Collins. Wally, this is Ray Lockwood, from my home town."

The men shook hands and Ray said, "I take it you're a ballet buff too?"

Chris's friend smiled. "You might say."

"What did you think of Stephanie Lang?"

"Incredible extension."

Ray tried to think what "extension" could mean.

"I didn't feel Danny used her extension at all," Chris said.

"Those *arabesques en air* weren't exactly *tiny*," her friend said, and then they were arguing, pleasantly, fluently, technical terms and French words spilling off their lips like running water.

Ray stood and listened and tried to make intelligent grunts. He saw that the young man's clothes had color and style and showed his body, and the body held itself with a rippling confidence. Ray was very aware that his own three-piece dark suit had no color, no style, did nothing to show his body.

"But could you believe those retards?" Chris's friend said.

"What retards?" Chris laughed.

Ray felt like a member of the audience, allowed to watch, allowed to applaud, not allowed to break into the dialogue. He pushed his way to the bar and ordered another drink to douse his irritation. He turned and stared at Chris. She was laughing and gesturing and as the intermission bell sounded she kissed her friend on the lips.

The vodka turned sour in Ray's stomach. He saw that he did not exist for Chris. The evening was lost time, lost money, lost effort.

Walking back to their seats, he said, "I take it that fellow's a pretty good friend?"

She caught something in his voice and looked up at him quickly.

He was still carrying his empty plastic cup and he crumpled it hard. He felt alone, suffocated, like a mole burrowing into darkness.

"What's the matter, Ray?"

He stopped and looked at her. He didn't know what he was

feeling and he didn't know if he could handle it. "You kissed him."

"Wally partners me," she said. "Didn't you recognize him?"

"No."

"And he's gay."

*He's gay and you love him,* Ray thought. *I saw.*

She touched him and hope sprang back, nagging at him that success was just one push away. Always just one push more.

"Come on," she said. "We'd better hurry."

# twenty-three

Even before the lights were up Anna was excusing her way past knees, pressuring a path out of the house before the intermission surge to the bar could block her or slow her, then not exactly running along the underground promenade but not exactly walking either, arriving a little out of breath at the stage door but not so out of breath she couldn't shout a "Hi!" and smile at the guard as she dropped into a chair to wait for her little girl.

In the old days—in her day—she could have talked her way past any guard in any house in New York, but nowadays—what with bomb threats and prop rip-offs and sopranos getting mugged in their own dressing rooms—why waste the breath? She took a copy of *Dancemagazine* from her purse, frowned at the Miss Nobody on the cover, skimmed ads, couldn't *believe* the price of leotards, what was going on, an Arab cotton embargo?

Suddenly the loudspeaker overhead sent out a staticky burst. Her eyes jerked to it. Her ears translated. Applause. They were still clapping in there. Hell, did she walk out on one of Steph's curtain calls?

"Anna—Anna, my dear."

She jumped.

Marius Volmar took her hand in his, bent down, came within a breath of kissing it, held it a moment.

She tried to collect herself. She'd heard that people aged but their voices didn't. In Volmar's case the manners hadn't either.

"You're looking very well, Anna. How are you?"

She tried to force some kind of reply up through her surprise. His cold, dignified distance of twenty years ago had turned no warmer. There still hovered about him a neatness that did not quite belong to the living.

"Why, Mr. Volmar—" she stammered.

She had prayed for this moment, planned for it, rehearsed it; but the reality caught her unprepared. Out of nowhere, the past was screaming in her ears, blotting out the present. She smelled a men's cologne—was it sandalwood?—that she had not thought of in all this time, and she realized now she had never forgotten it.

She sat silent, bursting with memory, hurting.

"May I sit?" He fixed a smile on her.

She glanced at the chair beside her. Empty. She tapped it. He sat. Still smiling. He'd smiled like that at her first *Lilac Garden*, and the smile had told her for sure she was a dancer. It was telling her something else now, something just as important.

"What a wonderful night this must be for you," he said.

"I'm loving it—but it's Steph's night." She laughed to ease her tension and the laugh felt girlish and false. "Steph did all the footwork. I just did the nagging." She shifted her purse in her lap.

"Then it's a wonderful night for both of you. May I be the first to say—congratulations?"

Come to think of it, he *was* the first. And she hadn't seen him come in, so he must have been here before her. Either it was a shorter walk from the grand tier, or he ran faster than she did. She began to see the outline of his intention.

"I'd be honored if you and Stephanie would join me for a glass of wine and a brief chat."

She pressed her hands down, keeping her purse still. "That's nice of you, Mr. Volmar, but Steph doesn't drink. Alcohol destroys muscle tissue."

"Ginger ale and a brief chat then?"

There. It wasn't just her imagination. He wanted Steph and

his wanting showed on the air like breath on a cold day.

"She's going to be tired. How brief is brief?"

"What I have to say won't take more than three minutes in a quiet place."

A voice in her whispered: *We've done it!*

"It's up to Steph." Anna picked up her magazine, wishing it wouldn't tremble so. She smiled—it was only polite to smile—and pretended to read. She wanted him to see she didn't care. He sat very still beside her. She could count each coiled tick of his mind.

Crowds flocked by. Dancers, reporters, hangers-on. And kept flocking by. She could see them glancing at Volmar, feel them wondering, *Who's that he's with?* Hands waved and voices shouted and there was almost a fight when a woman in sable tried to get by the guard without a pass.

And then Steph came through the security door, looking darling in her white rabbit hat, like a little Russian princess.

Anna called and jumped to her feet, arms outstretched in a big welcome-home.

"Mom!"

A flying kiss.

"Mr. Volmar." Handshake. "Thank you for those roses."

*And my lilies?* Anna wondered. Her smile froze when she saw who was with Steph: that Danny kid. He was hanging back a little, but even in shadow triumph glowed on him like a sun tan.

Steph turned, made introductions. The men batted compliments back and forth. It struck Anna as ridiculous, a dwarf trying to waltz with a giant. She pulled Steph to the side and whispered.

"Mr. Volmar wants to talk to us. Now. Private." Anna pointed with her eyes, leaving no doubt as to who wasn't included.

"But, Mom, I promised Danny—"

"Honey, this is important. Danny's a professional, he'll understand."

"But I can't just—"

Who was this Danny all of a sudden, some kind of fiancé? Anna looked at the boy and she didn't like what she saw. He was sharp. Jewish, she'd bet anything. Jewish *and* handsome, and those were the worst. He was trying to use her little girl.

"You *can* just. Mr. Volmar's waiting and he hasn't got all night, so say good-by to your friend."

Steph's eyes begged.

Impatience flared through Anna. Her whisper hissed, "You can see that kid *any* time!"

Didn't Steph see that in one swoop Volmar could leapfrog her over thirty ballerinas and three years' sweat? Sometimes—like right now—Anna wished she hadn't spoiled the child so. Okay, so it was Steph's big night, but there were a few things Anna could just call to Miss Overnight-Success's attention—like a career sacrificed and that drunk of a husband and twenty years' scrubbing floors and ironing shirts and pinching every penny and what for, to get talked back to by your own daughter in front of the whole ballet world?

"Do this for me." Anna's hands were coaxing on her daughter's shoulders. "Just this once. *Please?*"

Steph's face went through a tug-of-war. She was still wearing her stage lashes. She was too young for lashes offstage. She had perfect skin and they made it look breakable, like a doll's. Her eyes sighed.

"Danny, I'm sorry. I forgot. I promised I'd have a drink with Mom and Mr. Volmar. Would you mind if we put off our celebration till another night?"

Anna had never seen a human face collapse so quickly. Danny was wearing a smile like the window at Tiffany's, but when Steph said that it was as though a sledge hammer had smashed in the glass.

Anna grabbed Steph by the hand before anyone could start feeling sorry for the kid. "Good night, Danny," she called, edging the two of them through the mob toward the exit. "Terrific job, really terrific, it's a great *pas de trois!*"

*   *   *

"I care about you, Chris. And damn it, I try to care about dance. I try hard."

The apartment was almost dark. There was a lamp on the table by the sofa and it threw a pale glow on Chris's face. She was very pale and she looked up at Ray calmly.

"But you don't seem to realize there's a world out there with millions of people who don't dance or even know what a pirouette is."

"I know there are people like that," she said softly.

"They have lives too. A lot of them have good lives. Important lives. Happy lives." His eyes clutched at her face like fingers feeling out Braille.

"I know," she said.

"Don't you even *wonder* what other people's lives are like?"

"I know what other people's lives are like. I grew up with other people."

And suddenly all the injustices he had suffered began spilling out of him. "Damn it, Chris, I ought to be memorizing cases and decisions and instead I'm mememorizing names of steps and ballerinas and choreographers and it doesn't seem to make any difference to you."

Her eyes were blue and blank and blameless. "You don't have to memorize things for me."

"But I want to. I want to prove I care about the things you care about."

"Don't prove things, Ray. Please."

He sat down on the sofa beside her. His light brown hair had fallen across his forehead and he was breathing hard. He was thinking: *I'll dare to tell her. Maybe I'm not alone in my secret cave. Maybe in her heart she wants me too.*

"Chris—can't we have *something* together, just you and I?"

She stared at his handsome, pained face. "I thought—maybe we did," she whispered.

He reached a hand to stroke her and then he was gripping her shoulders and she could feel the strength in him holding itself back.

"Ray—don't—"

"Does it bother you to touch me?"

"No, but you're squeezing."

Without warning he pushed her back against the sofa. His mouth crashed roughly into hers. She tasted liquor and his probing tongue and suddenly everything was heat and motion and pain. She felt something jamming against her thigh and she knew it was his erection. Terror shot through her. This was sex, this ripping and clawing and liquor breath, this twisted face trying to smear itself against hers, these hands that bruised and crushed.

"No!" she screamed. With a desperate effort, she clawed her way free.

Silence thundered.

He was staring at her, a hand pressed to the red gash on his cheek. He swallowed. "I'm sorry, Chris. Very sorry. I guess we just don't understand each other." He got to his feet. "Are you okay?"

"I'm okay," she said in a voice that wasn't okay. Nausea and white, blinding panic were still spinning in her.

"I'll let myself out," he said, and a moment later she heard the front door close.

\*       \*       \*

They took a table at the café in Avery Fisher Hall. The marble and the boxwood made a corner that was almost private and Anna was finally able to catch her breath.

Volmar quizzed Steph about her teachers and Empire and Danny Gillette. Anna sipped and stirred her ginger ale and sipped and finally cut through the small talk.

"Mr. Volmar, you want Steph in your company, right?"

He turned toward her, slowly, and stared. Anna knew there was something she lacked, a knack of dressing or the right accent, something that made people...hesitate. So what?

"I mean that's why we're here, isn't it?"

"That's correct. I would like Stephanie in the company."

"Steph has had a long day." Anna placed a hand on Steph's. "And she's dead beat, and if we're going to talk contract, let's talk contract."

Volmar glanced thoughtfully at Steph. "Very well. Let's talk contract."

"What are you offering?"

"As far as money is concerned, I had in mind—"

"Money she can get anywhere." Anna felt light and springy, as though she were dancing on the tips of her toes. "First off, why should Steph give up a brilliant future at Empire to join NBT? What are you offering in the way of roles that she can't get from Lester Croyden?"

"Serious roles in serious ballets."

"Serious roles in the serious back row of the serious corps? No, thanks. She goes in as soloist."

"Very well. She goes in as soloist."

"I want it spelled out in the contract and I want a guaranteed minimum. You're not going to give her one Prayer in *Coppélia* and bury her."

"I can hardly spell out the solos when next season's repertory isn't even set yet."

All right, they'd haggle. Not because Anna intended to budge an inch, but because she understood men and she knew haggling was important to them. "I don't need the names, I need the number. And solo means she does her own footwork, hers and hers alone, no Ribbon Dances or four little swanlets."

"How many solos?"

While Anna was spelling out her conditions, she noticed something odd: there was no twinkle at the table, no twinkle in her little girl. It was as though Steph weren't there at all, but far away in some secret darkness, thinking thoughts of her own.

Anna winked, tried to catch her eye. *See what your mom's doing for you? Toughest agent in the business!*

"Really, Anna, ballet doesn't work like that."

"I got a lawyer who can *make* it work like that."

"Steph has great promise, but you'll forgive me for saying, she has a long way to go before she's a ballerina."

Steph's fingers lay on the cloth napkin, little and curling like the first tendrils of a vine. Anna touched them again.

"Fine. She'll go her long way at Empire. Come on, Steph."

Anna picked up her purse and made a move as though to rise. Volmar drew a deep breath of resignation, as though to let her, and a chill ruffled Anna's certainty.

"I accept your terms," he said, "on one condition. Stephanie must join NBT immediately."

"How immediately is that?"

"This week."

Anna couldn't believe it. The twenty years didn't matter. She had Volmar crawling. "What do you say, Steph?"

Steph had half turned away from the discussion. There was a quality in her voice that Anna had never detected before. "I'm sorry, Mr. Volmar."

*Dear God,* everything in Anna screamed, *she's not going to turn him down!*

"I'm awfully tired," Steph said. "I can't even think."

"Of course," Volmar said. "But you'll let me know—one of you—within the week?"

* * *

"What did I tell you?" Anna's heart was doing *fouettés* in her rib cage. "He loves you."

"I'm not ready for it, Mom."

"If Marius Volmar says you're ready, you better believe you're ready."

"Tonight I'm not ready for anything but bed."

"A cup of tea will do you good." Anna flagged a Checker cab and pushed Steph in first. They went to Anna's place.

They talked in the kitchen because it was in kitchens that all the important events of Anna's life had taken place. In a kitchen she could cope: the tools of survival were all there, copper-bottomed and shiny and neatly displayed. Steph fell into a chair. She looked white and slumped and used up. Anna filled the kettle, set it on the large burner so it would come to the boil fast.

"I heard those people whispering," Anna said. "'Who *is* she? Where did she *come* from? Why haven't we *seen* her before?' The critic from the New York *Post* doesn't understand why Empire's been hiding you all this time. He says it's a crime."

Steph bent down and pawed through her tote bag like a puppy digging up a bone. She came up with a cigarette, lit it. She looked like a little girl trying to act grown up. "Mom, I like it at Empire."

"Danny has a lot of talent, I agree. He'll go places—someday. But remember one thing: choreographers have a lifetime. Dancers haven't. A dancer has to make every second count."

"I want to do solos, but I want it to be with *this* company because—"

"Because you're in love with him."

"Because a dancer doesn't dance alone. A dancer creates with other dancers. Everyone at Empire from the youngest kid in the corps to the principals—we're collaborators. Mom, if I walked out on them after tonight—"

"You're not walking out. You have a better offer, you're moving up."

"If Empire had treated me badly, maybe I could. But they

haven't. Don't you see how it looks?"

"Okay, tell me. Tell me how it looks."

"It looks as though I squeezed Linda out of her role. It looks as though I used Danny and got him to squeeze Ilonka out. It looks as though I used the whole company and then threw them all away."

"You didn't have anything to do with Linda losing that role."

Steph gave her mother a sudden, long look. "You don't know that."

"I know dancers and I know this business. She lost that role on her own. And I'll tell you what it looks like if you stay with that company. It looks like you're an idiot."

"Then I'll look like an idiot. You can't just snap off a collaboration like a stick of celery."

"Forget the celery. Just don't throw away this opportunity. The top man in ballet wants you and he wants you on *your* terms. You'll never get this chance again."

Steph was silent. Anna could tell she was thinking. It made Anna afraid when Steph thought like that.

"If he wants me tonight," Steph said, "he'll want me next year."

"Honey: there are eighty good ballet schools in this country and they're turning out two dozen girls a day who could dance pirouette *piqués* around Anna Pavlova. You have competition, real competition, and it's going to get worse. So don't kid yourself. Don't do what I did. Don't throw away your one chance because you think you're in love."

"Stop comparing you and me. We're not the same."

It was one-thirty in the morning and Anna Lang was sitting on a straight-backed kitchen chair. She was suddenly aware of time, not just the hour but the years that stretched back and back and could not be stopped from stretching forward. She sat silently, her face turned away from the person whom for nineteen years she had called a daughter. Her eyes were staring into that dark future that she would enter in a moment, alone, as soon as she had collected the shattered bits of her strength and glued them together again.

She did not say that all her life she had been picking up pieces that other people had smashed.

She did not say that there would soon have to come a time

when glue could not hold shattered glue.

The shaking of her shoulders whispered it, the hands hugging her sides screamed it.

Her daughter watched and felt rotten and cruel. Steph wanted to touch the thin cotton protecting those bent, trembling shoulders.

"It just isn't fair," Anna said. "Sure, you have to do what you want and I'm not going to stop you. But they're a lousy nowhere company and Volmar's offering you—"

"What's he offering me? What's so great about NBT?"

"If he'd made that offer to me twenty years ago, I'd be a star today. Sure I'm jealous. I admit it. What I wouldn't give to be your age and in your place . . . there's nothing I wouldn't give. And to see you throwing it away like it was garbage—it's like you're spitting on *me*."

"You don't mean that, Mom."

Anna fought the temptation to weep. She would not be shameless in front of her own daughter. Instead she folded herself together, neat and brave, and allowed herself a little pain. She ached because she was a mother and because she had done her best. She ached for the youth that was gone and the chances that had vanished with it. But most cruelly of all she ached for this child who would not believe her.

"I'm Anna Boborovsky Lang and I say what I mean! It may be stupid but I say it and I mean it and if only once, just once, you'd *listen!* Doesn't a mother have a right to be listened to?"

"I've been listening."

"You've never listened. Never. What's the use? Do what you want. I love you but I can't do a damned thing to stop you."

*     *     *

Chris looked up from the sofa as Steph came into the living room. She pushed the tangled hair out of her eyes and tried to blink herself awake. "I didn't expect you," she said groggily.

Steph stared at her. "Are you all right?"

Chris pushed herself into a sitting position. "I'm fine. I just dozed off watching TV." Too late, she realized the TV wasn't on. She saw Steph's brow furrow.

"Is that a bruise?"

"Where?"

"On your neck."

Chris glanced down. Steph was looking at her oddly and it took her a moment to realize what the look meant. *She thinks I made love with Ray.*

Steph went to the phone and Chris heard her make an excuse to Danny about not coming over. *Sex is easy for Steph,* Chris thought. *She can handle it. If I tell her what happened tonight she'll think I'm a baby. I'll just say we loved her ballet.*

"I thought you'd be with Danny," Chris said. But she thanked God Steph was here, at home.

"I thought so too," Steph said.

Chris sensed something very much amiss. She said what a wonderful performance it had been and Steph said, sighing, "It could have been much better."

*She sounds just like me,* Chris thought. "But you were perfect!"

"It would have been ten times better with Ilonka. I'm just not on her level. I don't have her extension, I don't have her triple spin, I don't have anything...."

Chris watched Steph flop into a chair. "Steph, what's bothering you?"

"Everything. Danny, my mother, my job..."

Chris had never seen Steph helpless or glum or confused before. It made her feel needed and she forgot herself in a sudden surge of purpose, like a fleet of white corpuscles rushing toward an infection. "I'll make some hot chocolate and why don't you tell me about it?"

Chris made cocoa and Steph sat staring at the steam wisping up from her cup.

"It's all such a screwed-up tangle."

Chris took a tiny, scalding sip of cocoa. "Why aren't you spending the night with Danny? Tonight of all nights?"

"I couldn't look him in the face." Steph explained she'd had an offer from NBT and Chris bit back a little yelp of happiness.

"Chris, he could have had Ilonka Banska, it would have made him, and he gave up his chance for me. And now my mother wants me to drop Empire and move to another company."

*We'd be together,* Chris thought. *I'd have a friend.*

"That's like—" Steph seemed to fumble for words. "That's kicking the ladder over when you've reached the top. It's using Danny and dropping him."

Chris did not answer. It was better to let all the doubt and bitterness spill out.

"All my life," Steph said, "everything I've ever wanted—really wanted—my mother keeps taking it from me. I feel like a little kid at a birthday party playing pin the tail on the donkey. My mother blindfolds me and spins me again and suddenly I don't know where I am and I have to start looking all over again...."

After a moment Chris said softly, "She's only trying to help. She loves you, Steph."

"I've had her help and I've had her love up to *here*. If she doesn't ease up, I swear I'm going to hate that woman."

*She doesn't mean that,* Chris thought. "Would you rather have parents who didn't care?"

"God, I'd give anything. Just to be left alone. Just to be allowed to make my own decision *once.*"

*Funny,* Chris thought, *I'd give anything to have a parent who cared—even a parent like Mrs. Lang.*

Steph was looking at her, a blush of guilt fleeting across her face. "Chris, I know those parents of yours break your heart—but believe me, in the long run you're better off. You're traveling light."

"What if—you don't *want* to travel light? Steph, you don't know how it is. You buy tickets for them and the tickets are still at the box office after your premiere. Your father cancels at the last moment because of a board meeting he knew about a year ago. Sometimes there are flowers with a note someone else wrote, sometimes there isn't even a phone call. When your parents don't care you're more alone than anyone else in the world. Even a Danny can't make up for it."

Steph crossed her arms and laid her head down on the table. At first Chris thought she had passed out but then she saw the sighing rise and fall of the shoulders.

"Maybe you're right, Chris." The voice came muffled and thick. "But it doesn't help. What am I going to *do?*"

Chris thought a moment. "Decide what you want and just do it."

"I don't *know* what I want."

"You have time. You'll make up your mind. And whatever you choose—Danny loves you and your mother loves you. They'll accept it. That's what love is."

"I wish I could believe the world was like that."

Chris reached a hand and touched her. "Don't worry about it now, Steph. Sleep on it. You'll do the right thing."

## twenty-four

---

The next day Danny had good reviews in all three papers. Steph was glad for him. But the *Times* slapped her and that hurt. "Not a Banska by any stretch." The *Post* called her "adequate" and the *Daily News* didn't mention her.

"What do critics know?" Anna said. "You got the review that counts: Volmar."

After the performance Steph went to Danny's apartment. There was a longing to their love-making that she had never known before. There was passion but it was the passion of sadness. It was as though their bodies knew that this was their last time.

Afterward they pulled apart and she lay staring at their nakedness, smooth and strong and dancer-white.

"What's wrong?" Danny asked.

She was wondering if they would ever be this way again. "Nothing."

"Forget how to smile? You use these muscles—and these—" His lips skimmed her mouth.

"Will you tell me something honestly?" She sat up. "Did you drive Ilonka out of *Lacrymosa* on purpose?"

He stared at her. Something edged out of his expression, as

though a door had closed. "I didn't drive her out of it."

"You could have kept her. She wanted the role. It would have made your career."

"She was wrong for it."

"Was she, Danny? Do you really believe that?"

"It's my ballet. I know what's right for it and I know what's wrong."

"And I was right for it?"

"Yes."

"There wasn't any other reason?"

He stared at her a long moment. "No other reason would have mattered."

"It does matter. You gave up your chance for me."

"I didn't give up anything. Ilonka will hate me for a season and then it will all be forgotten."

"But will Empire ever let you do another ballet?"

"If they don't I'll go somewhere else. But that's a long way off."

"Danny—it's not a long way off for me. NBT has offered me a position."

She felt a terrible stillness flowing out of him.

"Are you taking it?" he asked.

She didn't know. That was the dreadful thing. She reached her hand toward his, hoping he would touch it, hoping his touch would tell her what the answer should be. "I want to be with you," she said.

"Then what's the problem?"

She tried not to cry. She wanted to say, *I wish there was some way I could have you and the other job too*. But suddenly she was crying, tears pouring down from under her eyelids. She took his hand and squeezed it hard as though she could wring an answer from it. *Danny*, she wanted to say, *help me, I'm so scared this will be the end*.

He listened to her crying and he didn't move, he didn't speak. There was no gesture, no hint, no help. If only he would put his arms around her, touch her, look at her . . .

She felt some terrible harm about to happen, already happening.

"They're a better company," she said. "The only decent thing at Empire is you. Hannah Meredith is a bumbling socialite.

Heinrich is a hack. Lester is a twit. All they do is mount museum pieces."

The reasons were real enough but they sounded obvious and dumb, like excuses. They fell into silence. For a long while Danny said nothing. He seemed to be staring down an empty road.

Finally he said, "Companies change. Empire could change. You and I could change it."

She loved him for believing that but she knew it was only a dream. "A dancer's life is so short, Danny. All we have is five, ten years."

"What makes you think you'd do better at NBT?"

"I'd be working with artists."

"Volmar hasn't done an original work in twenty years."

"But he's an artist. And he wants me."

Danny looked at her. "I want you. I'm an artist."

Why couldn't he understand? Why did he have to act as though she were asking the impossible? "But Volmar has a company."

"And I don't. I see." He shook his head, not seeing, not yielding. Refusing.

The realization hit her like a bottle crashing on her skull: there was truth to her mother's harping. Danny *did* expect her to give up her chance, he *did* believe he came first. She did not know whether this greed was typical of all men or peculiarly Danny's. But it was there in the dark room with them, a third presence breath-takingly physical.

She tried to be patient. She tried to explain. "Danny—you're a soloist. You ought to be a principal. Everything at Empire is political. Who's getting reviews, who's sleeping with who, who owes who what. They're not trying to develop you as a choreographer. They're trying to cash in. That's all they're interested in. They didn't stage your ballet because it was good. They staged it because you got a review. Suddenly you were a star. Do you think, without that review, they'd have even noticed you?"

"Frankly, yes. In time."

"At Empire it takes too much time. It takes your whole life. And then some girl in the corps gets her picture on the cover of *Vogue* and Hannah Meredith smells publicity and jumps her up to principal and they fire a real principal to make room for her."

"That's only happened once. With Peggy-Anne."

"It would never happen at NBT. Danny, it could happen to anyone at Empire. You, me, Ilonka."

"Who said ballet was a welfare state?"

The atmosphere in the room had turned argumentative. She felt her voice rise a cutting notch. "All right—maybe dance isn't a welfare state—but at least it ought to be an art!"

His face wrinkled like a bunched-up fistful of sheet. "Art? Jesus Christ, you talk like one of those girls who grew up watching reruns of *Red Shoes*."

He was trying to hurt her, but she knew that was only because she had hurt him. She didn't care. "One day I *will* be an artist."

"Artist?" he exploded. "The two of you are old masters already."

She looked at him with baffled eyes. "What are you talking about?"

"Your mother sets me up. You deliver the punch. That's real timing. You two are a team."

She shook her head, not knowing what he meant, knowing it was false.

"You know something? You had me convinced, Steph. I believed you. You know what's stupider? I believed *in* you."

"Danny—I never lied to you."

"Not in words. That's for sure. But you're pretty accomplished at non-verbal lying."

He got up, strode from the bed. He turned, naked and silent in his accusation. She felt dirty. She sat in the darkness, numb and chilled, her heart pounding. She could not look at him. She stared down at her feet. Dancer's feet. Arched and strong. And at this moment useless. Troublemakers. She couldn't find words. She sat still for a moment and then she rose and walked very slowly till she was standing within touching distance of him.

"Danny—I love you."

He stood motionless, walled into his anger. "Sure. Sure you do. Likewise. It's been a pleasure."

"You don't think I pretended!"

His face was turned away. He was dead to her.

"Danny, I begged you to let Ilonka dance that role!" If only he would touch her, make some move of reconciliation: she didn't want Marius Volmar, she didn't even want dance, all she wanted was for Danny Gillette aka Goldberg to tell her to stay with him.

But he didn't.

Words she didn't want to hear came spitting from him.

"Sure you begged. Right over there in the sack." He was hunched and heavy-shouldered, like a cornered bull.

"I was honest with you right from the beginning!"

"With a mother like that, you don't need to tell lies. Or stick knives in other people's backs. She does it all for you."

"My mother has nothing to do with this! It's *my* decision! I love dance and I love you, and if I want to go to the best company, that's my choice, and if you want to make some kind of conflict out of it—"

"If *I* want to make a conflict out of it?"

"Well, you *are!* I'll be dancing solos—principals—good ballets—if you loved me you'd *want* me to do well—just the way I want *you* to do well!"

"Sure you want me to do well."

She had never heard such a voice before. Not from Danny. It had dropped to a hiss. What it lacked in full breath it made up in venom.

"Thanks to you, I haven't got a friend left in the corps. There's not a soloist or a principal who'll talk to me. Lester and Hannah will probably cancel my contract next spring. As my yiddishe momma used to say about people like you, with a friend like that, who needs enemies?"

The whole situation had gone violently wrong. She couldn't understand. All she had wanted was to ask his advice and instead, suddenly, they were fighting and his lips were twisted like a half-healed scar and his face was an ugly red lie and his mind was made up and hers was just as made up as his.

"I *never* tried to use you, Danny!"

"Because I was dumb enough to volunteer. Well, now I am *un*-volunteering! So why don't you just get your shit together and stuff it in your tote bag and get the hell out of my life?"

He snatched her clothes from the chair and her tote bag from the floor and sent them crashing against the wall. There was a flurry of spilled change and scampering cat and then only the ticking of the clock.

Steph did not move. Instinct told her everything was lost. There was nothing to do now but wait and be sure he had used up all the violence in him. When she could hear his breathing slow she gathered her clothes and what her fingers could detect along the floorboards of her scattered small possessions.

She dressed as fast as she could but her movements had an exasperating underwater slowness. She heard his breath coming in gasps, trying to shape more words, more hate. She didn't want words. She didn't want light. She didn't want to see him. She wanted speed. She felt unmoored, lost, with only one direction to guide her: *out.*

She kept her eyes busy with buttons and pennies and lipstick cases and the clasp of her bag. She did not want to see if he was watching or if there was anything in his hand. Humiliation and emptiness drummed in her and with them an awareness that the moment was dangerous, it must be crossed quickly.

She sped across the room and shut the apartment door quietly and went down the three flights of stairs two steps at a time.

As she ran toward West End Avenue to look for a cab, tears stung her eyes.

*     *     *

Chris was fighting her nightly losing battle with insomnia when a sound made her start. She recognized the scrape of a key probing the front-door lock. *That couldn't be Steph,* she thought, *it's much too early. Someone's trying to break in!*

Her heart thudded and she debated whether she had time or courage to make a dash for the telephone. Just as she slipped one foot out of bed she heard the door bang open and shut. There was a stumbling in the other room.

A *junkie*, she thought. *Dear God...*

A light went on and Steph stood in the bedroom doorway, out of breath and disheveled, as if someone had tried to attack her. And succeeded.

Chris snapped on the bedside light. "Steph—what's happened?"

"I'll be okay—I just—" The voice had all the life squeezed out of it.

A fist of ice grabbed Chris's heart. Steph staggered to her bed and sat down. For a long moment she stayed slumped over some private pain, white and shaking, and then she looked up.

"Is there any vodka left?"

*What's wrong?* Chris thought. *Steph doesn't drink.* "There's a little—but we haven't got anything to put with it."

"Just an ice cube will be fine."

Chris fixed the drink, hurried back to the bedroom, and watched Steph down half the shot in a swallow. *This isn't Steph,* Chris thought, *coming home at two in the morning, belting back straight vodka.*

"Steph, you'll make yourself drunk."

"The sooner the better." Steph sat gazing at the vodka and then at Chris and finally she said, "It's over. Danny and I are through."

There was a long sighing silence. Chris felt a stab of surprise and then a rush of unthinking empathy. "Oh, Steph, I'm sorry."

"I feel numb. I can't believe it. I can't understand *why.*"

Chris sat beside her and Steph leaned against her shoulder and shut her eyes.

"We argued. Like two trains coming at one another on the same track. He wouldn't stop and I wouldn't stop. It was stubborn and ugly and stupid and neither of us wanted a collision but it happened."

"But if neither of you wanted it, can't you apologize?"

Steph smiled sadly. "There's no way. A wreck's a wreck. It's over."

She described the argument. Chris listened, feeling sympathy but feeling something else too. A strength was flowing back into her, strength she hadn't felt for weeks. *Steph needs me now. I'm not alone.*

"So it looks as though I'll be joining NBT." Steph frowned at her glass as though it had cheated her. "Funny, liquor gets you drunk when you don't want to be, and when you do—forget it."

"Do you want another?"

"No. Full day tomorrow at Empire. Even if I am about to walk out on them." Steph slipped out of her dress and moved toward the bathroom. Her steps lurched, as though one leg had grown two inches longer than the other. There was a quality about her that shocked Chris. It wasn't that Steph was drunk:

anyone could drink. But she was shattered and gutted, like a bombed-out city.

Defeated.

Chris couldn't believe it. She tried to think of something reassuring, something Steph would say if the roles were reversed.

"It'll work out, Steph. You'll see."

Steph turned and squinted at her. "You sound just like me."

"I don't care who I sound like," Chris said firmly. "It's going to work out because you're going to *make* it work out."

Steph stared a moment, then lurched to Chris and hugged her. "Bullshit but thanks."

"And, Steph—it'll be like the old days, when we were in school. We'll be working together again."

*The old days,* Steph thought, *when we knew how to believe, when nutcrackers were princes and swans were really enchanted princesses. . . .* How comfortable those old days seemed.

Steph smiled. "Remember the promise we made each other? That silly promise?"

Chris nodded. "Now it's come true."

# twenty-five

NBT was the worst mistake of Steph's life.

On her second day, as she came into the dressing room, she couldn't help overhearing the conversation.

"...complete operator. Steer clear."

"What did she *do?*"

"What didn't she do! She had Linda axed, she got Ilonka axed—"

"Ilonka!"

"Can you believe? And she walked all over Danny and dropped him. Linda says don't go near her—*ne touchez pas*—poison."

The girls saw her and suddenly it was so quiet Steph could hear Kleenex blotting cold cream. No one looked at her directly but eyes followed her in the mirror. It was a long aisle with dressing tables on both sides and she had to walk all the way to the end.

The hostility was so tangible she almost tasted it. Not just that day but every day. No one in the company talked to her. Except Chris, who always smiled when they met in the corridors or in class and asked how she was doing.

257

"I thought you were exaggerating," Steph said, "but, God, they're cliquish."

There was something sad in Chris's nod.

"I don't see how you kept your sanity," Steph said. "It's like persecution. They're really shits—every damned one of them."

"Two or three aren't."

"I sure haven't met them. This morning I was practicing a leap into arabesque. A half dozen girls were watching and they saw I needed help. But not one of them told me what I was doing wrong."

Chris shrugged. "You'll get used to it."

When Chris was busy Steph's only company at lunch was a book or magazine and the silent stares of strangers. At NBT she felt something she had never before experienced.

She felt hated.

She lived in terror of company class. Discipline hung in the air like tear gas. There was no late arriving, no early leave-taking; no hanging on to the piano instead of the barre; no chatting, no sitting-this-one-out; worst of all, no smiling. Every minute was work and sweat and *ouch*.

There were certain mannerisms to the style of any company, and Chris drilled Steph in NBT's.

"Space your fingers evenly," Chris corrected.

"I thought I did."

Chris smiled and shook her head. "At NBT *even* means all the time—whether you're taking a fish dive or leaping into the wings."

Watching herself in the mirror of the deserted studio, Steph did a pirouette with arms in low second. It didn't make sense, but somehow the spaced fingers completed the line of the upper body and the entire movement seemed just a touch more graceful.

"And when you come down from your *relevé*, do it with a tiny hop." Chris demonstrated.

"Why?" Steph said.

"You'll look lighter."

Steph tried it, and to her surpise she looked as though there were twenty pounds less of her.

"And when you jump, always begin on the upbeat."

Steph jumped, beginning on the accented *"and"* that dancers were trained to hear in their heads before the first beat of the measure. The result was a surge of movement, quick and clean as the flick of a scalpel.

"My God," Steph said, "how many other tricks do they teach you?"

Other NBT mannerisms were harder to pick up. For one thing, the speed of the company was frightening, and she found herself writhing in the coils of impossibly fast tempos. Dance masters invariably singled her out.

"You there—a bit more on top of the beat, couldja?" or "You in baby blue—don't drag so hard."

The tones of voice ranged from kindly bitchery to bitchy kindness, but the undertone was always there, the hint that she didn't really belong.

And, in a way, she didn't.

The virtuosity of NBT's dancers was of a level demanded only of principals at Empire. The entire company, from corps on up, could do double turns in the air, effortlessly. They could all do double, even triple *fouettés*.

All of them except Steph. Her body was so unaccustomed to the demands put on it that her life began to feel like one uninterrupted wince. Bunions erupted on her feet where there had never even been blisters before. She spent a fortune on sterilized lamb's wool, packing her toe shoes against disaster.

"You'll get used to it," Chris said. "It took me awhile too."

Steph got used to it—the way a sick body gets used to inoperable cancer. She ceased being surprised at the pain.

Until the day that Marius Volmar gave company class.

*       *       *

Freddy Branson, an aging principal who had been with NBT twenty years, had taken the dancers through most of the barre work when the door opened and Marius Volmar strode into the room. He stood watching a moment, hands on hips, and allowed the dancers to finish their combination. Then, with a sharp nod, he indicated that he was taking over.

He stared down the barres. His gaze took in Steph for one

hollow moment, then moved on.

"You've learned how to take class," he said, "now you'll learn how to dance."

He wasn't looking at her, but Steph felt her face flush. She knew the remark had to be aimed at her. A flutter of glances said that the others knew it too.

Volmar barked out the remainder of the barre. "Go to the center, adagio, please. You all look like machines dancing."

Steph flushed again, knowing she was his target. His eyes followed her through the adagio and pirouette combinations. During the *petit allegro* she kept her movements fluid and lyrical, maintained her turn-out. Volmar snapped his fingers to the beat. The noise was staccato, insulting, like something aimed at a waiter.

"Up to tempo, please."

Behind her, Ellis whispered, "This is the *petit allegro,* honey, not the adagio. If you can't move your ass, at least get out of *my* way."

By the time they reached the *fouettés,* she was dizzy from trying to pull herself up to the beat.

"Stop!"

The dancers froze. The pianist's hands recoiled in mid-phrase from the keyboard. The entire class was silent now, all heads turned to Volmar. His eyes raked the class and came to a stop at Steph. The skin of her arms and face began to burn.

Volmar clapped his hands, spanking out the beat. "Single, single, single, double. Single, single, single, double. We'll do it till we get it."

They did it over and over. It was a hellish combination. The other dancers were perfect, but Steph kept flubbing her double. Each time she flubbed, Volmar had the entire class start again.

At the end of eighteen minutes the dancers were exhausted, hanging off the barres. Volmar gave a wave, silencing the music. He lit a cigarette, stared at the dancers. His eyes were a paralyzing mixture of contempt and disgust.

*"Grande révérence."*

The dancers bowed. He turned his back, walked swiftly from the room, and slammed the door.

Silence dissolved into muttering. Dancers threw Steph glances. Their eyes said, *What are you doing here anyway? Why don't you go work in the corner?* She fumbled with her bag, wishing she were tiny, invisible, dead. Never in her life had she felt such humiliation.

Until Volmar's next class.

\* \* \*

He peered in her direction and she sensed a shaft of malice sliding through his smile, clear as sunlight through a stained glass window.

"Miss Lang—one moment, please."

That was all. She waited. He turned his back. He whispered with the ballet master. He beat time for the accompanist, indicating the tempo of a passage. He joked with several of the principals.

Steph stood shivering at the barre, needing to get out of her damp clothes. In chattering twos and threes, the other dancers left. Some of them glanced at her, but most were above showing any sort of curiosity. Chris saw the look on her face and stopped to throw out a hurried whisper of encouragement.

"He's not a monster—he only acts like one."

"I feel more than an act brewing. Chris, I'm still such a *schlep* in class!"

"He's probably going to whisk you upstairs and give you a solo."

Chris smiled and waved and then Steph and Volmar were alone in the domed emptiness of the studio. He had propped a score open on the top of the upright piano and was bent over it, tongue poking mountains of dissatisfaction in his cheek.

Steph pulled a wad of paper towels from her tote bag and sopped the moisture off her neck and arms, reached under her blouse to pat the goose flesh dry. Hopeless. She put on her wristwatch, wondered if he'd forgotten she was there, finally worked up the courage to clear her throat.

"Mr. Volmar—"

He raised a hand, silencing her. "In a moment."

And kept her waiting three minutes more.

Abruptly, he closed the score, tucked it under his arm, and with a glance at her went to the door. She stood shivering in speechless amazement.

"Come along." He was holding the door, frowning as though she were a stupid puppy. "We haven't all day."

She followed him to the elevator, through the third-story corridors. He made no allowance for her toe shoes; she had to run to keep up. He unlocked the door of his office, gestured her in.

"Make yourself comfortable. But don't sit in the leather chair—you're sweaty."

All the chairs in the office were leather. Except one. It was wooden, slatted and uncomfortable, something out of a high school auditorium. It did not belong in a room of glass and chrome and leather and signed Chagall lithographs. She speculated that he kept it there especially for occasions like this.

She sat, winced as the slats pinched, shifted. And waited.

With maddening slowness Volmar prowled the bookshelves, exploring till he found a suitable hole to slide the score into. Steph's muscles began to cramp. She shifted. Volmar went through an unhurried ritual of cleaning his pipe, stuffing it with tobacco from a leather pouch, lighting it.

"Mr. Volmar—if you're not in any rush—maybe I could come back? I really need to shower."

His eyes fixed her over the match flickering at the rim of the pipe bowl. "I am not interested in your hygienic problems."

Something in him goaded her. "Mr. Volmar, I *have* to be interested in them."

He glanced up as though she had suddenly made him curious. "I should like to see how you move."

"You've seen how I move."

"That was not movement. That was class. I am contemplating a minor ballet—very minor. And within this very minor ballet I am contemplating a very minor role for a female of your physique."

"Thank you."

He stared at her. His nose wrinkled. "What an absurd thing to say. You know nothing about the role—I haven't even decided whether to use you or not. And you sit there and thank me."

She wanted desperately to say something polite. "I mean thank you for considering me."

"I am considering your physique." After a long search he

took out another score. "Do you play the piano?"

"I never had time to learn."

He handed her the score anyway. "Anton Arensky—Suite for Two Pianos. The waltz. Last movement."

"Mr. Volmar, I don't read music."

"How can a dancer not read music? Music is the floor you walk on."

"I've had solfège. I can tap rhythms and I can sing with movable *do*. But I can't read a piano score. I can't read anything more complicated than a melody."

"Can you listen?"

"I'm an expert listener."

His eyebrows arched. "Then listen expertly to this, please."

He put a record on the phonograph. The piano music was babbling, busy, smoothly gossipy. There were too many notes. He lifted the needle at the end of the cut, let silence drift through the room.

"Well? What did you hear?"

"I heard a waltz."

"And did you like it?"

She had not liked it and she couldn't believe he liked it either. But she was not going to be goaded into thinking out loud, not with a role at stake. "Mr. Volmar, you told me you're choreographing the music. I tried to imagine it as dance."

"Ah—what a gift. You imagined my choreography."

"That isn't what I meant."

"It's what you said. You intrigue me, Miss Lang. Show me what you imagined. Don't be shy. Perhaps I can use it."

She couldn't answer. She couldn't move.

"Come now. You've heard the music; you've imagined the choreography. Show me."

She got to her feet. "Am I partnered?"

"Forget the partner. Do your own variation."

He put the record on again. She improvised. She tried to catch what she heard: the cascading inner voices, more meaningful as blur than as music; the thinly pretty melody dressed up as a symphonic beauty; above all the swooping retards, the grandly hesitant rubatos. What she attempted was not parody: the music was dead serious. She tried to exaggerate a little girl's dream of balletic prettiness.

He stopped her in the middle of it. "Enough." His eyes met hers, pricked with light like the tips of scalpels. "Do you fancy yourself a lyrical dancer?"

*He hates me,* she realized. *Absolutely hates me.*

"Not especially," she said.

"Do you fancy yourself a dancer?"

"Not yet."

He considered her one endless moment. "Studio 5—eleven-thirty sharp tomorrow."

\*   \*   \*

Knowing Volmar was an ogre for promptness, Steph arrived at studio 5, warmed up and ready, at eleven-twenty. Sergio Moritz, one of the older principals, was doing stretches at the barre.

"Good morning," he called.

Steph hung back for one instant of speechless surprise. It was customary at NBT, as at Empire, to save time by rehearsing alternate casts simultaneously, but she hadn't bothered to look at the cast sheet and it had never occurred to her that Volmar would use Sergio even as a cover. One of Volmar's charity cases, Sergio had been with the company a quarter century. He was now so hobbled by tendonitis and arthritis, there were days he couldn't get up on *demi-pointe* to pirouette. He did character and mime roles, non-dance parts, and from time to time gave a company class.

Sergio glanced up at her from a *plié*. "The first new Volmar in thirty years," he grunted. "Do you know anything about it?"

"Only that it's a waltz."

She caught a wince scurrying across his face. He shot up from the *plié* like a diver surfacing for air. His face was suddenly skeleton-white. *Either he's pinched a nerve,* she thought, *or he's very scared of waltzes.*

The studio door swung open and Carla Morris, a soloist with the company, came bounding in. "Hi, everyone. My, my—*two* pianos. Aren't we fancy!" Carla was a Minnesota blonde, and she had what was known as the Volmar body. Tall and flexible almost to the point of being overextended, she looked as though she belonged in tennis clothes, not leg warmers. And acted it.

Her smile was casual and cordial, but Steph sensed Carla sizing her up. One of them would dance the role at the premiere—create it—and the other would cover in case of sickness or injury. The rehearsals were, among other things, elimination tryouts. Steph and Carla were rivals, though for the moment Carla was spreading a cover of smiles and chatter over her steel.

Wally Collins was the next to arrive. He shot a cheerful round of hellos, got down on the floor to limber his hips. Steph hardly dared hope, but wouldn't it be wonderful if she got Wally as a partner: he'd make anyone look like a ballerina. The two rehearsal pianists came in and as they began practicing Wally made a face at the music. "Yech! Sugarplum syrup!"

On the dot of eleven-thirty Volmar arrived with Tanya Merrill, an ex-ballerina who coached for the company and, it was whispered, had once had an affair with him.

"Good morning. We will listen to the music." Volmar signaled the pianists with a nod.

The waltz finished in a cloudburst of silvery tinkles. Volmar slipped out of his black velvet jacket, slung it over a barre. He rolled up the sleeves of his plaid lumberjack shirt, rubbed his hands together.

"Carla, you will dance there—with Wally."

Stephanie's heart shriveled to a hard nut.

"Stephanie, you will dance there, with Sergio. Now, imagine, please."

He half talked, half demonstrated the choreography. He moved like an ex-dancer, a man who had once been good, still surprisingly graceful in his ability to suggest moves rather than dance them full out.

Gradually, Steph began to glimpse the kind of ballet Volmar had in mind. It frankly surprised her. She had been brought up to think of Marius Volmar as a serious man, a Picasso, a Stravinsky of the dance; and here he was blocking a cutesy piece of fluff.

A tough piece of fluff, too.

It was with the lifts that the real trouble came. Sergio couldn't lift Steph on time or high enough or steady enough, he couldn't set her down on time, and he was way late, gasping for breath on the second lift. She looked down at his hands on her waist. They were pink and wrinkled and trembling and it made her sorry to see that the nails were manicured.

By the end of the rehearsal, Volmar had blocked out the first half of the ballet, and Steph's lifts still didn't work.

Carla's were beautiful.

# twenty-six

Volmar did not come to the next rehearsal.

Tanya took over the coaching. She pointed to white masking tape that had been laid in strange geometric shapes on the floor, like cubist voodoo. "Be careful not to dance inside these spaces."

"Why not?" Carla asked, squirming out of her leg warmers.

"Because that's where the pianos will be."

Steph had never seen pianos with quite so many bends and curlicues. And the spaces were much too large. "I thought there were just two pianos," she said.

Tanya gave her an irritable look. "There *are* just two pianos and keep your asses out of the spaces, okay?"

Steph felt uneasy. It wasn't just the oddity of the tape marks: there were details Tanya didn't seem to remember of Volmar's choreography. She asked Carla, "Didn't Tanya move those *châinés*?"

Carla shrugged. "Who cares?"

"Mr. Volmar may care."

But that was the puzzling part.

Performance date loomed nearer. They hadn't yet learned, let alone seen, a step of the second half of the ballet. Tanya kept coaching them in the first half, adjusting details of speed and spacing and timing.

And Marius Volmar never once looked in on a rehearsal.

One night, waiting in the wings for her entrance in *Harlequinade*, Steph heard two boys from the corps whispering. "And he's using a real punk-rock band."

"Volmar doing *rock?*"

"He's been rehearsing Jimmy and Andrés for two weeks. They're not supposed to talk about it, but Jimmy says it's *wild.*"

"When's it premiering?"

"Two weeks."

"I don't believe it. Shit, there's my cue."

Steph didn't want to believe it either. After all, ballet was full of rumors. She checked the backstage call sheet, rehearsal room schedules, the season schedule. The only premiere in two weeks was "New Work"—Volmar's waltz ballet. There wasn't a trace of a new punk-rock ballet.

Which ought to have proved there was no such thing. But somehow didn't.

*     *     *

"You're dancing the premiere."

Steph had bent down to take a gulp from the drinking fountain. She looked up, saw Tanya, and clapped a hand to her mouth. *"Me?"*

"You. Congratulations."

Steph felt a flicker of doubt at the lack of congratulations in Tanya's narrow brown eyes. "But Volmar hasn't seen me. He hasn't even finished the choreography."

Tanya gave her an indecipherable look. "It's still definite."

Carla was at the barre, warming up with *tendus*, and Steph could tell she had already heard. Steph slipped into her leg warmers; right hand to the barre, she *plié*'d.

"Steph, do you mind if I say something about that pirouette going into arabesque?"

"I wish you'd tell me what I'm doing wrong."

"Your pirouette's fine. But as you go into arabesque, try not dropping your left shoulder."

Carla showed what she meant. Steph tried to copy. On the

sixth try the arabesque came out almost right and on the seventh she had it.

"The trouble was my *shoulder?* I could have sworn it was my foot."

"Sometimes it's hard to judge when it's your own body. Even with the mirror. I wasn't going to tell you, but it's such a little thing and—now—what's the point being mean?"

\*     \*     \*

The day before the stage run-through Volmar finally showed up at rehearsal. Sergio was having trouble helping Steph out of a finger pirouette, and Tanya had just signaled the pianists to take it again from "da da dee *dum*." The studio door opened and Volmar slipped in.

"Continue, continue." He waved a nonchalant hand. They continued. They continued. He strolled to the front of the studio. He watched, eyes bored and almost contemptuous.

When Steph and Sergio came to the altered lifts, Wally tactfully copied Sergio's preparation. There was not even a flicker of reaction from Volmar. Either he hadn't noticed—which struck Steph as hardly likely—or he didn't want to embarrass Sergio—even less likely—or he simply didn't give a damn.

The dancers came to the end of the choreography. They stopped, waited. Volmar let the music dribble on a moment. He lit a cigarette and then clapped for silence.

"That's fine, girls and boys. Just fine. Thank you."

He crossed to the door, a man in a hurry. Steph stopped him. "But, Mr. Volmar, what else happens?"

He looked at her oddly. The other dancers clustered near. She realized she was spokesman for the group.

"You've only choreographed half the music."

"The music repeats. Repeat the steps."

Steph couldn't believe she had heard him right. He had stuck her with the worst possible partner, he had wasted Wally as cover, and now he was telling her to improvise.

"But the music doesn't repeat in the same sequence."

Volmar shrugged. "So? Change the sequence of steps."

Steph could see the panic rise like a blush on Sergio's throat.

He'd never be able to partner her cold through a changed sequence. "Shouldn't we at least run through it?"

"Work it out yourselves," Volmar said. "You're dancers."

Then he was gone, and the dancers were staring at one another in amazement. Wally whistled slowly. "Stage rehearsal tomorrow, premiere the day after, and he wants you to *wing* half of it? I don't believe it."

"I'd just as soon cover this one as dance it," Carla said. "Just as soon."

*       *       *

Steph fought back the stirrings of uneasiness. She managed to get her stage make-up on, managed to dress herself in the Giselle-length tutu Volmar had specified. Even stretching the tasks, she finished her warm-up with two gaping minutes left to kill.

She didn't dare smoke another cigarette or gobble more honey. She fussed with eye shadow, fussed with her shoe ribbons, kept glancing at the clock. Stage rehearsal was scheduled for three. When the moment came, it was like the breaking of a dam. Tiny nameless terrors, a sense that something was about to go disastrously wrong, came gushing down in a flood.

*It's only a rehearsal,* she told herself. *Save your jitters for the performance.*

She went out to the stage. She could feel expectancy buzzing through the house. Off-duty company members curious to get an advance peek at Volmar's first ballet in thirty years, clustered in the wings, whispering and jostling. Three rows of the orchestra were filled with spectators—patrons who paid a thousand dollars a year for the privilege of watching what NBT brochures referred to as "the act of creation."

A scattering of anonymous faces dotted the dimness of the upper balconies. Steph wondered how many of the dance press were out there.

She excused her way past stagehands, went to the wing where she'd make her entrance. Tiny tendrils of menace stretched from the empty stage. The set was a typical Volmar nothing:

dusk-blue cyclorama, two grand pianos tail to tail shaping a single mysterious silhouette against the twilight.

Steph squinted.

The stage manager was down on all fours, laying lines on the stage with white tape. She tried to clamp down on a growing nervousness. The pianos were already there, so why the tape? And why five feet *behind* the pianos?

And why, mixed in among the dancers she recognized, those two hooligan types in leather? And why were Jimmy and André dressed the same way, leather jackets with flashy chains and dangling hardware? She frowned.

Sergio came up behind her. "Hi, Steph."

"Hi, Sergio."

He looked as though an undertaker had done his make-up, great glops of pancake and blush trying to cover age and exhaustion. They had rehearsed the changed sequence and it hadn't gone well. They clasped hands and his palm was sweating.

"All right, are we set to go?" An impatient Volmar stood in the third row of the orchestra, shouting into a mike. Beside him Tanya sat with a note pad open on her lap, ballpoint pen poised.

"All set," came the call from backstage.

"Then let's go. Curtain!"

The two pianists came onstage. Volmar had made them wear black tie. They went to their separate pianos and fussed with the height of the stools.

Steph flexed up and down, limbering her toe shoes. Something clanked overhead, making her start. She looked up. A lighting man had dropped a beer can on the steel catwalk four stories above. That was all it took to wipe out her concentration.

Sergio touched her and whispered, *"Merde, querida,"* and she realized her music had begun.

*"Merde,* Sergio."

She darted a kiss on his cheek. Something flicked across his face and she wondered if he had developed a tic. Her cue approached: four, three, two . . . *now.*

She *bourrée*'d out onstage, leaned against the piano like a teen-ager infatuated with the pianist, then let the music sweep her to stage front: arabesque, *plié,* arabesque, *plié,* turn . . .

Trouble, stage right: a totem pole of lights blinded her on the turn. She made a mental note to mention it to the lighting designer.

Sergio was moving out from the wing. Walking, he still managed to be the *danseur noble*. Their hands ached and he guided her in a pirouette. A line of sweat had seeped through the spine of his jacket. His shoulder was low, and she had to readjust her center. His shoulder stayed low, and she wondered if it was hurting him.

Now came the series of *chaînés*, the little hopping leaps from one foot to the other. Sergio stood to the side, presenting her, then stepped forward to guide her in a turn *en arabesque*.

A noise made her head flick to the right, almost knocking Sergio's arm out of position.

Leather boys were wheeling electronic equipment out onto the stage, lining up speakers with the white tape marks. They wore guitars slung across their chests like rifles.

"Keep going!" Volmar shouted. "Everyone just keep going!"

The pianists kept tinkling out their waltz. Steph tried to keep dancing, but she could feel Sergio losing the beat. The leather boys began tuning their instruments and punk rock came blasting through the waltz like bullets through paper.

Anger flashed through Steph. She lost her count. She came off *pointe*, dropped her *port de bras*. Volmar was shouting through cupped hands, but she couldn't hear. She could see the pianists' hands working imperturbably, but the waltz was obliterated beneath the blanketing electric shrieks.

Sergio managed the first lift, got her halfway up for the second and couldn't make it. He dropped her. She landed on one knee.

A strobe light began flashing. Overhead, revolving balls of metal glitter scattered pellets of colored light in a blinding disco snowstorm. Steph couldn't see or hear or recognize anything. She could feel Sergio beside her, frozen in disbelief.

Jimmy and Andrés came punk-swaggering out onstage. They circled Steph and Sergio, leering. There was a sudden mugger's lunge and Steph felt herself yanked away from Sergio and then someone was lifting her, not a ballet lift but a rapist's lift.

"On the piano!" Volmar was onstage, shouting above the guitars, thumping a fist on the piano lid. "The piano is a car!

Throw her across the hood! Make it look rough—Miss Lang, try to look stunned, will you? Dead if you can manage."

She lay absolutely still on the piano. The waltz vibrated beneath her. The knee she had fallen on began to throb.

Jimmy and Andrés thrashed through a male *pas de deux*. Amazement shielded her like a bulletproof plastic bubble. She could make out homicidal acrobatics, metal glinting through air, leaps and pursuit and wrestling, one dancer strangling the other with a chain, a body being dragged offstage.

Abruptly, as though a blade had sliced through an electric cable, the rock music stopped. The stage was dark except for two soft spots on the pianists.

There was only Arensky's waltz and Stephanie Lang lying on a piano top, yearning to move her arm and touch that knee and count how many pieces it was in. The music grew thinner, wispier, dissolved in one last silvery tinkle.

The spots dimmed out.

After an instant's silence the patrons broke into applause and bravos. Steph sat up, reached, felt. She still had a knee, thank God.

\*   \*   \*

The asbestos curtain came down and the dancers stayed onstage, wrapping themselves in robes and sweat shirts and towels. Volmar—yellow-pad jottings clenched in a gesturing fist—shot off his notes.

"Andrés, before you strangle Jimmy, could you play more with the chain? I want the impression of classical ballet *manacled*. Jimmy, when you're dead, *be* dead. Theatrical dead, not ballet dead. It'll be more shocking."

Andrés and Jimmy listened, nodding, agreeing, then tried it.

Sergio seemed to have turned his eyes to some blank inner wall of his mind. He reminded Steph of a man hauled bodily from a traffic accident. His face made no acknowledgment when Volmar spoke to him.

"Sergio, you were fine. Give us a little more panic when the boys interrupt, but act it, don't try to dance it. Let the audience think hoods really *have* invaded the stage."

Volmar turned to Steph. She detected an instant's hesitation.

"Miss Lang, you're supposed to embody the indomitable spirit of the white tutu."

*In other words*, she thought, *I'm supposed to be a damned fool?*

"Even after the interruption, please try to keep dancing as long as possible. Jimmy and Andrés will be doing their best to stop you, but the important thing is *don't stop dancing*. It doesn't matter if you miss a step or fall behind the beat—keep the dance going. Now when Andrés lifts you—"

"That's not a lift, Mr. Volmar," she broke in quietly. "It's an attack."

Volmar's gaze dusted over with sarcasm. "That's right. As he lifts you, your arms and feet continue the classical ballet movements. Don't try to fight back, don't defend yourself. Above all, don't give up the dance till Andrés lays you on the piano top."

Steph fought to control the anger building in her. "And then what?"

"Then you're dead. Just lie there. You can do that, can't you, Miss Lang?" He smiled for all of them, then turned and strode into the wings.

Steph followed him. "Mr. Volmar, why didn't you warn us what you were planning?"

Amusement flickered in the flint-gray eyes. "That would have killed the surprise."

"That rehearsal almost killed Sergio and me."

"My dear Miss Lang, you're a good deal stronger than that."

She knew the danger of letting him sting her into unguarded honesty, but she couldn't keep her rage to herself. "It was cruel of you."

A smile bent the thin line of his lips. "I could have been crueler. I could have let you go into *performance* not knowing."

Wariness stirred in her. His gaze flicked across hers, teasing as a hand-held fan. At that instant it occurred to her that he might have planned something even worse for the performance, some far crueler amputation.

But she didn't learn what it was till the night they premiered.

# twenty-seven

For the first time in twenty years, Sergio Moritz was happy.

Tonight he had a dressing room. Actually it was Raymond Johnson's, but Ray was out for the season with a fractured tibula, and so tonight Sergio Moritz had a dressing room of his own, a dresser of his own, a role of his own.

"Do you know, Harry," he confided to his dresser, "I was a little nervous about this role?"

"Nervous? But you're a pro, you've danced this type of schmaltz a hundred times."

Sergio watched Harry pluck invisible lint from the blue braided jacket that was the upper half of tonight's costume. Harry was forty, chubby, almost bald, but a nice boy. Two things the Harrys of this world never outgrew were boyhood and a love of ballet. Some had actually begun as corps members, but most had never even made it that far. They recognized their own lack of talent and—unembittered by it—catalogued music, fetched coffee, stitched costumes, dressed dancers, led under-paid, unrecognized lives in the kitchens and pantries of ballet and felt they'd been rewarded in gold when a dancer smiled at them or whispered a bit of gossip in their ears.

*The saints of dance,* Sergio reflected.

"The problem was the lifts," he said. "That Lang girl refused to *plié*. There's no preparation. I can tell you, it's like lifting bricks."

"She just has too much thigh. She's scared if she bends her leg someone will see."

Sergio smiled. "*And*, to be honest, it *is* my first role in ten years." Fourteen years, but he doubted Harry would remember.

"*Ten* years? But I saw you do an *Illuminations* only last—when was it, two or three years ago?"

"Ah yes." The poet. A last-minute cover, and a disaster. Critics had been kind. "Not my best work."

"But you *projected*. That gesture with your right hand—"

"What a memory you have, Harry. Tell me, did you watch my dress rehearsal yesterday?"

"And *loved* it."

"Interesting, hmm?"

"Fas-ci-*na*-ting."

Sergio had been utterly unprepared for the punk-rock onslaught on his pretty little waltz. It had left him shocked, depressed, a little suicidal around the edges. But with twenty-four hours to reflect, he had come to see the ballet for what it was: a major Volmar statement.

A Sergio Moritz comeback.

He had, of course, been jittery creating a principal role after so many years of covering. He had taken a Dexamyl for energy and a vodka for his spirits. Now he felt secure. The trembles were gone. His head was clear and logical. Since no one had seen the ballet before, since the punk rock wiped out the waltz anyway, no one would be sure whether he was making mistakes or dancing intricately self-destructing choreography.

He was safe.

He was happy. There were telegrams in his mirror, bouquets on his dressing table. Alonso had cabled from Havana. A dresser was helping him slip his arms into a lovely blue jacket.

He was home again. Home where he belonged.

Someone knocked. Two sharp raps. Marius Volmar asked if he could be alone with Sergio.

"I like that jacket," Volmar said.

Sergio rhumbaed his shoulders comfortably against the

robin's-egg blue. "My favorite color. I wish I could take it with me."

"You can."

Sergio's finger, on the verge of flicking an excess spot of blush from his cheekbone, hesitated. His eyes met Volmar's in the mirror, just beneath the telegram from George Balanchine.

"You mean after the season?"

"No. You can take it tonight."

"Wardrobe wouldn't like that," Sergio smiled.

"It wouldn't fit anyone but you. It's no good to us."

"If I take it home, my cat will chew it. Better to leave it here. You don't want your stars dancing in chewed blue, do you?"

The chew-blue rhyme was a sort of joke, and Sergio had hoped at the least for a sort of smile in reply. But Volmar's lips held a straight line, not smiling, not frowning. He pulled out a chair and sat and placed a hand on Sergio's knee.

"Sergio—you've been with us twenty-five years."

"A member of the family, yes?"

"You've worked hard, and loyally. Tonight is the company's way of saying thank you."

Sergio shifted uneasily. His knee stayed locked in Volmar's grip. "Tonight is special for you, Mr. Volmar, but for me—well, I'm just doing my work. I love my work and I don't need thank you's."

"Tonight is special for you, Sergio. Very special."

Sergio pulled his lips in tight against his teeth, determined to keep any expression from showing till he knew exactly what Volmar was saying.

"Sergio—this is your farewell appearance with NBT."

Sergio shut his eyes, blanking out the moment, the reality, giving himself an instant to breathe deep and tell him his ears had heard wrong.

Volmar's gaze awaited his patiently.

"Why?" Sergio was shocked at the whimper of his own voice.

"You're old."

"Forty-two."

"Forty-seven."

"In any business but ballet that's young!"

"But this is ballet."

Sergio saw himself in the mirror, a man made magically a boy, a brave smile framed in cablegrams and cut roses.

"You look fine, Sergio, you look twenty years younger than your age—but your movements—"

"Then why?" Sergio smashed a fist into the Kleenex box. "Why did you drag me back and give me the role? Why not just let me crawl offstage? Do I have to die out there in front of everyone? Is that what you want? Is that part of your new ballet?"

"The premiere is a present." Volmar's hands were on Sergio's shoulders, steadying. "How many dancers end their careers creating a role?"

"I don't care how many. I care about me, Sergio Moritz."

"You'll have full pension."

"I want to dance."

"You can teach class, you can coach. Perhaps you can even stage a ballet for us now and then."

"*Mother Goose? Valses Nobles?* No no no thank you." Sergio raised his hands, blotting Volmar out. "I'll dance your ballet, but I won't take your blue jacket."

"As you wish." Volmar stood, one hand on the doorknob.

"As for the pension, I'll have to consider it." Sergio's hand snatched blindly, yanking cablegrams from the mirror. "I've had offers: Balanchine, Alonso—Marcia wants me to come to Stuttgart."

"You'd do very well in Stuttgart."

Unthinking, Sergio pressed a fistful of cablegram to his face, blotting tears, wrecking make-up. When he stumbled to his feet it was Harry, not Volmar, who blocked his way.

"Let go of me." Sergio pulled free.

"Don't you want to fix that make-up before you warm up?"

"I'm not warming up."

Sergio wrenched his ballet slippers loose and dug his feet into a pair of loafers. He was halfway to the elevator before he managed to fasten his raincoat. He ignored greetings and *merdes* and stares, plunged across Columbus Avenue to the bar in O'Neals' Baloon.

"Double vodka on the rocks, please, with a twist."

\* \* \*

The voice on the box called, "Places, please."

Steph adjusted her tutu, made sure her toe shoes were securely glued to the soles of her tights. She hurried out to the wings. Stagehands, electricians, and lighting men were making their last-minute adjustments. The pole of lights was still in the third wing, still blinding, and Steph clutched at the lighting designer's sleeve as it wisped by.

"Mildred, you said you'd do something about those lights."

Mildred, a heavy-set woman who should not have worn slacks and who ought to have worn a bra and who could outshout any man in the stagehands' union, gave her a shrug of a glance. "Sorry, hon. Can't do anything about it now. Just lower your eyes." Then shouting up to the catwalk, "Can you see if that dimmer's working on 23?"

The stage went pitch-black. Sparks hissed down in Fourth-of-July rainbows.

Someone cried, "Shit!"

Steph banged her hip against something, and as the lights groped back up to half strength, she saw it was the pre-amp unit for the electric guitar, placed smack in the way of her entering diagonal. She called to a stagehand. "Could you help me? This isn't supposed to be here."

Heavy hurrying shoulders bunched in burly apology. "Sorry, miss, that's musicians' union."

"Can't you just help me move it two feet?"

"Not allowed to."

"But I make my entrance from this—"

The stage manager crossed the stage, calling, "Places! Anyone seen Sergio?"

"Let's give this mother a shove," a voice whispered in Steph's ear. It was Jimmy, leather-jacketed, charcoal-unshaved. He bent low like a football lineman, placed his hands low on the 300-pound switch-studded box. Together they budged it just far enough to let a ballerina *bourrée* past.

"Seen Sergio?" The stage manager's face blurred by anxiously.

Steph flexed her toe shoes and pressed her palms to the canvas floor.

"Who's covering for Sergio?" someone shouted, distant and desperate.

"That's all I need," Steph groaned. "I haven't rehearsed a step of this with Wally."

"Don't you worry." Jimmy pointed. Across the stage, a raincoated figure wobbled through a flickering cone of light. Jimmy cupped his hands to his mouth. "Wrong wing, Sergio! Over here!"

Steph gripped Jimmy's leather sleeve. "Something's the matter with him."

Sergio crossed the stage, weaving, colliding with a piano, fending it off. Steph sucked her breath in. Mascara and eye shadow had trickled to his jaw, tracing a network of cracks like shattered glass. The unmistakable sour smell of drunkenness floated three feet ahead of him. Steph recoiled.

"Get Wally," she whispered to Jimmy.

Jimmy's eyebrows flexed and hooked somewhere near his greased-back hairline. He turned and torpedoed a path through stagehands and dancers and vanished.

The chattering and buzzing of the audience that had come spilling through the curtain like sea surf suddenly dropped to silence. Steph realized they'd lowered the house lights. Her throat tightened.

"You're not dancing like that, are you, Sergio?" The stage manager was at Sergio's shoulder, helping him out of his raincoat.

"He can't dance," Steph said. "He's drunk."

The words made no dent on the wreck of Sergio's face. Not even his attention flicked up. He was somewhere else, beyond denting or further wrecking.

"Volmar says he dances." The stage manager crouched, twisted Sergio one foot at a time out of his loafers and into a pair of new shoes.

"But don't you see he can't even stand up?"

The stage manager darted a faintly amused glance in Steph's direction. "If Volmar says blow up the stage, I blow up the stage. If he says this is Sergio's farewell performance, this is Sergio's farewell performance. Knock 'em dead, Sergio boy."

The stage manager gave Steph a wry shrug and then the curtain was hissing up and a house of three thousand was holding its breath.

Sergio placed a hand on Steph's shoulder, bracing himself

against some inner sway. A death's head smile ran like a gash across his face. "Sorry," he slurred. "Very, very sorry."

One instant was all she could bear of the eyes, the breath. "It's not your fault. It's *his*."

Her music began. She went up on *pointe*, ready for her entrance.

*   *   *

Anna saw the fall from the twenty-third row of the orchestra.

She could not believe it had happened. A moment ago the stage had been a ballroom filled by one whirling couple. Now, barely two minutes into the ballet, it was a motionless graveyard, her daughter a heaped lump of tutu on the floor.

In the silence of three thousand held breaths, terror began to set on Anna like chilled gelatin. Needles ran pricking up and down her legs. She felt a strength flowing out of the audience, godlike in its power to forgive or destroy. The silence thickened like falling snow until it had the icy weight of a verdict.

Unthinking, she crossed herself. The pianos went on like a clock in an empty room, ticking off the instant of motionless shock.

Anna darted a sweeping glance around her. The audience sat frozen in darkness. She could not read them. There were too many faces with too many expressions, and when she narrowed her eyes to make them out, her eyelashes only made them dimmer.

A sudden rushing gasp filled the house. It exploded into a thousand-throated cry of dismay and shock and tut-tutting pity and hot, thrilled bitchery: this was the blood they had come to ballet to see.

A split second passed before Steph scooped herself up. She began moving in time to the music again, rapid and vulnerable like a bird with broken wings.

Anna clenched her eyes shut and wished she could die.

*   *   *

In the shadow of his first-ring seat Marius Volmar shifted weight back into the comfortable depth of his chair. He lifted one hand with elegant unhurry. His fingers moved up the side of his jaw and down again, unlacing the concern that had gripped his face. He allowed his eyes to close partially, almost blotting out the stage and its shimmering, insignificant figures.

Perfect failure was as delicate an achievement as success. Tonight he had achieved it, and he was satisfied.

\*     \*     \*

In the dressing room Steph sat at her mirror and stared at the bouquets from her mother and Chris, from Lvovna and Danny. She reread the notes, so full of hope and encouragement; lingered at Danny's *Fond best wishes;* and felt dull and used up.

If the fault had been Sergio's, for being drunk, or Volmar's, for springing leather boys and punk rock on her, she might have felt less shocked, less adrift on a sea of humiliation. But there had been no hidden trap door tripping her, no jealous rival's ground glass in her toe shoe: she had slipped on a single pirouette, alone and unsabotaged. There was no one to blame but herself.

She wondered if she would ever again have the chance she had thrown away tonight.

"Can I get you something, miss?"

Steph turned her head slowly toward the voice. It was Lily, a middle-aged Korean woman who was one of the seven corps dressers.

"Coffee? Something from the candy machine?"

Steph shook her head.

Dressers understood when dancers needed chitchat or needle and thread or a kind ear; and they understood when dancers needed to be left alone. Lily nodded and slipped away.

Steph sat a moment longer, listening. Over the loudspeaker she could hear the adagio of *Etudes Symphoniques*, the final work on the program, blurred to a soft secret whisper. The other girls in the corps would be in the wings, just lining up for their entrance. By now they would all have heard: Stephanie Lang *fell!*

She was glad she didn't have to face them right away. Company class tomorrow would be soon enough and awful enough.

She kept the cards and handed the bouquets to the dresser on her way out. "Could you take care of these, Lily? Maybe you'd like them or maybe one of the hospitals..."

Dressers wound up with half the dancers' bouquets, and the wards at Roosevelt Hospital, six blocks away, wound up with half of those.

"Sure I will, miss. Aren't they lovely."

*    *    *

At the stage entrance Anna paced and scowled and arranged every accusation and reproach in order of increasing magnitude. She set her tears and her betrayed looks and her shouts in neat, ready stockpiles. She was armed for war.

And then the door opened and Steph came out, pale and little and hesitant, and Anna couldn't. She was overwhelmed by an impulse to run to the girl and hug her.

They stared at one another a long moment. Something quiet and unexpected filled the space between them.

"Hello, Mom."

"Oh, honey, what a night."

"Thanks for the flowers."

Gently, Anna took Steph's arm. "First time I danced with your father, I was doing this beautiful schmaltzy jump on his shoulder. I had hours to prepare, and don't ask me how, but I jumped right over him and fell flat on my face. And you know what that rat Volmar said? He said, 'At least you kept your leg turned out.' I could have died."

A smile hovered but didn't quite settle on Steph's lips. They pushed through the street door, up the concrete steps toward the traffic. "How was my turn-out?" Steph asked.

"You held it like a pro—right till your ass hit. How do you feel?"

"Me or my ass?"

"Your ass I don't care about—that'll recover."

"So will I."

That was all Anna needed to hear. She was glad now that she hadn't shouted. "Do you want to talk?"

"No. But thanks."

They kissed good night, and then Steph walked east and Anna stood waiting for her bus. Her eye followed the child up the avenue. She thought of things she could have said, nice encouraging things, and she wondered why she always thought of the nice encouraging things too late.

Just before Steph turned the corner she looked back and waved.

Suddenly Anna felt happy. One of the worst nights of her life and for that single instant she felt happy.

\*    \*    \*

The next morning Chris went out early and bought the newspapers. She served Steph her reviews in bed, with coffee and high-protein health drink made in the blender.

"Have you looked at them?" Steph asked, trying to sound very casual and calm.

Chris nodded.

"And?"

"They liked the ballet. They *say* they like Sergio. But I think they're being polite."

"And?"

Chris shrugged. "Critics don't dance. They don't know anything."

Steph opened one of the papers. The critic hailed Volmar: "His first work in thirty years was well worth the wait. *Do I Hear a Waltz?* is a searing statement on the bankruptcy of romantic values." He patted Sergio on the back: "A brilliant farewell. Dance has lost in Sergio Moritz a loyal and dedicated servant."

And he crucified Steph: "Lacking the lyric brio to bring off the waltz, yet insecure outside the movements of traditional ballet, she makes little of her most dazzling opportunity, the apocalyptic final segment. What a joy it would be to see this role danced by a seasoned ballerina!"

Steph folded the paper. Chris had edged toward the door. Her eyes were helpless with embarrassment. *She's scared,* Steph realized; *she's more scared for me than I am for myself!*

"Come on," Steph said. "it's not the end of the world."

"It's so unfair. I *know* how hard you worked."

"But I stank."

A glaze of amazement dropped over Chris's face.

"And look at the bright side. I used to be scared of audiences.

Scared I'd fall on my ass or make a fool of myself. Now I've done it. There's nothing left to be scared of. You're looking at a former coward. A flop is the greatest therapy in the world."

Chris stood staring, mouth open, and then with a sudden cry she rushed from the room. Steph found her at the kitchen sink with a wad of paper towel bunched to her face.

"What's the matter, Chris? Look, *I'm* the failure in the family. What are you crying about?"

"I just know—if it happened to me—I could never be like you."

"It's not going to happen to you. And anyway, who the hell would want to be like me?"

"*I* do, Steph. *I* do."

# twenty-eight

---

In the season's schedule it had been a hole, a vacuum labeled "New Work." But now little stickers went up on posters outside the theater and inside the lobby, ads appeared in newspapers, correcting "New Work" to *Do I Hear a Waltz?* It was whispered backstage that people were actually standing in line asking for tickets to the five remaining performances. *Do I* was selling out.

The dancers were astonished. "Who'd want to see *that?*"

Two days after the premiere there was a change in the rehearsal sheet. Stephanie Lang was removed from the second and all other performances of *Do I.* Christine Avery was to dance in her place.

\*　　\*　　\*

"Why?" Chris whispered. Huddled in the rocking chair, she looked underweight, eroded. "Why *me?*"

"Because you can do it," Steph said. Though in her heart she wondered.

"With only six rehearsal days?"

"You can do it."

Chris had the darting eyes of a tiny trapped animal. "The

whole corps has been waiting for this. They're going to rip me apart and eat me."

"Come on, Chris. It's only a stupid second-rate ballet. Give it a try."

"Why can't he use Carla? She covered the role!"

"Maybe he doesn't like the way she covered it." Steph felt tired. She wanted to close her eyes. "You can't do any worse than I did, and I survived."

Chris's gaze met hers, direct and unswerving. "I can do much worse than you. That's why he chose me."

A sense of apprehension for her friend crept over Steph. "Would it make it easier if I came to rehearsal with you?"

Chris sighed and attempted a smile. Fear pushed ripples of sweat through her skin. "Would you mind?"

\*       \*       \*

Steph hardly recognized *Do I*. It wasn't the same ballet at all. With Wally partnering, everything in the waltz worked: the lifts, the spins, the sliding *glissades*. Volmar choreographed the assault. He rehearsed Chris with Jimmy and Andrés, leading her through every detail. This time nothing was left to chance or surprise or improvisation. The boys, meshed into fine nets of muscle, became one seamless ripple.

But Chris, trapped and alone in her fear, didn't mesh. She stood outside the rippling net, squinting and scowling, falling off balances and missing turns, staring down at her feet as though they belonged to her worst enemy.

Volmar went and put his arm around her. He sat her down in a chair and talked to her for a long time.

It didn't help. She was a lunging dagger, ripping the net, shredding movement into chaos.

Steph watched and wanted to hide her eyes.

At home, night after night, Steph marked the steps with Chris. Their fingers wiggled in the air like the chattering of two deaf mutes. They took the tricky parts over and over till Chris could mark them perfectly, without prompting. But the terror never left her eyes.

"Why is he doing it, Steph? First you, now me. What does he *want* from us?"

Steph couldn't answer. Like Chris, she wondered. But she had no idea what Marius Volmar wanted.

And Chris closed her eyes and crossed her arms and set her fear down in her lap.

\*          \*          \*

The evening of the performance Chris sat staring: not at television, not at Steph, but at walls, like a prisoner with two hours till execution. Steph prepared the last dinner, to the prisoner's specifications: yogurt, wheat germ, honey, lecithin.

"Smile," she said, wiggling fingers. Chris didn't smile and Steph was sorry she'd tried.

The phone call didn't help. "Mom? Where are you?"

"Still in Evanston. Ruthie has the flu and we couldn't get out of dinner with the Morgans."

Chris slumped into a chair. "I understand. . . ."

"Be realistic, dear. Your father has a very crowded schedule and you only gave us six days' notice."

"That's all the notice they gave me."

"We're bound to be coming to New York next month. You'll be dancing in something, won't you?"

"Probably a role in the corps."

"That's fine, we'd love to see you do a role in the corps. Dad sends love."

They left for the theater fifteen minutes before the usual time. Nights when they both danced they always went together, but tonight was different: Steph wasn't just *with* Chris, she was attached—like a seeing eye dog, and a bossy one at that.

Waiting for the elevator, Chris fidgeted. "I forgot the new toe shoes."

Steph caught her. "No, you didn't. I put them in your bag."

Chris's face went through eight shades of desperation. "My eye liner—there's none in the dressing room."

Steph caught her again. "I have eye liner."

"I need green."

Steph kept one foot in the elevator door and one hand reining in on Chris. "Borrow some of Carla's."

"Carla doesn't talk to me."

"Tonight she'll loan you her green eye liner—even if you both have to mime the dialogue. Oh, Chris, calm down."

They stood very stiff and straight in the elevator and all the way down to the lobby they carefully didn't look at one another. The elevator was up to its usual unpredictable tricks. As they got out the door decided to slam a little faster than usual, catching Chris on the hip.

"Ouch!"

"It's only a little bump," Steph said. She knew from experience how those little bumps could hurt but it seemed best, tonight, to treat everything as lightly as possible.

And to take no chances. She asked the doorman to call a taxi. It cost ninety-five cents to get to the stage entrance of the Met. She held Chris's hand all the way and gave a dollar-five-cent tip, bribing fate. They flashed their passes at the guard, and he waved and buzzed them through the security door.

They got looks from the other girls in the dressing room, a few nods—some of them almost friendly—and one hello. Chris sat at her dressing table and took a metal box from one of the drawers. It was a fishing tackle box, from Sears, and perfect for stashing theatrical make-up—half the girls in the corps used them.

Steph made chitchat and pretended she didn't notice Chris's hands shaking. Chris arranged jars and good-luck charms on the table top in some mystical private order. She placed a ragged little toy bear against the mirror where it could stare at her.

"What is *that?*" Steph cried.

"A friend I've had a very long time."

"I've never seen him before."

"He makes very few public appearances. Only on special nights, when I need him."

Chris began dousing her face in Formula 405. And stopped. And turned. Her eyes were huge black O's, all pupil. "Oh, Steph, I'm so—"

Steph knew: *I'm scared shitless.* She pressed a shushing finger to Chris's lips. *Don't let her say it.* "You—are—going—to—be—a—sensation."

Chris's eyes slumped. She glopped on another palmful of Formula 405.

"Chris, what are you doing?"

"Foundation. Why, shouldn't I?"

Steph wondered how Chris could have been with a company this long and not picked up pointers from the other girls. No wonder her make-up blurred onstage. "If the foundation's too heavy, the building sinks." Steph wadded a handful of Kleenex into a sponge and scooped off the excess. "Okay. *Now* build."

Chris poked a jittery finger into the green eye shadow, closed one eye and dabbed.

"Is that all you use?" Steph said. "Three pirouettes and you'll sweat right through it."

"I hate make-up."

"And I hate toe shoes. Here. Look at me." Steph took over. She blotted out Chris's eyebrows with thick pats of bone color.

"What are you *doing?*"

"I'm giving you eyes. Now sit still." Steph whitened out the bottom lashes completely. Good. Already the eyes looked huge. Like a ballerina's, not a little orphan's. "Close your right eye. *Right* eye."

Steph hesitated. *Why not try something radical?* She leaned and whispered to Carla at the next dressing table and Carla handed her a little pillbox of eye shadow.

Chris's left eye gaped. *"Pink!"*

"The whole corps wears green. Tonight you're a non-conformist." And then Steph drew a thin black pencil line above each eye socket, flicking upward at the outside for that almond shape. Then dark brown, as far above the eye as she dared, the phony eyebrow line.

"It's too high!" Chris whimpered.

"Just hold still and trust me." An eighth of an inch below the eye Steph drew the phony lower eyelash line.

"It's too low!"

"As long as it averages out. Want to put the lashes on yourself?"

Chris bent toward the mirror, squinted, attached her uppers, blinked, pulled them off, reattached them.

Steph watched her do the lowers. "Not on your lashes. Put them on the bottom line—like Cynthia Gregory's."

Dubiously, Chris spirit-gummed the lashes to the brown line. Beautiful.

"Mascara," Steph said. "Heavy. *Heavy.* You're not going to a debutante cotillion, you're *dancing.*"

Then the nose. Chris had a pug nose, so Steph drew a line

lightly down the center, extending below the tip. She shadowed the sides. Result: the quintessential Dame Margot WASP schnozz, straight and long. Then long strokes of clay-colored blush under the cheekbones, out to the ears.

"You're making me look like a clown!"

"I'm making you look like Maria Tallchief."

Finally the lips. Steph borrowed a dark, dark red for the lower lip and drew on a big luscious pout.

"See? The new you! Surprise!"

Chris looked at herself in the mirror. Who was that confident cat-eyed ballerina winking back at her? *That's not me, I'm pug-nosed and small-chinned and scared!* She felt the beginnings of nausea, like the banking of a plane, and she braced her hands stiff on the dressing table and pushed the image away.

"We'd better warm up," Steph said.

They went to studio 3, deserted this time of night. The voice on the intercom kept prodding: "Fifteen minutes . . . ten minutes . . . places, please."

Chris felt caught in the cool rising panic of *now.* Her mind scampered like a trapped dog looking for a way out. "I have to pee," she blurted.

Faces turned as she rippled down the hall.

She hurried into the bathroom. Which stall? The last stall, the farthest and safest. She ducked into it, pushed the door shut, slammed the rotating bolt clockwise.

*Safe!*

She sat. Gradually she became aware of sweat beginning to creep through her make-up. A voice paged. *Go away!* Blood drummed in her throat. The voice paged again. *Go to hell!*

People came whispering into the bathroom. "Chris, are you there?" Steph called.

And then they were outside her door. "Chris, are you all right?"

"I'm peeing."

"No one's going to hurt you. Please come out."

"There's something wrong with my pee. I can't come out."

"Do you want us to get a doctor?" That was Carla, who had loaned her the pink eye shadow.

"I don't want anything, I'm all right, please just go away and let me pee!"

"Chris?" That sounded like Heidi. Heidi didn't like her.

She closed her eyes, but she couldn't blot out the whispering, and when she opened her eyes a hairpin was working its way through the crack and under the bolt, nudging it up. She sucked air through her teeth.

"We're your friends, Chris. Please let us help." Who was that? She didn't know the voice. "It's just nerves, a doctor explained it to me: it's a panic reaction, the body tries to dump excess baggage, but there's never anything to pee."

They were right. There was nothing to pee. Her mind, balanced on tiptoe, swayed. She reached a hand forward and silently lifted the bolt. She squeezed back into a corner of the stall. The door swung inward. She squeezed herself smaller, teeny-weeny tiny.

Faces peered at her, silent cat faces with make-up amplifying eyes to shouts. "There's nothing to be afraid of. Once you're onstage you won't even have time to be scared."

She allowed herself to be pulled slowly forward. They walked her, Steph on one arm and Carla on the other and Heidi running alongside saying how scared she'd been when she danced her first Little Swan and how she absolutely had to *crap* and once she was onstage her feet took over, don't ask how it happened, just thank God for feet!

Chris nodded, not really seeing or hearing, struggling to stay afloat. A last wave of electricians and stagehands eddied past. Across an abyss she saw guitars and drums glittering like an auto wreck and she realized they'd brought her to the wings. Her body screamed refusal: *Not here, not now!*

She wheeled away from the stage but there was a circle of eyes closing her in. "Don't make me," she begged.

*"Merde,"* they chorused, hands pushing her back. *"Merde...merde...merde..."*

There was a whooshing sound, like wind sweeping down a lane of elms. The curtain rose. The house, dark now, opened out like a huge and perfect black rose with footlights sparkling at the stem.

The rose stirred, soft and beckoning. *I'm only a flower. You love flowers, Chris. A flower can't hurt you.*

She was paralyzed in an icy instant of not knowing how she had got here or where *here* was. Could it be the city street where her hand had slipped out of Nanny's, or the classroom full of strangers, or the swimming pool where a boy had shouted "Swim!" and pushed, or was this some greater and more terrible height than ever before?

She stared down, not recognizing the chasm. She waited for the insane golden courage of the dancer to descend on her. All that came was the music, the thread that tempted her forward like a voice shouting: *Jump! Leap from the cliff!*

END IT!

Her feet lingered one last moment, kissing the safe earth of immobility. Something within her counted. She flexed. She readied. She reached to take one hand of the void. Music, the seducing suicide voice, whispered—*Now!*

She arched, bent, plunged.

She fell into a stage-light galaxy that stretched in ribbons. Stars blazing the colors of flowers warned her: *Fall no farther, here are the edges of the universe!* The music, gusting up with the force of wind, fought her descent, caught her, held her, moved her perfectly along an unwavering upward slope.

The music signaled and her body understood. Eruptions detonated at the tips of her feet and hands. Bright feathered movements burst from her. Limbs and torso thrust and swam, leapt and ran, with not even a whisper of her own will.

Dimly, distantly, she was aware of a rush of air from a thousand throats, the gasp of the black rose.

There was no time to glance back at her fear: the signals came too fast. She let the motions happen. She let them take hold and mold her, use her, spin her across fragments of eternity.

And finally set her down in thunder.

The black rose opened and shut, shut and opened. An usherette took hold of the monster curtain and, pitting all her weight against it, held it open a pitiful crack.

Hands pushed Chris forward. She curtsied. The sweat stung her eyes like gouging fingernails but she remembered to smile, and when her partner handed her the bouquet that had fallen from nowhere she remembered to pluck out one rose and hand it back to him.

\*     \*     \*

Steph watched from the wing. Applause washed over her—Chris's applause. She turned away, puzzled. Somehow, miraculously, the ballet had meshed. Chris had danced it and danced it brilliantly.

Steph ought to have been relieved but she felt something else, a whispering itch that shamed her. She tried to ignore it.

Ellis came up behind her, grinning. "Looks like your little friend made it, eh, Steph. Overnight the worm turns into a butterfly. I'll bet you're real happy."

Steph stared at him. "Yes, Ellis, I *am* happy. Why do you ask?"

"Big-hearted of you."

"Maybe I'm not big-hearted. But Chris worked herself to death and she's good and she deserves a success."

Ellis bent to smack a cold kiss on her forehead. "And you, honey, deserve her."

*       *       *

Chris looked tired the next morning—no wonder—and Steph volunteered to go for the reviews.

On the way home she thumbed through the *News*, defying fresh ink and sticky pages. The review was there: *New Volmar Repeated.* Her eye dove down the column, past the fuzzy photo of Wally supporting Chris in arabesque, captioned *Dazzling Soloist.* Her eye slowed. The words were black lumps, like ants pressed together. Her mind tried to separate them, to sift meaning from "lyricism" and "long splashing leaps" and "fearless syncopation," all the poetic and wrong terms that made criticism a disturbingly foreign language. Gradually, she understood that the review was favorable.

She leafed through the *Times*—four unmanageable sections today. She managed not to drop the "Home" section. They came right out and called Chris "spectacular."

Steph shut her eyes. *My ballet*, she thought; *Chris's reviews.* A jealous stab went through her and for one ripping instant it was as though Chris had aimed an arrow at the exact center of her stomach.

She pushed the pain away, refusing it. She reminded herself of all the dancers who worked and worked and never got mentioned. Her mind saw a field of unmarked graves.

She stared up the avenue. Eight blocks away Chris was waiting. Chris the success.

Steph organized the papers under one arm. She straightened her shoulders and took two deep, fortifying breaths.

*       *       *

"Chris?" she called as she let herself into the apartment. "I've got them!"

Chris was sitting at the window, staring out. She didn't answer. Steph walked over and stood holding the papers.

"Every one of them mentions you. You're a hit."

Chris gazed at her blankly. "What?"

That was it. Not a *thank you,* just a *what.* Chris did not even reach for the papers.

"Your reviews," Steph said. "I brought you your reviews."

Chris's eyes sipped in a little of her and then turned toward the window again.

"The *News* says you're lyrical, the *Times* says you're terrific. Chris, I'm talking about your *reviews.*"

"I heard you," Chris said.

Steph could not check a sudden surge of exasperation. She thrust the papers into Chris's lap. Chris sat a moment without moving; then, like a dutiful child in school, she opened the papers one by one. She found the arts page in each. Her eyes floated up and down the columns of print. She closed the papers, stacked them, put them down as though they were too heavy to hold.

"What's wrong with you?" Steph cried.

Chris stared at her.

"What in the world do you expect, Chris? Most newcomers don't even get noticed, and you—you're on every dance page in town!"

"I danced badly." There was something flat and beaten in the voice that matched the dullness in the eyes.

*Maybe it's normal,* Steph thought. *Maybe after a terrible strain it's normal to sit staring out of windows, to let your reviews slide through your fingers like melted snow.*

"You danced beautifully," Steph said.

"I slipped on a *gargouillade*."

Steph was speechless. Chris's eyes squinted up at her, mute and uncomprehending. Steph crouched. She placed her hand on Chris's, let it lie there, feeling the slow pulse.

They stayed that way a long time. Steph fought to be kind.

"Chris, aren't you happy? Doesn't it mean anything at all?"

Chris sighed and turned away.

Steph couldn't think what more to say. Now didn't seem the moment. She went quietly into the kitchen and began measuring out brewer's yeast for the morning pep-up drink.

And then threw the goddamned blender into the sink.

# twenty-nine

That summer Steph and Chris were roommates on the company tour of Europe.

In London it worked. The language was English, the reviews were good, and Chris whooped like a child when Steph took her to see the changing of the guard at Buckingham Palace.

Paris was harder. They hiked up Montmartre to see the view from Sacré Coeur cathedral and Chris felt dizzy. They bought Belgian waffles from a corner stand in the Latin Quarter and Chris took a nibble and wasn't hungry and threw hers away. They went up the Eiffel Tower and the mob pressed them together and at the first level Chris whispered, "I've got to get out!"

Steph found her later in the hotel room, sitting with the curtains drawn. "Chris, it's a beautiful day, we're in Paris, pretend it's a vacation and enjoy yourself!"

Chris's eyes gazed into Steph's and seemed to peer beyond them. "I'll try."

And maybe she did try. But never hard enough. Steph had to keep prodding: cheer up, chin up. "We may never be in Madrid again, and the Prado Museum has the best collection of Hieronymus Bosch in the world!" And in Rome, "Now you're *not* going to come all this way and skip St. Peter's! What if the Pope puts in a surprise appearance, would you want to miss that?"

And in Athens, "You'll be the only one in the company who hasn't seen the Parthenon."

"I can see it from the window."

"If you'd open the blinds you'd see that you can't see it from the window. Come on, put on your sandals and load up your camera."

Steph pushed and Chris trudged. Something always went wrong, and suddenly. Chris had a headache or the trots or an ankle on the verge of strain, and she would scurry back to the hotel for shelter. Steph came to dread the *Do not disturb* signs dangling from doorknobs and the drawn shades and Chris huddled in a chair or under the bed sheets.

Steph felt her patience blowing away bit by bit. "Chris, is there anything wrong?"

"No."

"Nothing you want to talk about?"

"No. Could you just sit with me till I fall asleep?"

She tried to understand, but Chris was two people and nothing explained both of them. There was the Chris who sat in hotel rooms shutting out all of Europe. Then there was the Chris who came to life in performance, who danced whether she had a fever or diarrhea or her period—and got good reviews.

By the time the company reached Amsterdam, Steph felt shackled and drained. Her mind ached and her body was in constant bad temper. There was very little rehearsal space in the State Opera, and in class she was squeezed between Carla, who couldn't end her combinations correctly, and Ellis, who thought it was funny to blow on the back of her neck. To make matters worse, Volmar had jetted over the night before and was giving the class.

The pianist was playing a thumping waltz that only added to Steph's dispiritedness. Her body was an impossibly heavy, impossibly stupid weight.

"Turn—repeat on the other leg."

The dancers turned with smooth weariness. The piano thumped on. Outside, one of those North European rains was falling that seemed to leave the city dirtier. Water tapped the windows with the nattering sound of fingers. Feet drew silken whispers from wood.

Volmar began weaving up and down the barres. He stopped beside Chris, eyes taking measure. "Keep your right arm in second position, my dear."

The whole class could hear, as obviously they were meant to. Her arm was in perfectly decent second. He touched her shoulder, ran his fingertip out to her wrist. Always smiling. It was a deliberate movement, like the stripping of bark from a branch in one continuous piece.

Glances darted between dancers: *Did you see that?* A blush rose faintly on Chris's throat and Volmar continued his stroll.

Now he stood at Steph's barre, unsmiling. She became careful. She arched her foot. She froze her arm in good second unwavering, the fingers spaced and completing the line. There was nothing he could criticize.

"Two *ronds de jambe à terre en dehors*," he barked, "one *rond de jambe à terre en demi-plié* ..."

The words were aimed at her with the directness of bullets. Finishing the combination, she slipped: she did a *rond de jambe à terre* instead of closing in fourth. It was foolish and unthinking of her and exactly the sort of mistake Volmar loved to pounce on. A tightness closed across her chest. She braced herself for the demolition to come.

There was one flick of his eyes into hers, his gaze an alloy of steel and contempt. He moved on, saying nothing.

Ellis leaned forward, his whisper hot in Steph's ear. "Honey, when he doesn't even bother to scream, you're dead!"

That was the trigger. A wind stirred in her, whipping her hands and face to a burn. She felt a blinding surge of resentment. *If it weren't for Chris,* a voice in her shouted, *I'd have enjoyed the tour, I'd be rested, I wouldn't make idiot mistakes in class!*

And suddenly she detested the part of herself that loved Chris: she was an animal wanting to lop off the paw that held it in a trap. Her mind went skimming along the friendship that fenced her in. There had to be a loose slat. If she couldn't escape through it, then at least she could use it to beat Chris.

"I'm taking the tour boat," Steph said that afternoon.

"Can't we just rest?" Chris's eyes were moist and huge and soft purple, like bruises that had been powdered over. The summer had eroded whatever gift for aloneness Chris might once have possessed, and Steph knew just how to hurt her.

"I'm taking the tour boat. Are you coming or not?"

The boat took them through the harbor and canals of Amsterdam. It was a gray day, drizzling. The guide spoke five languages and Steph could tell Chris wasn't hearing a word of any of them. Then a bus took them to the flower market and the diamond market and finally to a small warehouse."

"We will now see the Anne Frank museum," the guide announced. "It was here during World War II that the Jewish girl Anne Frank hid with her parents and several friends from the Nazis. Please stay in line."

Steph had not known that the museum was part of the tour. It was a narrow building with cramped staircases. Several tour groups were going through it at once, whispering in different languages.

On the wall were photographs with captions. The line moved so slowly that there was no way of not looking at them. A German housewife going to the baker with a wheelbarrow full of paper money to buy a loaf of bread. Hitler addressing a rally at Nuremberg, arm thrust out straight as a leg in *développé*.

Chris clutched Steph's hand.

Anne Frank in what looked like a high school yearbook portrait, a girl with wonderful ballerina eyes. A mass of human limbs, not at first recognizable as corpses, dumped in fourteen-foot garbage heaps. A human head with the upper hemisphere of the skull removed, brain exposed and intricately veined and grooved.

Steph heard a scream and her hand was suddenly empty. "Chris!" she called. "Wait!" And she fought her way back through the silent mass of people.

\*   \*   \*

She found Chris in the hotel room sobbing. "Is that what happens."

"Steph knelt and tried to stroke comfort into the shaking body. "It only happened once, Chris."

"Why?"

"I don't know why."

"They passed laws against her. They wouldn't let her go to

school. They wouldn't let her go to the movies. They wouldn't let her walk in the streets."

"The laws weren't just against her, Chris."

"They wouldn't let her have friends!"

"She had friends. She had good friends."

Chris's voice was shrill and her eyes were on fire. "They killed her! She didn't do anything to them and they killed her!" All of Chris's nightmares were upon her. Terror had finally forced a passage through all her flimsy pieced-together barriers. The certainty of pain and death, so carefully buried, had erupted into the open. It was running wild in her.

"They're gone now," Steph said. "They're not killing anyone any more."

"How do you know?" Chris stumbled to the window and pulled the curtains shut.

"It's history, Chris. That was a museum. It was all long ago." Steph had supper sent to the room and Chris didn't touch it. A cathedral bell chimed and Steph said, "We'd better get ready to go to the theater."

Chris stared as though she were insane. "I can't go out there."

"Yes, you can. You're dancing tonight."

Chris shook her head, three violent *no*'s.

Steph put her hand gently on Chris's cheek. "It's only three blocks. I'll be with you."

The back of Chris's neck was damp. Steph bathed her and dried her and dressed her and walked her to the theater. Chris sat in the dressing room, thin and pale and rigid, hands folded in a lump on her stomach.

The stage manager called for places and Chris didn't move. "Chris," Steph said, "you're dancing in five minutes. Hear the orchestra tuning up?"

Two silent tears crawled twin tracks down Chris's face.

"Come on. You're wrecking your make-up." Steph grabbed a Kleenex to blot and a mascara brush to repair.

The stage manager rapped lightly on the door.

"Can you hold the curtain two minutes?" Steph said. Chris wouldn't stop crying. Steph shook her. "You're a dancer, damn it. Now start acting like one."

There was no response and it dawned on Steph that Chris didn't even hear her.

"Chris." She snapped a finger in front of Chris's eye. No

blink. Steph hesitated, then slapped Chris forehand, backhand, hard across the cheeks.

"Girl talk or can I butt in?" Wally stood in the doorway, chewing gum. He bent to pick at loose lint on a leg warmer. "May I have the honor of the next dance with one of you two superstars?"

Steph's glance shot from Wally to Chris and back.

"She's zonked," Wally said. "You're covering."

"But I've never danced *Cantabile*."

"You've rehearsed." Wally pulled out a strand of gum and sucked it back in.

"I don't even remember how it starts."

He tossed a nod in the direction of the house. "Neither do they."

Steph's mind clutched for excuses. "I'm not in costume."

"So? It'll be *Cantabile* in a tutu. This is not a formal dress ball. You'll notice I'm wearing the wrong schmatta too."

Steph stared. *"Spectre?"*

He nodded. "Not one *Spectre* on the whole tour, eighteen *Cantabiles*, so what do they pack? Look, you'll be a Sylphide, I'll be a rose, now let's get off our asses."

Steph threw a last worried glance back at Chris. Wally tugged her toward the wings.

"What's my entrance?" She suddenly couldn't remember.

"Your entrance is lying down. I do all the heavy work. Want me to cue you?"

"You're going to have to."

"Took you long enough," the stage manager said.

Wally plucked the gum from his mouth and slapped it onto the stage manager's nose. "Tell them Anna Pavlova's subbing."

Steph had marked the role in rehearsal, but she was used to a piano and the sound of the string orchestra threw her.

"Not yet," Wally whispered when she began her *port de bras*, prone position. "You've got eight more counts, so enjoy the nap." The eight counts went sobbing by in the cellos and then Wally whispered the movements to her. The company choreologist stood in the wing hissing directions, and Wally *jeté*'d over and said, "You're confusing the lady. I'll handle it."

And he did exactly that.

As the lights dimmed for the final, romantic *penché*, Wally gazed yearningly into Steph's eyes and said, "Hear about the mixed-up bank robber?"

"I'll kick you if you make me laugh."

"This mixed-up bank robber went into the bank and said, 'Hands up, mother-stickers, this is a fuck-up.'"

The curtain dropped smoothly and Steph kicked him before it came up again.

"I'll bite your ass," he muttered as they took their bow.

"Try it."

The curtain came down and he bit her ass. "Jesus, next time rinse the Woolite out!"

They took eight bows in all. Afterward Wally hugged her. "It's a shit ballet but with you dancing it almost looked good."

"Thanks for getting me through it."

Other members of the company came up and congratulated Steph. Some of them had never spoken to her before. Volmar asked why she'd changed the steps. She was too tired even to apologize.

"Mr. Volmar, I didn't change them. I didn't know them to begin with."

He looked at her thoughtfully. "In that case you have talent."

                    *        *        *

At two o'clock Amsterdam time Steph placed a transatlantic call to her mother.

"What's the matter, what's wrong?"

"Nothing's wrong, Mom." Steph spoke in a near whisper.

"I can't hear you. Something's wrong."

"It's a satellite call. We have to talk one at a time."

"I am talking one at a time. What's wrong, why the call?"

Steph glanced across to the unmoving figure on the other side of the room. The hair was a spill of pale silver on the pillow, and in the light that filtered through the window shade the eyes seemed to be open, feeling out the upper surface of the room.

"I danced Chris's ballet tonight."

"*Cantabile?* That mess?"

"They loved it, Mom. I got eight curtain calls."

Steph tried to tell the story. Her mother kept breaking in, machine-gunning questions: who partnered, did the conductor rush the retards as per usual? The two women's voices kept colliding in mid-Atlantic, waves blanking one another out. Anna overrode.

"What about that lighting gimmick at the end, does the State Opera have a decent lighting board? Did Volmar say anything?"

Steph reassured her mother on every point and Anna's voice relaxed to an almost natural pitch. "I always said, a good dancer can put anything across. Send me the clippings. Special delivery. And insure them!"

"If there are any, they'll be in Dutch."

"*Dancemagazine* can translate. So can the *Times*."

"Mom, the New York *Times* isn't going to be interested."

"You do the sending, let me do the interesting." Half-beat pause. "And what's the matter with Chris, how come you went in for her?"

The shadow on the other bed stirred. Steph cupped the receiver closer.

"She's a little tired, that's all. Look, Mom, I can't—"

"Figures, the way she eats. Two nibbles of bee pollen and that's breakfast. Breakfast is a dancer's most important meal, and don't you forget—"

"This is costing money, Mom. I love you."

"I love you too. Don't forget those clippings."

Steph hung up. Silence. Small black room. Chris was holding out her arms. The voice pleaded.

"I'm sorry. I'm ruining everything for you."

"Go to sleep," Steph said wearily.

"I'm weak and I'm scared and I'm draining you."

"*Please* go to sleep."

"I don't want to drain you, Steph—you're my only friend. I'm trying so hard to be strong, please believe me I'm trying."

"Please believe I'm tired," Steph snapped, wheeling on her.

Chris bunched the bed sheet in fistfuls to her eyes.

"You're an adult!" Steph exploded. "You're not a baby! I'm not your nurse!"

Chris began sobbing and Steph took a deep breath and went to her and put her arms around her.

"I'm here, Chris," she soothed. "I'll be here."

But she was only reassuring herself. In the secrecy of her

heart she counted the minutes limping by. A cathedral bell chimed again. The sound died lingeringly. Then there were only the two of them, buried in the little black room, and Chris had gone to sleep in her arms.

Steph thanked God there was only one more stop on the tour.

# thirty

To celebrate NBT's opening night at the State Opera in Copenhagen, the Danish Ballet hosted a party across the square in the grand reception room at the Hotel d'Angleterre. Rumor said it was the only decent company party between London and Bucharest and all the dancers swore it would be a blast.

Steph was bored with midnight affairs where you tried to make small talk with the same people you'd been seeing twenty-four hours a day for the last seven weeks. But she didn't want to look standoffish just when the company was beginning to accept her. So she put in an appearance.

She ducked the receiving line of Danish and American cultural officials and got caught in the drift of guests, a mix of dancers and bureacrats and Danish balletomanes. Waiters circulated with foaming bottles of champagne. A piano and string trio played current American pop tunes as though they were of *Merry Widow* vintage, and half the Americans probably weren't even aware what they were smiling at.

Always starved after a performance, Steph searched for food. The buffet table was laden with whole smoked salmons and bowls of chilled gray caviar and great jellied oblongs of pâté. In the crush she bumped into Wally. He was trying to choose a canapé out of a variety as eye-boggling as a field of butterflies.

"Why don't you take a plateful?" Steph suggested.

"And why don't you come over to the corner? One of the Danish corps girls has some incredible pot."

They went to an open window where a small group of dancers had struck comfortable poses against the blue silk curtains and matching Regency chairs.

"Is it true," a Danish boy asked Steph, "that in New York they have sex bars?"

"Is Jerome Robbins working with the Royal Ballet next year?" a girl asked.

The NBT members and their Danish counterparts dressed in the smart eccentricity of their profession, but Steph's eye detected a certain national accent in clothes: Danish boys still wore blue jeans, and Danish girls hadn't yet discovered lounging pajamas.

"Is Balanchine really coaching Baryshnikov in *Apollo* and *Prodigal?*"

Just as Steph was running out of "don't know's" Wally passed her a joint. She pretended to take a drag.

"What are these yellow things?" Wally held out a canapé.

"Custard," a girl said.

"Custard on a *sandwich?*"

"Why not? It's Danish."

"It's delicious."

"I think that you have the munchies."

"I'm going to get some more. Anyone else want some?"

Steph went with him.

"Where's the basket case?" he asked.

Steph wished the dancers wouldn't talk about Chris like that: at least not to her. It made her feel she had to choose between being Chris's friend and being popular. "Chris is at the hotel. She was tired."

"Scared, you mean. Are you two gay?"

"God, is that what people are saying?"

"I just wondered why else you'd put up with her."

A shadow loomed out of the glitter. "Good evening," it interrupted. It was an old woman, short and slight and alone. She had a deeply hollowed face, white hair drawn back in a jeweled bun, and she wore a long gown of black satin that might have been in fashion a hundred years ago.

Wally's eyes dilated. His voice stuttered. "Good evening, Madame Tamarova."

Steph drew in a breath. Tamarova the legendary, this little old thing? Tamarova, star of the Imperial Russian Ballet, dictator of the Royal Danish Ballet school? It didn't seem possible.

"Young man, who is your friend?" the old lady demanded.

"Ah—Madame Tamarova, this is Stephanie Lang."

"How do you do, Miss Lang. Are you enjoying Copenhagen?"

"Very much, Madame," said Steph, mystified why Tamarova should seek her out.

"You've seen the Little Harbor Miss—the Little Mermaid, I think you call her?"

"Not yet."

"You must. Not because she's great, but one must see the legends for oneself."

*I'm seeing one now,* Steph thought. *She looks like someone's grandmother.*

"And Tivoli," Tamarova went on. "You must see that. And the brewery tour. You wouldn't think so, but it's interesting. But beware. Carlsberg gives you free beer. Anything free is dangerous."

Wally stood on the periphery of the conversation, nervous and excluded by Tamarova's back. His hands retreated into his pockets and suddenly he blurted, "Excuse me." And was gone.

Tamarova stepped closer. "I saw you tonight. You're not bad."

"Thank you."

"Don't thank me. It's not a compliment."

Steph judged the woman to be eighty or more. The years had made cold black caverns of her eyes. Her gaze was dark and hard as onyx and the eyes seemed to say, *We may not see much at our age—but what we do, we see through.*

"You're not good in the corps. You don't have the gift. To be corps, one must be like the others. If they are a beat late, you must be a beat late. If they do timid little *bourrées*, you cannot sweep with your arms. I am sorry to say, in the corps you look like a soloist."

"I try to fit in."

"You'll never fit in. Don't waste your time. You must aim at ballerina."

"Doesn't everyone?"

"No. Many girls in this room dream of ballerina—but maybe three know how to aim at it. Volmar can help you."

"I wish he thought as well of me as you do."

"Trust him." Tamarova's voice blazed with conviction. "Trust him four years, no more. He will give you bad roles. He will break down your confidence. He will destroy you. But he will rebuild you his way, and he will make you a principal. Be careful. If you stay too long, he will ruin you. Volmar is good for the feet, mediocre for the arms, disaster for the head. Do not become his mistress."

"He hasn't asked me to."

"Volmar does not ask. Too bad you are not a man, he would leave you alone. But I think he is already playing games with you, yes? You are his type."

\* \* \*

Setting his champagne glass down on a waiter's tray, Marius Volmar happened to catch sight of her across the room.

Her back was toward him, but he recognized her from the unmistakable tilt of her head. Proud people choose to carry their heads high, short people have to. Tamarova was both short and proud. Especially at parties she gave the impression of peering at a star forty-five degrees above the horizon, as though the last surviving prima ballerina of the Imperial Ballet had no friend or equal nearer earth.

She was talking to Stephanie Lang. Perfect. Saved him the trouble of inventing a pretext to introduce them. He made his way through the guests.

"I see you've met," he cut in.

"Naturally we've met," Tamarova said. "I always like to see if your new faces have any brains behind them."

"And does she?"

Usually Tamarova hid things well. But there was an excitement in her tonight that was very near the surface. It kept her fidgeting. Volmar was quite certain of the cause: she saw in Stephanie Lang what he did: the Aurora for whom Petipa created the dream *pas seul*.

"Marius, your allegros are beginning to worry me. Why so fast? Are you trying to squeeze in everything before you die."

A wrenching change of subject, and typical of Tamarova's autocratic ways. Volmar distrusted strength in others. Sometimes, when people like Tamarova gave their lives to one thing, it was because the one thing could not fight back. Volmar had been unable to decide about her. Determined, she was. But dedicated? In all the years of their friendship, he had never known for sure whether she was a ballerina or a bully.

"Which allegro?" he asked pleasantly.

"*Symphonic Études.* I find it revolting. It's like a panic. Even the audience is relieved when it's over."

Volmar answered in Russian. Steph listened quietly, feeling lost and at the same time lucky to be standing with the two greatest names in ballet. The party babbled on around them. She was aware of a ticking sound like a tiny bomb hidden at the end of Volmar's gold watch chain.

Tamarova returned abruptly to English. "Young lady, are they still serving champagne?"

"I think so," Steph said.

"Could I trouble you to bring me half a glass?"

"I see you like her," Volmar said, alone now with Tamarova.

"Who?"

"You don't fool me. You never bother to insult a dancer you don't like."

"I think you fool yourself."

"I could tell you something about that girl that would interest you. She dances a fascinating solo. Only you and two other living people have seen it."

Tamarova had to tip her head far back in order for her gaze to meet his. "Why don't we talk privately?"

"*Volontiers, chère amie.*"

Tamarova snatched his hand. She led him from the party through the lobby and into the elevator. The graceful brass cage slowly lifted them through layers of softening light, deepening silence. Volmar could scarcely keep his excitement from showing. Something in him was convinced that tonight, at last, he would see Tchaikovsky's lost pages for the *pas seul.*

Tamarova took him to her room. Volmar sniffed. A thin layer of the past lay, like faintly scented powder, over everything.

"Charming," he remarked.

"You don't need to be so kind," she said. "It's comfortable, that's all."

"It's very—tsarist."

"A dancer must keep her stretch. Since I already have one foot in the grave, I keep the other in my cradle."

His eye roamed. She had made a museum of three walls: framed water-color sketches for ballet sets, doubtless Benois and Bakst; autographed photos of the last generation of the Imperial Ballet; in a fan case over the door a red feather fan that she must have waved in the 1912 *Don Quixote*.

Of the fourth wall she had made her little altar: a small table with a heavy lace cloth, a single candle burning behind a curved ivory shield, throwing a crescent of light up onto an icon of St. Cyril. Beside the candle she had placed a little enamel box of blue and white panels.

He recognized the box. His mother had had one, long ago. It was one of the Fabergé-designed boxes that Tsar Nicholas had filled with chocolates and given to the members of his ballet on his last birthday.

Volmar wondered, wickedly, if Tamarova had ever unwrapped her candies.

"Now what are you trying to tell me about that girl?" she said.

"You like her. Don't deny it."

"She's charming. The best sort of American girl."

"I'm not talking about her charm. You like her dancing."

Tamarova offered him a cigarette from a gold case with Cyrillic engraving. He accepted. They sat on a small sofa that looked as though it had shed many skins of pink satin upholstery.

"What did I see her in?" Tamarova asked. "There's been so much dancing lately."

"You saw her in *Valse Nobles, Alborado, Jeux d'Enfants*."

"Of course. *Jeux d'Enfants*. A delightful Pierrette. And her feet—so exact. She could make lace with those toes. But she's overextended. It ruins the arabesques."

"Not Pierrette. The corps. Second from the right."

"A treasure like that you bury in the corps?"

"One always buries treasure. Even nature puts gold underground. And your opera glasses were glued to her throughout the ballet."

"But I'm a trained prospector. The public is not."

"I'm not interested in the public's reaction. Only in yours."

"You hid her just so I could discover her?"

"I try to invent ways to delight you."

"And you do delight me. I think you'll make something of her."

"She knows the solo."

Tamarova's cigarette hesitated at her lips. "What solo?"

"*Sleeping Beauty*. Act One. Aurora's dream *pas seul*. The dance Petipa made for your mother that no one has ever danced."

"You're mistaken. There's no dream *pas seul*."

Volmar looked down at Tamarova. It seemed further down than in years past. She looked up at him, old and frail and furiously erect, as though straining for a higher position that was rightfully hers.

"In all our years of friendship," Volmar said, "I've heard you lie more often than any other woman."

"I haven't lied to you so very often."

"You tell only one lie. But you tell it over and over and over."

"Because you nag at me over and over and over. There is no dream *pas seul*."

"Then come to the theater tomorrow. Stephanie Lang will dance it for you."

"How can she dance a dance that never existed?"

"Lvovna taught it to her."

It was wicked of him to mention her lifelong rival, but the situation called for wickedness. A ghost of blush beat in her cheek. Her voice trembled indignantly.

"Lvovna has made a career out of her photographic memory. Well, if those are photographs, I'll tell you one thing: her camera wobbles badly."

"Then why don't you come and correct the photograph?"

"I'll break her camera and expose the negative." Tamarova went to her altar and lifted the lace cloth. A key clicked. A drawer slid open. She turned, holding a small flat parcel almost the size of a phonograph record. "This is what you mean—and it's no photograph."

She handed him the package. A dryness clogged Volmar's throat. His heart was pounding. *Good God,* he thought, *I'm not going to have an attack now!*

"Open it."

The pounding subsided. He broke the seal. It seemed as violent an act as the breaking down of a door. A dust of eighty years ago seemed to spill from the envelope, filling the room. He reached his fingers inside, into the past.

"Act One—number twelve," Tamarova said. "Aurora's *pas de deux rêvé*. By Pyotr Ilyich Tchaikovsky."

Holding the yellowed pages, scanning the small, neat musical notation, Volmar felt a rush of desire to press the manuscript to his lips. He had completed a journey that had begun a half century ago: the quest of his life. He trembled and began to weep silently.

For a long time he sat staring down at his treasure. Then, slowly, he began to read, putting the orchestra parts together. When he touched the first page to turn it his thumb left a faint crescent slightly lighter than the rest of the paper. The music surged in his head.

"*Pas de deux,*" Tamarova said. "*Pas de deux.* Not *pas seul.* Doesn't anyone speak French any more? Doesn't anyone know ballet?"

"Maybe with this we can help them remember."

"God grant," she said.

"May I have it?"

She didn't answer. Just stared at him with those great silent eyes. Impatience flared in him.

"You didn't show me this just to torture me. Or to correct my French."

"To me, those pages are sacred. They are Tchaikovsky; Petipa; my mother. They are what dance—could have been. How badly do you want them?"

"How much are you asking?"

"Money? I have my pension, I have my school. I'm not interested in that."

"Then what do you want?"

"Something you could give far more easily than I can part with those pages."

She paced three steps, turned, paced back and faced him. Her eyes were like the window of a cash register awaiting a figure to be rung. Volmar's impatience foamed up into anger.

"Tell me the price then."

Tamarova moved quietly and quickly across the room. There

was a set of double doors that Volmar supposed led to the bedroom. She flung them open. A sudden brightness came crashing in. Volmar had to squint.

A tall male figure stood silhouetted against the light, motionless.

"He is the price."

He seemed to have been waiting a long time. He seemed willing to wait longer.

"Marius, this is Aleksandr Fedorovich Bunin. Sasha—Marius Volmar."

The stranger came to life, stepping into the room with a swinging stride. Now Volmar could see him. Brown hair, brown eyes; strong facial bones; a handsome beard that unraveled at the top to reveal smiling teeth. He wore a red knit sweater and blue jeans. He could have been a sailor.

With a sudden surrendering movement he bowed his head, as if to an executioner—or an audience. "I am honored," he said.

"Sasha comes to us from Leningrad."

"I have long admired your work, Citizen Volmar."

"Sasha—*Mr.* Volmar, not 'Citizen.'"

"Forgive me. I have long admired your work—*Mr.* Volmar."

Volmar could not help smiling. So thorough was Soviet conditioning that even anti-Communists had difficulty mouthing the forbidden word *gospodin.* They ranted against Marx and Lenin but they called you *grazhdanin*—"citizen."

"You've seen my work then?" Volmar asked coldly.

"When you toured my country, three years ago."

"A most uncomfortable tour."

"Even if we haven't enough money to repair our shoes, we Russians will spend eight, ten rubles for a ticket to the ballet. You cannot imagine what ballet means to us. It is our sole link to the nobility of the past, the one thing in Russia the Communists have not ruined."

"I am not political," Volmar said. "Not in the least."

"Nor am I, Mr. Volmar. Not in the least."

"Ah—then you're a dancer?"

Gravely, the young man nodded. Volmar knew the type. They had the skin of princes, the marrow of peasants. Lacking wit and grace, they got by on shrewdness and strength.

"And for many years it has been my highest ambition to dance one of your roles."

And by pushiness. Volmar turned to Tamarova. In English, "Another of your defectors? I hadn't heard about this one."

"This one they are keeping secret."

"Kirov?"

"But of course. Look how he stands. That they haven't forgotten."

"Bunin. I don't recall that name." Then, in Russian, to the young man: "You couldn't have been a principal."

"I would have been if I had chosen to stay. But I could not tolerate the dictatorship—"

"Nor the constant intervention in artistic affairs," Volmar sighed. The same line they all parroted when they realized they'd never make a success at home. "In other words, you were tired of the corps."

"Sasha was a soloist," Tamarova said. "He's been in Copenhagen since the last tour. And they'd take him back in an instant. I think he could even negotiate and become a principal. They want him very badly."

The beard was probably a disguise to make him look less a dancer. It made him look less a youth, too. Volmar subtracted five years from his first impression. He put Citizen Sasha Fedorovich's age at twenty-four. The Kirov's superstars generally bloomed into principals a little earlier than that. Obviously there was practicality to the boy's defection.

"I will never go back there," Bunin said. "They crush the human spirit."

Volmar lit another of Tamarova's cigarettes. "Everything crushes the human spirit. Governments, landlords, taxes, pollution."

"The Soviets have been very careful about Sasha's departure," Tamarova said. "There has been no publicity."

"They publicize the principals," Volmar said. "Nureyev, Baryshnikov, Makarova make headlines. When it comes to a soloist like Citizen Bunin..." He shrugged.

"He is more valuable to them than Nureyev or Baryshnikov or Makarova." Tamarova paused as though preparing for a triple turn in the air. "His father is *Minister of Agriculture!*"

"Then his father is in trouble."

"My father and I are not friends."

"Certainly not now," Volmar said.

"I want to go to America, where dancers are free. I want to

dance modern roles. Balanchine, Tudor, MacMillan—Volmar."

"Dancers are not free anywhere," Volmar said. "Not in Russia, not in America, not in this room. Dance is a tyranny of the old over the young, the ugly over the beautiful, those who no longer can over those who can."

"Sasha needs an American visa and working papers," Tamarova said. "The consul will give them to him if you'll promise him a place in your company."

Volmar was strongly tempted. In the balance of his mind he weighed the manuscript against the boy. There would be problems if he let a Soviet fox into his sheepfold. On the other hand Tchaikovsky was worth a problem or two.

He decided to make one last attempt at negotiation. "We're not that sort of company. With all due respect to Citizen Bunin and the Kirov, we are not a showcase for Soviet sensations. Why don't you try American Ballet Theatre or the Canadians?"

"I have seen Sasha perform," Tamarova said. "He is good."

Volmar could not explain the stubbornness that flashed over him. He was a man who knew his prejudices and was rarely blinded by them. Yet every instinct in him shouted *No* to citizen Aleksandr Fedorovich Bunin.

"We don't do *Spartacus*," Volmar said. "We don't do class-conscious *Giselles* and happy-ending *Swan Lakes*."

"He is good at everything," Tamarova said.

"We have nothing for him. There are no solos available."

"Marius, let us be frank. Your company is the best. Sasha must go to the best. He is willing to join the corps."

Volmar saw she was serious. He almost had to laugh. A Kirov soloist in an American corps? The other boys would look like morons and sissies. Absolutely impossible.

"Yes," Bunin said. "To go to America, to go to Volmar, I will go backward."

Volmar maintained a silence, hoping to chip away at Tamarova. Her hardness strained. And held.

"Take Sasha," she said, "and the Tchaikovsky is yours. Refuse him, and . . ."

"Why are you doing this?" Volmar said.

"Why do I do anything? Why do I bother to stay alive when I am old and tired? For dance. Only for dance. You'll let me know in twenty-four hours, Marius?" She gave him her hand to kiss. "Otherwise Sasha goes to the Paris ballet."

"And he takes Tchaikovsky with him?"

"Of course. It's his safe-conduct."

# thirty-one

The plane was forty-five minutes late taking off. Rumors buzzed. Volmar was not on board; Volmar was sick, missing, had been in an accident, and decided to stay behind in his native Copenhagen.

By now, the dancers didn't care. They had been worn out by currency exchange and passport formality, worn out by stages that sloped and stages that weren't deep enough and rain-mushy outdoor stages that held onto your feet like mud. They were tired of hunting down Band-Aids and Woolite in five different languages, tired of tiny hotel rooms with musty mattresses, tired of one another.

They had spent their money, their patience, their strength. All they wanted now was to go home and sleep.

At nine-thirty a black car with two American flags on the hood came plowing across the runway. Marius Volmar and a stranger stepped out and hurried to the boarding ramp. With a thump, the stewardess pushed the door open. There was a gray splash of daylight and Marius Volmar and his companion stepped on board.

The stranger's gaze swept the cabin, methodically, neutrally.

A stewardess handed Volmar a telephone. His voice came crackling over the public address. "Boys and girls, I should like to present to you Aleksandr Fedorovich Bunin. Sasha for short." There was a groundswell of whispering. "Mr. Bunin will be joining the company. Since he does not speak very much English, any helpfulness you can show him will be appreciated."

Volmar handed the telephone to the stranger. The bearded face shaded with anxiety. And then, with a heavy Russian *l* forced up from the back of the throat, "Hello."

The stranger smiled. The dancers broke into applause. Heads turned row by row, like leaves flipped over in a sudden breeze. Rumor silted back through the chartered jet: *He's a defector. . . . Got to be Kirov. . . . Looks Bolshoi to me. . . . Who wants Bolshoi? What we need is a Rudy or a Misha!*

Steph and Chris had taken seats near the rear of the cabin. Magazines and hand luggage were piled on the empty place between them. Chris leaned toward Steph to whisper, "God, he's handsome!"

"How can you tell? He's all beard."

"Those eyes . . ."

"Russian blue. So are Brezhnev's." Steph opened yesterday's Paris *Herald* to the Royal Ballet review.

"Brown," Chris said. "Very pale brown."

Steph glanced at her friend. "Watch it. For all we know, he's gay. We're not going through *that* again."

Chris was shaking her head. "He couldn't be gay."

Steph sighed. "Why don't we leave that question to the experts?"

Chris didn't answer. She was too busy staring.

The newcomer made his way slowly down the aisle. Silence rippled out around him. Gossip stopped. Eyes stared. He had the smile of a little boy in a toy shop—a gaze so openly eager, so harmlessly greedy, that every face it touched had to smile back.

Volmar stood apart, at the front of the cabin, watching. What he saw disturbed him. The girls' eyes moved with Aleksandr Fedorovich Bunin as if they'd been caught on fishhooks. Though the boys' eyes were more skilled at deception, Volmar could still read the signs: longing in the gay boys, a bristling defensiveness in the straights.

Trouble. Most definitely trouble.

*      *      *

"Please?" The Russian nodded at the seat.

Chris threw a glance at the empty place beside her, began scooping magazines and packages into her lap.

"Thank you much." He squeezed past Chris's angled knees and dropped into the seat. He smiled first at one girl, then the other. "I am Sasha."

"I'm Chris."

"Steph. Hi."

He offered his hand, gravely, to each of them. They shook it, gravely.

"Is great pleasure." He adjusted his seat belt and shut his eyes and fell into the instant easy sleep of a cat.

Steph was uneasily aware of the male next to her.

His fingers, resting on his knees, had the long taper of a concert pianist's. The dark nicotine stain on the third finger of the right hand must have been years in the making. She saw that he chewed his nails. For some reason that made him likable. No rings. Even more likable. His jeans fit snugly and even in relaxation she could follow the definition of the thigh muscle. What she could infer through the sweater was more of the same, strength without bulk.

She tried to tell herself she was evaluating him as a partner, nothing more. Her eye roamed up to his profile. A partner didn't *need* a profile, but . . .

He had a high forehead, pale and smooth, and an oddly pleasant upturned nose. A very full lower lip pouted through the beard. She suspected his chin would be strong, and she prayed it didn't have a dimple.

Chris's eyes had followed exactly the same path and were fixed on the sleeping face. Steph looked quickly away and concentrated on the whine of the jets. She felt the plane lift off. The bright patchwork of Denmark faded gradually to pastels. The horizon tilted. She braced herself against the sideways pull, the sudden bite of the safety belt.

Chris huddled forward in her seat, face rigid and white. A choking sound was coming from her mouth. *Good God,* Steph wondered, *does she think we're going to crash?*

The Russian's eyes flicked open. His glance wandered over to

Chris, seemed to stumble a moment at the neckline of her blouse. It was a good deal lower in her forward position than she probably realized.

"Chris," he said gently, "okay?"

She shook her head.

"Chris." He snapped his finger sharply, caught her eye. He pried her hand loose from its grip on her waist, tucked it between his two hands, patted it. He smiled. "Now okay?"

She nodded. "Now okay."

\*       \*       \*

The captain's voice announced that they would land a half hour ahead of schedule. *Damn,* Volmar fretted, shifting in his seat. Every change in timetable meant more uncertainty and complication. The plan depended on the State Department's men being at the airport to meet them. *Pray God they have the sense to check arrival times.*

The Long Island shore came bursting through the fog. There were shouts and applause as the plane touched down. A stewardess' voice urged everyone please to remain seated. Volmar could hear that no one was remaining seated. Coats were being reached for, packages collected, bodies were pushing for position in line, voices were laughing and calling.

The stewardess brought Sasha forward ahead of the others, handed him over to Volmar like a parcel.

*"Kak proshla vasha poyezdka?"* Volmar asked. How was your trip? Russian was a good language: they had a formal pronoun. You could keep the Sashas of this world at a distance.

"Where is the Statue of Liberty?" Sasha asked. His tone left no doubt that he'd been cheated.

"New York Harbor. You'll have plenty of time to see it."

They left the plane directly behind the captain and the flight officer. The State Department had promised an escort but there was no one at immigration to meet them. Sasha's papers were in order—no trouble there. But as they came into the baggage area Volmar was aware of a jibbering excitement on the other side of customs. He knew that sound.

"Forget the bags." He pulled Sasha with him.

"My guitar!" Sasha whimpered.

"We haven't time."

The customs officer, surprised that they had nothing to declare, shrugged them through. As they hurried into the waiting area there was an explosion of shouts, the eye-stabbing shock of a hundred flash bulbs.

*"That's him!"*

A barrier of potted palms went down and the flood of reporters was upon them, hungry-faced, ugly, trampling. Voices climbed on one another.

"Which one's Bunin—you?"

"Not the old one, asshole!"

*Flash*.

"Why did you defect?"

"What do you think of America?"

*Flash flash*.

"Do you like American ice cream as well as Russian?"

"What does your dad think about this?"

The State Department had promised no leaks. So much for promises. Sasha's eyes darted in panic from one screaming reporter to another. A woman thrust a microphone into his face.

"Do you like girls?"

*"Nye ponimayu,"* Sasha cried, *"nye ponimayu!"*

Volmar squinted over the dipping, rising, whirlpooling tide of newsmen. His eye found the exit.

"You—who are you—do you speak English?"

The woman's microphone waved insultingly in Volmar's face. He knocked it aside.

"You're goddamned rude, whoever you are!"

Gripping Sasha's hand, Volmar threw all his weight into his shoulder, bulldozed a sideways opening, pressed forward, ignored shouts and flash bulbs, lunging arms and spittle-caked questions. His heart was battering like a kettledrum and it was a miracle he reached the taxi alive.

\*     \*     \*

"Why don't you just call him Sasha?" Volmar spoke slowly, hiding his shortness of breath. He wanted to keep his heart trouble secret. Till the end, if possible.

"Well, it's certainly easier," Dorcas said. She smiled and

Sasha returned her smile—with compound interest, it seemed to Volmar.

They were standing in Dorcas' living room. Sasha's eyes took inventory. They did not simply sparkle. They were bonfires. From everything his gaze brushed he seemed to draw little increments of audacity, till finally he touched his finger to a brass lampstand, stared at the dustless fingertip, and whistled softly.

"That's all right," Dorcas said, seeing Volmar about to chide. "Let him touch what he likes. He can look at those books—there's some Pushkin in French—or he can play the piano or go stroll on the terrace."

Volmar translated Dorcas' offer. The Russian smiled with a naïveté that could have projected to the top of the Metropolitan Opera House.

"He says he'd like to sit."

"Oh, let him sit, by all means. Excuse me if I stand. I'm much too excited to sit still."

Sasha dropped into a richly upholstered armchair near the fireplace. He stretched cozily as though drawing extrasensory comfort from the unlit birch logs. Volmar could not help smiling. Even amidst luxury like this, the Soviet chameleon could make himself at ease.

"I've prayed so many years for this opportunity," Dorcas said.

"I didn't know you prayed," Volmar said.

"For a Kirov dancer? Of course I pray! Marius, ask him what roles he knows."

"My dear, he was only a soloist."

"He must have covered *something*. Ask him."

Volmar asked.

"*Lac des Cygnes*," Sasha answered, by-passing his interpreter.

"*Swan Lake,*" Dorcas said thoughtfully. "And you dance Siegfried?"

He nodded again. *"Et aussi Giselle."*

"You do Albrecht? Or Hilarion?"

"Albrecht, *naturellement*."

Naturally, Volmar thought, this hammer-and-sickle peacock would claim to have danced the lead.

"*Et aussi La Belle au Bois Dormant. Florimund.*"

"Marius—what would you think of a *Sleeping Beauty?*"

"I'd like to do one very soon."

Dorcas glowed. Volmar did not bother telling her he had no intention of perverting his company or his *Sleeping Beauty* into a showcase for Soviet upstarts.

"We'll have to change the entire schedule." She was a flurry of hands and pearls. "It's going to be an awful rush. I just hope I can keep my head."

She gazed at Sasha, and Volmar could see the self-deception at work in her eyes, magnifying the boyishness, the smile, blanking out any hint of calculation in the gaze that met hers.

"He can change everything for us, Marius. Have you seen the papers? We're on the front page."

"We?"

"He. But it's all the same thing."

Volmar sighed. "When will your war be over, Dorcas?"

"War? What war?"

"This war with tickets and box office and government grants."

"Never. It will never be over. Ballet will always be in the red and we who love it will always have to battle for it."

"But this war mentality of yours is ridiculous."

Dorcas lifted a silver box from the coffee table, offered Volmar and Sasha cigarettes, took one for herself. Sasha sprang between her and the silver table lighter, a lit match in his hand.

She gazed at the boy a moment, exhaled a Berlitz *"Spasibo,"* and angled her cigarette to the flame.

"You're ready to seize on him"—Volmar gestured toward Sasha, who sat listening and staring, eyes narrowed in undisguised fascination, head turning to follow each of their moves—"as though he were your last available weapon."

"He'll be our H-bomb. All we need is the delivery system. And you can leave that to me. I've got a few ideas. We'll call in professionals."

"Professional what—fighter pilots?"

"Publicists."

"And who is this enemy that you intend to crush with your publicists?"

"The enemy is ignorance and apathy and prejudice."

"In other words, the public?"

Her eyes were dreaming and fierce. "The *real* public. We'll get tourists and gawkers and idiots. People who've never seen a girl on *pointe* or a jump or a lift or a fish dive or a double turn in the air. And when they leave that theater, they'll be stark raving converts. Balletomanes."

"That kind of balletomane we don't need."

"You handle your dancers, I'll handle my audience. That's our arrangement, Marius. It's worked in the past, it'll keep working."

There was a slight stiffening of her spine. Volmar recognized the emergence of Dorcas the box-office expert. He had met this creature once or twice in the years of their working together and he preferred to ignore her.

"I'm tired," he said, "of people who know nothing about art and everything about ballet."

"And I'm tired," he said, "of people who know nothing about business and everything about box office." Dorcas gazed pityingly at Volmar as though she understood mysteries he never would. "Oh, Marius, we're both tired. You especially. You've just come back from a gruelling tour and the State Department was *no* help and those reporters were revolting. Now isn't the time to talk. We'll only say things we don't mean."

"I've never said a word I didn't mean."

"You *are* in a bad temper." Her eyes flicked toward Sasha. "It's embarrassing—with him here."

"He doesn't understand English."

"He certainly understands a shout—and the look on your face doesn't need translation."

"Neither do the dollar signs in your eyes."

Sasha had been studying them both. He looked up at Volmar and said, in Russian, "Forgive me, Mr. Volmar."

"What do you want?"

"Is Madame angry?"

"That's not your concern."

Sasha looked in curiosity from Volmar to Dorcas. She stood by the French windows staring out at her landscaped terrace, out toward the great space over Central Park where no one had yet built skyscrapers.

"I hope she is not angry because of me," Sasha said.

"What if she is?"

"Then I must apologize."

"You'll only make it worse. Just keep quiet."

"She keeps looking at me. I should say something to her."

"What can you say? Your English is terrible."

"I would like to tell her she is beautiful."

"I'm sure you would like to tell her that."

"And her house is beautiful. She is rich?"

"It's lucky you don't speak English."

"I would not ask her if she is rich. I am asking you."

"She is very rich and if you behave *kulturni* she can help you."

"I would like to live here. It is a museum."

Dorcas turned on her heel, leaving a tiny welt in the carpet. Her eyes met Volmar's with the authority of a finger pressing the hold button on a telephone. For a moment she did not speak and then, coming slowly out of her calculations, she said, "Has he got a place to stay?"

"I'll take care of it."

"Don't be stupid. The maid will make up the guestroom."

"My dear Dorcas, he can't stay here."

"Of course he can. There's plenty of room."

"Be sensible. If he stays here, it looks—"

"I'd be flattered if people think I have a young lover. Besides, we can't talk to one another so we should get along perfectly."

"I'm thinking of the dancers. If he stays here, he's your protégé. I would prefer no protégés in the company."

"Nonsense. He's a refugee. Why shouldn't I help him? It's my duty as an American."

Volmar looked at her with concern, with a little compassion too.

"Marius, either you translate for me or I'll say it myself. My Russian may be World War II, but I do know how to invite a man for the night. I just don't know the word for 'week.'"

Volmar's eyes sank with fatigue. He thought carefully a moment and then he said to Sasha, "Madame has invited you to stay here."

"I cannot refuse such an honor."

"He says yes." And now Volmar was tired of talking to imbeciles. "I'll be going. Phone me if you run into any insurmountable language barriers."

"You go straight to bed and take that phone off the hook. You're looking very peaked."

Dorcas came with him to the front door.

"By the way, Marius darling—can he dance?"

"I've never seen him perform."

"Ah. Then we'll just have to take our chances."

# thirty-two

The first company class of the season pulsed with curiosity.

"I hear he dances like Nijinsky."

"I hear he dances like Nikita Khrushchev."

"I'll bet he's gay."

"I'll bet he's straight."

"They say he's a KGB plant."

"Gotta be CIA."

A crackle of silence swept the room. He was standing in the doorway, a tall, pale, uneasy bundle of muscle and nerve. He had shaved his beard, and when he smiled there was something sad and soft about his mouth.

Conversation rose again to a listening whisper.

He stood looking for a space. Eyes tracked him in the mirror. He crossed the studio to where Lucinda Dalloway had set her bag down at the barre.

"Please," he said, pointing, "is room?"

Dalloway's leg was hooked in *développé* over the barre, and she shot him a frown up from under it. A narrow-hipped bad-tempered redhead, she was the top ballerina, the top bitch, and the top barre-hogger in the company, and one thing you did *not* do in NBT was ask Dalloway to move her bag.

Unless you were a young Russian defector with glossy dark hair and brown eyes who came nimbused in rumor and mystery. Dalloway's frown softened to a shrug of the eyebrows. Sasha thanked her and moved the bag to the wall.

Marius Volmar arrived on the dot of ten. He was wearing a faded lumberjack shirt and dungarees, impeccably clean, impeccably unpressed. "Good morning, girls and boys." He was always cheerful at the beginning of a new season, but cheerful or not, he didn't waste time. He nodded to the accompanist.

"Left hand to the barre. *Plié*, *un—deux—*"

The piano thumped the ½ rhythm and the dancers *plié*'d and watched Sasha. Even in the very simple knee bend they saw his litheness, his buoyancy, the arch to his back. In the *rond de jambe* they saw the extension of his leg, the arch of his foot, the soft silken circles he drew on the floor.

He was good. There were shrugs. So what?

Volmar fired out pirouette combinations. At each command Sasha shot into an explosion of perfectly centered spin, stopping dead on the beat, facing dead front.

He was perfect. The dancers exchanged "So what?" glances. They had expected something more than perfect, a Rudy or a Misha.

And then as class wore on he changed. His eyes glazed with a fierce absorption in his work. It was as if, till now, he had been trying to show he could be one of them. With the grand allegro he seemed to lose the strength to hold himself back.

His first *grand jeté* came with such unexpected speed that the other dancers backed off. There was a sudden burst of elevation, a soaring through space with legs and arms perfectly extended; and then a slowing of time, as though the air didn't want to let go of him, and he drifted to the floor with the floating softness of thistledown. There was hardly a sound as his foot touched wood.

Marius Volmar's gaze—serene and almost priestly—circled the dancers. From time to time it brushed the newcomer but it never lingered on him. Marius Volmar could see more with a brush of the eye than most men in an hour's study. The class gave him time to look Sasha over. He wanted to see flaws, but he saw nothing worse than mannerisms, the typical Soviet striving for dash and splash. The boy was no Fabergé egg, but he was no boiled potato either.

*I will have to be careful with that one,* Marius Volmar realized. *Very careful.*

Sasha left class with Lucinda Dalloway. They were chatting and smiling and he was carrying her bag. The dancers rushed into huddles.

"He can dance."

"And he's not gay."

"You hope."

"Lucinda wouldn't waste her time."

"Where are they going?"

"Coffee."

"Who invited who?"

"She invited him."

"Think it'll be a thing?"

"I give it a month."

"A week."

"An afternoon—her husband comes home tomorrow."

\*   \*   \*

"The government is *crazy* for him! We could pull down three quarters of a million in supplemental grants next year." Dorcas' eyes were green and shining and triumphant. "And have you *seen* this year's subscriptions? We're selling out! *That* impresses the corporations. They'll up their contributions to get bigger credits in the programs. Our federal matching funds will skyrocket!"

She had caught Volmar in his office, darted in, and shut the door. "Just a chat," she had said—a chat buttressed with fistfuls of box-office receipts and press clippings. It seemed there wasn't a paper in the country that hadn't run the wire service bio of Sasha, or a magazine that hadn't stretched out tentacles for an interview.

"Of course we've got to handle him carefully. Those TV interviewers can be killers."

Volmar looked questioningly at her. "Live interviews?"

"Maybe not live. Not till his English is better. But we'd be fools not to take advantage of every medium we can." She sat forward in the chair, bursting with plans. "And he *has* to dance principal roles this season."

Volmar had no reply but a dry smile.

"You can't tell me he's not ready," Dorcas said. "Everyone says he's a sensation in class."

"Class is not performance."

"Then put him onstage. Give him something big. That's what they're screaming for. That's what they're *paying* for."

An objection swelled within Volmar's chest. He mimicked her intonation. "We don't have anything *big* to give him."

"What does it take to stage a *Corsaire* or a *Don Q pas de deux?* A blue cyclorama, one orchestra rehearsal."

She waited for his answer and it didn't come.

"Well, why *not?* What in the world have you got against Sasha?"

"It's called artistic principles. I happen to place mine above political fads and press campaigns and moneygrubbing."

Anger blinked through her face, fierce and unguarded and wrinkled. "You may call it moneygrubbing, Marius, but the rest of us call it survival. The dancers have to be paid. We need costumes. New sets. The musicians are already grumbling about a spring strike. For three decades this company has operated on the brink of extinction. Sasha could be our salvation. He's gold. Pure gold."

"And what if the other dancers come to resent this highly publicized ingot?"

"Dancers aren't fools. They know we have to sell tickets. They know we have to balance our books. With Sasha—it's all possible."

"Over thirty years we've worked to build this company."

"Of course we've worked," she cut in sharply, "and now we have a chance to *keep* the company."

"We don't have stars," Volmar said. "*That* is what makes us good."

"Well, if we don't catch this star and tuck him in our pocket, he'll go to American Ballet Theatre or Balanchine. They'll wipe us out. You just don't know, Marius. You don't understand the public. You never have."

He put his forehead in his hand for a moment.

"Marius, I know you have your vision of this company. It's not a vision I've always shared, but I respect it. I've worked for it every bit as hard as you. Now we have a chance to win a public.

To win broad support. I'm sorry, but to me that's every bit as important as your private vision. After all, it's not tearing down your life's work if we schedule one or two solos for Sasha."

Darkness crept into Volmar's thoughts, an apprehension of loss blacker than any he had known since childhood.

"If you're so dead set against him," Dorcas cried, "then why the *hell* did you bring him to America?"

Volmar was not ready to tell her. A plan could not be put before Dorcas half formed or with blank spaces. The woman had too many free-floating ideas of her own, most of them dreadful. Given the slightest opening, she didn't hesitate to thrust them into other people's projects. No: he must work out every detail of his *Sleeping Beauty*, make it totally, irrevocably his, before he even whispered of it to this meddling dilettante.

He stood up and nodded his head, momentarily helpless. "Very well. Sasha will have a ballet."

"Something big and splashy with a lot of cymbals and leaps—like Rudy and Misha do."

Volmar winced. It seemed all a Russian dancer had to do was defect and the public would rank him with Nureyev and Baryshnikov. Could people really be so stupid?

"Promise now. Lots of leaps and barrel turns."

"I promise," Volmar said. "He'll have a ballet."

\* \* \*

Marius Volmar summoned the Russian to studio 3. "Dance for me."

"What you want?"

"Anything. Just tell Muriel."

Muriel was the company's worst rehearsal pianist. Volmar kept her on out of loyalty—she had been with the company a quarter century—and because bad pianists sometimes came in handy.

"You give me male variation from *Bluebird?*"

Muriel put her liverwurst sandwich down on the piano lid. She wiped her hands.

"I do my own treatment?" Sasha said.

"Anything you like," Volmar said.

"Good. I show you everything."

Sasha counted out two measures. Muriel thumped into the allegro.

Sasha danced.

He had strength, he had speed, he had balance. There was an undeniable maleness in that body and cunning and even art of a sort. Since company class Volmar had known he'd made a mistake: but not till today, till Sasha Bunin's first *tour en l'air*, did he realize how grave a mistake. Now he saw with sickening clarity that his life's work was in danger of annihilation.

A ballet company is many warring elements: it is dancers, musicians, choreographers, designers. But above all it is the single vision, the single idea of one man. If it has not that singleness, that unity, it is chaos—nothing.

This Soviet did not fit in with Marius Volmar's idea. He kicked it down like a paper house and set up his own idea, a brilliant idea perhaps, but not Marius Volmar's.

Volmar hunched forward in his seat, squinting. *There is a flaw here,* he told himself. *There has to be something wrong with this rush of movement, this sculpture speeding through time.*

"Stop." Volmar clapped. "What do you call that—that thing you just did?"

"I do not call it. I do it."

"Well, is it a *cabriole* or is it an *assemblé?*"

"It is Sasha. There is no name for it."

"Dance is a language, like music or mathematics, and every movement in it has a name. If it's a *cabriole*, it's not completed. And you're very far off the vertical."

"It does not matter. I can do it vertical, horizontal, anywhere in between."

"It matters. I want to see a correct *cabriole* and a correct *assemblé.*"

"Very well. Correct *cabriole*, correct *assemblé.* Would help if I could have correct music, please. *And!*"

Sasha began again. The *cabriole* was correct. The *assemblé* was correct. *I don't want to watch this,* Volmar thought. *But I must.*

Dimly, paying keenest attention, Volmar at last began to sense the flaw. It was an artistic, not a technical flaw, far too subtle for the untrained eye to detect. The variations in speed and placement were icily symmetrical. Everything was icily symmetrical. Sasha Bunin's dancing had the precision not of living matter but of crystal.

He was *too perfect*.

It went on two minutes longer, till finally Sasha rose on half *pointe*, in attitude. He shifted his weight back. With one leg hooked up he whipped into triple pirouette and landed on one knee, the other leg extended, arm in perfect arc, head cocked back and grinning.

The boy came down knife-clean on the final beat. Then, after a moment, got to his feet.

"There. You have seen Sasha. Is genius, yes?"

Marius Volmar's mouth was dry. Truth stuck to the roof of it. "No."

"Why not genius? Who else can do it?"

"Genius isn't a question of who else can or can't."

"Who? Who else? Tell me! Who else have you seen rise in turn from extended fifth?"

"I've never seen anyone else do it. I've never seen anyone who'd want to do it."

"In all Kirov, only Sasha Bunin can do it. You cannot deny: it is good, very, very good."

"It's not good. It's not good at all."

Tiny pink ridges rose like hen's scratches on Sasha Bunin's cheeks. "What is wrong with it?"

"Everything. From the desire to the execution. The same as with the rest of your dancing. It's all acrobatic, all childish, all bad."

"You don't like me?"

"I like artists, not children."

"But children can grow and I am talented, very talented, yes?"

Marius Volmar took his time. He lit a small cigar. He savored the first inhalation. He let the proud young Russian stand before him, out of breath and waiting and hurting.

"You're strong," Volmar conceded.

"Is bad to be strong?"

"You're too strong for your talent. You're too ambitious for your strength."

Sasha Bunin stiffened. "I want to learn. I want to learn from

Marius Volmar. You will teach me right ambition and right strength and right dancing."

"I can see I'll have to."

Sasha Bunin dropped to his knees and his voice became tight in his bowed head. "I shall work, *cher maître*: and you will be proud of me."

*Never,* Marius Volmar vowed, *I will never be proud of this cock-a-doodling barrel-turning Soviet rooster.*

\*    \*    \*

"Well?" Dorcas nagged. "Well?"

"Well what?" Volmar snapped.

"Well, what are you going to give him to dance?"

"Oh, a little something . . ." Marius Volmar's voice trailed off. He wanted for Sasha a role that was small but difficult, a role that demanded gifts Sasha did not possess and displayed none that he did.

Volmar scavenged the past repertory. He searched scores and squinted through sheets of Labanotation and spent hours viewing film and videotape. He hit upon something altogether inspired, a corpse that had lain twenty years in the company vault: ugly libretto by Jean Genêt, ugly music by Darius Milhaud, ugly steps by a choreographer who had died, leaving Volmar free to make them even uglier.

There were roles for three men, condemned murderers in a prison cell. The first raped the second, the second killed the third. No *grand pas de deux*, no leaps, no turns, no lifts, no lyricism, no line, no solo—no woman.

"It will do," Marius Volmar decided. "It will do perfectly."

He told the librarian to Scotch-tape the orchestral parts back together.

"There's a bassoon part missing, Mr. Volmar—should I have it recopied? It'll be $280."

"Forget the bassoon."

On Tuesday afternoon Marius Volmar announced to the press, with satisfaction, "The noted Soviet artist Aleksandr Fedorovich Bunin will make his American debut in one of the most technically and dramatically demanding of all ballets in the contemporary repertory: *Deathwatch*."

On Wednesday he announced it to Sasha, and on Thursday they began rehearsals.

At first Volmar felt sure of victory. Sasha's body strained and grimaced. And failed. Exaggerated extensions, wrists flung at right angles to the arm, flexed feet, all exactly opposite to classical technique—the positions and movements were utterly beyond him. He was a tongue trying to twist itself around an unknown language.

"Thighs turned *in*, Sasha, *in*—like Wally and Joe. Knees in. Hips forward. This isn't *Giselle*. Come on. *And!*"

Volmar made the dancers go over and over the deadly movements, knowing Sasha would have to give up in helplessness. The Russian's forehead was raked with worry and his limbs writhed in the trap. But the persistence of his efforts began to disturb Volmar. He could see determination glint in Sasha's eyes; he saw the blind, survival-minded animal gather all its strength and cunning.

"Sasha, we've got to do better than that. We've got six days to pull this together. *And!*"

With each attempt, lips pressed tight, brow streaming sweat, Sasha failed a little less. Volmar watched. Where three days ago the dancing had been rotten, today it was only mediocre.

"Four days, Sasha. Knees *in*. *And!*"

Volmar hunched in his chair, eyes sour. It wasn't bad enough. It wasn't bad. It wasn't bad at all. Like an ignorant child playing the piano by ear, Sasha had somehow caught the brittleness, the angularity, the jagged thrusts and lunges. He had caught the *idiom*.

The day before dress rehearsal he looked as good as the other two dancers. At the dress he looked better. After the rehearsal he turned in breathless sweat, like a horse wanting a lump of sugar. *"Cher maître?"*

"It will do," Volmar sighed. "It will have to do."

# thirty-three

Volmar stood in the wings that evening. The audience gave Sasha an ovation before he had even risen from his prisoner's cot. *Fools*, Volmar thought. *If they applaud him lying down, they'll bravo his backward somersault.*

And they did.

Dancers crowded curiously into the wings. Volmar kept a policeman's eye on the performance. But Sasha did not simplify the difficult movements, he did not exaggerate the showy ones. There were no Kirov interpolations, no corkscrews in the air, no barrel turns across the cyclorama. He stayed exactly within the music and the choreography, and Volmar could see the intensive adjustments to body and mind that it cost him.

When Sasha went effortlessly on half *pointe*, then in one quick jerk forward and down into *penché*, Volmar felt a grudging respect for the Russian: as an athlete, not an artist. Languidly, Sasha let his arms droop till the fingertips grazed the canvas stage cover. His eyes were huge and fixed and staring into the audience. Good eyes, Volmar had to admit. Perfect eyes for a dancer.

Then, in a movement that made the audience gasp and wonder if he'd hurt himself, Sasha dropped his head to the floor.

There was no face now, only waves of dark hair. A flute trilled, forever and low, stretching the stillness.

Volmar could feel the house holding its breath.

The orchestra broke into crashing polytonal discords. Still on half *pointe*, still in *penché*, Sasha began a mad, quickening series of blind backward hops. At least from the front of the house they looked blind. There was a trickle of white tape on the floor to guide him.

As Sasha spiraled backward a dancer whispered at Volmar's shoulder, "He's too good to be true." It was one of the girls, the Avery child.

True, Sasha's speed was remarkable, and when he reached the circle it was downright astonishing, like Kafka's cockroach running crazy on LSD. There came a final hop, a sudden thrusting out of all four limbs, a fall flat onto the stomach. The spotlight now caught the knife planted in his back.

Amazement rippled through the audience: how had the knife gotten into his back? An instant of silence from audience and orchestra alike, a flick of the conductor's baton, a final screeching dissonance, down with the curtain, and instantaneous thundering applause, throats bravoing themselves sore.

Utter *grand guignol*, Volmar reflected, utter trash, utter success. He had miscalculated and the Russian had won. Still, it was only a battle, not the war.

"He's a natural, an absolute natural." Dorcas was at Volmar's elbow. Her hair had been teased back and tinted in hundred-dollar waves and great clusters of Cartier fresh from the safe deposit box dappled her violet evening gown. Her eyes glowed. "It's a bitch of a ballet and you were a pig to give it to him, but you have to admit he's a natural."

"I admit nothing."

"Listen to that applause." Dorcas cocked her ear toward the curtain, rising for the third time.

"Publicity," Volmar said. "Politics. It has nothing to do with dance."

"It has everything to do with a sold-out house. And he's not a bad dancer either."

"There are flaws."

"We've all got flaws."

Volmar felt sorry for Dorcas. From the trembling in her eyes he suspected she might actually be in love with the Russian. He pitied her. She had natural bad taste and the money to indulge it. She would always be a slave.

"Are you going to keep Sasha on a leash," she said, "or are you going to let him dance something good?"

"By good you mean *Sabre Dance?*"

"We haven't had applause like that in fifteen years," she said dreamily. "It's like the old Ballet Russe."

The applause died a much too lingering death. Stagehands shifted scenery. Lighting men changed gels and the angle of spots. A growing flurry of inactivity onstage caught Volmar's attention.

"Why are they holding the curtain?" he said.

"Herb Kiley sprained an ankle warming up," the stage manager said.

"Who's covering?"

"Tony Likiourdopoulos."

"Well then, is he warmed up?"

The stage manager's face darkened. "He's in Rochester."

Volmar stared at this tall, stooped underling, eyes scampering evasively beneath the pudgy eyeglasses. It was an old game with stage managers. They played dice with fate, allowed covers to give recitals in Rochester high schools when they were needed in New York as stopgaps against disaster.

"Why Rochester?" Volmar said. "Why not here where he's scheduled?"

"His grandmother died."

"And he went to revive her?"

"Marius," Dorcas said, shocked and shushing.

Volmar ignored her. She doubtless believed in Santa Claus too and he knew for a fact she wept at TV reruns of *Wuthering Heights*.

"Who danced the role last week?" he asked.

"Phil Branson. I phoned. He's on his way in a taxi."

"In a taxi from where?"

"West Nineteenth Street."

"Too far. He won't have his costume or make-up. He won't be warmed up."

"I will dance the role," Sasha Bunin cut in. He stood bulging in leg warmers and towel-stuffed sweat shirt. "I am warmed up."

"You don't know the role," Volmar said. "You've never danced it, you've never even covered it."

"I saw it last week. My *entrée* is second retard, *grand jeté, piqué, tour,* assist Lang—"

*Your entrée,* Volmar thought, marveling at the gall.

Sasha's fingers marked, head bobbed. He hummed the Rossini. He was in the right key and, unlike the orchestra, he even caught the modulation. There were such dancers: they learned a role by watching a single performance. They danced a ballet once and they remembered every step of every other dancer in it. Living encyclopedias.

Lvovna was such a dancer.

So, if he was telling the truth, was Sasha Bunin.

"Marius." Dorcas clutched at Volmar's sleeve. "Let him."

Volmar had no choice. "Very well. Go get into some green unitards. We'll hold the curtain five minutes."

*"Merci, maître."*

Sasha scurried in one direction and Dorcas was about to scurry in the other. Volmar clamped a hand to her shoulder so sharply that brooches rattled.

"There will be no announcement, Dorcas. No drama."

Her eyes seethed at him. "You're being a bastard about that boy."

It made no difference.

Sasha *entrée*'d on the second retard, unannounced and anonymous in his green unitard, and a storm of applause swept the house. A flock of dancers pressed into the wings to watch. Volmar could see young faces glowing with astonishment and admiration.

*Sasha will ruin it,* he told himself, *he will dance too full, too strong, he will make the other men look weak.*

But Sasha danced with restraint, deferred to Stephanie Lang in the *pas de deux,* took no solo bow even though the other dancers tried to push him in front of the curtain.

*I was wrong about him again,* Volmar thought. *Maybe that's why I dislike him. He proves me wrong too often.*

After the last curtain call Dorcas steered Sasha into the dressing room of a principal who had been with the company twelve years. "Alex, would you be an angel?" She thrust Alex's clothes into his arms and hustled him off to change with the corps.

Through squinting eyes Marius Volmar watched the explosion of rot. A spill of reporters came flushing through the backstage corridors, sweeping dancers and dressers to the wall. Sasha received them bare-chested and quotable.

"Mr. Bunin, why did you come to the United States?"

"I came to America to extend myself. In the Soviet Union it is all *Swan Lake*—flap, flap. Here it is jazz, Balanchine, Martha Graham, nudity—Volmar. I want to show I am good at it all."

Flash bulbs flashed. Cassette recorders buzzed. *Clever little bastard*, Volmar thought, *he knew English all the time and never let on*.

"If you had stayed in Russia, would you have become a principal, like Nureyev and Baryshnikov?"

"I do not know if's."

Sasha took off his dance shoes. Sondra Kessler, who reviewed for a weekly and had a daughter at the School of American Ballet, lunged for one of them. Volmar could not see who grabbed the other.

"Has your defection to the West helped your career?"

"Not yet. I am still soloist—not principal." Sasha smiled with all the resources a face could muster. It was irresistible, the smile of an orphan boy with gonads. "Mr. Volmar says I am very bad dancer, with Russian habits. But he says I will learn to be better."

"Do *you* think you're a bad dancer?"

"No. I am great, like Stradivarius violin. Volmar is great, like Oistrakh. We are destiny for each other."

"Why did you defect?"

"Why you think? To get big publicity, big stage, big audience."

"I *do* beg your pardon, Mr. Bunin!" Ivor Noble's shrill lisp topped the uproar. "But aren't those pretty shallow reasons for defecting?"

Sasha glanced at the drunk little man with the bottom button of his blazer plugged into the top hole. "Do I need deep reason to shit?"

Volmar had to say one thing for the boy: he didn't ass-kiss the press.

"Are you heterosexual?" a woman asked.

Sasha peeled off his unitard. "Better you ask the girls."

"Are you living with Dorcas Amidon?"

He sat scratching an itch through his shorts. "Better you ask Dorcas."

\*     \*     \*

The next morning's papers howled and Marius Volmar frowned.

*More Sasha! More Sasha! Sasha is a national treasure!* In the same review, Ivor Noble—one of the greatest dance illiterates ever to cover drama, ballet, and cooking for one newspaper—singled out Stephanie Lang. "Miss Lang, alas, is not even a trinket, though, in the words of the late Hilaire Belloc, Marius Volmar appears to be preserving her as the 'chiefest of his treasures.' This critic is second to none in his admiration for Herr Volmar's many past achievements, but one must question the judgment of any company director who would pair an artist of Bunin's international stature with a novice of Miss Lang's lack thereof. The results, kindly put, were excruciable."

*And all because I wouldn't pay that vulgar little cockney three thousand dollars*, Volmar thought. It was a shame. Worse, it was false. Stephanie Lang had danced well. The mistakes had been those of her last-minute partner, not hers. She was good, getting better, and soon Marius Volmar would make her a ballerina.

*She'll stand up to this review*, he thought, crumpling it. *She's strong.*

Later items from the company's clipping service included color photographs of Sasha Bunin wearing Yves St. Laurent slacks ("$85 at Bloomingdale's St. Laurent boutique, New York residents please add sales tax"); a page of Sasha Bunin's favorite recipes ("low-cal cotelette à la Kiev: Sasha's secret is to take half a cup of cottage or farmer's cheese and half a cup sweet butter, and blend in his Cuisinart food processor—$225 at Altman's—'And then I take my poodle, Merde, for a walk around the block!'"); and an inch of newsprint from a gossip column ("'What do I care if she is principal or soloist or corps or cigarette girl so long as she is girl? Perhaps,' adds Sasha with a twinkle in his soulful brown eyes, 'is because I have no class distinction, am what you call pinko?' If you spell that word m-a-l-e, Sasha you hit it on zee button, da da da!")

\*     \*     \*

At dinner that night Volmar asked Dorcas, "Have you hired a press agent for Sasha?"

She mumbled through a mouthful of the restaurant's pâté and he waited for her to wash the swallow down with wine.

"Two. They're brilliant youngsters with the most incredible contacts. Can you believe they're getting us a spread in *Sports Illustrated?*"

Volmar turned on the banquette to face her directly. "It's cheap."

"And we're broke and it's selling tickets."

"Those innuendos about his sex life aren't even innuendos."

She shrugged and the Barbados tan of her shoulder slipped a half inch further into view. "Sex sells."

He studied her. "You don't care?"

She arched her head back and laughed softly. "My poor dear Marius—it's publicity, just publicity. Would you like a piece of my pâté? They've made it with Calvados, it's sublime."

\*     \*     \*

In the dressing room after performance Chris heard two of the girls gossiping about Sasha Bunin and some jet set party.

"How the hell does he have any strength for class? He couldn't have gotten to bed before seven in the morning."

"*Women's Wear Daily* says nine in the morning."

"It's not fair—he even photographs well. Do they say who he went home with?"

"Some millionaire from Texas. She's a model and very in."

Chris was dressed and ready to go home but she sat back down at her mirror and neatened her drawer, choosing powder puffs to be thrown out and powder puffs to keep, shoe ribbons that might make it through one more class and ribbons that definitely wouldn't.

"Is that her? Jesus, he likes them skinny."

"Novelty. There aren't any skinny rich girls in Russia."

"It's lucky Dorcas doesn't subscribe to this paper."

"How do you know she doesn't?"

"Unbelievable."

Chris heard paper crumple and hit the watebasket, and after the girls had gone she went and retrieved the clipping. She smoothed it out on her dressing table, weighting the corners down with a cold cream jar and bottles of bee pollen and vitamins. She read the article three times and each time she felt more hollow inside. She recognized the names of pop singers and socialites; it sounded like a lot of drugs and money and disco and she wondered what an artist like Sasha saw in people like that.

She was staring at the photograph of the millionaire Texas model, thinking the blond hair couldn't be natural, when something furry brushed her leg and made her jump. She looked under the dressing table. A huge gray poodle was chewing one of her dropped powder puffs.

"Hey, whose dog are you? Don't you know you're not allowed in the theater?" She petted the animal and pried the powder puff out of its mouth. One of the good puffs, thoroughly ruined. Damn. "Come on, pooch. They're turning out the lights."

She was buttoning her raincoat when a voice called, "Merde! Where is my sweetheart! Here, Merde!" and Sasha Bunin came bounding into the dressing room. He stopped short at the sight of Chris.

"Forgive—I thought girls all gone home." His eyes became shiny as chocolate drops. The poodle nuzzled his leg and he dropped easily into a chair. "Is all right I sit? I have been chasing Merde all over theater, no breath left."

Chris nodded. She noticed how strong and straight his neck was, almost feminine in its smoothness and length. Sasha gazed at her, smiling. She lowered her eyelids, unaccountably embarrassed.

"You are here late, last one, yes?" he asked.

She nodded.

"You dance *Alborado* tonight?"

She nodded again, intriguing him because she was still giving no clear hint as to whether she was an opportunity or a waste of his time. He snapped his fingers suddenly.

"Second gypsy, yes? I knew I recognize you. Very nice elevation. Very nice balance. Very, very nice."

A blush began to flicker in her face. *He doesn't remember me,* she thought. *We held hands over the Atlantic and he doesn't remember.*

Her hand went to the dressing table and before she placed her tote bag over the clipping he saw his photograph. A pleasant certainty came over him. He was not wasting his time.

"Do you like dogs?" he asked.

"I've never had one." A doctor had told her she was allergic. She wondered why she wasn't sneezing now.

"This is regulation show poodle. My very best friend in all America. I tell him all my secrets. What is your name?"

"Christine Avery."

"Of course, Christine Avery, second gypsy in *Alborado*, how stupid I am. Christine, this is Merde. Merde, say hello to Christine, she is very good dancer."

The poodle nuzzled Chris's skirt and she reach down to pet its neck. Her hand touched something through the thick gray curls. Sasha Bunin's fingers. The two of them stayed that way, the touch of their hands hidden in a poodle's fur. The air around them smelled of soap and rosin and powder and sweat. Chris felt outside the moment, aware but not taking part.

Sasha stroked her fingers and the dog, fingers and dog, until he felt her relax and become trusting and calm beneath his hand. "Where you go now?" he asked.

"Home."

"Walking?"

She nodded.

He studied the bridge of freckles across the nose, the sweep of ash-gold hair, the shyly bulging underlip. It came to him that she did not know she was beautiful. He smiled.

"Merde and I will walk with you. Merde needs to walk."

For a moment Chris looked away from the brown eyes that seemed to be memorizing her. Sasha watched with interest. Her uncertainty pleased him. She was the first uncertain American girl he had met. Finally her shoulders dropped as if there was very little strength left in them.

"Sure," she said. "I'd like to walk."

She felt safe walking with him. He was lean and strong, with narrow hips and broad shoulders, and he talked and laughed and got her to talk. She didn't feel lost or lonesome as she usually did walking home alone. Merde kept tugging on the leash, dragging them across streets in search of the perfect hydrant or tree, and finally settling for the white-wall tire of a Rolls-Royce.

"Merde has good taste, yes?" Sasha said.

She laughed. "The best."

She couldn't believe she was walking on West Seventieth Street at eleven thirty-six at night with the newest and maybe the greatest star of international ballet. Later, lying in bed, remembering, she would have time to believe it. For now she would just enjoy it. She felt alive and happy, but odd, as though she were on the moon, not earth. A different gravity pulled at her. She was lighter.

They reached her building.

"Will you invite me and Merde up?"

Without even thinking, she shook her head. "I don't live alone."

He seemed surprised and a little hurt. "Boy friend?"

"I room with a girl friend. She's with the company."

Sasha nodded. "I understand. Is okay." He put two fingers to his mouth and whistled a Checker cab to a brake-grinding stop. He held the door and Merde jumped in and he kept holding the door and she realized he was holding it for her.

"We go to my place," he said.

Something warm and whispering gusted through her and her knees felt liquid. "I can't."

"Why not?"

She didn't know why not. Maybe there was no why not and that was what frightened her. "I just—can't."

His eyes showed concern. "Wrong time for you?"

She nodded. "Wrong time."

"You very nice girl, Christine. Not like other girls."

She stood silent before him, breathing rapidly. His hand brushed her hair and then gently, reassuringly, lifted her face. The movement was grave and compassionate. An arm went protectively around her waist and another around her shoulder and he pressed her to him.

*I will never forget this moment,* she thought. *This moment is complete, nothing can be added to it.*

And then he kissed her and she felt her mouth dissolve under the kiss.

"You not forget me, Christine?"

"No, I won't forget."

"Next week we make date, my place?"

"Yes." She didn't dare but she still said yes.

Her hand clung to him and to the moment, and then he was in the taxi and the taxi was moving away. He turned and waved through the rear-view window and she saw the furry ball of Merde's head beside him.

She rode up the elevator in a glow of excitement. *Somebody cares*, she thought. *Sasha Bunin—cares.*

# thirty-four

There was a very short period in Chris's life when she awoke each morning to joy. *He'll talk to me today*, she thought. But in class Sasha nodded only one day. Another day he didn't see her and another he was talking to Lucinda Dalloway.

*He'll phone*, she thought, and she hired an answering service just to be sure of not missing the call.

"You're crazy," Steph said. "No one phones us except wrong numbers."

But he didn't phone and Chris realized he didn't know her number. *He knows the address,* she thought, *he'll write*. But there was no letter.

She began to feel betrayed and helpless, trapped in her own longing like a bird in an oil spill. The need to see him suffocated her. She had never known anything so strong in her life. She took to hanging around the theater after his performances. She lingered in the corridor near the men's dressing room. She heard voices laughing and Merde barking but she always panicked before Sasha came out and she ran and hid.

She saw him with women: Dorcas Amidon and Hedi Luftig, who danced with ABT, and Sondra Kessler, who reviewed for one of the news weeklies. *He's busy,* she thought. *He never knows till the last moment when he'll be free. He'll put a note in my box.*

She took to checking the A box four and five times a day. But the only note for Christine Avery came from Marius Volmar, and when she went to his office he asked if she knew the Danish composer Jakob Gade.

She shook her head.

"Years ago he did a very nice little tango. Light, but no lighter than Lehar. I'm thinking of a tango rhapsody. I'm going to make the part on you."

Which meant she was not even covering roles at Sasha's rehearsals. She was cooped up learning Volmar's new steps. The loneliness and lostness in her screamed. She wrote Sasha a note—*Please phone!*—underlining the words three times. She slipped it into the B box and then she thought of the company gossips and the humiliation if someone else should open it, and she went back and ripped it up and stood trembling, wanting to scream and not able to.

"Hey, what's the matter?" Steph stood staring. "You look like you need to hiccup and can't get it out."

Chris did not dare tell the truth. She knew Steph would laugh at her. She grabbed at the nearest excuse. "Volmar's making a new ballet on me and I'm just nervous, that's all."

She described the *enchaînements* and the leaps and the feet pointed in instead of out. She made it all sound harder than it was so that Steph wouldn't suspect how weak and stupid and in love she was.

Steph listened and looked at this girl with skin the color of bone. *She's not a conniver and she doesn't sleep around,* Steph thought, *and she's climbing up through this company faster than a surfacing shark.* Steph felt a terrible weight of envy. Perhaps no matter how hard she worked Chris would always be ahead of her. Perhaps Chris had some essential talent that she did not.

She watched Chris leave for rehearsal and she moved restlessly to the pay phone. Her dime hesitated at the slot. *I can't live like this,* she thought. *I can't be jealous of my best friend.*

She had to tell someone or she would explode.

She dialed her mother at work. There was a background of shouts and Anna Lang was shouting in the foreground.

"Mom, can I talk to you?"

"Make it fast—it's a madhouse here today."

"No, I have to sit down and talk to you. Now. Please."

"Honey, you sound like a mess. What's wrong with you?"

"I don't know. I just have to talk to you."

"Christ, I have an exercise class in five minutes. Tell you what, I can take a fifteen minute break at four. I'll meet you in the coffee shop, four on the dot."

*    *    *

Anna listened to her daughter, nodding and sympathetic. Her face revealed nothing and she said nothing.

But her mind was working. She sifted the evidence of the last two years. She sorted fragments and where she found matching edges she assembled them. She could begin to make out bits of a pattern, and the pattern was Marius Volmar.

She felt an anger unlike any other in her life. It did not blind her or sicken her. It gave her sight and strength. She saw she had been patient for too long. She saw with an absolute certainty that she must strike in her little girl's defense, strike now, immediately.

"Calm down, you're all worked up over nothing." She placed a reassuring hand over Steph's. "Chris is Chris and you're you and you're both talented. Sooner or later it was bound to happen. Just go home and soak in a hot bath. And don't worry. When you're doing Giselles and Juliettes and Odile-Odettes she'll still be dancing fandangos."

Anna told the people at Arden's she had to leave for the afternoon. She didn't even wait for their *no*. She strode out onto Fifth Avenue and hailed a cab, to hell with the three bucks, this was important, this was her little girl's *career*.

She was a familiar face, and the guard at the stage entrance nodded her past. The doors on the third floor of the State Theater had been outfitted with slots so that black and white plastic nameplates could be slipped in and out. The nameplate reading *Marius Volmar, Director* had been fastened with bolts.

The door was partway open. Volmar sat at his desk, gloomy and rocklike, chin propped on one hand and the other holding a grease pencil to mark an orchestra score. He bobbed time to some rhythm inside his head.

Anna stared a moment at the neatly bald head, the muscular neck. She inhaled sharply, gathering strength, then cleared her throat.

He did not hear.

She rapped on the door.

He looked up. For an uncomfortably long moment his eyes seemed to pull themselves back from a dream into an irritating reality. He nodded and got to his feet. "Yes, Anna—can I help you?"

"You can give me three minutes."

His eyes were politely curious. "You're angry?"

"I'm angry."

"Why don't you close the door? It's better to be angry in private."

She closed the door. He reached into a bookcase and placed a wine bottle and two glasses on the desk. The bottle had been uncorked and was already half empty.

"Now then." He blew dust off the stem of one of the glasses. "Would you like a drink?" The bottle gave a telltale xylophone rattle against the rim of the glass. He was nervous. Anna allowed herself a tiny smiling satisfaction.

"No thanks."

"One of the ballerinas brought me a case from France. I assure you, it's not bad."

She shook her head. "I never touch liquor."

"This is wine, Anna. Not liquor."

"I still don't touch it. Alcohol destroys muscle. And a lot else too." Anna sat down. Her hands were like restless children and she had to concentrate to keep them from squirming in her lap.

"And how much muscle do you need for an angry little chat?"

"I'll keep my head straight, thanks. But don't let me stop you. Go ahead and drink."

"Dear Anna—do you deny yourself all the pleasures of life? Or just the civilized ones?" He lifted the glass and drained it. His eyes watched her. She sensed a mockery in them that he did not bother to disguise and that she wasn't going to waste time trying to understand.

"I want to talk about Steph," she said.

"Naturally."

"Why do you hate her?"

An instant's silence slid by and he said, "Anna, you have no sense of other people. To you, that little girl is the world. To me, she's nothing. She's hardly developed enough to notice, let alone hate."

Anna sucked in her breath. The nerve of the man. "I happen to know for a fact that you hate her. And I want to know *why*."

"Anna, you're quite, quite mistaken."

"I think it's because of me. I think you hate her because I stood up to you and *no one* stands up to Marius Volmar. If Volmar tells sixty-two girls to pirouette *à la seconde*, they pirouette *à la seconde*. If Volmar tells them to bang their heads into a wall, they bang their heads into a wall." Anna's hands began shaking uncontrollably, like a drunk's. *Damn*. "You run an army, not a ballet company, and when I was one of your soldiers I rebelled and it's been stinging you ever since."

"I don't keep grudges," he said. "Life is too short."

"We all keep grudges."

"I've had a good deal more on my mind these last twenty years than the departure of a soloist."

"Principal," Anna corrected.

Volmar shrugged.

"And I know what you hate most of all," she said. "You hate what's inside Steph."

Volmar's eyebrows arched up.

"Talent," Anna said. "You've never had it. Not in yourself, not in your dancers. All you can do is boss the cowards who don't trust themselves. If one of your dancers has *real* talent you have to warp them or hide them or wreck them. If you ever let a *real* dancer on that stage, the whole world would see that NBT is a bunch of Volmar-programmed zombies. Faster than anyone else, more accurate than anyone else, and who cares?"

"You're right." His voice narrowed and his eyes were cold. "She has no speed, no accuracy."

A sense of raging justice made Anna strong and certain. She felt she was looking down at Volmar from a great, safe height, reading him as easily as an X ray. "Then how come she's in your company? How come you bid for her and when I turned you down flat you came crawling back with a bigger bid? You want her, *Mister* Volmar. She's *good*. One day she'll be great. You know it and you want in on it!"

His lips shaped a smile. His teeth showed, jagged and

undeniably his, but with the gray translucence of old china, as
though the cleanings that had removed the red wine stains had
taken off most of the enamel too. "Do you honestly believe what
you're saying?"

She kept her voice cold and flat, but her eyes were fingernails
ripping at the calm of his face. "Oh, I do, Mr. Volmar. I do. I'm
not clever and I never had an education, but I have eyes in my
head and I can balance the figures in a checkbook. And I can add
*you* up like two and two. I know exactly what you're up to with
Christine."

"Christine who? We have three in the company."

"Steph's roommate and best friend, that's who and you know
it." She was shouting but she didn't care. Let the eavesdroppers
in the corridor hear: they knew it already. "You're promoting
Chris into roles Steph should be getting and you're doing it to
make Steph a jealous wreck."

"What do I care who's jealous?"

"You care because that's the way you control your puppets."

He was motionless an instant. "Puppets? What are you
talking about?"

"*Puppets!* What else do you call them? Dancers? Boys and
girls?" Anna threw the words out like spit. "They come to
Volmar to find out what kind of food they should eat; how long
they should grow their hair; who they should room with; who
they should sleep with; whether they should be straight or gay or
a little bit of both. And you give them answers. Even if you don't
know or care, you give them answers. You're the boss. You're
Einstein. You're God."

"You make me sound like some sort of medieval alchemist."

"You're a crooked psychoanalyst." She knew she was saying
things that could never be forgiven. So what. He disliked her
already, considered her a pushy ballet mother. Most people
disliked her. She knew it and she was used to it. Life wasn't a
popularity contest, after all. "You get those kids to open up their
heads to you and you change the wires around so they're scared
stiff and hooked on you and screwed up without you."

At first she had felt a certain caution in confronting him, but
that was gone now. The words poured out. He was staring at her
with such surprise, such helplessness, that she didn't know
whether to laugh or reach a hand to comfort him. She gave him
two beats. There was no denial of anything she'd said.

"I'm wise to you, Mr. Volmar, and your tactics won't work with Steph."

"Anna . . . Anna . . ." He sipped from the second wineglass. "I can understand that you're worked up. Your child hasn't made the progress we'd all hoped for. But aren't you being just a little unfair to me?"

"Unfair? Tell me about unfair!" She stamped both feet on the floor. "I've *seen* the Volmar technique! I've *seen* you in rehearsal! You tell a joke and they're laughing two minutes before the punch line—because if they don't laugh you'll bury them in the back line of the corps! You give company class and you can't even demonstrate the movements but they all show up because Mr. Volmar remembers who takes his classes and who doesn't, and they can't afford to displease Mr. Volmar, not if they expect to dance solo in *his* company; or keep the solos he's given them; or stay a principal. And afterward they have to sneak off to a *real* class. They're scared shitless! You've got them so stuffed with hooey about Volmar and New York and art, they feel *lucky* wasting eight years in the NBT corps when they could be in Atlanta dancing leads!"

"My dancers are free." His voice was quiet now, subtly shadowed. "Any one of them can go to Atlanta, at any time."

"Damned right—and the suckers don't even *know* it!"

"I'll release Stephanie from her contract any time she wishes."

"Big deal. She doesn't need your permission."

"Whose permission *does* she need?" He aimed a level, inquiring stare at her. "Yours?"

"She takes my advice. What about it?"

"I fail to see the difference between being a puppet and being a momma's girl."

"The difference is, I'm on her side."

"Are you?"

"I've spent twenty years fighting for that girl and I'm not going to stop now."

"Anna . . . Anna . . . Do you ever slow down to think, or are you too busy kicking up dust storms? Did it ever occur to you that I might be on Stephanie's side too?"

"Then where are her solos? When are you making her a principal? How come Chris has got this fandango rhapsody and Steph doesn't have a *Do I?*"

"Did it ever occur to you that what's holding Steph back might be—her mother?"

Anna could hardly believe he'd said it. "I'm the only thing that keeps her *going!*"

"You drive her." Volmar nodded. "Undeniably you drive her. But there's a difference between being driven and being motivated. Now the fact is, she has very little motivation. It shows in her technique."

"How in her technique?"

"She can't hold her turn-out, for one thing."

He was calm now. Anna could see it was a false, lying calm, like a lid pushed down on a boiling pressure cooker.

"Steph has the best turn-out in this company—except for MacInness maybe, and she can outjump MacInness any day."

Volmar steepled his fingers thoughtfully. "Like you, Anna, I trust in Stephanie's talent. I'm willing to go on working with her."

"Oh, you're so generous with your praise, Mr. Volmar. And your precious time."

Now came a hissing, whispered shout. "I am willing to work with Stephanie, but I am not willing to work with the ghost of *Anna Barlow!*"

For a moment she could not answer. "What the hell is that supposed to mean?"

"It means you will never be a ballerina again." Volmar's voice had dropped from a shout to a cajole. She sensed trickery. "Stop trying. Hang up the toe shoes. Toss them into the Black Forest. Bye-bye, ballet."

"I'm talking about Steph, not me."

"I'm talking about you, not Stephanie."

"I can take care of myself."

"No, you can't. That's why you try so hard to take care of her. You're a fine mother, Anna. I wish *I* had had such a mother."

She studied him carefully. There was a disturbing kindness in the smile that lined his tanned face. Suddenly there was no breath in her.

"But you're a ferociously lonely woman. It shows and it breaks my heart."

"We're talking about Steph," she said through clenched teeth.

"It breaks *her* heart too. You see, Anna, your daughter has youth. She has ability. She'll take care of herself because time and nature are on her side. But who'll take care of *you?*"

The sudden gentleness of his voice stabbed at her.

"Who's on your side, Anna?"

"*I'm* on my side."

"Are you? Do you even have the time?"

Anna had not expected this. She retreated momentarily into silence, looking away from his eyes. "Steph's on my side too," she said softly.

"No, Anna. The debts of the children are never repaid to the parents. How could life go on? They're repaid to the grandchildren."

"I don't have grandchildren."

"My poor, poor Anna. You expect her to be your little girl forever."

Anna shook her head. She closed her eyes but she could not slow the reeling of her thoughts. "She'll always be my daughter. Nothing can change that. Not even you."

"You're *your* mother's daughter, Anna, but does that make *you* a little girl all your life? For twenty years you've been a woman. Soon you'll be an old woman. Why don't you wake up?"

"We're talking about *Steph*."

"We're talking about Anna Barlow—who could have lived her own life but instead chose to be a dybbuk in her daughter's body."

"What's a dybbuk?"

"A dybbuk is a woman who wants a second chance. There are no second chances, Anna. Not even by proxy. Don't waste another quarter century looking for one."

"Can we *please* talk about Steph?"

"Who was the last man to kiss you? Was it Marty? Was Marty the last man to hold you?"

"This is crazy!" she cried, but he went on.

"And the last man to say he loved you was Marty too. I can see that. And there's been no one since. In all those years. Poor Anna. Even you deserve a little better than that."

"Marty was my husband! Of course he loved me! Of course he said it!" But had he? Anna couldn't remember. She was losing direction. She felt she'd waded into a stream, seeking a shortcut to the other bank, and been swept into an undertow.

"Do you remember the first time I saw you?" Volmar said. "It was scholarship auditions for the company school. Do you remember the way I looked at you?"

"How do I remember if I remember? That was a hundred years ago. I was a kid, a dumb kid."

"I remember it very clearly. You *were* a kid. Tall and red-headed. Soft-skinned. And I was a young man."

"I don't want to remember!" Anna whipped the shout out at him. "There's no *point!*"

"I wanted you. But I was shy. And when you married Marty I was jealous. I fired you. I thought you'd give him up and come to me."

Volmar looked up at her. He was the same man as a moment ago but now he seemed pathetic and hurt. Anna tried to answer. There was no protest, no voice in her. Her throat was dry and her palms were moist and her heart was thumping.

"Don't *tell* me this," she whispered. "There's no use."

"When you came back I wanted you more than ever. And I tried to steal your little girl."

"I'm going," Anna said. "I'm not listening to this." But she didn't move. Some weight held her in the chair.

"You wouldn't let me have Stephanie. I took Christine instead. And you're right. I gave Christine roles she's not capable of. But not to make Stephanie jealous." He leaned forward. "To make *you* jealous."

"I don't believe this."

"You've always known."

Anna's jaw dropped. Her hand fell. She tried to remember all the sharp and true and killing remarks she'd stockpiled but they all seemed blunt and dull and of no help. "I don't believe you," she sighed. "I don't believe *this*."

"I know what I want and I'm a patient man. I want you, Anna."

"It's too late." She shook her head. "Even if it was true, it's too late."

"You're not going."

She struggled to her feet, both hands clamped to her ears. She moved quickly toward the door, ignoring the dizziness that tugged at her. Her fingers fumbled with the push-lock doorknob.

"I said *don't go!*"

He yanked her hands from the knob and now he held them,

crushed together in his fist, and they no longer seemed to belong to her.

"What's the matter with you?" she screamed. "Are you *drunk?*"

She saw Volmar's hand poised in mid-air and then she felt a stinging slap below her ear. Suddenly the room spun ninety degrees and she was staring at blank wall. A moan built in her lungs and swelled in her throat. It spilled out low and wounded and long like the pleading of a dog caught in a leg trap. Her control deserted her now and she began to sob.

"There, there . . . my poor dear Anna . . ."

He touched a fingertip to her tears and drew her head down to his shoulder and kissed her softly on each shut eye. The smell that came from him was a mix of soap and maleness and the clean mustiness of leather bindings on shelves. She could feel how strong and lean he was, surprising in a man his age. She could see how clean and neatly cut the nails were that rested on the sleeve of her forty-dollar dress.

She allowed his hands to graze on her shoulders and her face and her cheeks.

"I hate you," she whispered.

He stroked her patiently, soothingly. "I know," he whispered. "Let it out. Don't be ashamed. Don't be afraid of it. Don't be afraid of anything. You're safe now, Anna, safe. . . ."

\*    \*    \*

Afterward, Marius Volmar was not ashamed.

Not when Anna Lang clung to him. Not when she said she had to see him again. Not even when he said he loved her.

Everyone lacked something. The difference between Marius Volmar and most people was that he knew what he lacked.

Conscience.

Anna Lang thought she needed a mission and Stephanie Lang thought she needed a mother. Today he had shown Anna Lang what she really needed. With one simple act he had lifted her daughter's reins from Anna Lang's hands and taken them himself.

It was better that way.

Marius Volmar knew exactly what to do with reins.

# thirty-five

Steph sensed Chris edging into another of her breakdowns. The signs were creeping back again.

Early Sunday morning, before the rush of matrons with plastic laundry baskets and New York *Timeses* and loud voices, Steph was feeding dirty clothes into one of the coin-operated washing machines in the basement. She felt something in the pocket of Chris's blue jeans. She tugged out a stained, ragged envelope. To her astonishment, it held an uncashed NBT payroll check.

"Chris, I found this in your blue jeans. I don't think it could have survived another wash and spin-dry."

Chris stared at the pay check. It seemed to take her a moment to recognize what it was. An embarrassed smile came over her face. "I was wondering what I'd done with it."

"Wondering? I would have been screaming. Chris, that check is three weeks old. Those jeans were at the bottom of the hamper. Don't you budget your money?"

"I don't know—should I?"

A strange questioning look made Chris's eyes look bluer and larger.

"What's the matter with you lately? Last night I came home

and you were sound asleep and the door was unlocked. You leave the TV on when you go out. You forget everything—mail, toothpaste, groceries."

"Don't be angry with me, Steph."

"Not angry—just concerned."

"I'm all right."

"Sure?"

"Yes . . ." Chris let her shoulders droop. "No."

"Want to tell me about it?"

"Promise you won't say I'm a dope?"

"Promise." Steph sat down at the kitchen table facing her. They stared at each other.

"I think I'm in love," Chris said. "Does that sound awfully stupid?"

It didn't look like love to Steph. Love was pink cheeks and blushes and darting eyes. This was a wasting disease. "Does he feel the same way?"

"I don't know. We haven't talked. He's busy."

It sounded like another one of Chris's gay treasures. "Want to tell me who the guy is?"

"Sasha."

"Oh, my *God!*" Even worse.

"You promised you wouldn't say it."

Steph's patience deserted her. "If you get hung up on him, you're not a dope—you're a lemming! Look what he did to Ursula. He broke up Helena's marriage. When he ditched Molly she had to go to Payne Whitney for depression and they had to feed her intravenously."

"I wish someone would feed me intravenously."

"Chris, he's not even a Don Juan. He's a pinball player racking up a score. Girls aren't human beings to him. They're rosin to grind his dance shoes in."

Chris was silent. There was no denial, but she veered back from the force of Steph's warning. "I can't help it," she said in a tiny, white voice. "I love him."

"Yes, you can help it! You can just stick to your dancing and let Sasha wreck other people's careers—not yours!" Steph squeezed her hand. "And remember to deposit your pay checks—okay?"

\*     \*     \*

Chris tried.

She deposited her next pay check. And when at long last Sasha spoke to her after class—"You like picnic?"—she tried to say "No."

But it came out "Yes."

"Today?" His eyes were on her, warm and soft brown.

"All right."

It was a sunny day, mild for February, and she'd thought he meant a picnic in the park. But instead they took a taxi to a brownstone in the West Seventies. He let her into a studio apartment that smelled of new paint.

"Home," he announced. "You like?"

There was very little furniture: a Victorian framed mirror; a king-sized mattress on the floor with candy-striped sheets; and Merde, the poodle, prowling circles around a bowl half full of dog food nuggets.

"It's very bright," she said.

He threw open a closet door. She had never seen so many blue jeans in her life: there were dozens, stacked on shelves, dangling from hangers, piled on the floor—all shades from brand-new to washed-out.

"How many?" she asked.

"Forty."

"But—why?"

"Promise I make myself in Russia. I want blue jeans, I want dog, I want everything Soviet say no, you cannot have."

"Are you happy now?"

"Why should I not be happy? In America I have everything. Except furniture." He touched her cheek. "Will be better with furniture. Maybe you help me choose?"

"Sure," she said. "I'd like to."

He spread a tablecloth on the mattress. "Sit. We have picnic."

She sat on the tablecloth. He brought out a loaf of French bread, cheese and sausage, a straw-wrapped bottle of Chianti. He reminded her of a magician setting up his table.

"I make you sandwich."

He was so near to her that she could feel how warm his breath was. She was trembling. She drew back.

He gave her the sandwich and a plastic cup of wine. *"Zdoroviye,"* he proposed. "To health."

She sipped, and just as she was smoothing down her skirt

over her knees, the dog came bounding between them. Chris's wine spilled.

"Your bed!" she cried.

"Is all right. Merde, you have no table manners." Sasha struck the animal lightly on the nose. It ran immediately to a corner and sat cringing. Sasha brought a towel from the bathroom and sopped up the stain. "I would be crazy without Merde. When I have nightmares, Merde is here—to keep me from jumping out of window."

His eyes met hers. There was such gentleness in them that she felt he had caressed her and she had to hold her breath.

"What kind of nightmares do you have?" she asked.

"Memories—Russia—my family."

"Were you unhappy?"

"Aren't families always unhappy?"

"I don't know. I had some happy moments with mine."

"My family never had happy moment. Not one." His eyes were not solid brown. There were tiny gold-colored flecks in them that seemed to turn like pinwheels.

She could not look at his eyes too long without feeling dizzy.

"My father put my mother in house for crazy people. She was not crazy. But in Soviet they know how to make you crazy. My father tells doctors, 'Make Natasha crazy.' They give her drugs. Soon she cannot move. She cannot talk. She cannot choose when to piss, when not."

Chris shuddered. "Why did your father do that?"

"He was in love with other woman."

"Oh, Sasha, I'm so sorry."

He put away the uneaten food. He left the wine out.

He told how the doctors confiscated the presents he brought his mother; how they gave her electric shock, cut off her hair, destroyed her memory, turned her into an old woman. By the time the doctors released her his father had divorced and remarried and the government gave her one room to live in.

"Seven stairways to reach this one little room."

He told how his mother pulled a chair to the window in the one little room and jumped out. And then he sat silently staring into his wine.

His story had a mixture of effects on Chris and the mixture disturbed her. She was sad but at the same time excited that Sasha Bunin had confided in her. She did not like to admit that she could feel sadness and excitement at the same time. She tried to concentrate on being sad.

"Oh, Sasha."

She shook her head. She could not imagine a life where such things happened. She could not imagine people who survived such lives.

He was looking beyond her, into the mirror. He turned his head and smiled at her. There was such bravery and loneliness in the smile and such boyishness that she could not bear it. She wished she had the courage to reach a hand and comfort him.

"You are first person I ever tell this to."

"I'm glad," she said. "I'm glad you told me."

"I am glad you let me tell."

"I'd let you tell me—anything."

He looked at her and she began to blush.

"Ten minutes ago I was alone," he said. "And now I have friend, yes?" He touched a hand to her hair. 'Your hair is very soft. Like feathers on baby chicken. Have you ever held baby chicken?"

"No . . ."

He closed his eyes and brushed his cheek against her hair. "I think I am holding baby chicken now."

He laid a hand on her shoulder and drew her close. His lips moved gently along her throat and under her chin and up to her mouth. They kissed. And then they were quiet. She remained pressed against him, breathing fast.

"You are very kind to listen to Sasha."

"No," she said. "I'm not kind at all."

"Sometimes Sasha is very foolish."

"You're not foolish."

"Is foolish to say I love you?"

"No. It's not foolish. Not if it's true."

He smiled. His features were odd and uneven and one by one almost ugly, but his face was the most beautiful she had ever seen. *Or is any face beautiful when it's this close and smiling?* she wondered.

He lay back on the mattress and eased her down beside him. She let her head rest pillowed against his shoulder. She tried to master the rise and fall of her bosom, the unwanted blush that covered every inch of her body.

"Be peaceful," Sasha whispered.

"I want to."

"Are you afraid of Sasha?"

The poodle had come back to the foot of the bed and stood gazing at them. She took refuge in embarrassment.

"The dog," she said.

"Merde bothers you?"

He got up and snapped his fingers. Merde followed him into the bathroom. He said something in Russian. When he came back he had taken off his shirt. She could hear the dog pawing and whimpering at the closed door.

Sasha stood looking at her and for a moment she felt bewildered as a child. She heard the snap of his belt buckle and she looked away, snared in uncertainty. She did not know if she was supposed to take off her clothes or if he was supposed to. She did not know how these things were done.

She undid a button of her blouse.

"You are virgin?" he asked.

She felt a paralyzing rush of shame. She could only nod mutely. Her eyes went to his face, watching for some movement, some sign. Nothing in his expression changed, but she sensed something secret behind the smile.

"Do you mind?" she said.

"Do you?"

She lowered her eyes. "Not if you love me."

He came to her and nuzzled his face in her hair. Her hand closed on his neck. The strength and smoothness of it reassured her. "You will tell me when you are ready," he said. "I will be very slow. Nothing to worry."

She nodded, wanting to believe him. For a moment she was terrified and then he kissed her, deeply this time, and the terror drifted away. She shut her eyes and let her head rest against him. He undressed her, bending her this way and that as easily as the stem of a flower.

Then he held her a long caressing moment. His arms were strong but she could feel them being gentle for her. He stroked her and kissed her and all the time her eyes were shut. His whisper was warm and soft in her ear.

"Now?"

He didn't wait for her to answer. In one smooth move he was on top of her, taking her. There was an instant of stabbing pain that blotted out everything. She struggled not to struggle. She bunched her fist into her mouth and closed her teeth on it to keep from crying out.

And then something astonishing happened.

There was no pain, no fear.

*I've done it,* she thought: *I've leapt the abyss!*

She felt a warmth and closeness she had never known with another human being. She clung to him, weeping and grateful. The aloneness was gone.

Now there was Sasha.

When she opened her eyes and saw that he was really there, she was amazed and happy and she said his name over and over.

He put a finger to her lips, pulled away from her.

They lay side by side. Not talking. Not touching. After a moment he got up and opened the bathroom door. She watched the naked man and the panting dog.

She wondered, *What will Steph say when I tell her?*

And then, like a warning signal, her mind flashed memories of all the gossip and headlines, Sasha and this girl, Sasha and that girl.

*This will be different,* she decided. *I'm not going to tell Steph. I'm not going to tell anyone.*

*This is mine.*

*And I'm going to make it last.*

"Everything's different now," she said dreamily.

"Different?" He slipped into his blue jeans. He did not wear underpants.

"Now you're part of everything."

He smiled vaguely.

She couldn't quite understand the smile. She didn't know men but she thought she knew smiles. Perhaps this was a Russian smile. Perhaps it was his way of telling her how much he loved her.

"Now get dressed," he said. "We take Merde for walk."

# thirty-six

They never slept together again. He never phoned or spoke to her or even looked at her. There was no explanation, no reason. Chris was crushed.

She retreated into a private cave of shock and despair. For days she tried to feel nothing, to shut out everything. But she couldn't shut out the company; the whispers and rumors and eagerness pressed in on her. She couldn't help hearing.

Every day fresh rumors of Sasha's escapades ran through the theater. They were communicated by quick meaningful glances in class and whispers in the wings and hoots in the corps shower.

"He's been seeing Ernestine Paley."

"Ernestine Paley—who's that?"

"Rich."

"But he has plenty of rich girls."

"And he wants more."

"No kidding," another voice cut in sarcastically.

Dance gossip can be vicious; and blind. Nobody noticed Chris, turning her head away. Or did they? Rumors kept jabbing at her, almost as if they were aimed.

"So how long can he keep it up?"

"Until he has a heart attack. And he will."

"Come on, he's just a kid."

"Kid? He's going on twenty-six. Joanna saw his *passport*."

Like seagulls scanning a beach for dead fish, dancers searched newspapers and magazines for any Sasha tidbit that might have floated in on the tide of yesterday's gossip. Articles were clipped from *Women's Wear Daily* and *After Dark* and *Playboy*, from Rex Reed and Earl Wilson and the Sunday *Times* second section. They were passed from hand to hand at lunch and coffee break until they grew translucent with mayonnaise thumbprints.

Dancers read out the headlines, and their voices were mincing and pinched.

"'Sasha and Bianca, any fire to the smoke?'"

"'"Is crime to like girls?" quips Sasha Bunin, Soviet Russia's latest annual gift to American ballet.'"

*Why do they hate him*, Chris wondered, *and why can't I hate him?*

One day a new note, raucous and triumphant, sounded in the rumors.

"She's dropped him!"

"Who?"

"The actress—Lolly Popp—she got her Academy Award nomination and she ditched him!"

"Whoop-*ee!*"

Something fierce and jubilant flared through the company. Sasha Bunin, who could *entrechat huit* and double *cabriole*, who could fill every seat in the house and screw every girl in the company and outside of it, Sasha the invincible had failed and failed on page one.

He came to class late the next day. The dancers made room to let him through. They were silent and watchful now. They did not want to miss a single one of Sasha's movements or expressions, a single word or gesture that might betray the inner hurt.

Chris fought the force tugging her eyes but finally she turned and looked.

He moved his leg in a slow, perfect *rond de jambe à terre*. She loved him. She loved the pale beauty of his face and the smooth column of his neck and the strength that controlled his long, straight legs. She loved to see his body move without strain. His eyes were dark tragic wounds and they did not see her and she loved them too.

When she looked away she felt a despair, a finality such as she had never known. *He will never love me*, she realized. *He will love only those girls who stride through gossip columns with the golden confidence of goddesses. And they will never love him.*

It ripped at her.

After class the dancers leaned close together and whispered. They were bitchy and they were certain.

"He doesn't space his fingers."

"The footwork's slowed down."

"He *basted* those shoes in rosin."

Everyone was pleased. Except Chris. The image of Sasha ate into her solitude, into her waking and her sleep. It spread like a blot. If she saw a boy and a girl holding hands in the street or on television, she felt something corrode inside her. She had to look away.

She didn't want to eat and she had no appetite for sleep. All she wanted was to cry. Alone, she gave in to tears that racked her throat sore. She took her temperature and it was a hundred point one. She must have forgotten to shake the thermometer down, because she was aware of Steph observing her.

"Are you eating enough, Chris?"

"Lots."

"Sleeping?"

"All the time."

\*      \*      \*

Steph knew Chris and she knew the symptoms when Chris was preparing a new role. She knew Chris's sleeplessness and staring at walls. But this time there was more.

Chris's eyes were dark and unseeing, like windows shuttered against the cold, and silence lay over her like banked snow, and she sat in the rocking chair, not moving her body, the very life in her seeming to come and go like waves on a beach.

Steph wanted to help but she knew better than to push. She knew she could do most just by being there, silent and supportive.

The night of the premiere Steph sat with Chris and with a

fresh Kotex napkin wiped the thickening fear from her face. Chris had lost weight even since the final costume fitting, and the floor was littered with muslin snippets of last-minute adjustments.

Chris stared dazed ahead of her. "I forgot to invite my parents. Not that they would have come."

"Next time," Steph said, trying to sound light and cheerful, as though it were the most natural thing in the world for your parents to skip every one of your premieres in favor of some board meeting or Social Register bash. She brought Chris water to drink in a Dixie cup and Chris tried to refuse it.

"I'll bulge."

"Two swallows of water isn't going to make you bulge! You're wearing a skirt, not a body stocking."

A fine sheen of sweat had crept down from Chris's scalp, not enought to blur her make-up but enough to make Steph wonder why she was dehydrating.

"Come on," Steph prodded, "time's a-wasting." She helped Chris into her toe shoes and practically had to pull her to her feet.

"I'm dizzy," Chris said.

"You're scared. Every dancer is always scared, so stop making a production out of it."

Chris looked at Steph. The tone of voice had wounded her. Steph put an arm around her, partially for forgiveness but mostly to start her walking.

Steph walked her to the backstage barre. Chris was wearing leg warmers and a robe over her costume and Steph held the head shawl that she would wear onstage.

The orchestra was playing the final measures of *Mother Goose*. There was a rush of dancers' and stagehands' feet. The applause came loud and soft, like the volume on a TV turned up and down, as the curtain fell and rose and finally stayed down. Stage sets rumbled.

"I shouldn't have had that water," Chris said. "I have to pee."

"So pee."

Steph stood outside the stall. It sounded like a phony pee but it was one of Chris's rituals and every dancer's right. In the wing Steph helped Chris out of her leg warmers and robe. She draped the shawl around Chris's head and under her left elbow.

"*Merde.*"

They hugged. *Something's wrong*, Steph thought, *she just warmed up and she's ice cold.*

Chris waited silently for her entrance.

Behind the Moorish arches, the cyclorama was lit the noon-white of an Iberian sky and it blinded her. The curtain rose hissing and the footlights came up and she could feel their heat.

Across the stage's blazing abyss, cool and shadowed in the wing, she saw her grandee, Wally Collins. He was wearing Spanish-dancer trousers and a high-cut black jacket with flamboyant gold embroidery. He smiled his huge white smile, telegraphing it to her.

*I loved him*, she thought. *And he hurt me. Does he know how much, does he care how much?*

The music cut in: a solo violin sob, punctuated by two commanding orchestral chords. A downward skitter of woodwinds, bird-delicate and panicky: her cue.

She obeyed, went on *pointe*, skittered forward into the light and the applause. The violin sang, low and throaty and gypsy. Her feet did what they had memorized, a very, very slow turn on *pointe* that filled her skirt and caused her feet to wink in and out of her eyesight. Her hands made a partner now of her shawl. She came to a slow rotating stop, still on *pointe*, a balancing in attitude, a glance toward the conductor as gravity eased her down.

And then it was tambourine and tango and Wally sliding like a Valentino. Chris did not bother watching her own performance. Her body piloted for her, precisely and automatically. The stage filled with grandees and not one of them was Sasha. A dozen hands held and spun and tossed her and not one was his.

And when the applause came it had nothing to do with her, it was an ocean hurling itself at a shore. She went back and faced it six times. She gave Wally a rose from her bouquet and he bowed to her and finally the stage manager let her go back to her dressing room.

Steph was waiting. "Come on, Chris—smile."

"I'm smiling."

"That is *not* a smile." Steph shook her head. The dressing table and the chairs were banked with flowers. Applause was still coming over the loudspeaker.

And Chris looked as though she wanted to break into tears.

"Chris—they loved you."

"Nobody loves me. I danced horribly."

It was too much, too much of the same, and Steph cut in almost shouting: "What the hell is *wrong* with you? What the hell do you *want?*"

Chris did not answer. She knew what she wanted and it had nothing to do with applause. She wanted Sasha to want her. She would give anything, she would give dance, she would give life, if only he would want her just once more.

"You've had bows after every solo—three roles made on you—reviews—success—tonight you have your own dressing room—you've got everything a dancer dreams of!"

*Not everything*, Chris thought.

"If you don't know how to be happy, can't you at least be a little bit *grateful?*"

Chris did not know why her best friend, her only friend, was screaming at her. But she knew enough to make herself a blank, to remain perfectly still. The room was silent and then Chris took off one silver-hoop earring and it clinked as she set it down.

"I've worked every bit as hard as you, just as long as you," Steph shouted, "and I've got *nothing!*"

"You have so much more than I do," Chris said softly. "You have courage. I don't have courage or technique or control or feet. I'm a freak. But you're a dancer. A real dancer. And people love you."

"I can't believe this. Tonight of all nights, when they're tearing down the house shouting for you, you're sitting there counting mistakes and weeping tears for little Christine Avery."

"Why are you angry with me?" Chris whispered.

Steph stared at Chris's wide-open eyes and then her lips sprang back from her teeth like a tiger's. "Because I can't stand any more of this, and I can't stand any more of your goddamned self-pity!"

There was an instant of annihilation, of shock whooshing into the space where Chris had been, and Steph dashed from the dressing room and slammed the door and stood in the corridor feeling her heart hammer, trying to choke back the poison that was raging in her.

Her mind hopped in disconnected little lurches. A tiredness

came bombing down on her, spraying an ashen fallout of
hopelessness. Long after her breath had come back, long after
the poison had spent itself, shame burned in her. Shame not at
what she had done, but shame at feeling no shame for it.

She needed a darkness to pull over herself. She fled to the
shadows of the prop bins, of the canvas flats with their broad
brush strokes and patches, the electrician's cables and the totem
poles of dead lights. She listened to the theater going to sleep for
the night, the receding waves of voices, the distant slamming of
iron doors, the soft creeping hiss of silence through the wings.

It was twilight here, peaceful and sad and somehow not part
of the city. She sat on a stool, waiting for her thoughts to knit
together.

She did not know when she became aware of the man and the
dog. But gradually she knew they were there, fifteen feet away.
The man was seated on a ladder. She sensed he was gazing
inward at some hurt in himself. The dog seemed part of the
man's concentration. There was a flicker of a hand when the
man leaned down to pet the animal. The face bent into a ray of
light.

It wore a look of utter desolation and she saw that the man
was Sasha Bunin.

*He's crying*, she realized. There were no tears, no sound, but
he was crying. And the dog heard him. She knew all the stories
about Sasha and the girl friends he changed as often as he
changed blue jeans, but she had never thought of him crying.
She had never thought of him alone, eight thousand miles from
home, with no friend but a dog.

It came to her that she had been wrong.

Not only about Sasha Bunin. She had been wrong to be
jealous of Chris. Wrong to lose faith in herself. As she stared at
the man who was staring into shadows, she felt her muscles
stiffen and her will harden.

A fierce glow of certainty came into her.

*I'm jealous and I'm frightened and I'm human,* her blood
whispered. *But I'm something more.*

*I'm a dancer. Like him. No one will take that from me.*

*I will fight what is weak in me and I will win and I will dance.*

She thanked Sasha Bunin silently and left the wings on
tiptoes.

\*    \*    \*

A thin rain of applause was still spilling through the speaker. Chris heard a knock at the door. She looked up, saw herself in the mirror, and realized she'd been crying. She grabbed the cold cream.

"Come in," she called, glopping over the tear tracks.

She'd expected the dresser, but the door opened softly and Ray Lockwood stepped in. He had a girl with him.

Chris stood and tried to smile. "Hello, Ray."

There was an instant of eye contact and then he pulled his glance just a little to the side. "Brought a friend," he said. "A fan of yours."

An odd jauntiness radiated from him, filling the room with a faint unreality.

"Claire Morgan, Christine Avery. Chris, Claire."

"I really adored your performance." She was a dark-haired girl with dime-shiny eyes and a small blunt thimble of a nose and she spoke with a Social Register drawl.

"It was sensational, Chris," Ray said. "As always."

He saw that Chris had lost weight. Every sinew and tendon of her birdlike body stood out in the glare of make-up lights. His throat filled with the old grieving ache.

"I've never been in a dancer's dressing room before," the girl said. "Mind if I explore?"

"Go right ahead," Chris said.

The girl began prowling. She brushed the chair where Chris had laid her robe and brown and red silk splashed to the floor. Chris could almost hear a rasping sound as the girl drew her eye along the wall. A photograph attracted her and she went and snatched it off its hook.

"Who's this?"

"My teacher. But it's not mine—this isn't usually my room."

"Lvovna?" the girl said sharply. "You studied with Lvovna?"

"That's right."

The girl stood examining the picture, frowning at Chris as though to superimpose her on it.

Ray's toe tapped softly on the floor. "Claire studied dance," he said. He was looking at Chris as though he'd asked a question and was waiting for an answer.

"That was years ago," the girl said. "And I never studied with anyone quite so well known as Lvovna."

A swell of voices came gusting over the speaker.

"At the moment I'm a market analyst with Kidder Peabody," the girl said. "The stockbrokers."

Chris nodded.

"Claire and I are engaged." The words came from Ray in such a low rush that Chris was not certain she'd heard right. She looked at him blankly. He was watching her, measuring the response in her eyes.

Her gaze went curiously from Ray to the girl and finally she said, "Congratulations."

Her reaction bit physically into Ray. He saw that she had never cared and never would care. He took his fiancée's hand. "We'll be married this spring."

"You're invited," the girl said. "And if it wouldn't be too pushy of me to suggest a wedding present, I'd love the shoes you danced in tonight. Could you autograph them?"

"Sure," Chris said quickly. "Do you want them now?"

"Why not, while they're fresh."

Grateful to have an excuse to sit down, Chris unlaced her shoes and took the ballpoint pen that Ray was holding out.

"Could you put the date," the girl said, "so we can tell our grandchildren it was the premiere?"

Chris signed the sole of one slipper and wrote the date and name of the ballet on the other. The slippers were still warm when she handed them to the girl. "They're a little stinky, I'm afraid."

"We'll give them the place of honor," the girl said, "stink and all."

Without warning Ray bent to kiss Chris on the cheek. "You were beautiful," he said.

There was something desperate in his eyes and Chris couldn't answer it.

"I think Chris needs to shower," the girl said. "And, Ray, you've got Max Factor on your mouth."

They went and the thought stabbed Chris, *I'm losing everything...everyone.... Soon there'll be nobody, nothing...*

# thirty-seven

"What's that?" Dorcas said suspiciously.

Volmar had phoned to warn her he was dropping by, but not that he was dropping by with champagne. He handed it to her, smiling. "For you."

"And that?" She nodded, not smiling, at the package still in his hand.

"For us. Open yours first."

She did not bother unwrapping the bottle. She pulled off a strip of paper to expose the label. The *Taittinger brut* gave her pause. "Nineteen sixty-three. And chilled. Damn it, Marius, I'm not confessing to any more birthdays."

"Am I asking you to?"

"If I open this—and you know I'm going to—you'll take it as an admission. You've always had the ridiculous idea that I was born on February nineteenth."

"I assume you were born one day or another. What's wrong with February nineteenth?"

"What's wrong with it is that it's today."

"My dear, you're not getting any older. But the champagne is. Why don't we taste it before it turns to salad dressing?"

Dorcas summoned the Bolivian maid and dispatched her

with a burst of Spanish in which Volmar could discern only the word *champaña*. Just as teacups never appeared at Dorcas' without platefuls of cakes, the champagne glasses arrived with a bowl of lady fingers. Volmar opened the bottle, was pleased at the healthy pop of the cork.

He poured and raised his glass.

"Not to me," Dorcas said. "Not to us. Not to auld lang syne."

"To Pyotr Ilyich Tchaikovsky."

"All right, I'll drink to that. What's the occasion?"

"This is the occasion." Volmar slid the package across the coffee table.

Dorcas shook it, made a face. "An art book?"

"Not even warm, my dear."

She undid the wrapping paper, opened the loose-leaf binder, stared at the Xeroxed pages. Puzzlement rippled over her face and then a dim sort of understanding. "But it looks like his autograph."

"Most definitely."

"I'm a lousy sight reader. What is it?"

Volmar had completed his plans for the ballet. Every detail was fixed and glowing in his mind and he held in his hands Sleeping Beauty's reins. He was ready at last to share his vision with Dorcas. "Aurora's Act One solo—dropped from the Petersburg premiere. Not a note of it, not a step of it, has ever been performed in public."

Dorcas' eyes scanned down the page, skepticism and interest mixing in them like a yin and yang wheel set spinning. "This is the full orchestration?"

"The composer's own. And"—Volmar leaned across the table and gave the pages a flip—"the short score of the Act Three prelude and Aurora's variation. Tchaikovsky's scoring—not Stravinsky's. We could restore the original."

For an instant Dorcas' gaze was dreaming and hungry. Her lips took a kiss of champagne. "What a coup that would be. . . . But Petipa's choreography for the solo—it must be lost."

"Not lost." Volmar shook his head. A smile teased at the corner of his mouth. "*Dazzling*. He conceived a *pas de deux* danced by Aurora alone. The partner is invisible—imaginary— and yet he is *there*—visible—in Aurora's reactions."

Volmar stood, hands sketching the movements in air.

"He supports Aurora. He lifts her. There is even a passage, a variation for the absent partner—which of course refers to Florestan's Act Two variation. But the harmony is open, ambiguous. It works beautifully."

"You've seen it?"

"Several times."

"But how?"

"Lvovna taught it to one of the girls."

Dorcas stared at him one girlish instant, then hugged him. "Oh, Marius, this *is* worth having a birthday for. Will you play it for me?"

Dorcas Amidon was one of the two thousand New Yorkers rich enough to pay the maintenance on a living room big enough to house a nine-foot concert grand piano. She was also one of the two hundred New Yorkers who had been rich enough long enough to own a Steinway Model A concert grand. The last A's had been built before World War II, when the government conscripted seasoned piano wood for gliders.

Volmar lifted up the music stand and propped the Tchaikovsky open to page one. "This is going to be a very inaccurate impression. The harp—her preparation. Fortissimo brass, three chords—his entrance. His spotlight is empty, of course. Kettledrums, light soft strokes, set the adagio tempo. Melody in winds, it's a fascinating doubling, flute and bassoon unison, not octave. . . . She arabesques, he supports her—she has to overbalance, very few dancers can do it. Forgive me if I sing here, there's a countermelody here, cellos."

He was no expert at sight-reading orchestral scores, but he managed a reasonable likeness. As the last notes of the *pas de deux* died away Dorcas was staring off at some far horizon.

"A restored *Sleeping Beauty*. It could be the spring gala." A crisp practicality tiptoed into her voice. "We have the sets from the '66 production—if they haven't grown fungus."

"We can clean them up."

"And with new costumes for the principals—how many principals are there?"

"If you count Puss in Boots and all the storybook characters, two dozen."

"We could pinch the courtiers' gowns from *Giselle* and *Swan Lake*."

"We'll have to."

"Who do you see as Aurora?"

"I was considering somebody new."

She stared at him appraisingly. Under the company charter he had the final say in casting: she became acting director only during his absence or illness. "Do I dare ask who?"

"You do not."

"We need names, Marius. A gala runs from twenty-five to two hundred fifty a seat. For that kind of money, people expect brilliance."

"Brilliance will be no problem. We'll pack the production with principals."

Dorcas nodded. He could see the notion ignite her.

"Cameo appearances," Dorcas said. "Lucinda could do the Lilac Fairy. Sally Shelley for the Enchanted Princess." She smiled. She loved galas. "And for Bluebird—Wally could do that brilliantly."

"There are several roles he could do brilliantly," Volmar said—including, he was careful not to say, the male lead— Prince Florimund. Let her think it could go to her adorable Sasha if that would make her an ally. After all, he needed her vote to get the project past the board of directors.

"And Prince Florimund?" Dorcas said.

"My dear, we don't have to cast the entire ballet this minute."

"We should know who our principals are going to be. There's the publicity to think of."

"We'll think of that in due course."

"You're too casual, Marius. A gala is business. It's practically high finance these days. We could make a fortune out of this. We might even be able to interest Public Television. If we had the right names ..."

She didn't finish her sentence. Volmar turned, following the direction of her glance. In the open foyer door stood Sasha Bunin, boyishly trim in his blue jeans and Adidas sports shirt, glowing as though he had just come from class or some girl's bed.

Volmar had heard no doorbell, no maid. Obviously Sasha had been promoted: he now had his own key to Dorcas' co-op.

"Why, Sasha," Dorcas said, "I didn't hear you come in."

"He's as quiet as Puss in Boots," Volmar said.

Dorcas bridled visibly at the remark linking Sasha to a subsidiary role in *Sleeping Beauty*. As though to show he was very much the *premier danseur*, Sasha gave a forlorn, Petrouchka-like shrug of shoulder and face that was worthy of Misha Baryshnikov.

"I did not wish to disturb," Sasha said. "You are working?" He plunked a kiss on Dorcas' cheek that was downright proprietary in its nonchalance.

"It's grown-up talk," Dorcas said. "You'd better scram for a while."

Sasha's eyes lingered on the champagne, the two glasses. He smiled. Volmar felt a tremor of irritation, distant and suppressed, like the passing of a subway train twenty-two stories below.

"Very well, I shall scram and shower. It is nice to see you, Mr. Volmar."

An awkward silence followed.

"He's not living here, Marius. It's just that he has an awful landlord and the plaster's falling down and there's no hot water in his place."

"His English has improved miraculously."

"Yes, isn't he a wonder? Marius, for Prince Florimund, don't you really think—"

"I really think that decision comes later, my dear."

\*     \*     \*

Afterward, Dorcas lit another cigarette, gulping down smoke as she paced.

She wanted Sasha to dance that gala. She sensed that Marius, perverse as always, was veering toward opposition. Persuasion would be required. She had to catch Marius like a fly, and the flypaper had to be scented with Chanel.

She cocked an ear to those inner whispers that had been her automatic pilot for fifty-four years. The silence of the apartment flowed over her.

It was a New York silence: honks and brakes of Fifth Avenue traffic, the whine of a jet passing four miles overhead, the whispering of water pipes in the walls, the footsteps of neighbors, muted though foot-thick ceilings, reminders that even at your loneliest you were never more than twelve feet from someone else in this city.

If she stood absolutely still she could hear Josefa in the kitchen, humming and clattering dishes; farther away, very faintly, she could hear Sasha's tape recorder—the piano music he used for exercising at home. When she lived alone the apartment had had one sort of silence and now with Sasha it had another. She preferred the silence now. She liked knowing that he was in the house somewhere, running a bath or reading a book or napping. It gave a comfortable explanation to the sorts of noises old co-ops make.

Of course he wasn't in the house as much as she'd have liked. He was young, and independent, and sensitive about appearances. She'd agreed when he wanted his own place.

For appearances, he said.

Appearances kept him out two or three nights a week. She minded, but not unbearably.

Suddenly it came to her: a dinner party.

She would invite a who's who of money, arts, and glamor. Sasha would be the centerpiece. The guests would simply assume he was dancing the lead. The assumptions of the powerful, after all, had a way of becoming public policy. The ballet might not even be mentioned, but the party would amount to an announcement and Volmar's presence to an endorsement. Rumor would spread through ballet circles and the media, the top-priced tickets would be snapped up long before the first mailing, and it would be impossible—short of a humiliating retraction sure to alienate the company's major supporters—for Volmar to cast anyone else.

Eagerness pulsed though her. She slid aside the glass-paned door and stepped into the dining room, mentally roughing out table placement and seating. Her heart beat with the hot certainty of success.

*     *     *

"Christine Avery, please?"

"Speaking."

"Christine darling, this is Dorcas Amidon? I'm giving a little dinner party on the ninth for Sasha? We'd be just delighted if you could drop by, eight o'clock sharp?"

Chris stifled a quick intake of breath. Sasha wanted to see her, after all these weeks of silence? Before she could stammer a yes, another thought shot through her mind: Why wasn't Sasha phoning? Why so far in the future? And why did they have to meet at a party?

Her mind skimmed for an excuse. "I'm dancing."

"It's a Sunday, Christine, the theater's dark."

"But I'm dancing Monday."

"Well, if that's a problem, we'll just arrange it so you're *not* dancing Monday." Dorcas' voice slid from one gear to another. She was no longer courting the daughter of a Chicago industrialist who could add luster to her party: she was instructing an employee, a corps girl who'd better stay in good with the boss if she ever expected to make principal. "This is important, darling."

"I'd love to, but—"

But she was scared. She wanted to see him: more than anything she wanted that. But she was achingly aware that she'd need support.

"Good. Sasha will be so happy. We'll count on you then?"

"I've already made plans," Chris blurted. "Could I bring my friend?"

A chill whooshed from the phone. "Darling, you'll just have to unmake your plans."

"I'm sorry, but I can't."

"Now really." There was a silence. Christine stood dripping wet from her bath, beginning to shiver. The phone sighed. "All right. Who's this friend?"

"My roommate—Stephanie Lang."

*       *       *

She didn't see him.

Chris stood in the foyer and didn't see Sasha anywhere in the cool dim churning of gowns and jewels and dinner jackets. A maid took their coats. "Go right on in, please."

Chris and Steph went right on in. Three steps. Chris's eye searched. Waiters wove deftly though the crowd. Hands reached toward trays of drinks. Rings and bracelets and cuff links shot

out needles of light. A hundred conversations jumbled together
and arrows of tipsy laughter came flying above the gray roar.

"We should find Dorcas," Steph said.

Chris's eye swept the mobbed, perfumed twilight. "You look
for her. I'll be along."

"You're sure?"

"Sure."

Steph got scooped up in the mob and Chris stood alone and
squinting and uncertain. A humming white noise of chatter
came whirling up around her. She took five deliberate steps into
the crowd and felt swallowed up, lost, unreal, as though she
weren't there at all.

She didn't see Sasha anywhere.

She struggled to ease a way through the guests, whispering
"Excuse me's" that were sucked into the chatter. She recognized
some of the faces: the Rockefeller who had been Vice-President;
the New York senator whose wife had almost been caught in an
Iranian conflict of interest; Jacqueline Onassis.

With a courage she had not known she possessed she raised
her voice. "I said excuse me, please."

She pushed. There was a pocket of silence and Jacqueline
Onassis turned and looked at her.

"Why, hello," Jacqueline Onassis said.

Chris gulped out a hello she did not mean and pushed past.
She stood on tiptoes. She didn't see him by the piano or in the
groups by the sofas. A waiter stopped her, offering a tray of
shrimp and hot cheese puffs and bits of liver wrapped in bacon.

She shook her head.

And then she saw him. He was standing in a corner. He was
wearing a slimly tailored tweed sports jacket and if he'd had a
tan he would have looked like a model with his grinning face and
curled dark hair.

The guests were pressed thicker and it took more chopping,
almost shouted "Excuse me's," to get through.

She saw he was wearing blue jeans, too.

She stopped.

He was listening very carefully to a girl in a strapless print
gown, a tall brunette with huge breasts. His expression was sad
and laughing and astonished and attentive all at the same time.
The girl kept gesturing with little strokes of a slender jeweled

hand and he nodded as though his attention were tied to that hand with a thread.

Chris tried to look cheerful and unconcerned as though the tide of the party had just happened to sweep her there. But her heart was pounding painfully and she wanted him at least to look at her, to give some acknowledgment.

She kept darting glances up at him through her eyelashes, and finally she cleared her throat. *He must see me*, a voice inside her screamed.

"Now I'll be furious if you're not here when I get back," the girl said.

"I'll be here," Sasha said.

"Promise?"

Sasha laughed and Chris did not find the sound of that laugh encouraging at all. His hands were on the girl's shoulders, two flashes of white on tan, and he bent to kiss the tip of her nose. The girl turned, smiling. She had triumphant emerald eyes that flicked over Chris as she slid past.

Chris felt a faint blush spreading over her cheeks and she felt a coldness flowing out of Sasha like a door of a refrigerator left open. The silence between them grew till it had the weight of a tombstone. His gaze swiveled toward her. The "hello" froze on her lips.

For one instant, one instant only, he looked at her with eyes that were clear and cool. Her heart turned over. He said nothing. The gaze moved on.

It came at her like a slap: for Sasha she did not matter, did not exist, was not even there.

"Sasha darling," Dorcas Amidon cut in, and Chris stepped back. Tonight Dorcas was tall and confident and lightly dabbed with jewels. She wore a lime gown perfectly tailored to her slimness, and her chestnut hair was perfectly swept back to accent her green eyes. She might have been exhibiting her prize thoroughbred stallion. "I'd like you to meet some dear, dear friends, Bunky and Binnie Finch."

The Finches were a conservatively dressed gray-haired couple in their sixties, both very handsome.

"Binnie's a great ballet fan, and Bunky's with Coca-Cola."

Sasha accepted the introduction with solemn courtesy.

"I'm something of a ballet fan myself," Mr. Finch said.

Gently, Dorcas pointed her thoroughbred. "You've drunk Coca-Cola, haven't you, Sasha?"

There was an exquisitely timed hesitation. Sasha broke into a smile. "But of course. I adore Coca-Cola. Cannot get in Soviet."

"You people have a deal with Pepsi, don't you?" Mr. Finch said. "How's that working out?"

Sasha made a face. His Petrouchka face. "Pepsi? No comparison."

Dorcas was pleased. The press had made Sasha a national hero, an overnight American. In a moment Bunky Finch would ask him to endorse Coca-Cola and NBT would be ten thousand dollars nearer its gala.

Dorcas lingered long enough to make sure conversation was moving in the right direction. Then she excused herself and mingled.

The party was a success.

Her rich guests adored the darling, talented, fiery Russian with the cunningly broken English; and Sasha obviously adored being adored.

Dorcas chatted with the Duponts, who'd flown up from Wilmington, and the Havemeyers, who'd flown up from Philadelphia, and that took care of two Ford Foundation votes. Her rule was sixty seconds per guest, and it was a coup to find the Taylors and the Terrys and the Creasys all standing together at the bar—two Wall Street brokerage houses and an airline in one swoop.

"His English is so *good!*" Amanda Terry cooed.

Dorcas took a glass of Perrier from the bartender. "Completely self-taught," she said. She didn't know who the hell had taught him but it sounded good.

"He seems to have a great respect for free enterprise," Farley Taylor said.

"Who wouldn't, coming from *that* hellhole?" Dorcas said.

"We're thinking of an ad campaign on ideas that made America great. Would he be interested?"

Dorcas smiled. Farley's airline was losing two hundred million a year and he was still trying to buy the public, the Congress, and the President. Dorcas had a second rule at parties: save the no's and the negotiating for tomorrow.

"I'm sure he'd love it."

She moved on to chat with a cancer specialist from Sloan-Kettering—she hardly knew the man, but something about cancer specialists loosened guests' purse strings. Sixty seconds with the new photo-realist painter—his work was awful but *Vogue* had done a spread; sixty seconds with that dreadful girl from Louisiana, a piece of swamp trash that the President had put in charge of the federal arts giveaway—no way of not being nice to her; and then Dorcas spotted Marius Volmar sitting by himself at the end of a sofa.

"Marius, you're being sullen."

"I'm being bored."

"Stop being bored. Go out there and raise some money."

Dorcas turned and collided with Harry Hirsch from the board of directors of the second largest cosmetics company in the United States. They'd given lights to last year's gala; he was carrying two drinks, so it was safe to pretend she was dying to chat.

"Harry, wait till you see the costume sketches, I just know they're going to start a whole new trend."

"We're coming out with a line of costume jewelry," Harry said. "It's going to be sold at perfume counters."

It sounded *revolting*. "But that's marvelous, Harry. We haven't even *thought* about Sleeping Beauty's crown—I'll bet we could work in some of your brooches, with a nice credit in the program."

She watched for the shift of calculation in his eyes. She saw it.

"I'll give you a ring," he said.

"Let's have lunch." Dorcas moved on into another near collision. "Why, Emily Brontë!" she cried.

Emily Brontë Bateson had flown up from Dallas. You had to remember to call her Emily Brontë, because that was her first name, not Emily.

"Where is he?" Emily Brontë said.

"Where's who, darling?"

"Your Russian."

"Oh—where the women are thickest, I suppose."

"I want to sit next to him." Emily Brontë wore too much jewelry and she had a habit of getting drunk early at parties.

"Keep your fingers crossed, darling. You might be at the same table."

"I want to sit next to him."

Emily Brontë was oil. To her, culture meant giving the Metropolitan Opera seventy-five thousand to put new ponchos on the knights in *Parsifal*, then buying out the boxes and jetting a private planeload of friends to New York to see her name in the program.

"I'd have to change the place cards," Dorcas said.

"What do you need—sets, lights, costumes?"

"Oh, darling, don't be ridiculous."

"I want to sit next to him."

"Let me go take care of it right now." Dorcas hurried into the dining room. A snow-colored twilight hovered expectantly over the tables. The candles floating in Baccarat bowls lent a shimmer to the crystal and china and silver. The centerpieces were fresh orchids and they gave the air a faint pleasing sweetness.

The seven waiters from the agency prowled about in their cut-aways, checking place settings.

Dorcas located Emily Brontë's card, went quickly from table to table. It wasn't a question of exchanging two cards but of recalculating entire balances and chemistries. It took eighteen switches before Dorcas felt she had reapproximated order.

She told the butler, "You may announce dinner."

*       *       *

Throughout dinner something bothered Steph, a feeling she could not quite define.

The senator on her left and the fashion designer on her right made interested, interesting talk, the food was delicious—she had never tasted veal scallops in madeira before—but a sense of incompleteness nagged at her. After coffee, as the guests drifted back to the living room, she looked for Chris.

She didn't find her in the living room or in any of the bathrooms. A couple was necking on a pile of mink in one of the bedrooms, but the woman wasn't Chris. Adrift in uncertainty, Steph found herself on the terrace. At first she thought she was alone with the boxwood hedges and garden furniture.

"Chris?" she called.

She stood a moment listening. Traffic moved in waves twenty-two stories below, almost gentle at this distance. There were potted trees that had been wrapped in cloth shrouds. She peeked at one. It looked as though it might turn out to be a dogwood in a month or so.

And then from the corner of the terrace came a soft scraping sound. It could have been troubled breathing or the scrape of a shoe on tile. It came again and she saw it was a man lighting a cigarette.

Recognition thumped in Steph's breast. It was Sasha Bunin.

In the dimness and in a tailored jacket he looked taller and thinner than in company class. In profile he seemed almost fragile. For an instant she caught a hovering sadness on his face, and then he saw her and smiled.

She'd had wine with dinner and she was sliding into giddiness and she smiled back. "I was looking for my roommate," she said.

There was something steady and appraising in his eyes. "If you are looking out here, the only thing you will find is me. I am Sasha Bunin." He took a step toward her and offered his hand.

"We've met," she said, surprised he didn't remember.

He stared. "Of course. You are in the company."

"You've partnered me," she said.

"Yes. The night of my debut. You are—"

"Stephanie Lang."

"But of course. How stupid I am. Forgive me. This party has made me crazy."

"Aren't you enjoying it?"

He stared between the boxwoods, still winter skeletons, down at Fifth Avenue and Central Park. "I thought America would be different."

"From what?"

"From Russia."

"Isn't it?"

"Different but same. Everyone desperate. Talk desperate. Act desperate. Always 'Hello we love you.' Before you even know them, 'Hello we love you.'"

"Maybe they do love you. Maybe they'd like to."

"No. They exaggerate. Must be loneliest people on earth." He tugged at a twig of boxwood. "And you—you enjoy party?"

She shrugged. "The food was good."

"I could not taste it. These people make me too nervous."

It was cool on the terrace and Chris had vanished and Steph

felt a numbness creeping in from her shoulders. "I'd better go look for my friend."

"Tell me your name again? I want to remember you." He smiled and it was impossible not to believe that smile.

"Stephanie Lang. Good night."

"Good night, Stephanie."

\*  \*  \*

As Steph tiptoed into the darkened bedroom Chris managed to bring her sobbing under control, but she couldn't stop shivering. Steph saw the head buried face down on the pillow.

"Chris, are you awake?"

She turned on the table lamp. Chris pulled herself up on one elbow, eyes wincing away from the light. Steph stared at her a moment.

"Why did you leave the party like that?"

"I'm no good at parties," Chris said.

"Oh, come on. Everyone noticed you and wanted to talk to you. That man from Indiana kept asking where you'd gone."

Chris gazed at Steph, at the pale-as-birch-bark hair and the confident smiling eyes. She began to understand why people were drawn to Steph and why they would never be drawn to her. She couldn't fight the weariness that descended on her. "I don't remember any man from Indiana."

"The junior senator. Very handsome. Reddish hair. Divorced. He has some kind of position on the Joint Committee on the Arts."

Chris tried to reach back but all that came was the memory of voices like wind in a tunnel and eyes empty as light sockets and a dull void where Sasha should have been. Before tonight she'd had no idea of the strength of his indifference. She felt caught and helpless and despised. "I honestly don't remember."

"Well, he certainly kept asking. You made a conquest." Steph wiggled a good night with her fingers, switched off the light.

Chris lay on her side, her stomach pumping wretchedness, her eyes fixed on the darkness that thickened and thinned with a heartbeat of its own.

Steph was hardly aware of the jagged breathing on the other

side of the bedroom. Her thoughts were full of Sasha: how sad he seemed, how sensitive, so walled up in his fame and success and unhappy love affairs!

Her blood raced and her temples drummed. She couldn't explain her elation and she didn't want to. Perhaps it had something to do with the tiny, newborn suspicion that Sasha Bunin needed someone.

Perhaps.

# thirty-eight

Marius Volmar did not ask how it had happened or why.

He simply knelt at the altar of his art and gave thanks that at last some dry dead wood within him had ignited. At first he had felt only the glow of the single spark, tiny and vulnerable. He had nursed it, knowing too much air could snuff it out, too little could starve it. His spark had not gone out. It had thrown out sparks of its own that had grown and spread till now there was a flame in him, feeding off the air in his lungs, choking him and warming him at the same time.

The flame crept nerve by nerve through his being; it grew into a running fire, a glare of color and movement in his eyes, a blaze of sound and rhythm in his ears, a leaping contraction and release of every muscle in his body and mind.

He was burning with his ballet.

He did not know how much fire he had in him, but he knew fires were as mortal as men. He knew he must not squander a spark or an instant. The fire was ready. He was ready. The girl was ready to be made ready.

He yanked Stephanie Lang from the corps of *Fille Mal Gardée*. She stood before him, trembling that she had done something wrong.

"You'll be dancing second girl in *Sanctuary*," he said.

She darted a glance up at him. She had looked into Marius Volmar's eyes before but they had always been closed to her, steel doors bolted shut. Now the doors had opened a crack, letting escape a trickle of warmth that she had never suspected in him. In her surprise she stepped back, as if brushed by a ghost.

"Tomorrow," he said. "Studio 3, eleven-thirty."

She nodded her head slowly and she was there at eleven-thirty.

"I've been cruel to you, haven't I?" Marius Volmar said.

She swallowed. The silence stretched and fear ran prickling up and down her legs. His cruelty had became familiar and in its way comfortable, like a partner whose shifting weight and balance she instinctively anticipated. But his kindness left her defenseless. She had no way of counterbalancing. She stood with her hands hanging limply, staring down at the floor.

"Have you ever seen *Sanctuary*?" he asked.

"Once," she said. It was a contemporary Dutch ballet, abstract and crystal-hard. The score was a jagged rush of dissonance and the movements matched. "I saw Pat McBride."

"You're frightened. Don't be. Save it for the performance."

"But I'm not fast enough."

"That's why we're going to start slow."

She had never heard a father's tone in any man's voice. She had never expected to hear it in his. She fought to stay in one piece, to stay solid.

He led her gently into the role. First they worked out her solo passages, alone with the pianist. He explained the distortions of classical patterns. "It's only a *pas de bourrée*—but one foot's nailed to the floor."

Her fear melted in the patience of his instruction. He demonstrated lifts, taking her gently between his hands and lifting her as easily as a pillow. *He's strong,* she thought. *I never knew he was strong. I never knew anything about him at all.*

Sometimes he showed the movement and she watched. Sometimes he took her hand or foot, her neck or knee, and made her feel the movement. Sometimes he stood back and said. "Do your own treatment, let me see." And then he might say, "We'll keep that and just hope the choreographer never sees it," or "That's terrible," and they would both smile with the quiet gaiety of collaborators.

When it was time to learn the *pas de deux*, he gave her Wally.

"Just imagine you're warming up at the barre. Wally, you're the barre. It's a simple *battement tendu*, pure classroom. But the barre is sinking and you mustn't let go."

"But it throws my hip out."

"Exactly."

When the *pas de deux* was right, Volmar rehearsed the five soloists. Steph was as good as the others. Volmar had nursed and coaxed something out of her that she had never known she had in her.

The day of the performance she was frightened. "I know I can do it, but I'm still frightened," she said. "That's silly, isn't it?"

"No," Volmar said. "I'm frightened for the first time in thirty-two years and it feels absolutely wonderful."

She felt very close to him at that instant, very grateful to him, and sad that she had no way of showing it. *I'll show him tonight,* she promised herself. *I'll show him in my dancing.*

* * *

At four o'clock that afternoon the spokesman for the musicians' local asked to speak with Marius Volmar.

"The men have been working for seven months now without a contract," he said.

"But not without pay," Marius Volmar said.

"Just so you won't say we didn't warn you—this is the new deal." He was a short, bald man, and fat rimmed his neck like a goiter. He dumped a pound and a half of paper on Volmar's desk. The pages were Xeroxed, the type single-spaced and tiny.

"We want thirty per cent, retroactive to expiration of the old contract. Annual increases of eight, plus cost-of-living, for the three-year life of the contract. A maximum of five performances per week. Maximum rehearsal of—"

Volmar lifted the pages of the contract in wads, peered between them as though a cat had defecated in a linen closet. "What's your name?"

The man smiled, showing crooked stained teeth. "Harnett. Seymour Harnett. Good to make your acquaintance."

Volmar ignored the hand. He detested hypocrisies and besides the nails were filthy. "We dance eight performances a week. You want to play five. What do we do for the other three—hire another orchestra? Pay you overtime, which is double your normal robbery, which amounts to hiring two extra orchestras?"

"You do what you want, Mr. Volmar. I'm just telling you what you'll do if you want an orchestra after June 1."

"If you had your way, Mr. Harnett, we'd never mount ballets to new scores. Our music costs would triple. We'd have to double ticket prices. We'd be wiped out."

"We got a right to a decent wage the same as any other American."

"You think those dancers are getting decent wages?"

"They don't have mortgages. They don't have wives. They don't have kids."

"Some of them do."

"The only thing those faggots are supporting is color TVs and poodles and you damn well know it."

Volmar could feel his heart hovering on the brink of spasm. *No anger*, he warned himself: *do not waste precious anger on this dog.* Slowly, he spoke. "I don't recognize your name, Mr. Harnett. But I do recognize your bald head. You play triangle."

"And wood block. And tambourine. And xylo. Any percussion you can name."

"During *Coppélia* you spent most of the performance reading. Now and then you picked up your little steel stick and tapped your triangle. Now and then you forgot to. You're not an artist, Mr. Harnett. You're not even a workman. You have no business corrupting the honest efforts of honest artists."

Indignation purpled Harnett's face. Volmar raised a hand, staving off interruption.

"But if I fired you—and I ought to have after *Coppélia*—the orchestra would go on strike. The stagehands would go on strike. The ushers would go on strike. The AFL-CIO would have garbage men picketing the theater. We would not be able to perform. So I have no choice. I can wait for you to retire, on full-salaried pension. Or I can wait for you to have a heart attack, on company insurance. But then your place will be taken by another bald man from the same union—most likely your bald brother-in-law or your bald son—and he'll play triangle just as badly as you do, picking his nose and missing his cues, wandering in and out of the pit when he wants a drink or needs to empty his bladder."

A jangle of shock seemed physically to strike Harnett. "You're bald too!"

"But I am not little, Mr. Harnett. And I don't earn three times what a dancer in the corps earns, or twice what a principal earns. And I don't whine at having to work five days a week—or seven—and if I need to rehearse I rehearse till I'm right and I don't expect to be paid for mistakes!"

Silence slammed down between them.

"You're going to regret that, Volmar. I could have been on your side."

"You could never have been on my side, Mr. Harnett. I deal with artists and I deal with humans but I have no dealings with livestock. Now do you want to take this rubbish with you or shall I throw it out myself?"

"We're going to fuck you, Volmar," the little man screamed. "We're going to fuck you but good!"

Volmar shoved the contract over the edge of the desk and let it thud into the wastebasket. "Be so good as to close the door when you leave, Mr. Harnett."

Volmar had known for a decade of escalating union demands that this moment would come. It surprised him how little surprise he felt, how little anger. His heartbeat was perfectly normal as he reached for his telephone.

He spoke first to Dorcas and then he said to the operator, "Belgian consulate, please."

*       *       *

Volmar went to her dressing room to tell her himself. "I won't be here tonight, Stephanie."

She turned away from her mirror, an eyebrow pencil clutched in one suddenly rigid hand.

"It's a labor problem. The company may not survive. I have to go to Brussels this evening. My plane leaves in an hour. Forgive me."

Her mind raced to fear, and the fear became a deep sustained underbeat within her. "I'll miss you," she said softly.

"I'll miss you," he said. "I wanted to give these to you later, after you'd danced the way I know you're going to. But I won't be here, so please accept them now."

He handed her a basket of flowers. It was so huge she had to put both arms around it to hold it to her.

"If you're susperstitious you'd better not read the note till afterward."

She turned to set the flowers down and when she turned back to him he brushed a kiss on her lips.

"I'm counting on you, Stephanie."

It was a tiny kiss, quick and light and barely there at all. She shut her eyes and out of some storybook memory came a fireside and two parents holding hands and the soft gold tick of a grandfather clock and the knowledge that nothing could ever hurt her.

The kiss stayed with her when she warmed up and it stayed with her as she waited for her entrance. It stayed through the *pas de deux* and her variation and the coda, beating on her lips with the soft pleasing sting of brandy.

*Volmar kissed me!*

She knew she was dancing well. She could tell when Wally winked at her. She could tell when the conductor held a retard for her, courteously, unhurryingly, like a gentleman holding a door for a lady, and then went right along, not even grimacing at the faster tempo that suddenly came spinning out of her feet and felt exactly right.

She could tell when her dresser patted a towel over her face and arms and kept pushing her around toward the stage. The audience called her back for five bows and she hardly cared: all she could think of was Volmar's kiss and his flowers and the unopened card. She hurried back to her dressing room.

More bouquets had arrived. She glanced at the note on a dozen pink gladioluses. *Best of luck tonight and always. Danny Gillette.*

Sadness stirred in her. She pushed it away. She opened the note that had come with two dozen red roses. *Merde. Sasha.*

She sat a moment, surprised and pleased, and then she found Volmar's card and tore it open and almost cut a finger on the heavy paper. *Congratulations, Stephanie, on a job beautifully done.*

The words wobbled in front of her eyes. *He . . . believes in me!*

There was a knock at the door and her mother came in, glowing like a Christmas tree. "Honey, you were terrific."

"Honest?"

"Honest."

Steph plunked herself down at the dressing table, as bright as a marquee with its make-up lights bordering the mirror. She peeled off eyelashes and worked cold cream into the layers of make-up.

"I just wish Volmar could have seen you tonight." Anna stared at all the bouquets and baskets heaped on the chair and spilling onto the floor. There must have been a dozen. Anna inventoried.

Flowers from Lvovna: ten cents of daffodils but nice of the old bag. Flowers from Danny Gillette.

"You still seeing Danny what's-it?"

Steph shrugged. "It's been over a year."

Red roses from Sasha Bunin. Well, well. "Didn't know you were friends with Sasha."

"Neither did I."

Anna came to a hundred dollars of roses and lilies and gardenias and camellias. She looked at the card. *Volmar?* Her eyes narrowed. Marius had never so much as taken her out to a French restaurant or offered to bring a steak over for dinner and if he was throwing away hundred-dollar floral arrangements on Steph . . .

"Nice of Volmar," she said. "Too bad he couldn't have seen your extension in that lift. And your double *fouetté*—"

"Oh, Mom, he saw those."

"How? Ship-to-shore TV in a 747?"

"He's been coaching me *weeks* now. He really cares about me."

Anna squinted. The note was not one of those over-the-phone-to-the-florist jobs: it was in Marius' own handwriting. *Congratulations, Stephanie, on a job beautifully done.* That was payment in advance and it wasn't the Marius that Anna knew.

"Of course he cares about you," Anna said. "You fall on your ass and he falls on his."

"More than that. Mom—he kissed me."

Anna slid the card back into its envelope. Steph's eyes were green and radiant. Emeralds. "Kissed you?"

"For twelve months he's been treating me like I wasn't even here, and tonight he *kissed* me!"

Anna got up quickly and paced to the shower and pretended to check whether there was soap and a towel. She didn't want Steph to see her face because suddenly her face didn't feel it could keep any secrets. That kiss nagged at her, *nagged* at her: how had Marius kissed Steph, on the cheek, on the mouth, long, short, or what, had he held her, had he touched her, where had he touched her, if that bastard touched her Anna didn't want to know, Anna *had* to know.

There were thoughts whirling in her no decent mother would want to admit to and she wished she could bury them under a ton of dirt. *I'm jealous*, she realized, *I'm jealous of my own little girl*, and she was ashamed.

"You're a dancer," she said, "not a kiss booth at a county fair." Her voice was wrinkled and old and hoarse and she couldn't help it. "Stay away from that old goat. He could be your father."

Steph was staring, eyes big and baffled and embarrassed. "Mom, you don't think—"

*He's my old goat and twice the lover your drunken pop ever was, that's what I think.*

Steph was smiling. "Mom, sometimes you're too much."

It was Steph's night and with one flick of her tongue Anna could take it away from her. *I could tell her she stank tonight. I could tell her what happens to girls who put out for the director.* Anna fought that tongue and it was one of the hardest fights of her life and she almost won.

"Honey, you're a dancer and a good one. Someday you're going to be a great one. And you don't need to make it that way."

Steph came to her and hugged her, careful not to smear cold cream on the dress Anna had bought at the Bendel's sale and saved for the occasion. "Mom, you're sweet."

*Am I?*

"But he's not like that."

*Isn't he?*

"And I'm not a kid."

She got into the shower and Anna looked at her. She had grown beyond girlishness and prettiness. She had real breasts, not a dancer's breasts. Her face was sure in its femininity and her eyes were unashamed. Tiny ripples of envy and regret washed the skin at the back of Anna's neck.

That much was true. Steph wasn't a kid any more.

\*   \*   \*

Steph bought all three newspapers the next morning.

It was raining great slaps of water on the pavement, and she dashed from the newsstand across the avenue into an arcade of the Gulf and Western Building. Strangers had taken up positions around her, fellow exiles from the downpour.

She thumbed excitedly through the *Times*. Twice. No review. That didn't mean anything. Sometimes the *Times* was a day late.

She searched the *Post*. There was a two-inch article, *Dutch Revival*, a photograph of Lucinda Dalloway in arabesque that certainly hadn't come from *Sanctuary*, no mention of Stephanie Lang.

The *News* showed Dalloway again, same arabesque: Steph's name was in the credits, misspelled *(Stephane Laing)*, and nowhere else.

She felt a crushing disappointment. For a long while she had no will to move from the arcade. Finally she stepped into the rain. *Tomorrow*, she told herself. *The* Times *will have something tomorrow*.

And it did: an interview with Aleksandr Fedorovich Bunin running five columns; a photograph of Sasha cradling his poodle Merde; and a half-page announcement of changes in the NBT program that Steph had not even seen posted in the theater.

*Sanctuary* was dropped completely, *Do I*'s were cut to one, the abstract ballets were gone. In their place were *Spectre de la Rose* every night, Bunin and Dalloway; three *Le Corsaire pas de deux*, Bunin and Fowles; and four *Don Q pas de deux*, Bunin and Banska.

The interview quoted Dorcas:

*"Ilonka is an artist in the grand style. She and Sasha have been dying to dance together ever since Sasha's hairbreadth escape from Soviet tyranny. Empire have been absolute dears about loaning her to us."*

Sasha was quoted:

*"Would not call it Bunin festival, no. Is romantic festival. These days people like what is romantic, yes?"*

And again Dorcas:

*"Romantic, Bunin—what's the difference? The name 'Bunin' is synonymous with everything romantic in ballet. Did you know that last year alone there were over 18 million paid admissions to ballet in the U.S.A., 6 million more than to professional football? We're on a definite upswing and a lot of the credit has to go to Sasha."*

Steph searched, but there was no mention of *Sanctuary*.

\*     \*     \*

As Deputy Minister of Culture, Pierre Huygens had no choice.

Marius Volmar was a distinguished guest of the government. If he wanted breakfast with the Deputy Minister, he got it. If he wanted two breakfasts, he got them. Or three.

And so every morning for a week they breakfasted in the bar of the Hotel Bruxelles, always at a quiet corner table not visible from the lobby. Aside from occasional darts of Flemish or French piercing the screen of potted palms or the overzealous waiter offering fresh café au lait, they were undisturbed.

Pierre Huygens had heard rumors, but they were contradictory. If he was to believe one source, Volmar had nothing more mysterious in mind than next summer's NBT tour. If he was to believe another, Volmar was discouraged with America and wished to return to Europe.

Whatever country he chose, Marius Volmar would be a catch. And so Pierre Huygens was patient.

There were scattered hopeful hints: a disparaging remark about commercialism in America; an admiring reference to the depth of the stage at Théâtre de la Monnaie. Pierre Huygens did not press. He tried to show no annoyance, no hurry. He sipped coffee, spread thin glazes of peach preserves on hot buttered croissants, waited for Marius Volmar to unlock his secret.

At the sixth breakfast, Volmar changed his pattern.

"How about the ballet tonight?" he suggested.

Ambition nagged at Pierre Huygens. Tonight was his anniversary and his wife Berthe would be broken-hearted. But

Marius Volmar was worth an anniversary. "I'd be delighted."

The ballet was an oddity, one of Béjart's nude mythologies, danced rather calisthenically to a mix of raga and Wagner. Volmar tactfully refrained from expressing an opinion.

Afterward they went to Mère Mathilde's, Brussels' best seafood restaurant. The filet of flounder stuffed with lobster was so light in texture, so delicately seasoned, the two bottles of Pouilly Fuissé were so perfect a complement, that for almost an hour Pierre Huygens forgot he was a very baffled and eager man.

With brandy, Volmar offered Havana cigars. They smoked.

Volmar did not like to make a move till he was sure. He had studied the man and the Brussels situation for a week. Now he was sure.

The waiter cleared away dessert plates. Throughout the city churchbells chimed midnight. Volmar leaned forward in his chair and Pierre Huygens waited for him finally to tip his hand.

"Quite soon," Marius Volmar said, "I may be looking for a new home."

"A new home in Belgium?" Pierre Huygens inquired cautiously.

"Just a place for me and my family."

"I didn't know you had a family."

"A family of eighty-six."

"Ah—your dancers! You want to move your company to Belgium?"

"I would like to create a Belgian company."

"But we have a Belgian company."

Volmar observed his guest. The face, taut and skeletal and hungry-eyed, had a papery look, like a ledger page itemizing twenty years of bureaucratic strain. "I would like to create a Belgian company that employs American guest artists."

"But we have a company."

"My Belgian company would not perform in Belgium. There would be no competition with your company."

"I don't understand. Where would you perform?"

"In America."

Pierre Huygens' mind roamed over the mountain of paperwork that would be required. "You want to bring your Americans here and turn them into Belgians and take them back to America—why?"

"It won't be necessary to bring them here. All I'll need is a Belgian charter for the company and a Belgian address for legality."

"May I ask why you want to do this?"

"You've heard of our American musicians' unions?"

"You have many good musicians."

"And many greedy unions. Our orchestra plans to strike. Its demands will bankrupt us."

Pierre Huygens shook his head in amazement. He had heard that American recording companies could no longer afford American orchestras, that the Boston Symphony worked for German marks and Dutch guilders. He was sorry for America and for the suicide of her soul.

"There is only one way for us to survive as dancers in the United States," Marius Volmar said. "We get rid of the orchestra. We pay musicians on a performance basis. We perform as a foreign company on tour. As Belgians." Volmar pinned Pierre Huygens with his gaze. "How soon can you let me know?"

Pierre Huygens stirred uncomfortably. He had eaten his *mousse au café* too quickly. He felt Marius Volmar fencing him in to a most premature, most unwise yes/no. The decision would require time; research; discussion with the Minister.

"But surely there couldn't be any immediate rush," Pierre Huygens said.

"There is."

"But I saw in the Paris *Herald Tribune*, Bunin's *Corsaire* is a sensation, the house is selling out. You've raised your prices, orchestra seats are being scalped for thirty dollars, no?"

For an instant Volmar stared in openmouthed surprise. And then a curtain of frost dropped. "I don't know about the scalping."

"But Bunin must help your situation considerably."

"Very little."

Pierre Huygens took up his cigar again. With deliberation, he tapped the dead tip into the ash tray. "I understand your situation, and I'm sure the minister will sympathize. Nevertheless, it would help if we could make the proposal as attractive as possible."

"And what will attract the Minister?"

"Aside from your very great prestige, Monsieur Volmar—

which is the only consideration—it might speed the paperwork if
Bunin could be persuaded to come to Belgium."

"Permanently?"

"We would not dare hope that, no, we could not expect you
to give up your most brilliant dancer. But perhaps if Bunin could
be persuaded to dance one or two guest appearances with our
National Ballet..."

*         *         *

The weather had turned murderously cold as Volmar hurried
back to his hotel. Anger thudded in him, sending his heart
skipping like a soccer ball.

His eye tried to pierce the scrim of drizzle and mist that
blacked out the city. The news kiosks were dark, boarded up for
the night. There was not a Paris *Herald Tribune* to be had in
Brussels.

He had to find one. He had to know.

"What's that in your wastebasket?"

The night clerk regarded him in astonishment. "Monsieur?"

"That Paris *Herald Tribune*—give it to me, please."

"But, monsieur, it's old—and used—" Before handing the
paper over the night clerk attempted to smooth out the wrinkles.

Volmar snatched it from him. He found the review on the
center page, reprinted from an earlier New York *Times*. Words
leapt out from the column of print, stabbing his eye:

*Bunin... Bunin... Bunin...* Corsaire pas de deux... *a virtuosity dazzling even to a generation grown jaded on the
pyrotechnics of Nureyev and Baryshnikov... a sheer riot of
kinesis... a* Spectre de la Rose *recalling Nijinsky...*

His stomach rolled over inside him like an unborn creature
that was all claws.

"When is the next flight to New York?"

"Nine o'clock monsieur—Sabena."

"Nothing earlier?"

"Alas, no, monsieur."

"I'll need a reservation. My name is Volmar, V-o-l-m-a-r.
Initial *M*."

# thirty-nine

Volmar took a taxi from the airport straight to the theater. He didn't waste time waiting for the elevator but dashed up the fire stairs two steps at a leap.

At stage level he could hear the piano thump-thumping. His stomach made a fist. He recognized the abominable drivel of Leon Minkus, *Le Corsaire*. He stood in the shadow of a wing, watched in disgust.

There were three figures onstage: Sasha, stripped to the waist, sweaty and posturing; Lucinda Dalloway, packaged in wool and plastic wrap, lotus-positioned on the floor; and Frederick Branson, who ran a creditable company class, standing uselessly.

Sasha was arguing. "Maybe would be better I put in double turn."

The dance master sighed. "We have turns in the air, turns on half pointe, barrel turns, turns on the knee—it's a helluva lot of turns for one little variation."

"No problem. I can do it."

Volmar hurried down into the darkened orchestra. His eye picked out the row where Dorcas was sitting, hands on chin propped on the seat in front of her. She had bloomed into a

403

producer-director: hair pulled back in a no-nonsense pony tail; instead of pearls, horn-rimmed glasses dangling around her neck on a dime-store chain; baggy sweater and—blue jeans.

Volmar wondered if there was some boutique that pre-dirtied jeans.

Dorcas stood, her voice raised and crisp as celery: "Freddy—why can't we use both?"

Freddy glanced from Sasha to Dorcas as though they'd caught him in a tug-of-war. "Both what, Dorcas?"

"Both your choreography and Sasha's."

His shoulders rose and fell in silent helplessness. "There's not enough music. We have to make up our minds."

Dorcas was threading her way through seats, approaching the stage. "How many bars does Sasha need for the two turns?"

"Four counts," Sasha said. "If I had eight I could *sous-sus* back up..." He dropped into an extended kneeling position. Abruptly, like motion picture film reversed, energy bursting from nowhere, he corkscrewed up, did a double turn, and came to a knife-clean stop exactly on the beat.

"I *like* it," Dorcas said. Then, to the accompanist. "What happens if you repeat the last eight counts?"

"The musicians get overtime."

"Very funny. Will you just play it?"

He played the phrase, repeating the final eight counts. Dorcas stood with her head cocked, like a hostess in the kitchen sniffing dinner.

"That doesn't sound any worse to me than the rest of it. What do you think, Freddy?"

Freddy sighed. "The music doesn't bother me. But there's no logic to the movement. Why not sixteen and let him do a somersault?"

"My, my, what a lot of wits we have here today. We'll keep the extra eight. Someone remember to tell the conductor."

"It's a hell of a lot of oompahs for those horns," the accompanist said. "Their lips will be ragged."

"They're paid for oompahs and Blue Cross can pay for their lips. Okay, Freddy, what's next?"

"Lucinda's variation."

Dorcas scowled. "I wish there was some way we could perk *that* up."

"How about thirty-two *fouettés?*" Freddy didn't bother to hide his sarcasm.

"It's *not* such a bad idea," Dorcas said. "But let's save it for a last resort. Sasha, how do they handle that variation in the Kirov?"

Sasha marked with his fingers, a grinning puppeteer. "Very nice little *coupés jetés*, getting faster and faster."

Dorcas shut her eyes a moment, visualizing, and nodded. "Do you remember enough to show Lucinda?"

"Of course. Lucinda darling." Sasha beckoned Dalloway up from her lotus postion. "Just watch and follow. Music, please. *And.*" With a delicacy amazing in a male dancer, and breath control amazing in a human body, Sasha demonstrated at tempo, calling out the steps. *"Pas de chat, trois fois . . . bourrée . . . bourrée . . ."*

"Dorcas," Volmar whispered sharply. Fury hammered in him.

Dorcas' head jerked back, her attention shattered. She squinted in Volmar's direction. "Why, Marius." Holding her note pad to her bosom, like a shield between him and her, she shifted weight away from him. "What are you dong back so soon?"

"You know perfectly well."

"How was your trip—mission accomplished?"

"I want to talk to you."

"Can't it wait ten minutes? We're in the middle of—"

"I can see what you're in the middle of. Come to my office."

\*       \*       \*

"Dorcas, you are a mediocrity."

"If that's meant as an insult, try again."

"You are a pretentious, self-serving, self-deceiving second-rater."

She leaned over the desk, teeth bared. "Wrong, wrong, wrong, right. I have no pretensions when it comes to dance. I am serving this company, not my ego. I do not fool myself. I know I'm a second-rater, the same as half the people in this world, which is why I'm able to speak their language."

"And choreograph their ballets too?"

"The audiences want Sasha. Do you realize what our ticket sales have been?"

He was aware of a changed Dorcas, a woman drugged with new exhilaration. Enthusiasm and cockiness were pumping in her blood, working a chaotic and dangerous synergism.

"We're subscribed through next year! Marius, that has never before happened in the history of this company!"

"And if people wanted pornography, you'd have sex shows onstage?"

"Why are you scared of good honest bravura dancing?"

"Because it's bravura shit and it belongs in a stable."

"It pays for your elitist crap! If we program ten minutes of Sasha dancing *Le Corsaire*—they'll sit through two acts of anything! Happily! What's wrong with that?"

"We are a company—not a showcase for Soviet buffoons."

Dorcas' fingers jabbed the air, enumerating. "You did a *Coppélia* for Lucinda. You interpolated an adagio from *Sylvia* and a *pas de deux* from *La Source*. You gave Beverly a *Dying Swan*. You massacred Grigorovich last season so that Christine of yours could get through it—and might I remind you I didn't even raise a *whimper* at *Do I Hear a Waltz? Or* at your choosing Stephanie for the premiere?"

"That is all beside the point."

"No, Marius. It *is* the point. There's a great sign above our door: *Women only will be showcased here. Males not allowed.* Well, now we've got a male and the public wants him. They want him more than they'll ever want your Lucindas or Beverlys or Christines or Stephanies. And you are jealous."

The blindness of her accusation so astonished him that for a moment he couldn't answer. "Of those cheap acrobatics?"

"Of that man."

Now he began to see the depths of the charm Sasha had worked on her. "You're infatuated with him."

"No more than you are with your ballerinas."

"He's using you, Dorcas. He's a Tartar shark with a baby mongoloid smile."

"And a very well trained male body that people pay money to see. He's saved us, Marius. *Saved* us."

"That vaudeville is salvation?"

"Then go out there and give him something good. Give him

your plotless ballets. Get Jerry to let you do *Goldberg Variations*. Ask Mr. B. for *Symphony in C*. Anything. Just *use him!*"

Volmar felt the warning onrush of anger, his heart tightening into a fist. He forced himself to be gentle and explanatory this one last time. "We are a company. We do not have stars. We do not leapfrog outsiders into principal roles over the heads of our own dancers."

"He *is* our own dancer. We have him under contract for three years."

"Perhaps in three years he'll be ready."

"He's ready now. He's a natural prince and you know it and the public is *dying* to see him sink his teeth into a good prince role."

"We don't do prince ballets."

"And what do you call *Sleeping Beauty?*"

He had known, of course, what she was aiming at. He was still surprised. In the past she had pursued her aims with a certain timidity and deference. Now she had slipped out of character. He did not know this screaming, demanding harpy.

"That man," Volmar said, "is not dancing *Sleeping Beauty*."

"I don't believe you seriously mean what you're saying."

"With every fiber of my soul."

"You're insane."

"Furthermore, I am removing your *Corsaires*, your *Don Q*'s, and all your lovely little *pas de deux*. We are going back to our original schedule."

"That's a grave mistake."

"Until my contract expires, *I* control the casting. *I* choose the repertoire."

"Marius, be reasonable. Sasha is a miracle. He's a force of nature. He's a tornado, a tidal wave—why don't we just harness him? I know I had no right to tinker with the schedule and I'm sorry. But look at the box office—oh, God, just look. Marius, we could put him in *anything*. He could dance Beethoven quartets, Mexican hat dances, they'd still love him. Sasha is a chance for *all* of us!"

"I'm not ripping down the building just because someone has found a pretty column for the façade. If you want to harness Sasha, go hire a Broadway theater."

"Marius, if you let him dance *Sleeping Beauty*, we can pay off this year's deficit. Just give him *Sleeping Beauty*. I won't ask for anything else."

The voice was openly pleading. He had beaten back this flurry of independence. Close call. Only now did Volmar realize how hard his heart was pounding.

"No," he said.

She gazed at him a moment of long sorrow. He resolved he would be kind: he would forget they had ever humiliated themselves with this exchange. He waited for the words of apology that would close the matter.

But her tone was oddly lacking in repentance. "In that case, Marius, I'll talk to my lawyers."

She went.

For a while Volmar was able to put her out of his mind. He was able to think of important matters—like the schedule she had so thoroughly botched. With scissors and Scotch tape and grease pencil he began repairing the abortion she had made of his season.

But he couldn't lock the back door of his thoughts. He kept seeing Dorcas, her face eaten with acid rage. Behind her he saw Sasha, all smile and twinkling feet. An electric jolt went through him. His heart gave a jump. He felt a stab of pain in his left arm and a nausea that was terrifying in its swiftness. He slapped his hands to the desk top, gripping hard, held himself back from the sudden emptiness that loomed beneath.

*Hold on*, he told himself. *You shall not be scared by those two children*. And yet for a long spiraling moment his hands refused to let go of the desk.

Finally the moment passed. The emptiness slid away.

He put his schedule away, slipped into the corridor, took his fear for a walk. It was five-thirty. Most of the dancers and stagehands were home having early suppers. The house was almost deserted.

As he walked, he tried to think. He had to separate Dorcas and Sasha. He had to shatter the alliance. Exploit its inherent weaknesses. To do that he would have to know more.

"Hello, Mr. Volmar." A trio of girls from the corps slipped past, giving him wide berth, giggling nervously. Volmar was perfectly aware what his dancers thought of him. They were

terrified by him; more than a few hated him. He was not a man
who cared about being loved or hated.

He cared about being obeyed.

He glanced after the girls and thought what a pity it was he
didn't have a dancer friend, someone placed low in the company
who could pass on garbage and gossip. Garbage and gossip,
intuition told him, would have to be his weapons.

"Evening, Mr. Volmar." A man wearing dark glasses
wheeled his double bass past. Volmar grunted. Musicians, like
stagehands, were swaggering adolescents who traveled in gangs
called unions and periodically went on looting rampages called
strikes. He did not so much as waste his breath on a "Hello" to
them.

Two armloads of male unitards brushed past. "Hello, Mr.
Volmar."

It was Harry Burns, one of the men's dressers. A tiny buzz
went through Volmar's head.

"Well, Harry, have you been keeping an eye on things for me
while I've been away?"

Harry Burns stopped in surprise and almost dropped his
unitards. "Pardon?"

Volmar made a point of knowing a little about all his dancers
and dressers, just enough to fill a two-by-four-inch mental filing
card. Harry Burns had spent five years in the NBT corps, gone
straight from that to twenty years in the dressing rooms.
Seventeen years ago his lover, a promising Cuban dancer, had
caught polio, pulled himself to a window, and thrown himself
out. Since then Harry had blossomed into a loverless, gossiping
lush.

"Do you have time for supper," Volmar suggested, "or a
drink?"

Harry Burns looked shocked. And eager. The director of
NBT did not, as a rule, invite dressers to dine with him. Harry
glanced at the embarrassments in his arms. "Sure—just let me
hang these up. It'll only take a sec."

\*       \*       \*

Harry Burns sipped at his fourth Black Russian. His blood
was bubbling with excitement. In the last ten minutes he had

counted over two dozen dancers hurrying along the Broadway sidewalk, and every one of them had instinctively glanced at the Theater Pub window and seen Marius Volmar and Harry Burns in a tête-à-tête at the front table.

The word would spread like a brush fire tonight. *Harry Burns is a somebody, Marius Volmar consults with him.* The new kid, the scholarship boy NBT had just taken into the corps, would be sorry he'd been so snooty.

Volmar nursed a coffee and picked at a half canteloupe. He nodded through Harry's chronicles of fornication and betrayal, slipped discs and tendonitis. He only half listened to the tale of Marsha Hamlin's slipped *fouetté*, marveled that Harry could talk through mouthfuls of liquor.

"The regular clarinetist had a bar mitzvah in Scarsdale, so he sent in his cousin, who'd never even been to rehearsal. Well, you know that part in *Baiser*, her adagio with harp and clarinet?"

Volmar nodded. He knew *Baiser de la Fée* very well. Dancers hated it because it was difficult without being showy. He loved it because it was a perfect mesh of music, movement, and story. Dorcas had dropped it from the season.

"Get this. It's scored for A clarinet, but the schmuck only has a B-flat mouthpiece. So he tries to transpose, but halfway through he loses his way. You wouldn't believe the sounds he was making—strangled chicken. Marsha wasn't counting—she was doing it by the music. Well, he left out her cue, she began the turn late, and *bang!* It's incredible Pete didn't lose his kneecap."

"Substitutes can be dangerous," Volmar said. "Tell me, Harry, how is the company reacting to the changes in our season?"

Harry stirred uncomfortably. "It screws up wardrobe. Last week we almost had to send eight sylphides onstage in *Firebird* princess shimmies. The tutus were at the cleaners. You can't reschedule like that—cleaners close at six."

"I'm not too happy with the changes myself. Bad for company morale, wouldn't you say?"

Harry shrugged. "Morale's okay. We're selling out."

"But I sense resentment."

Harry's chubby fingers toyed with the plastic mesh on the candle glass. "Maybe . . . a little."

"It's because of Sasha, isn't it?"

Tiny prickles of excitement were galloping across the skin of Harry Burns's face and neck and arms.

"I'm not asking you to be an informer, Harry."

"Course not." Harry nodded. *Volmar's informer*. He liked the sound of that. Important. The boys in the corps would start showing a little respect.

"Do the dancers feel Sasha's getting too many solos?"

"That doesn't bother them," Harry said. "What can you do? He's a Russian, people buy tickets to see Russians do barrel turns. Frankly I've seen Cubans do better barrel turns, but who's going to argue with the box office? No, the solos aren't the problem. The trouble is . . ."

The voice trailed off in indecision, like a music box needing to be rewound. Volmar signaled for another Black Russian. "I don't need to tell you, Harry, that anything you say goes no further than this table."

The Black Russian arrived. Harry took a long, fortifying swallow.

"The problem is, Sasha is a sex machine. He just loves to screw. He's screwing in broom closets, he's screwing in his dressing room—"

"He has a dressing room?"

"Sure—Ray's old room. He's had it two, three weeks now."

"So Sasha is a great lover, is he?"

"Great, I wouldn't know. But determined. It's like he's keeping a score card. I swear, he's laid half the girls in the corps and the other half he's made dates with. He has this pattern. He comes on like gangbusters, champagne and roses and the whole seduction bit—and once he's had the girl, boom, he drops her. Half those kids still don't know what hit them. Not just the corps either. He's had four soloists I know of, two principals—married principals—you want me to name names?"

Volmar did not let his face even hint at the satisfaction he felt. He kept his expression somber, concerned. Harry Burns named names, and by the time he had finished, Volmar had formulated his strategy.

If chattering dressers and the entire company knew of Sasha's amours, it could only be a matter of weeks before rumors reached Dorcas. Humiliated, publicly betrayed, she would have no choice but to turn on her protégé. Indian giver that she was, she'd strip him of every cashmere sweater, every door key, every solo that she'd lavished on him.

All Volmar had to do was to train two dancers for the lead prince in *Sleeping Beauty*—Sasha and Wally. He would leave it open who was covering for whom. Dorcas would be satisfied thinking Sasha had the lead; and after the rupture she'd have no objection to Wally's taking it. Of course, to avoid suspicion, Volmar would have to do the same with the female principal: train two Auroras, leave the cover open.

Stephanie Lang and . . . who?

An idea came to him. The perfect cover.

"Thank you, Harry." Volmar slapped a twenty-dollar bill down on the table. "You've been a great help. We really must do this much more often."

# forty

Sasha Bunin baffled Steph. He could give a girl a bouquet one day and not a glance for two weeks afterward. In fact, not a glance for two weeks and three days.

She counted.

And then two weeks and four days after the bouquet, as she finished a solo in *Patineurs*, she almost smashed into him in the wings. He did not step aside and dancers were watching. She had a premonition he was going to do something show-offy to embarrass her.

"Why you not say thank you for flowers?"

"I never see you," she said. "You're always busy." She felt her face redden.

"You do not want to see me?"

"I didn't say that."

"Then you see me Sunday—you show me New York?"

She knew all the stories by heart: Sasha and this girl, Sasha and that girl, and instinct told her to say no. But he fixed her with all the brown innocence of his eyes and there was a pucker at the top of his ugly-beautiful nose. Instinct went out the window.

"All right," she said, dashing back for her bow. "Sunday."

413

For the two days and four hours and thirty minutes till Sunday noon she kept wondering, *Why the hell did I do that?* She waited for him outside the Gulf and Western Building, and at five after twelve she was certain she'd been had. At seven after she saw him two blocks away, running. He saw her and waved.

"You think Sasha forget you?" He kissed her hello on the cheek.

"In New York five minutes is normal," she said.

"In Leningrad"—there was still that Russian *y* sound after his *l*—"thirty minutes is lucky."

They laughed and he showed her the hip pocket of his blue jeans bulging with ten-dollar bills. "Today we take taxi. No walking, no subway. Today is holiday."

First he wanted museums: the Metropolitan, the Guggenheim, the Modern Art. The crowds pressed them close together and now and then he put his arm around her. She let herself lean against him, comfortable and careful not to think it was anything special to be leaning against Sasha Bunin.

His eyes were avid as a child's, gobbling up the big bright Tchelichews and Légers and Picassos. "Never see this in Soviet. Need special pass."

Now and then, not minding it at all, she felt his eyes gobbling her up too. *I'm foreign to him*, she realized. And she felt brisk and alive and exotic.

At the Whitney there was a storm of recognition: *"Bunin . . . defector!"* Heads turned and voices changed key and she was afraid for him. But he was large in his hulking knit sweater and strong-jawed and despite the ivory skin and the colonies of freckles he had a trick of putting menace in his face when he wanted, and not one person who came up and said, "Excuse me, aren't you—?" finished the question.

When Sasha had had enough of museums he said, "And now you show me city."

"What do you want to see?"

He wanted to see people: Chinese, blacks, Williamsburgh Jews, American Indians. Steph had to smile. They went to neighborhoods: Yorkville, Chinatown, the Lower East Side.

They strolled down a cross street. There was an iron-fenced garden with huge shade trees. It turned out to be a graveyard run to flowering weed.

Across the street was a church with boarded windows that had once been stained glass and a double transverse Russian cross and strange carved lettering above the doors.

Steph stopped. "What does it say?"

Sasha stared at the lettering. His eyes narrowed. "Is Ukrainian, not Russian."

"Aren't they the same?"

He shook his head firmly. "Different. Ukrainians anarchists."

"Can you read any of it?"

His face wrinkled and worked and he slouched his shoulders in a shrug. "God father, God son, God ghost. Is silly. Opium for people."

There was a pause and she stared at him. "Is that bad?"

He must have caught the blank on her face where he had expected agreement because he gave his hair a thick toss of his forehead and showed her the clear merriment of his eyes. "Is not bad, but cocaine better."

He burst out laughing and she was glad it was loud laughter because he didn't hear her not laughing. He took her arm and kept walking. That changed the subject and she was relieved.

The cross street took them to Second Avenue. It was Sunday and sunny, easy and tolerant and who-cares, and a dozen civilizations flowed through one another. There were old couples strolling in clean old clothes and smartly dressed blacks and Latin boys whizzing on skate boards; there were last decade's hippies, still beaded and stoned, and staggering winos rapping on windows of taxis stopped for the light; there were sidewalk fruit stands and illegal pushcart peddlers and Con Ed construction barriers that made mazes for traffic and strollers. The signs in English said *Closed* and *For Sale* but the signs in Spanish and Ukrainian were alive with exclamation points.

They went into a Jewish restaurant. The tables were crowded and the old waiters looked persecuted. They ordered cheese blintzes. When the food came Sasha examined his blintz. He cut into it. Tasted it. Shook his fork.

"Is Jewish?"

"It's Jewish."

"No, is Russian."

She saw he was honestly confused. She smiled. "Maybe it's

both. A lot of Jews came to American from Russia."

"Why they want to bring Russia with them? I come from Russia. I tell Russia to stay home."

"Maybe someday you'll change your mind. Maybe someday you'll miss Russia."

"Never."

"Not even your family?"

"Why should I miss them? You know what my father did to my mother?"

He leaned forward, head sinking almost to his folded arms. In a flash she knew he was going to tell her something dreadful.

"My father put her in a house for crazy people. She was not crazy. But in Russia they know to make you crazy. My father tell doctors, 'Make Natasha crazy.' They give her drugs. Soon she cannot move. She cannot talk. She cannot choose when to piss, when not."

Steph had not foreseen this. She pressed her lips together, silent, determined to qualify as a kind listener.

"Every month visitors' day I take train to see my mother. Every month worse. They cut off her hair. They give her electricity. In one year she is old woman. I say, 'Hello, Mama, remember me, Sasha?' She does not answer. To her I am no one. I bring her flowers. Books. Apples from private market. Doctors take everything. Is bad for her, they say. But I know what is bad for her is those doctors."

Steph looked at the pain in his face and all she could think of to say was, "Did she ever get better?"

"One day doctors say, 'You are cured, go.' I take her home. Is not true home. My father has new wife, my mother cannot live there. The government give her one room. Seven stairways to reach this one room. I carry her two suitcases. 'Mother, I help you unpack.' 'No,' she says, 'later.' She kisses me."

He touched a finger to his cheek.

"I go to class. *Petit allegro* piano stops. 'Sasha, come here,' they whisper me. 'Terrible accident. Your mother fall out window. Your mother dead.'"

He shook his head.

"Window comes down to here."

He placed his hands at his heart, shaping a window ledge.

"My mother pulls chair to window and she stands on chair

and *then* she falls. Is not accident."

Steph was suddenly aware what a very unstable place the universe was. "Sasha, I'm sorry."

Sasha shrugged and blinked at a tear. "That night my father and his wife go to theater. Best seats. Comedy. No, I do not miss Russia. I never will go back. You are first person I ever tell this to."

He moved her and he baffled her. She felt a terrible need in him. The sympathy in her surged higher, wanting to burst out. But something checked her.

He was playing with his knife, doodling lines on the tablecloth.

"Why?" she said. "Why am I the first?"

"I don't know," he said in a low voice, not lifting his head. "Because maybe I am stupid."

"You're not stupid."

"Because I think maybe you understand. Maybe is stupid."

"It's not stupid."

He raised his eyes and looked straight at her. "Could you want to be friend with someone like me?"

"I don't know," she said. "I feel sorry for you. Very sorry."

"Feeling sorry is not friend. I do not need feeling sorry. I need friend. World is no good alone. Is like blind and deaf. Nothing has taste. Nothing has feel. What can I do alone? Eat sleep wash. Watch television. I cannot work alone or talk alone. I cannot dance alone. I cannot love alone."

"You don't need to be alone," Steph said gently. "Everyone likes you."

"Do you, Stephanie? Do you like me?"

She hesitated. "I think I do now."

"You think but you do not know?"

"I don't know you, Sasha."

"You could know me. We could spend time together. I would like that."

Steph didn't answer. He had shared his unhappiness with her. It was a secret and painful treasure. She was proud he trusted her and she was determined to protect his confidence. But she would not let him move her into something rash.

They strolled and they chatted about other things. He was like silver polish stripping off her outer shell of electrons. She felt herself shining. But there was seriousness now too: he had laid a foundation beneath the smiles and jokes.

They reached her building.

"You live here too?" he said.

She was amazed how quickly the day had gone, like a feather blown by a breath. He kissed her good-by. It was a quick kiss, masculine and unsentimental. He turned to go and she watched his odd mix of gawkiness and grace, ugliness and beauty.

*I'm luckier than he is,* she thought: *I have a past to keep me company. He has none.* She felt a surge of responsibility of the have toward the have-not.

"Sasha!" she called.

He stopped and turned.

"We could go to a movie," she said. "Or have dinner."

His funny nose crinkled. "Are we friends?"

"All right. Friends."

"Shake?"

Very formally, the dark-haired Russian and the blond-haired American shook hands.

Friends.

# forty-one

Tuesday, Marius Volmar called Steph and Chris to his office.

"Sit. Please."

They had showered and changed to street clothes and there was no company class sweat left on them. He did not object when they deposited themselves on the leather armchairs.

"Our spring gala this year will be *Sleeping Beauty*." He explained the restored cuts. From time to time his glance touched each of the girls, absently, unimportantly. They nodded, wondering why he was telling them this, why both of them.

"In the ballet, Aurora is a girl on the verge of womanhood. I could give the role to a mature woman. Older dancers sometimes project youthfulness far better than younger ones: think of Fonteyn's Juliet; or Ulanova's Giselle."

The girls shifted on their cushions.

"On the other hand, a young dancer is—young. A body in its twenties can perform miracles that a body in its thirties cannot. Youth does not get winded. Youth does not need half a beat to prepare a turn. I've decided in favor of youth and miracles. We shall have a young Aurora, as Tchaikovsky and Petipa intended. Since Aurora moves from girlhood to womanhood, the girl dancing her will—with this role—make the transition from soloist to principal."

Volmar turned to Chris.

"I'm pleased with you, Christine. You have fire and you have something that very rarely goes with it: accuracy."

Chris dropped her gaze. For one unguarded moment she smiled with girlish embarrassment. Volmar's eyes remained fixed on her. Her feet crept together nervously.

"As for you, Stephanie—I've always had great hopes for you." Volmar's eyes grazed Steph now. "You memorize fast, you're musical."

*What's he saying?* Steph wondered. *I have no fire, no accuracy, just a little do-re-mi and a barn of a memory?* She felt glanced-over, omitted, like the only child at Christmas with no present under the tree.

Volmar swiveled back comfortably in his chair.

"As dancers you two are not at all alike. But you each have a quality that illuminates a different aspect of Aurora. Stephanie, you have the virtuosity for the Act One solo. Christine, you have the sincerity to lift the part out of simple Bolshoi sentimentality."

Chris looked frail and small and suddenly she was sitting very straight on the leather chair, like a little girl who'd been complimented on her posture. *He likes her better*, Steph realized. A sour-tasting envy flooded her. Partly in shame, partly in self-protection, she fixed her eyes on the neutral confusion of Volmar's desk, the double-decker chrome basket of *In* and *Out* mail, the set and costume sketches with tissue overlays, the scribbled-over cast lists.

"Stephanie, would you object to learning Aurora? It's a very, very difficult role."

A stab of surprise went through Steph. "Object? How could I object?"

His eyes were on Chris now, and suddenly Steph understood what he was doing: he was playing her off against her best friend, doing it coldly and manipulatively and on purpose. But why?

"Understand, I can give no guarantee that you'll dance the role."

"Guarantee—?" Steph stammered. Now he had lost her.

"I'm asking if you would cover the role for Christine."

Steph's hands tightened around one another. He wasn't

asking: he was commanding. For an instant her lungs seemed to be pushing air out and pulling it in at the same time and she couldn't get a breath or sound past her throat.

Finally she managed to blurt, "Yes—of course."

"Mr. Volmar." Chris's face was blushing and she was struggling to hold her voice steady. "That's not fair. I should be covering for Steph."

Steph sank against the leather backrest. She wished it would close over her like a coffin lid. She felt humiliated enough without the sting of Chris's bumbling generosity.

"My dear Christine, that's exactly what I was going to ask you next. Do you object to covering the role for Stephanie? Do you object to learning the part—with no guarantees?"

Chris's voice came faint and late like an echo of something that had been shouted very far away. "No."

"You both agree then?"

Neither answered.

Volmar smiled apologetically. "I cannot judge before I see. Until we rehearse, I can't be sure which of you I prefer. It's a dreadful thing to ask of any dancer. But dance is dance and we are professionals. So, if you are willing, each of you will learn the role. Sometime between now and the gala, we'll make up our minds."

Steph's instinct told her nothing was ever so simple as Volmar presented it. Not even the truth. She wondered which of them he was trying to hurt and why.

Chris forced out an objection, tiny and hesitant. "Mr. Volmar, Steph and I are friends, and I wouldn't want anything to—"

"But of course you're friends. Could I ask two dancers who weren't?"

\*       \*       \*

In the elevator, Steph and Chris tried to smile. And then the smiles thinned away and Chris burst into tears.

"Chris—don't. Please."

"I can't help it. You're my best friend. You're my only friend." Chris's eyes blinked up at Steph. "I don't want to lose you."

"Come on. No one's going to lose any friends."

Chris's eyes had a haunted glow. For a long time now Steph had sensed something unidentifiably wrong with her friend: there had been lapses of attention and memory and judgment and they formed an ominous pattern.

"I'm going to dance badly," Chris said suddenly. "Every rehearsal, I'll make mistakes. I'm going to make sure you get the role."

It was an absolutely crazy thing to say and something cold shot down Steph's spine when she realized Chris meant it. *I could take the role right now, I could just tell her I want it.*

She pushed the notion away. But it kept slithering back.

*She's so scared she'd give it to me. Without a fight. Without a whimper.*

Suddenly there were two scared people in the elevator: Chris drying her eyes on her fists, Steph staring deep down at something she'd never seen in herself before.

She shook her head, a hard snap of a shake. "No, Chris. We'll both do the very best we can. And whoever gets the role, we'll always be friends."

\*     \*     \*

"Well?" Sasha asked proudly. "What do you think?"

Empty, it was a New York nothing, with all the earmarks of five hundred a month rent: twelve-foot ceiling, marble fireplace, wood parquetry floor; two paint-splattered windows with a view of two windows across the street; a front door scarred with locks present and ghosts of locks past; a door with perforated tin panels tucking away the two-burner kitchen with its two-quart sink and one-ice-tray refrigerator; two newer doors, battered as welfare children, anyone's guess which was the closet and which the bathroom.

"It's—it could be—really terrific," Steph hedged.

"I am glad you love it. If you knew how long I look!"

There was a naked king-sized mattress, no other furnishing, and the poodle had already claimed it. Sasha flung himself down beside the dog, a very energetic pantomime of exhaustion. The poodle stirred.

"Needs things," Sasha said. "Paint, plaster."

*Needs an exterminator*, Steph noticed, watching a six-legged black dot scuttle out of the sink.

"I will buy rugs—pictures—furniture." Sasha waved, a set designer summoning props into existence. "Will be knockout, yes?"

"Is it big enough for you and Merde?"

Sasha cuddled the huge animal to his chest. "Big enough for me and Merde and anyone else."

"Does the fireplace work?"

Sasha nodded. "And wonderful Madison Avenue shop is going to find brass andirons for me. And you will help me choose furniture, yes?"

She hesitated. "I'm not much of a decorator."

"I do not want decorator. I want real home, place to hang my blue jeans. Monday you come help me choose furniture, yes?"

Steph summoned up a mental image of Monday in her date book. Masseur, class with the new man at Harkness House, that revival of *Turning Point* at the Little Carnegie that she'd promised to catch with Chris.

Nothing she couldn't cancel.

"Is problem?"

"No—no problem. Only, could I ask you a favor?"

"Ask."

"Please don't tell anyone."

His face went through the motions of shock. "You think I gossip?"

"Other people gossip. I wouldn't want it to get around."

"What can get around? Choosing bed does not mean spending night in it. You are scared of me?"

"You've been a perfect gentleman, Sasha." Too perfect, damn it all. "But rumors travel very fast in the company, and I don't want to hurt my roommate."

"My furniture—your roommate—I do not understand connection."

"Christine."

Something flew through his eyes too fast for her to catch. "Christine Avery? Second gypsy in *Alborado?* So what?"

"She has a crush on you."

"What means 'crush'?"

"She's in love with you."

"Not possible."

*How would you know?* Steph thought. *Your English isn't that good, you don't pay attention, all sorts of people might be in love with you and you'd never notice.*

"Sasha, I live with her. She's very naïve but she's my best friend. And she thinks she's head over heels in love with you. She'd be terribly hurt if she knew I was seeing you."

Sasha smiled and patted the mattress. She sat beside him, snuggling comfortably against his shoulder.

"We will wear big dark glasses," he said. "Like spies."

\*     \*     \*

They went to department stores and furniture shops and they didn't wear dark glasses.

Salesmen showed them chairs and sofas and just the fabrics to go with a standard gray poodle. Some recognized Sasha and a pleasant giddiness rose up in Steph when she sensed them trying to recognize her too.

"What you think?" Sasha said. "Big enough?"

They were staring at a Brazilian steerhide sofa. She tried to imagine the firelight in Sasha's apartment and the luxurious encircling sweep of leather. Sasha sprawled and motioned her to sit beside him. His arm went around her and he laughed, showing his Soviet dentistry.

She laughed, too, a hundred times in that one day. They chose sofas and chairs and rugs and lamps, all expensive, all beautiful. It was good to be with Sasha, good to be piecing together a home even if it wasn't hers.

"Day after tomorrow," Sasha said, "we choose curtains, okay?"

Her life paused while she waited to hear from him. A day went by and two days. He didn't mention curtains in class and he didn't mention them after performance. He rushed past her in the wings and smiled and showed his steel molar and that was all.

Her happiness was dashed.

One evening in the supermarket, waiting in line at the checkout, she picked up a magazine out of the rack. There was a photo of Sasha discoing with a TV talk-show hostess. The text called him the up-and-coming ladies' man in the United States, "making such venerable girl-watchers as Mikhail Baryshnikov and Warren Beatty look positively in need of French ticklers."

She worked out the date of the party. It was the day Sasha had said they would choose curtains. She put the magazine back and left the store without buying her groceries.

\*     \*     \*

It was heart bruise and it was stupid, the sort of hurt that happened to girls who fell in love at first sight, not to Stephanie Lang. The anger and the ache pounded in her stomach like a stab wound. She tried not to let the thought of him interfere with her work.

But it did. She was slow in class, sloppy onstage.

She tried not to let him butt into her dreams.

But he did—funny Russian *l*'s and steel molar and long smooth neck.

"What the hell have you got on your feet," her mother demanded after Thursday's *Lilac Garden*, "hiking shoes?"

Steph let it pour out.

Anna tried to show understanding about Sasha. "But, hell, this is ballet. You have to expect the machos to come on to you once a month, regular as your period."

"I don't know what's happening to me," Steph said, and there were dark circles beginning around her eyes. Anna knew exactly what was happening: too much coffee, too many cigarettes, not enough red meat, no sleep.

"You're in love with a prick," Anna said. "If it's any comfort, honey, you're not the first. Take a good look at your mom."

Steph stared at her. "But I thought he *cared* about me."

"You and two dozen other nitwits thought he cared." Anna made her eyes big with compassion and she hugged her little girl and wished she weren't quite such a little girl. "All that little Commie cares about is money and a poodle called Merde and getting his picture in the paper. He's got the brains to hire a press agent and you better have the brains to forget him."

"Mom, you don't know him. . . . He's not like that."

"They're all like that!" Anna burst out. "Honey, I'm Polish. I *know* Russians. I don't care whether it's Misha or Sasha or Kasha or Cashew! They make good partners onstage—*period!* You just get some sleep and start eating calf's liver for breakfast and for God's sake clean up your technique."

# forty-two

Steph took her mother's advice like doctor's medicine—held her nose and swallowed. She wrapped herself in work like a cocoon. She cut cigarettes to half a pack a day, coffee to three cups.

And it almost killed her.

She made sure there were fresh greens and red meat or fish for dinner. She fixed calf's liver for breakfast three times a week and she even persuaded Chris—who was looking pale and dangerously underweight—to try eating it.

At supper she and Chris usually kept to themselves, locked into separate silences and respecting the other's privacy. But sometimes if Steph had seen Sasha's name in the evening paper a wave of sadness would sweep over her and her throat would refuse to swallow and she would have to lay down her fork.

Once she looked across the table when Chris was staring hauntedly into space, not eating either. For an instant, seeing her roommate dejected and silent with shadows creeping under her skin, Steph had the uneasy impression of gazing into a mirror.

*It's the* Sleeping Beauty, she thought, *we're competing against each other and it's poisoning us.*

She almost said, "Chris, let's talk about it." But she wanted the role. Perhaps she wanted it even more than their friendship, and perhaps that was why she kept quiet.

She saw Sasha three times a week at *Sleeping Beauty* rehearsals. They spoke, hello's and hi's and How's Merde? and when Volmar paired them they touched. But they didn't really talk, and that hurt her. After two weeks the hurt was past its early wanting-to-weep stage: it became something deeper, less consciously felt, like a low note on a church organ.

She still checked the answering service several times a day from work and she made a point of getting to the mailbox first, just in case Sasha phoned or sent a note. She wouldn't have wanted Chris to know. Chris was hurt and mysterious and they were competitive enough these days without that added pain.

But there were only phone and electric bills and letters from Mrs. Avery and envelopes from Lenox Hill Hospital that piled up in the wicker catch-all basket on Chris's dresser. One day when she was cleaning Steph knocked the basket over. She had to crawl under the bed picking up the bracelet charms and pennies and all the odd childish things Chris collected.

She found four newspaper clippings about Sasha and eleven unopened Lenox Hill envelopes. It was none of her business, but she opened one.

*       *       *

"Chris," she said at supper, "why aren't you going for your checkups?"

Chris looked at her with a caginess she'd never seen before. "Who says I'm not?"

"The hospital says you're not. They've sent eleven reminders."

Chris slammed a fist down onto the table and the water glasses jumped. "You have no right to search my mail!"

Steph swallowed, knowing she was in the wrong, but in the wrong for the right reason. "Chris, you're not looking well."

"Because I'm not feeling well," Chris shot back.

"Then you should go to the hospital."

"This has nothing to do with the hospital. It's personal."

"Do you want to tell me about it?"

"I did tell you about it and you laughed at me."

Steph's brow furrowed. "I never laughed at you."

"I don't want to talk about it and I don't want you searching my mail!"

"Chris—listen to me. You can't keep skipping appointments. You've got to look after your health."

"I haven't been skipping appointments! I've been *busy*, that's all."

"You're not a child playing hooky, Chris."

"Then stop *treating* me like a child!"

"Go for a checkup. This week. Tomorrow."

"All right!" Chris screamed. "I'll go!"

"Tomorrow."

"All right, tomorrow! Just leave me alone—all of you! I'm old enough to take care of myself!"

But was she?

At a *Sleeping Beauty* rehearsal, a grueler with Volmar screaming, she told Steph, "You're doing your balance wrong. Don't grab it from your partner. Let him hand it to you."

And she was right. She was right and she was a fool, because they were competing in dead earnest now, and what one won the other lost.

The problem was the Rose Adagio in Act One, where Princess Aurora meets her four suitors. Neither Steph nor Chris had any difficulty with the opening steps: the movements were soft and flowing and supported as each of the princes in turn partnered Aurora.

The difficulty, for Steph, began when Aurora stepped back and rose on *pointe*. The choreography called for an attitude, one leg raised behind the other at an angle of ninety degrees, knee bent, right arm extended and left arced overhead.

"Fingers *spaced!*" Volmar shouted, and Steph couldn't help remembering another shout, Lvovna's how many years ago? *"In attitude the fingernails must be clean!"* Her fingernails were clean. Superstitiously, she scrubbed them before every rehearsal with a brush bought specially for the purpose.

Taking her right hand with its beautifully clean fingernails, each prince in turn walked round her, revolving her full circle. The attitude had to be perfectly, unwobblingly maintained.

So far, so good.

But then she had to recenter, bringing her balance back into herself, and at a signal of her eyes the prince let go of her hand.

Here she was on her own and here she was in trouble. Still in attitude, still balanced, she had to raise both hands overhead, shaping an imaginary crown, and hold the position for one instant of perfect motionless equilibrium.

Steph managed to hold her *pointe* and her balance, but she could feel her center skittering around inside her like a panicked hamster and she knew it just had to look forced and jittery, the opposite of everything Aurora and the Adagio represented. The pattern was repeated three times, and the hamster inside her skittered more wildly each time, and then came the worst.

As the last prince released her hand, she was in profile to the audience. Maintaining her *pointe* and her balance and her attitude, she had to straighten her raised leg very, very slowly till it was fully extended. At the same time she had to stretch both arms slowly forward, ignore the hamster turning somersaults, and hold the muscle-murdering arabesque "forever," as Lvovna would have said.

Chris's forever was a hell of a lot more forever than Steph's, and everybody at rehearsal saw it. Steph could feel the role slipping away from her.

"You're pushing into arabesque," Chris told her afterward.

Chris was right and it hurt. But Steph listened. She needed to know how Chris managed it, and like an innocent fool Chris told her.

"What I do is imagine silk ropes pulling me into arabesque, and I fight them—just a little—like Lvovna said to."

Steph had forgotten Lvovna's silk ropes. But now it all came back. She asked Wally to practice with her. The silk ropes worked. She got her arabesque and her attitudes and her Adagio into shape.

But she didn't return the favor. She saw Chris kicking off early in a double *fouetté*, dropping her shoulder. She kept her mouth shut. Just because Chris volunteered advice didn't mean she owed Chris any, did it?

"*Owe* her!" Anna cried. "Why not just cut your throat and mail her the role in gift wrap? Honey, this is war and you're entitled to use every weapon you can—short of sabotage."

Anna's voice lingered on that word "sabotage," and a feeling of apprehension descended on Steph. She couldn't shake it. *Sleeping Beauty* rehearsals left her drained and edgy: Volmar was always screaming—there were rumors that the orchestra was planning a walkout, so he had reason to scream; and Chris was always making suggestions, good suggestions, and Steph felt like a Judas; and Wally was the perfect gentleman partner and Sasha was the perfect gentleman partner prick.

Not even an apology for not having phoned or written or spoken. Not even an acknowledgment that anything was the matter.

Her head was throbbing from photos and headlines and gossip about Sasha up to all hours in discos with this woman and that woman and he had the nerve, the utter colossal nerve, to be utterly colossally perfect in every lift, in every supported turn and arabesque.

The perfect prince.

The perfect shit.

She was in a cold fury by the time she got back to her dressing room, and it didn't help to find her mother waiting for her.

"Okay, young lady, I got a few things to talk over with you."

Anna snapped an Elizabeth Arden message pad out of her purse, flipped through phone numbers and tic-tac-toes, and stopped at a page of ballpoint scrawl. She stared at it and then at her daughter. She sighed. It was the this-hurts-me-more-than-it-does-you sigh.

"Did I raise a dancer or an idiot?"

Steph felt a rim of irritation rise in her chest. "Maybe I'm an idiot, but I'm a very tired idiot, so whatever you have to say, please say it fast."

"Tired? If you'd eat right maybe you'd have some strength. Look at Shura Danilova. When she was twice your age and then some she had more stamina than forty Olympic shot-putters—because she knew how to *eat!*"

"I'm not Shura Danilova."

"To say the least. Honey, when you're good, I tell you, right? When you stink, I tell you, right? The truth is the truth and if you can't take the truth, then you don't belong in ballet, right?"

"If you say so, Mom."

Anna detected a whine and the last thing she was going to put up with at this juncture was whining. "I'm telling you facts, so don't try to yes me. Two and two's four no matter who says so."

"Mom, for all I care, two and two's five if it'll get you out of here any quicker."

Anna stared at this thing called a daughter. "Have you got a brain in your head or not?"

"Why don't you tell me, Mom?"

"Okay, you *haven't* got a brain in your head. You think people are going to go to the A & P for hamburger when Grand Union's got filet mignon at the same price, that's what you think."

"I don't even know what you're talking about."

"Your variation, that's what I'm talking about. Colleen Neary can do five unsupported pirouettes in her *sleep*—so get off your keister! Suzanne Farrell's got an extension from Lincoln Center to Tennessee. Now *that's* an arabesque and that's what people expect for their money, not some kid hanging off the rung of a fire escape. Honey, you got competition—and I don't mean Chris, she's so dizzy she'd bow to the backdrop. I mean when I was growing up and Millie Hayden walked onstage you could see those eyes move from the family circle. Even Nora Kaye doing *Symphony in C* had *eyes*, for Chrissake! You're dancing for people who remember *Fonteyn's* Rose Adagio! They can turn on their *television* sets and see Gelsey Kirkland, and frankly, after what I saw out there today, I wouldn't blame them!"

Steph was staring at her, hard and fixed. "You watched that rehearsal?"

"Damned right."

A silence vibrated in the room. Anna could have sworn the reflection in the mirror trembled.

"That was a closed rehearsal. You are *not* a member of this company."

"I happen to be your mother."

"You happen to be a pain in the ass. I take notes from Marius Volmar, not the exercise teacher at Elizabeth Arden's."

Anna's jaw dropped. A cold drizzle of shock glazed her. "You just watch your language, Miss Know-it-all!"

Steph inhaled through clenched teeth. "Mom, you may have put twenty years into me—I've put my whole *life* into me. My career depends on getting this role. I'm fighting for it. I need every ounce of fight I have in me and I don't need you picking fights and wearing me down."

"Picking fights—" Amazement gusted through Anna. "I'm

*fighting* your fights. I could have lost my job taking the afternoon off—but I took it off anyway—for you! Honey, I'm going to *bat* for you! You just listen to me and this time we're going to hit a home run!"

"Mom, every time you've gone to bat for me, the only thing you ever hit was me—smack in the face."

Anna was speechless. She clutched for some sort of twinkle, some sign that Steph was joking. But the girl was dead serious. A coldness sliced through Anna. Her hands were rigid and trembling.

"If you can say that to your own mother—after all I've done for you—you're crazy. You belong in an insane asylum. If you mean what you just said you belong in hell."

Steph's eyes didn't even flinch. "There's a lot more I could say, Mom, but what's the use? I'll just say this, and just this once: don't you dare ever come to one of my rehearsals again—*in your life!*"

Anna began quivering. Spasms shot through her. She pressed a Kleenex to her face. Tears were coming out everywhere—eyes, mouth, nose. She sat shivering in the chair, a polka-dot dacron-polyester-wrapped lump of shock.

"I love you, Mom " Arms went around Anna. A little warmth. Too little too late. "But you can be a hell of a nuisance."

"I was only trying." Anna stumbled to her feet.

"I'm trying too, Mom. Harder than I've ever tried in my life."

"Okay. Do it your way. Don't say I didn't tell you."

Steph smiled. "Mom, one thing I'd never say to you is, you didn't tell me."

"Okay. See you around." Anna fumbled from the room. Her mind scurried. She couldn't lose the girl. Not now. Not yet. There had to be a way to hold on.

Outside the dressing room it came to her: *Marius.* She'd phone Marius, cook him dinner, make love. Sure. *Should have gone straight to him instead of Miss Know-it-all.*

Marius Volmar was a pro. He appreciated pros. *He'd* want to see Anna Lang's notes.

# forty-three

The first company class in May, Sasha did his barre next to Steph.

"Hello, Stephanie."

"Hello, Sasha." She didn't look at him. She pretended her *tendu* needed all her concentration.

"How have you been?" he asked.

"Pretty busy."

"Like me. I am so busy I am a wreck."

"So I see in the papers."

"Do not believe papers. As bad here as in Soviet."

"I only look at the photographs."

"Awful photographs. Awful party. I hate big parties."

She wanted to say, "Then why do you go to them?" He wouldn't have heard. He had one leg in *développé* against the barre and his foot was practically in his ear.

"You like big parties, Stephanie?"

"Not especially."

"Little parties better, yes?"

"Sometimes."

"If I give little party, you come?"

She looked at him. His face was still ugly in the handsome

433

way she remembered. The dimple and the misshapen nose and the deep shadowed eyes still made her heart trip. And she hated herself for it.

"Depends."

"Tonight, after performance, I make dinner for you and me, all right?"

She wanted to say, "Why the hell should I eat with you, you've ignored me all these weeks, you could at least have had the decency to phone!"

"I can't."

"Please, Stephanie—why can't you?"

"Because I've forgotten the address."

\*     \*     \*

He was on the telephone when she arrived. He mouthed a "Hello" and kissed her lightly on the cheek.

"Yes, darling, yes." He was talking into the phone but his eyes were on her and she had the feeling he was dividing his "darling." "We talk about it later, yes?" He made a kissing sound and hung up. "Dorcas. She wants to be my mother, I let her be my mother."

He stood looking at her.

"Is still raining?"

"Pouring," she said.

"Let me get towel and dry you."

"I'll be okay if I can just get out of this."

He helped her out of the raincoat. His hands lingered gently on her. "Better I hang it over bathtub." He vanished a moment and she heard the dog barking in the bathroom.

She studied the room. He had furnished it in a way that looked modern and bright and expensively cozy. There were two chairs and an ottoman in gleaming dark leather and a king-sized bed set very low to the floor with a curving wrought-chrome headboard and a shaggy white spread that looked like fur but couldn't have been, could it? There were hanging bookcases of records and books and tiny Eskimo sculptures and a full-length mirror with a border of theatrical make-up lights. The desk had bright enamel boxes to hold clutter neatly.

She recognized a few pieces she had helped him pick. But most she didn't recognize.

He came back with a bath towel. "Tie this around your head. Your hair is wet."

"Then I'll look like your Russian grandmother."

"She looked wonderful, you look wonderful."

"So do you, Sasha." She quietly dropped the towel on a chair. She was used to seeing him in skin-tight practice clothes or perspiring and stripped to the waist. Here he was casually dressed and bathed and groomed. It surprised her how young and fresh and handsome he looked.

"Are you hungry?" he asked.

"Starved. Something smells good."

"Is very good."

He had a beautiful glass and chrome table but she saw they were not going to eat there. He had put two bright cushions by the fireplace. The tablecloth on the floor between them was set for dinner, with linen napkins in ivory rings. He had lit a small fire. The apartment smelled sweetly of pine.

"Sit." He patted one of the cushions. "And take off shoes. This is your home."

She kicked off her shoes and sat. It didn't feel like home but it felt good. He made scampering trips from kitchen to fireplace, refusing to let her help. The tablecloth filled with unrecognizable but delicious-looking cold hors d'oeuvres that turned out to be eggplant and minced salmon and calf's-foot jelly. There were tiny seasoned meat pastries and hot borscht with dollops of sour cream and chopped fresh dill. And two small glasses of clear liquid sitting in a silver dish of crushed ice.

He told her the Russian name of everything. "Is traditional Russian meal."

"I can't believe people eat this way in Russia."

"Is not whole meal—much more coming."

"But it's a feast!"

"Of course." He lifted a chilled shot glass. "To Stephanie and Sasha. To friends."

She stared at her shot glass. "Is it vodka?"

"Of course is vodka."

She shook her head. "I can't. It's too strong for me."

"You do not want I should drink alone—is bad for health. You can drink one little toast, yes?"

"All right. One little toast."

To a Russian, it turned out, one little toast meant tossing your head back and taking the whole shot in one swallow. She made the attempt. And felt like a flame swallower who'd seriously miscalculated.

He brought out a little copper burner and worked like a boy scout trying to light it. In a copper frying pan he made thin little crepes that he heaped with thick-lumped gray caviar—wasn't that the most expensive kind?—and more sour cream and lemon and melted butter.

"Sasha, I'm going to burst!"

"Nobody burst till dessert."

The crepes—*blini*—were delicious and she gobbled her way through four. And smiled. And found herself worrying about sex.

Because there wasn't a hint of it.

She wondered if he found her cold or unfeminine or built too much like a boy. He talked about jealousies at the Kirov and the fruit juice machines at Hammacher Schlemmer. She didn't know what to answer, how to meet his eyes. He kept filling her plate and her glass. She'd had so little experience at being seduced that she wasn't even certain this was a seduction.

Maybe he just thought she was one hell of an eating buddy.

She fumbled with spoons and bite-sized cheese pastries and she even fumbled with words.

"Stephanie." He slid his cushion nearer and her bare foot could feel the warmth of his. "Do you know how much I have missed you?"

She looked at him. "No, Sasha. I honestly don't."

"I did. Very, very much."

She inhaled and then she asked as casually as she could, "Why didn't you phone?"

"I did not want you should think me pest." He took her hand and held it tightly. "Did you miss me, Stephanie? Please tell truth."

She looked down at their hands. A longing came over her. She wished the two of them could be as naked and close and trusting as those hands. She didn't know how to answer. She knew what he wanted to hear but it frightened her to admit it.

"Don't you know?" she said softly.

"Say you missed me," he said. "Make me very happy."

She bit on her lips. He was crouched beside her cushion, fixing her another crepe.

"Sasha?" she said through a full mouth.

"Stephanie?"

"I missed you."

His face broke into a grin. For an instant his hand rested very gently on the back of her neck. And then he got up and brought chilled cranberry pudding and baklava.

"Russian, not Turkish."

And coffee.

"Turkish, not Russian."

"Sasha," she groaned, "I couldn't eat another mouthful!" But she could. And did. And felt relaxed and warm with all the food and too much vodka in her.

He put another log on the fire and then he went to the window and stood a moment looking out. He pulled a cord and venetian blinds tumbled down in a clatter, blotting out the rain and the world. He turned off the lights and crossed the room. There was only the firelight. He was sitting on the bed staring at her.

"Stephanie, do you not know I wish we should make love?"

She didn't answer.

He took off his shirt. He was wearing a small silver cross. It caught the light and sparkled. It was Russian, with two crossbars.

Her head felt cloudy and warm. She went to him and touched a finger to the cross. "I thought you weren't religious."

"Sometimes I am."

"When?"

His hand went around her wrist. "Now."

She pulled back just a little bit.

"Come to bed with me, Stephanie. Please."

"I have to go home. Chris is waiting."

"Am I such a silly, unimportant boy? I wait weeks for you. I cook beautiful meal for you. And now you leave me to run back to your little friend."

His hands crawled back into his lap. He looked terribly

unhappy. She thought he might cry.

"I never feel like such silly little boy in my life."

She hadn't thought it would happen like this. She sat on the edge of the bed and leaned over and kissed him very quickly. His eyes were watering.

"What do I do wrong? Why you do not want me?"

"I've heard about you, Sasha. We've all heard about you."

He blinked. "Terrible things?"

"Nice things. Very, very nice things." She placed a hand softly against his cheek.

"And you do not want some nice things for yourself?"

"Sasha, I like you very much and I'm drunk. If I don't get out of here in thirty seconds I'm going to make a fool of myself."

"Stay. We both make fools of ourselves. Is nice."

Her mouth was dry and her blood was beating like wings in her ears. "I'm scared."

"You virgin?"

She smiled. "No."

"Then why scared?"

"I'm scared..." *Out with it, Steph.* "I'm scared you'll only want me once."

He shook his head violently. "No, no—much, much more."

"Maybe not. You have other girls. You don't know how I'll be."

His face was serious. "I am not animal. I am very bad boy but when I am in love I am good."

"Would you be? With me?"

His eyes were wide and brown and aching with vulnerability. She looked away.

"Stephanie..." He put his hands on her shoulders. "I will be so good with you, you will wish I was not."

"I'd never wish that."

"Enough of wishing."

He kissed her and pulled her down. She felt her heart skitter like a baby pigeon cupped within his hand. He was affectionate and murmuring and his arms were strong. She had never suspected such gentleness and consideration in him, such hunger in herself. He went slowly and sweetly with her, and afterward, when she finally opened her eyes, he was looking at her.

"Do I do what you want?"

"Yes. You're perfect."

He drew her to him again. It was one of those silent floating moments when everything makes sense and none of it matters.

"I have to go home," she whispered. "It's late."

She got up to dress. She went to the window and lifted the blinds to see if it was still raining. There were trees on his street and a taxi going by. The headlights made bright streaks on the wet pavement. She sighed.

She saw Sasha's reflection in the window. He was looking at himself in the mirror, one hand to his hair.

"Come back," she heard him say.

"It's late. I can't."

"Stephanie—I think you use me once and throw me away?"

She looked over at the bed. He was smiling. She shut her tote bag and set it down softly. She went and sat on the bed. They kissed.

"Stay, yes?"

"I'll phone Chris and say I'm at my mother's."

His finger traced out her eyebrows and the line of her nose. "You are beautiful liar. Dangerous."

"You're a beautiful everything. That's even more dangerous."

\*　　\*　　\*

In the morning Sasha made coffee—French, not Turkish.

He said he loved her. She was the one woman he'd ever met who was his friend, who wasn't pursuing him for celebrity or sex, who understood him. He was tired of playing around: he wanted someone that he could ...

"How do you say *fidèle?*"

"Faithful?" Steph guessed. She was wearing his bathrobe.

"Someone I can be faithful to. Can it be you, Stephanie?"

She wanted to believe him. She wanted them to be lovers. She weighed obstacles: girls in the corps who loved to gossip about Sasha; Chris with her crush on him; Mr. Volmar, who was known to dislike him.

"It has to be secret," she said.

"Secret?" He scowled.

"No one can know but you and me."

He stared a moment and then burst out laughing and hugged her. "Stephanie, it is perfect! You are perfect!"

For Steph everything happened all at once and beautifully. Sasha gave her his key. They became secret lovers. She planned her time so not a moment was wasted. There was work and there was Sasha. Nothing else.

She had never been happier and she had never danced better. She began getting nice small mentions in reviews. She barely glanced at them. She couldn't wait to dash from the theater into a taxi to West Seventy-eighth Street. All she wanted was to be with him.

Two or three times a week—some lucky weeks four—they met afternoons, between rehearsal and performance. There were beautiful sunny days when they shut out the sun and lay in bed. There were beautiful stormy days when they lay in bed and listened to the rain. If she could think of a plausible excuse for Chris, they met at night, and nights were loveliest.

In rehearsal they made miracles.

At the end of the *Sleeping Beauty* Act Three *pas de deux* Steph had a dizzying rush of turns on *pointe*. It climaxed in a *pas de poisson*, a headlong suicide fish dive toward the floor broken at the very last moment when the prince caught her. The first time she and Sasha rehearsed it the other dancers applauded.

Even Volmar looked astonished.

After that, whenever Steph and Sasha were scheduled together, dancers crowded into the rehearsal to watch that final catch. There was an understanding between their bodies that she had never known with another dancer. Giddy with the certainty of him, she took risks she never before had dared. And when he caught her or lifted her or crushed her against him she almost cried out in happiness.

She wondered if anyone in the company suspected. Especially Volmar, whose eyes watched everything and gave away nothing.

\*      \*      \*

Marius Volmar kept close watch on his four leads: the two he wanted and the two he must pretend to want. He rehearsed all four together, careful to pair them in all combinations. He distributed praise and blame so as to suggest a mind still open.

"Wally, you're going to marry Stephanie, you love her—now can you put a bit more gallantry into those lifts? And let your hand linger on her waist when you bring her down—as though you were sorry to let go."

"How many beats?" Wally asked.

Volmar smothered an exasperated sigh. "It's not a question of beats, it's a *feeling* you must project. Your feet have the beats, your hands are free to express."

"It's easier if I know the count."

Which was the reason, Volmar was tempted to say, that very few gay men became *danseurs nobles*. Luckily, Wally Collins had Marius Volmar to guide his career.

Sasha, of course, had no trouble letting his hands linger on the girls' waists, and he didn't need to be told to extend his thumb. But he had trouble partnering Christine. And that bothered Volmar since he intended to team Christine and Sasha as covers.

Volmar watched them carefully. At first he could not tell where the fault lay. And then it came to him that the problem was Sasha. Not his dancing, but some psychological effect he seemed to have on the girl.

In solo variations, Christine responded intuitively to tone colors and harmonic shadings. She danced with her entire body, from eyebrows to fingertips to toes.

But when Sasha partnered her the musicality vanished. The line became hard, staccato. There was no link from one step to the next. She rushed her lifts, touching down early. She was cringing from Sasha's touch.

Volmar clapped the piano to a stop. "Christine, my dear, what on earth is the matter?"

The girl stood breathing rapidly. Her face was pale with a fever brightness in the eyes and it occurred to Volmar that she might be taking some sort of amphetamine.

"You're hurrying everything," Volmar said. "You jump two feet in the air before Sasha can even lift you. This is a *grand adage*—lyrical. *Pas de deux*. You're in love. Can we take it again from the *entrechats volés? And!*"

The piano began again. Christine did her first *entrechat*, then stopped almost in mid-air. "I can't."

There was silence. They all looked at her.

"What did you say, Christine?" Volmar asked mildly.

She kept her eyelids clenched, pressing back tears. "I can't do it."

"But you've done it before, my dear, and you will do it now. Come." He snapped a finger in the air, gave the beat. *"And!"*

\*     \*     \*

Another envelope came from Lenox Hill Hospital.

Even before she opened it, Steph knew what it was. Her heart dropped three stories. *What am I going to do about Chris?*

She telephoned Ray Lockwood. At first he tried to refuse. "It's not my business," he said.

"You're still a friend, Ray—aren't you?"

"So are you."

"I've been through it with her a dozen times and she won't listen to me. You're a man. You're a lawyer. You can reason with her."

"So can her parents."

"It has to be face to face and it has to be *now*. Ray, it's been months since she's had a checkup." There was a silence and Ray said, "When do you want me to come over?"

"She's always home around five."

\*     \*     \*

Steph let Ray into the apartment. "She doesn't know you're coming. She's in the kitchen."

Ray crossed to the sofa. He was about to sit when Chris appeared in the doorway. She stood there a moment looking at him. His heart gave a bang like a backfire and he forced his eyes to meet hers.

What he saw shocked him. *My God,* he thought—*she's dying*.

"How are you, Ray?"

"Fine. And you?"

She came into the room, white and tired and carrying a coffee cup. She sat down, saying, "I'm working . . . working hard."

He'd thought about seeing Chris again and he'd thought that after all this time he'd be able to handle it. Now he wasn't sure.

His voice felt strange in his throat, as though it belonged to someone else.

"You don't want to work too hard," he said. "You don't want to seal yourself off. I did that, studying for exams. I lost twelve pounds in a month."

*Why is he here?* Chris wondered. *Why is he lecturing me?* She sensed the same false jauntiness she had felt in him the last time and it put her on guard.

"You've lost weight too, Chris."

"Maybe a little," she admitted.

Ray leaned forward to toy with the ash tray on the coffee table. He glanced up at Chris as casually as he could manage. She seemed tiny in her chair—tiny and nervous and terribly breakable. He had an impulse to gather her up in his arms and cradle all her tiny nervous vulnerabilities.

Instead he made himself bully her. *For her good,* he told himself. *For her.* "You don't look well at all, Chris."

"I'm a little tired, that's all." She shifted impatiently. "Do we have to talk about people's health?"

"Don't you think we ought to talk about yours?"

"I've got doctors for that. Let's talk about something pleasant. Are you married yet?"

There was an odd look in her eyes and he couldn't tell how she meant the remark.

"You know I'm not."

"No," she said quietly. "I didn't know."

"Chris." He took her hand. "What the hell's the matter?"

He could feel her wanting to withdraw but the chair walled her in. She yanked her hand free.

"Why did you come here, Ray? To pick on me? Just stop it."

"He came because I asked him to," Steph said.

Chris whirled to stare at her. "Why?"

"Because she's your friend," Ray said. "Because you're run down, you've lost weight, there are circles like moon craters under your eyes " *There ought to be police,* he thought, *to keep dancers from killing themselves.* "You can't even hold that cup steady."

She held it steady, defying him.

"You shouldn't have to clench and struggle to go through the normal, everyday acts of living. Face it, Chris. Something is eating at your health. Don't you see the change in yourself? Don't you *feel* it?"

She leaned back and closed her eyes wearily. "I've had a very hard season."

"There's something else."

"I've been working hard. I've lost a little weight. I'll gain it back after the season."

"How many pounds, Chris?"

"Two or three."

"Ten or twelve," Steph said.

Ray decided to wade right in. "Chris—why the hell have you stopped going for your checkups?"

She spun and her hair whipped out straight behind her. "That's none of your goddamned business!" And then, abruptly calm, "I've had to shift my schedule around, that's all."

"You haven't gone for *six months*," Steph said.

Chris jumped to her feet, shaking. "I'm busy! I can't spend Wednesday mornings shuffling around labs! I have class! I have a life!"

"You have a body too," Ray said, "and you'd better start paying some attention to it."

"It has nothing to do with my body and it has nothing to do with checkups!"

"Then what is it, Chris?" Steph said quietly.

"Will you stop interfering, both of you! You don't understand and you never will!"

"Understand what?" Steph said.

Chris's lips drew apart in a sudden scream. "All right. It's Sasha!"

Shock hit Steph in a slap. She did her best to mask it. "What about him?"

"I love him." Chris collapsed back into her chair.

"Oh, Chris," Steph said. *"Still?"*

"Yes, still—and why not?"

"But it takes two people—to love," Steph said gently. "You want someone who can love you back."

"He *can* love me back."

*Why am I forcing myself to hear this?* Ray wondered. *It's over and done, I've had enough pain. Let her love who she wants.*

"Chris," Steph said, "you're just—wishing."

"And I'm going to keep on wishing and please just stop meddling!"

"We only want you to be well."

"I love him and I'm not a machine and I can't turn myself on and off—like some of you!" Chris stood and swerved, almost crashing into a standing lamp, and then she tore from the living room.

An instant later the front door slammed and Steph stared at Ray, biting her lip.

Ray steepled his fingers together. His voice was thoughtful, with a lawyerly sort of worldliness. "I suppose love happens to a lot of people and it wrecks a lot of them."

"She's not in love. She's a child and she's heard about love and she's making things up. Sasha would never have encouraged her."

"Are you sure?"

His eyes cross-examined her. She felt, after dragging him into this, she owed him some particle of truth.

"Maybe Sasha is two-timing your friend."

"I live with Chris. I know her schedule. She dances—and she sleeps. Here. Alone."

"In that case, Chris had better get help. Or a lover." Ray sighed and heaved himself to his feet.

"You're not walking out, are you, Ray? Now?"

"Walking out?" *Do I have the face of a saint,* he wondered, *or a martyr? What in the world do people take me for?* "There's nothing to walk out on. She doesn't want me. She never has."

"But she needs you."

Something soothing and vast washed over him. It was the calm of surrender. Finally he admitted to himself he was not a repairman or a nanny. He had done what he could and it had not been enough and now he had his own life to tend to.

"She needs you and her family and a doctor," he said. "Not me."

He kissed Steph lightly on the cheek.

"I can't care any more, Steph. I tried, but I can't go on caring. I'm sorry."

And then he was gone and Steph sat alone, realizing nothing had been solved.

*Tomorrow*, Steph thought, *if I have to chloroform Chris and drag her to Lenox Hill in a mailbag, I'll get her to that hospital tomorrow.*

But tomorrow came and, with it, the explosion that changed everything.

*     *     *

It happened at rehearsal.

The pianist banged into the adagio three beats before Chris's cue.

She froze. She could not will her feet to move. She felt Volmar watching. His eyes were grave and they were waiting to see what she was made of. Now was the moment to swallow back tears and torture and prove she was a dancer. Her eyes were burning and blood was thumping in her cheeks. She struggled. She lost.

"I can't dance with Sasha!"

Something changed in Volmar's expression: there was an infinitesimal realignment. "But you must. That's your job."

She could only stand, hands limp at her sides, and whisper, "I'm sorry."

She sensed the other dancers holding their breath. Volmar came to her. A hand rested on her shoulder. A voice soothed.

"I'll tell you something, Christine. What you are feeling—*now*—will help your dancing. Use it. Go. Move." He gave her a tiny push.

She felt desperate and trapped. She looked at Sasha in his dark green T-shirt and tights. She imagined those broad shoulders supporting her and the curling dark hair pressed into her face with its familiar faint smell of sweat. He was waiting with the godlike patience of a statue. Instinct or accident had guided him into a spotlight. His smile was a beacon. It beckoned.

Her body screamed refusal. She exploded in tears and ran from the stage.

Volmar sighed. Then, with heavy irony: "Sasha, I think you have influence on Christine?"

Obediently, Sasha went and stood in front of Chris in the wings. She was backed against a carpenter's ladder and her eyes would not meet his.

"Christine—come." He took her hand.

She jerked away.

"They are waiting," he said.

"And how long do you think *I've* been waiting?" The cry was torn out of her and there was something young and shrill about it, like the yelping of a puppy, that made her even more ashamed of herself.

"Christine, we must be professional."

She saw the other dancers hovering near. Their eyes were level with hers, curious but encouraging too. They meant to give support, but she knew she was not one of them.

"I still love him," she heard herself sob.

Silence swept the stage and beat deafeningly on her ears. She collapsed whimpering on the ladder. There was nothing left now, neither hope nor pride.

"I still love Sasha but he's dropped me for someone else!"

Steph stood at the edge of the circle of dancers. The shock came so swiftly that for an instant she couldn't react. Her eyes took in Chris, brittle and broken like a stick-candy doll, and Sasha, stiff and barricaded in his cool lack of denial.

She moved through the dancers and faced him.

"Sasha—is it true?"

His gaze fixed Chris with undisguised contempt.

"Answer me, Sasha," Steph said.

His face was sullen. He shrugged. "So what?"

There was a deathly silence in the wings. Tears were running down Chris's face. For an instant Steph and Chris and Sasha were alone, cut off from those around them, three solitary people waiting for something to explode or die or vanish.

Anger and disappointment swelled within Steph. There was no explosion, no death. Nothing vanished.

"You weren't honest with me, Sasha. You weren't honest with Chris."

"You are babies, both of you!" he shouted. "Are there no women in this country?"

He strode past her, shaking his head violently, making it clear he had been wronged and martyred. *He's very good at that,* Steph thought. *He can imitate anything. Even love.*

She crouched beside Chris. She spoke softly. "Chris, I didn't know. I swear I didn't have any idea."

Chris stared at her with shattered blue-button eyes. "But I told you."

"I thought it was puppy love."

"If I'm in love it's puppy love and if you're in love it's real, and that gives you the right to do what you want?"

"I didn't know, Chris. I'd never have—"

Chris stared at Steph with her long blond hair and her soft insinuating pity and she knew this girl was not on her side.

"You knew," Chris said. "You *knew.*"

Marius Volmar stood observing. His eyes were cold and bored. He clapped his hands. He had wasted enough rehearsal time.

"All right, everyone—back to work. You too, Christine. We're paying you for dancing, not for tears."

Chris stood. Her neck and back were very straight. Her voice was even as a grade-school ruler. "I won't dance with him."

Volmar said nothing. She was handing him the opportunity he needed, saving him the trouble of inventing a pretext for dropping her. He knew better than to grab at it. He gave her four beats to retract.

"Very well, Christine. You are excused for the day. And from the role. You will cover for Stephanie. Go have your tears and storms in private."

A murmur flashed through the dancers and Chris ran from the stage.

It took Steph an unbelieving instant to realize what had happened. The role was hers. She sank onto a chair. *I wanted the role, yes, but not like this.* She felt eight million kinds of confusion and elation and disappointment.

"From the coda," Volmar commanded. *"And!"*

Steph obeyed. She managed somehow to complete the rehearsal, to block out every awareness but the movement of her body. Afterward, Sasha followed her into the wings. He looked back toward the stage. There was no one. He grabbed the sleeve of her robe.

They were standing just outside the stagehands' room. Transistorized disco rock came in pounding waves through the half-open door.

He stepped nearer, eyes and voice angled low. She knew he was going to try to kiss her. She pushed him gently away and her hand lingered a moment, clinging to the warmth and dampness of him.

"Come with me," he said.

She shook her head.

"I want you to come with me now to my dressing room."

"No."

"I have to explain."

A balance had shifted between them. Before, she had been the child. But now it was Sasha pleading and Steph, like the parent, standing firm.

"You do not understand about Christine and me," he said.

"Don't I?"

He paced to the stage manager's console. His glance brushed the TV images of the empty stage, the dark orchestra pit. She could feel him gathering his justifications. *Maybe there is an explanation*, she thought. *Please God, let there be an explanation.*

But he ripped that last hope from her. "Christine is baby. I felt sorry for her, that is all."

For a moment Steph couldn't answer. "But she loved you."

"Baby love."

Steph dropped her eyelids, wishing sleep would come and blot out everything. He must have interpreted the movement as a sign of surrender. He was beside her, an arm coaxing at her waist.

"Don't let the baby ruin it for us. Please Stephanie."

His finger found a rift in her unitard, stroked the bare skin beneath her ribs as though they were alone in his apartment with only the fire for light. She felt the involuntary response of her nipple and anger flashed through her. She jerked away.

"You take one hell of a lot for granted."

"Only because I love you." His lips were purring along the side of her neck. Breath brushed the inner curl of her ear. Her heart beat shallow and fast.

*Why not,* she wondered, *why not settle for sex? Other girls do.*

Faultlessly timed, like a leap landing on a downbeat, his mouth glided in for the kiss. Her hand swung back and caught the side of his face in a firecracker slap.

He recoiled, looking as stunned as if she'd plunged a hatpin into his heart.

"You're a beautiful dancer, Sasha, and an arrogant lying bastard."

"All American girls same," he spat. "Go to bed with man once and think they own him. If you are jealous of that baby, then you are baby too."

"That baby happens to be my friend—something you'll never be to anyone."

"I have plenty friends."

"Good. You'd better invite one to dinner tonight."

"You are breaking date?"

"You're goddamned right I'm breaking date."

"But why?" He looked at her in wild bafflement.

"The fact you have to ask why is why. Get this straight, Sasha. I'm never eating with you again or drinking with you again or smoking pot with you again. I'm never going to be alone in the same room with you, I'm never going to be in bed with you again. There's only one thing I'll ever do with you again and that's dance, and that's the only time you're going to put a finger on me. *Capeesh? Ponimayesh?*"

He stared at her coldly. "Okay. Keep your little friend."

"I intend to try to. Good-by, Sasha."

# forty-four

Steph dashed into the apartment.

"Chris?"

She flung open doors: kitchen, bathroom, bedroom. Nobody.

"Chris!"

The bureau drawers were a pawed-over jumble of panties and chemises. A cyclone had hit the closets. Dresses dangled half ripped from hangers. Overcoats were puddled on the floor with galoshes and spilled shoe trees. Two suitcases were missing.

Chris was gone. She had stuffed some clothing into two suitcases and fled.

Steph sank into the rocking chair. She felt very alone in the empty apartment. A thought stirred in her, soft as a warning breeze.

She went into the bathroom and pushed aside the mirrored cabinet door. Chris's medicines were still there with their typed labels: the fat three-times-a-day bottle, the skinny once-a-day bottle, and the white plastic for-emergency bottle.

She felt tumbled and drained and melted. She did not know what she had done. She did not know what to do about it.

She waited. *Chris might come back. Chris might phone.*

She waited. The apartment grew dark. She got up to turn on a light. She had been sitting with her back to the television set and she had not noticed the note Scotch-taped to the screen. Now it hit her like a fist.

The crazy, slanting letters were spattered in blood-red lipstick. Chris's lipstick, Chris's crazy handwriting. *I HATE YOU!*

She ripped the note loose and balled it in her hand and broke down helplessly in tears.

Ten minutes before she had to leave for the theater the phone rang. It was her mother, just phoning to say hello and wondering how rehearsals were going and by the way was the cast going to be settled in time to print programs for the gala?

"I'm dancing Aurora, Mom."

There was a gasp. "Didn't I tell you?"

"Chris had a breakdown."

"So?"

"She walked out."

"So?"

"Mom, I'm worried. She's moved out of the apartment but she didn't take her medicine."

"She's got a key, she'll be back. Just don't let her walk back into the role, okay?"

\* \* \*

Seymour Harnett—triangle player and percussionist with the NBT orchestra, chairman of the musicians' strike committee—called the meeting to order.

He reminded the men of their grievances. He described Marius Volmar's fuck-you attitude. He folded his hands across his stomach, settled down in his seat, and let questions and answers whiz past.

"How much we holding out for?"

"Eight per cent annual after the thirty."

"Risky," the second oboe said.

"Bullshit. Show of strength is what counts."

"And if they say drop dead?"

"How they gonna say drop dead?"

"And if they still say drop dead?"

"Cancel their season? You kidding? They think that

Russian's going to save them."

"Can you see their faces when we shut down that stinking gala?"

"Ever think they might close down the company?"

"Don't be an idiot. They got matching funds from Uncle Sam, grants from Coca-Cola, has-been ballerinas selling pencils on Central Park West, tax write-offs, they make more money losing money than you or me do working our asses off. Who the hell lives in a Fifth Avenue penthouse—you, me, or Madame Dorcas Fuckface?"

Seymour Harnett said this was getting no one nowhere, all in favor of the strike please raise their hands, only one hand per man and no goofing, please.

He counted.

"All opposed."

He counted. He smiled. Three-vote margin.

"Motion carried. Unless management ratifies the new contract, we walk out the day of the gala. Anyone care to stop at the bar, the beer's on me. And, Harry, you'll get out the press releases, okay?"

*        *        *

"Wouldn't go out that way," the stage door guard said.

Volmar peered through the double glass doors at the chaos of illegally parked TV trucks, the milling disorder of reporters brandishing microphones and flash cameras. There was menace in their idleness, like the dammed-up violence of a teen-age gang.

"Better try the front of the house, Mr. Volmar. They won't be expecting you."

But they were.

Volmar had taken barely ten steps toward the fountain when the reporters converged screaming on him.

"Gonna pay the musicians?"

"True you're gonna hire scabs?"

Instinct told him to duck back into the theater, not to meddle with press and publicity and matters he didn't understand.

"Hey, Volmar, think they timed the strike to hit Sasha's premiere?"

The question jolted him. He stood rigid, speechless. His eye sought the face that had thrown it out. The plaza was mined with exploding lights. Reporters jostled like rats in a trap clawing for a hunk of moldy cheese. Their mikes and their cameras and their scribble pads pressed nearer. Ignorance and beer breath pressed nearer.

"What premiere?" Volmar shouted.

The answer came back in fragments: "Sasha—the big shindig—the gala—*Sleeping Beauty!*"

Anger surged up in him. His heart contracted painfully.

"The prince in *Sleeping Beauty*," he shouted, "will be danced by Wally Collins, one of our leading native-born American dancers, as befits a major production of an American dance company funded in part by American taxpayers' dollars. And that, ladies and gentlemen, is all I have to say to any of you."

\*   \*   \*

He sat working at his desk. Rehearsal music drifted in through the open door, washing over his half-listening mind like the reassuring sound of waves. He heard someone breathe his name.

"Marius."

He looked up. Dorcas stood in the doorway.

"The news said—they said you're not letting Sasha ..." She bent her head silently and just stood there.

He rose from his chair. The wings of phantom possibilities brushed him. He could lie. He could hedge. He could go put a hand on her arm. But he was tired. His mind ached.

She looked directly at him. The uptilted eyes caught the light of his desk lamp. "Couldn't you at least have told me first?"

"I'm truly sorry, my dear." And in a way he was. "I meant to."

She raised a white-knuckled fist to her mouth. "You *meant* to! That's all you have to say to me?"

He listened to her heavy-breathing silence. He had done nothing illegal. He was still director till his contract expired. It was his job to make such decisions. What could he say to this weeping woman?

"You hate him so much?" she said. *"Why?"*

"I hate no one." He hated only mediocrity, but he'd never make her see it.

"After all we've built together—"

"We've been through that."

"We've been through a great deal, Marius, but this—I'll never forgive you for."

"As you wish."

She tried to cuff the shiny streaks from her face. She looked like a smudged portrait of herself. "I've spoken to the lawyers. You can have your gala. After that, I'm buying out your contract. You won't be working for NBT any more."

For an instant he felt gravity sucking him down. He took a deep breath. "I can talk to lawyers too."

"You don't have money. You don't have contacts. You don't have friends. You'll never be able to keep the company."

His eyes probed hers. Had he underestimated her strength? *No. Her weakness.* "You'd destroy NBT—because of *him?*"

"You've destroyed the company, Marius. No one else. I'm sick. I can't discuss it any more. I hope the musicians let you have your gala. I hope it's the gala of your dreams. Good-by, Marius."

The phone on his desk buzzed. The girl at the switchboard said it was Mr. Seymour Harnett of the musicians' union. Marius Volmar had not planned to do what he did next. The words spat out of their own accord.

"I've stated my position, Mr. Harnett."

"Come off it, Volmar. We've all stated our positions. Now let's get down to some real concessions, or you won't have an orchestra."

"And your men won't have jobs. I've made every concession I intend to. I've had enough of your greed."

The voice bridled. "You *what?*"

"I'm negotiating no further. You may take my terms, Mr. Harnett, or send your men to the unemployment office where they belong."

*       *       *

Confusion settled on the company like twilight on an unknown city. No one knew whether the musicians would strike. No one knew whether the company would survive.

The dancers of NBT—like all dancers—lived every day of

their lives with ailment and injury. They could cope with cramps and strains and sprains, with shin splints and soreness and lost nails and half the itises known to the human body. But uncertainty was a different sort of injury. It attacked the dancer's most vital, most vulnerable organ: the spirit. And there was no way of massaging it out or bringing it down with cold packs.

The corridors of the theater bustled with rumor. There were whispers in the dressing rooms. There were bills overdue, rent overdue, loans coming due. Bee pollen was expensive and brewer's yeast had gone up again. There were pets to feed and it cost money to soak leg warmers in Woolite. The other companies wouldn't be hiring till fall and anyway there were never enough openings and those always went to the youngest.

The dancers were scared. They had staked their short dancing lives on a gamble. For all they could tell, these next few weeks might be their last.

Marius Volmar gave no sign of caring or even of knowing. Shouting and stamping and business-as-usual, he drove the company through grueling rehearsals of a ballet that might never be staged.

He was almost satisfied with his principals and their covers: Stephanie and Wally partnered well; Sasha instead of marking danced full out, as of course he would; and Christine brought a strangely smoldering competence to the role.

But Volmar was satisfied with nothing else.

Even though he choreographed every movement and gesture and floor pattern from his notes; even though he tolerated no experiment or accident or deviation—still, in his mind's eye, there was no complete picture, no whole *Sleeping Beauty*. This had never happened before in his life. The fire was in him but he could not focus it.

He wondered if he was getting old.

He found himself forgetting things. When he wanted the corps to step forward with more accent, he couldn't find the word. "Here we must have a little—" His mind groped helplessly and finally he had to demonstrate the upbeat with his body.

Tiny details irritated him horribly. Feet in the rosin box sounded like the crunching of broken glass. A girl watched her reflection in the mirror and he stopped the rehearsal and stood on a chair and shouted: "You there—yes, you—what were you watching?"

"My *sauté en arabesque*."

"Well, you're not going to have a mirror onstage. It's ridiculous at your age to have to *see* how you're dancing. Your muscles should tell you, and if they don't, you'd better learn something practical, like shorthand."

He saw the signs of declining morale: the girls had untidy hair, the boys wore long pouts; the corps no longer moved as one but waited a telltale split second for a leader to emerge and move first. Dancers who were covering marked their parts like ghosts trailing twenty paces behind. Dancers not rehearsing played cards instead of watching.

He heard whispers.

"Volmar's never been such a bastard before—what the hell's eating him?"

"He has his notes right there on his lap and he doesn't even remember the choreography."

He knew rehearsals were going badly and he didn't know the reason. *I'll pull it together*, he told himself. *I've always pulled it together.*

\* \* \*

"Unless somebody's willing to change course," the man from the mayor's office said, "we're deadlocked."

"You dragged me from rehearsal to tell me that?" Marius Volmar said.

The mayor, the governor, the President himself had called the possibility of a strike a scandal, a cultural disaster. What Marius Volmar found scandalous was that he had to attend meetings like this.

"Look," the man from publishing cut in, "nothing in ballet ever runs a hundred per cent smoothly." He was a balletomane and he had volunteered his services as arbitrator. *He knows his ballet*, Marius Volmar was thinking, *but he doesn't know union musicians*. "There are always misunderstandings and lost tempers and never enough money, but somehow or other, with a little good will, the show goes on. Come on, gentlemen—and Mrs. Amidon. There's no reason we can't get together on this. We all love ballet."

"Do we?" Marius Volmar said. "Do Mr. Harnett and his men love ballet?"

Seymour Harnett sucked at a large cigar. He had the face of a once predatory animal that had roamed indoors and lived too long off heavy cream.

"I'm here negotiating, aren't I?"

"I'd call it a holdup," Marius Volmar shot back. "There's no love of ballet in you or your men, no love of anything I can see except money. Certainly no love of music."

The man from the President's Council for the Arts lifted a hand. "Keep it to a dull roar, gentlemen."

"Mrs. Amidon," the man from publishing said, pushing back the silence, "you haven't told us your position."

Dorcas Amidon stared down at the table. Her voice was carefully controlled. "Mr. Volmar and I disagree on several points. I'll probably form a new company next year—in which case I'll certainly not be hiring Mr. Harnett or any of his men who voted to strike."

"That's not legal!" Seymour Harnett cried. "Did you hear that, she's threatening a lockout! That's intimidation!"

"Gentlemen," the man from publishing said. "Mrs. Amidon. Please."

"Musicians aren't people? Musicians aren't supposed to eat?"

The man from the President's Council drew in a deep breath. "Fellas, there's a line outside the loo. So either make up your minds to use the potty, or let someone else have it. Now either you reach an agreement, within non-inflationary guidelines, or you lose your federal matching funds. It's that simple."

"Why doesn't the President stick to his own goddamn guidelines?" Seymour Harnett cried. "Why is it always the musicians subsidizing this country?"

"The musicians don't subsidize me," Volmar said. A storm of anger was beginning to rise in him. Belgium had said yes, and now was the time to let these parasites know. "Mr. Harnett believes he has NBT trapped. He is mistaken. The Belgian government has offered us a home and a charter—and freedom from American unions. If the orchestra refuses reasonable terms, NBT will move abroad—beyond the clutches of Local 802. Mr. Harnett and his men will be free to eat picket boards and welfare checks for a change. NBT has fed them long enough."

There was panic in the eyes of Seymour Harnett and Dorcas Amidon and the President's man. Marius Volmar didn't need any of them. They had no hold. He smiled.

"Feed us!" Seymour Harnett cried. "You been stealing the bread from our mouths."

"Thirty-two thousand a year for tapping a triangle?"

"This is an expensive town—we're entitled to the cost of living!"

"A dancer gets nine thousand five hundred."

"Who gives a fuck what a dancer gets?"

For an instant the room was a whirlpool of gray spots and Marius Volmar could not find breath to answer. *I must speak,* he prodded himself. *They must not know.*

"I do," Volmar said. "I give a fuck what a dancer gets." His heart was battering furiously against his lungs. He rose. "Gentlemen, Dorcas—delightful as this is, I still have a ballet company to attend to."

There was a clattering rush of heels and Dorcas caught up with him in the hallway. "Marius, can't we talk?"

"Why?"

"Must we be like those people in there?"

"Why not?"

She was pained at the change in his appearance. His face had lost weight and he looked like an eagle gone old and shabby. "We shouldn't argue. It's bad for us. You're not looking well, Marius."

Her eyes were pleading and oddly brilliant and her make-up showed the smudges of hasty blotting.

"You're looking badly yourself," Volmar said.

She flinched but recovered. "Oh, Marius, we're squabbling like children, and if only we could all calm down—if at least you and I could calm down—"

"I'm perfectly calm."

"I'm not. I'm not calm at all. I've never been so miserable in my life."

"Then you have a lot to learn about life."

"I never thought I'd have to learn it from you."

"You American women are all virgins," he snapped, "and there's nothing more grotesque than a rich foolish old virgin."

He'd never seen a woman look so stunned and vulnerable, not even his mother when the Germans took her away in the police car. Dorcas stared at him one instant. Then her eyelids fell and she turned away.

\*    \*    \*

The rehearsal that Volmar returned to was a disaster.

"What do you do before you catch the girl?" he asked a dancer.

"Stand around," the boy said.

It hit Volmar like a blow. Was he losing his gift for authority?

"You have *échappé?*" he asked a girl.

"Yes."

"Then why is everyone else doing *chassé?*"

She shrugged. "Ask them."

It was incredible. Where was the respect?

"Are you dancers or dolts?" he cried. "We're going to rehearse this till we get it right!"

The problem was in the grand promenade of guests in Act One, Aurora's birthday celebration. Something had gone wrong, and kept going wrong, in the placement of the dancers.

"Let's take it from the third phrase—two groups once more. Piano, very, very slowly—slow motion now."

Volmar watched, squinting like a police inspector trying to spot a culprit. He stopped the guilty-looking couple.

"Let me see how you promenade out."

They promenaded out. Innocent. He was baffled.

"*Maître*, if you will excuse." Sasha Bunin gave a quick, almost apologetic bow of the head. "In the Kirov we avoid this trouble by—"

"No," Volmar said quietly and very firmly. "No legends of the Kirov, thank you. We're going to walk through this like turtles, one beat at a time, dead stop on every beat, till we see who's right and who's wrong."

The dancers knew he was furious. Usually, though it stung, they were grateful for his fury: it drove them to dance better. But this was a wrong fury. The grand promenade was not worth an hour of rehearsal. Besides, the mistake was there, in his notebook, and not in the dancers' feet. They stood resentful and humiliated. They had not earned this abuse. He was wasting their time.

The grand promenade was still a confusion when the rehearsal finally ground to an end. Volmar watched his dancers straggle toward the door. No: he would not permit this defeat, this Waterloo. He clapped his hands sharply.

"Girls and boys, one more moment of your time, please."

He waited till they were absolutely silent and absolutely still with all eyes fixed absolutely on him.

"You are professionals. You wouldn't be under contract to this company otherwise. You are also artists, and while in this theater you will conduct yourselves as artists. It is true that we're having difficulties with the orchestra. I don't know what rumors you may have heard. Put them out of your heads. When there are facts, you will hear the facts—from me."

He saw the sullenness in their bodies. He saw the fatigue in their faces. He found it obscene that young people should permit themselves fatigue. Discipline must never again slip as it had today. If they ever doubted the whip in his hand, the company was doomed; the *Sleeping Beauty* was doomed.

"Today you disgraced yourselves. Tomorrow you will dance. You may go."

\*   \*   \*

Volmar hurried home, shaken. He had never distrusted himself before.

He lived in two rooms on West Eighty-seventh Street. Few people ever saw them. A cleaning woman came twice a week; the rooms were dark but neat.

He pulled a chair to a closet and searched the shelf.

He found what he was looking for: a small leather case of his mother's possessions. Inside the case he found a small parcel wrapped in time-parched tissue paper that crumbled at his touch.

He took it gently, as though it were a mouse sleeping in his hand, and set it on a table and sat gazing at it.

The little candy box with white and blue enamel panels was one of three hundred filled with chocolates that Tsar Nicholas had given the imperial dancers on his last birthday. Naturally there were no chocolates left: his mother had been sixteen at the time, a little Maryinsky ballerina with strong legs and a very sweet tooth.

He was not a sentimentalist and he did not know why he had kept the box or why it had come into his thoughts today of all dreadful days. But as he stared at it the battering of his heart subsided.

He thought of the tsars and shook his head. They must have been odd men to have given the world such misery and such ballet and such little enamel boxes. The tsars were gone, but there was still misery and there was still ballet and there was still this little enamel box.

He touched it. His finger traced out the copper edging of the panels.

This box had traveled seas and continents. It had survived political and artistic revolutions. And here it sat on the table of a dark little apartment in New York City.

*A box like this,* Volmar thought, *never stops traveling. Never stops surviving. Long after me, there will still be this box.*

*Long after me.*

The thought gave him a strange smiling comfort, and when he dreamed that night, he saw his *Sleeping Beauty* at last.

# forty-five

---

After performance Steph sank down into the chair. Her head was throbbing. She crossed her arms on the dresser, made a pillow out of them to rest her head. Over the call box she could hear the massive rhythms of *Symphony in Three Movements*. She tried to shut it out, thanked God she wasn't dancing it tonight.

Layered laughter and gossip came drifting in from the corridor. She raised her eyes to the mirror, winced at the wreck staring back at her. She summoned energy, began brushing her hair. Electricity crackled in the bristles.

"The *Pierre?*"

Dimly, at the edge of her awareness, she heard a voice curling with incredulity.

"That costs a fortune!"

"What does she care? Her parents have a charge account. She can get all the grapefruit and yogurt she wants on room service."

"Yeah? Well, I'll bet even the Pierre doesn't have bee pollen à la carte."

The voices were coming from behind her. It flashed through her mind that the girls must be talking about Chris. She stopped brushing. Her ear clutched for another strand of the conversation.

"Sasha really flipped her out, did he?"

"Oh, come on, that little debutante was never flipped *in* to begin with."

Maria Coelho, a new Brazilian girl in the corps, approached and asked if Steph would like to go for a hamburger. *Oh, hell,* Steph thought, *do we have to chitchat now?*

As pleasantly as she could, she said, "Could we make it another night?"

During that instant of distraction she lost the voices, lost hold of the link to Chris. There was only blanketing chatter and waves of Stravinsky surging from the speaker.

She made a quick scribble in her address book with an eyebrow pencil: *Pierre.* She took a taxi home, telling herself it was because she was dead tired.

The Hotel Pierre answered on the twelfth ring.

"Do you have a Christine Avery registered there?"

"One moment, please."

Steph switched the phone to the other hand, wriggled out of the other sleeve of her coat. She felt a growing nervousness. What the hell was she going to say to Chris?

"Miss C. Avery is in room 1012. I'll connect you."

Relief went through her and then a smothering fear. She jammed a finger against the cradle, broke the connection.

\* \* \*

"Hello?"

Chris stood in her bathrobe holding the receiver.

"Hello?"

After a few seconds the phone began making a scraping sound. Sweat began to creep down the back of her neck. She hung up. She hurried to check the front door of the suite. It was double-locked and chained.

She felt helpless, like a chick trapped inside an egg in a nest.

The bedroom door had a push-button lock and she pushed it and crawled back into bed and turned off the light and curled up beneath the bedclothes. Very gently she tried to ease herself into a position that did not ache.

She lay listening to all the tiny sounds that made up silence.

The phone rang again. She held her breath, prayed it would

stop. It kept ringing. She sat up.

*If I take a very long time answering it will go away....*

Her hand inched to the night table, found the switch, hesitated. She thought the ringing had stopped and then it came again. She pressed the button. For an instant light blinded her. She lifted the receiver.

Warily, voice neutral, she said, "Hello?"

"Chris? It's me—Steph."

*No,* she thought, *no!* Time moved with nightmare slowness, like an anesthesia mask clamping her down.

"Chris, I've got your medicine."

With her last fading strength she laid the receiver on the pillow.

*       *       *

No answer.

Nothing.

At first Steph thought the line had gone dead. And then, from a great distance, her ear made out the sound of breathing. Chris's breathing—quiet, stubborn, as familiar as the neighbors' voices through the bedroom wall.

Steph stood holding the phone, adrift in Chris's refusal, not knowing what to say or do next.

"Chris, you need your medicine."

No reply.

"You've missed three days."

Still no reply.

"I'll come down to your hotel tomorrow morning at nine o'clock."

*       *       *

At eight fifty-five Steph was sitting outside Central Park, gathering resolve, grateful for a bench to rest on.

She had her tote bag beside her, securely gripped against snatchers. She'd stuffed it with practice clothes and Chris's medicines, and—a last-minute inspiration—the book Chris had been reading for the last three months, St. Exupéry's *Little Prince.*

She stared across Fifth Avenue at the sand-blasted elegance

of the Pierre. Traffic was different here from the rest of New York: there were limousines and double-decker London buses and flocks of cruising Checker cabs and they looked waxed and clean, like the fresh vegetables at a luxury grocer's.

At eight fifty-nine she crossed the avenue and went into the hotel. For an instant she was lost among the shifting patterns of people. Their clothing and voices suggested money, many different sorts of money, but a great deal of it. She went direct to an elevator and up to Chris's floor. She buzzed at the door and when there was no answer she knocked.

"Chris? It's me."

A chain slipped noisily and the door swung open.

Chris looked very small and thin. Her hair was unkempt, her face pale, and her eyes were like huge ash-rimmed burns in a bed sheet.

Steph tried to mute the shock on her face. She hesitated, one foot touching the doorsill, and waited for Chris to say the first healing words.

There was only silence.

"You forgot these." Steph held out the tote bag. The medicine bottles were on top.

Chris barely glanced at them. The three days seemed to have wasted her totally. Steph was overwhelmed by a sense of terrible guilt, as though she'd ripped the wings off a butterfly.

"Chris, I'm sorry." Her eyes pleaded for a hug, a handshake, a friendly glance, anything.

Chris's small hands were bloodless and taut and unforgiving. Her mouth unclenched and very quietly she said, "I'm not afraid of you any more."

She held a tiny balled-up wad of Kleenex in one hand. She had been crying, but she was not crying now. She was standing back from the door beside a table with a huge porcelain vase of roses. Her empty hand caressed the dark scarlet buds.

Steph reached out. "Chris, please—friends?"

Chris stared at her. "You can be so blind when it suits you."

"I didn't *know* you were seeing Sasha."

"You knew I was in love with him."

"But everyone thinks they're in love with him."

"All those nights—all those phone calls when you said you were at your mother's—you were with him. I was going crazy and you were the reason he wasn't seeing me."

"Do you think for a minute I'd have seen him if I'd *known?*"

From somewhere, some small untapped pocket of rage hidden deep within Chris, the reply came bursting: "Yes! You knew and that's why you did it! You took him from me!"

"I'd never take anything from you. You're my best friend."

"I'm not your friend—I'm your charity. I make you feel generous." Chris's voice took on a mincing viciousness. "'Poor Chris, always so nervous, she wouldn't get through her performances if I didn't wheel her onstage.' 'Poor Chris—always falling in love with gay boys. What *am* I going to do about her?' But let poor Chris fall in love with a man and you've got to grab him! 'Sasha's not for babies—Sasha's for big girls. Here, little Chrissie, I'll take Sasha.'"

Suddenly Steph felt very weary. Sadness filled her. "Chris, I've broken it off."

"You never wanted him. You just had to prove you could take him from me."

Steph's jaw dropped and she stood staring. She had never heard such quiet, coiled conviction in Chris's voice before and it frightened her. "You don't mean that."

"You've always had to prove you could take things from me."

"Like what?"

"Like *Cantabile*. Like *Graduation Ball*."

"Chris, I was covering. You've covered for me—you've walked into my roles. And you've done some of them better than me. Look at *Do I Hear a Waltz?*"

"And you'll never forgive me for it."

"Forgive you? Chris, I'm proud of you!"

"Proud of the baby—good little Chrissie, noble Steph. So noble and proud you have to steal *Sleeping Beauty!*"

Steph felt herself very near to exploding. "I didn't steal it. You walked out."

"I didn't walk out—you *drove* me out."

"Chris—I really think you're disturbed."

"Disturbed? You kick down my life and I'm disturbed? What the hell do you expect? Thank you? Roses? Okay, here are your roses—catch!"

Chris snatched the vase from the table and hurled it.

Steph ducked.

At first she couldn't believe it had happened. She stared down at the water and petals and razor-edged porcelain strewn like a suicide on the carpet. Her hand went to her face. The truth slowly soaked into her. *Chris could have scarred me—and she doesn't care.*

Chris's gaze met hers, righteous and cold. There was no remorse. No apology.

"You spoiled, stupid rich brat," Steph said.

"Rich and how you hate me for it."

"No, Chris. I don't waste time hating you for anything. You're doing a terrific job of it yourself. You could have had a career. You could even have had Sasha. And you could have had a friend. A good friend "

"A good friend like you?"

"Yes, like me. But you had to throw it all away on one of your little-girl breakdowns. Let me tell you something, Chris. Whether it's a role or a man—you'll never get it whining. You have to work and you have to fight. Like a woman. Something you seem to know nothing about being."

"I'm going to surprise you, Steph." There was a crazy calmness in her voice more frightening than anything she had yet shouted or thrown. "I'm going to fight you—just the way you've been fighting me all along. And I'm going to win."

Steph stared at the tiny figure trembling with hatred. *This was my friend. How did this happen?* Half of her wanted to burst into tears. Half of her was relieved: this burden would never again be hers to carry.

"I'm through with you, Chris. Through with your tears and your tantrums and your panics. Go change your own diapers."

"Now that that's settled, get the hell out."

"Gladly."

Steph was almost at the lobby door when she realized she still had the medicine bottles and *The Little Prince* in her tote bag. She went to the desk and plunked them down in front of an astonished clerk.

"Tell Miss Avery she has a package."

\*     \*     \*

Steph and Chris did not talk after that. In class they instinctively took different corners of the room, like cats stalking out separate territories. In rehearsal they watched one another for style and form, coldly, but their glances were careful not to meet.

Before performance there were no more hugs or help with the make-up or *"merdes"* in the wings. The other dancers sensed it. The eyes of the company were on the two girls, measuring, comparing—waiting. Whatever it was between Steph and Chris—competition, hatred, instinct to murder—it burst into the open the night of *Graduation Ball*.

The ballet was set to music by Johann Strauss. The story was comic and slight: students at a boarding school for young ladies gave a party for cadets from a military academy. The divertissement included a competition where two girls each tried to do more *fouettés* than the other.

In *fouetté*, the dancer went on *pointe*. One leg whipped out to the side, then in to the knee, and the momentum whirled her in a full cirle. *Fouettés* were single or double—or triple—depending how many turns you made on a single whip of the leg. It was a spectacular step, the triple most spectacular of all. There were no triples in *Graduation Ball*.

Until the night that Steph and Chris played the two girls.

They squared off, as the choreography required, taking up positions on opposite sides of the stage. Chris went first, whipping out four sets of three singles. They were neat, fast, scalpel sharp.

Steph went second, duplicating Chris exactly.

When Chris's turn came again she did three sets of singles. But for her fourth set she whipped out a *single, single, double*. Which wasn't in the choreography.

An appreciative murmur went up in the audience, and the dancers onstage exchanged glances.

From deep down in Steph came an energized bubble of anger. She wasn't going to let Chris get away with a trick like that. She whipped out two sets of singles, then *two* sets of *single, single, double*.

And then stepped back to watch Chris try to top it.

By now the other dancers had come out of character. Usually they mugged their way though the scene with "gee whiz" arched eyebrows. But now the choreography had been flung to the winds and they were actually wondering which girl would top the other. The audience sensed an electric charge onstage and sat forward in their seats. Opera glasses lifted and lips counted silently.

Chris threw herself straight off into a *single, single, double*.

That meant only one thing: there would have to be a triple. The only question was, when? It came in the fourth set: *single, single*, then with a blinding blur of acceleration *triple*.

The house broke out in applause that drowned Steph's music. She didn't give a damn. She had the last set, which gave her the advantage.

Chris had forced her up, like a rival bidding at the auction, and Steph had to open *single, single, double*. She kept the same pattern for her second set.

The dancers knew exactly what was coming now. If Steph was going to top Chris she had to do it in the next set.

And she did: *single, single, triple*.

The house began applauding and by the time Steph whipped out the last *single, single, triple* they were braving. She stepped back, caught her breath, shot a "Who, me?" smile into the audience and milked the applause with a little ad-lib curtsy.

Afterward, in the jostle to get offstage, Steph and Chris bumped into one another.

"Sorry," said Steph, before she saw who it was.

"Nice going," Chris said icily.

"It's your own stupid fault," Steph shot back. "Don't start things you can't finish."

Chris's eyes nailed her. "Don't you worry. I haven't even begun."

Word of the rivalry swept the company. At the next *Graduation Ball* the dressers and practically everyone who wasn't dancing crammed into the wings. Word had even leaked to the public, and everyone who had the pull to get walked in used it. There had been a three-quarter house for the first ballet on the program, *Concerto in G*. For *Graduation Ball* it looked like a sellout.

Chris led off with a wild rush of *single, single, double*. She kept to it for the whole set. There were shrugs in the audience, glances between dancers.

Steph took her strategy from Chris: three *single, single doubles* and a *single, single, triple*, just to keep ahead.

So far it wasn't anything that hadn't been seen the other night, but there was a spattering of applause.

Chris's turn again. Two *single, single, doubles* and then, pulling up to Steph, a *single, single, triple.* Applause. Then a *single, double, triple,* and the house began screaming.

Steph readied herself. Determination was drumming in her blood. She flung off two *single, single, doubles,* ripped into a *single, double, triple.* Applause. Saving herself, she finished with another *single, double, triple.*

It was the homestretch now.

Chris kicked off with a *single, single, double,* a *single, single, triple,* a *single double, triple.* The sweat was spitting out from her in whipslaps that lashed as far as the faces in the wings. And then, whirling in dizzying circle up and down and around, leg in, leg out, a *double, double, triple.*

There were shrieks of "Brava!" and even the dancers onstage, under cover of their roles, applauded.

Steph didn't have a choice. There was no way she could humanly top Chris's *double, double, triple,* so she had to open higher than Chris had. She spun out a smooth *single, single, triple.* Her body and mind were riveted to one objective: *stay equal with Chris.* Her next *single, single, triple,* came well, but on her *single, double, triple* she felt her balance slipping and she wasted momentum correcting it.

For her final set she did a *double,* a *double,* tried for a *triple*—managing a *double* and a sloppy fall into fifth.

Shit!

Steph was left simmering in a pool of anger. There were no more *Graduation Balls* that season, but the schedule had her and Chris both dancing the *Sylvia pas de deux* three nights apart.

Chris came first.

Steph watched from the wings, memorizing, determined her *Sylvia* would be twice whatever Chris could do.

And what Chris did was to balance in the adagio. Wally, who was partnering, stepped aside, presenting her. She went onto *pointe* and into arabesque and held it.

And held it.

The conductor looked searchingly at her, eyes puzzled.

She didn't come down. She didn't wobble. The audience began applauding. She held the balance till they were bravaing, then with a flick of her eyes she told the conductor he could go on.

*Okay,* Steph vowed, *I'll outbalance her.*

Three night later Steph held the balance till the audience was shouting. The conductor's eyes inquired and then they beseeched.

Steph ignored him.

She held the balance and held it and held it, floating on her bravas. It was like walking motionless in a dream through stretched time. She felt euphoric; victorious. She knew Chris was watching; smarting; hating.

Sasha was partnering, and his eyes began to plead too. If he moved before Steph he'd disgrace himself. He had to stand statue-still and it was obviously beginning to hurt.

The applause came like water rushing through a dam. The conductor shook his head. He took out his pocket watch and began winding it.

The water was rushing through two dams now. Gravity and time nudged. Steph let the balance flow through her and finally, drop by drop, out of her. She began the descent. Never hurrying. Now her heel touched canvas. Now.

She had won round two.

\* \* \*

Round three was *Voluntaries*.

It was an abstract ballet, full of tricky counts and soaring lifts, and it was cunningly dovetailed to the Poulenc organ concerto. It gave the ballerina one of the most dazzling leaps in all contemporary dance: after a shattering organ chord that sounded like a cathedral coming down, there was dead silence. In that instant of shocked nothingness the ballerina had to dash the full length of the diagonal, jump into the male dancer's arms, and—as he held her—execute a complete split-second turn.

It happened so fast, and the turn *after* the catch looked so contrary to physics, that audiences could never believe they'd actually seen it. The reaction was always the same: silence, a "Did you see what I saw?" exchange of glances, and applause that ripped the house apart.

There were dancers—very few—who could do a double turn after the catch. Natalia Makarova, who starred with American Ballet Theatre, was one of them. Stephanie Lang, who wasn't even a ballerina yet, decided that she was going to be another.

She was scheduled the night before Chris.

Sasha was partnering her, and just before performance she told him, "I'm going to do a double turn after the catch, so be ready."

His eyes bulged to twice their normal size. "You crazy."

She nodded. "That's right. I crazy."

By now the whole New York dance world knew about the two competing soloists, and the wings were jammed for *Voluntaries*. Not just with NBT dancers but with dancers from other companies who'd been able to wangle passes or con their way past guards.

Steph backed up for her dash—a little farther than she'd rehearsed.

Sasha was waiting, white-faced and braced.

Mentally she crossed herself. She muttered, "This one's for you, Chris." She waited for the chord. Readiness crept up from her feet, up through her calves and thighs.

The chord hit her heart with the impact of a starting gun.

She ran.

There was a commotion alongside her. The backstage audience rushed like hunting hounds from front wings to back, keeping her in view.

She jumped.

Her momentum crashed into Sasha's immobility. With a sideways twist of his hand he redirected speed into spin.

One turn.

Another turn.

And snap to a stop and screaming, stamping applause.

"*Bozhe moi*," he gasped. "Never do that to Sasha again. Bad for heart."

*     *     *

The next night was Chris's turn.

Six counts before the chord she backed to the very edge of stage. She would have stepped into the orchestra pit, but the heat of the footlights warned her.

From somewhere within her, some secret place where body and mind were once, came the spark, the *I will*. The weakness fell away from her like a dropped cloak. Now there was no headache, no chill, no dizziness.

Her face was dark. Her pupils had become huge, leaving no irises. Her eyes were hard, black pearls. She stared over the abyss toward Wally. Their gazes met and for one instant he was terrified.

He knew exactly what she was going to do.

The chord thundered out.

A dizzying determination seized Chris by the feet, catapulted her forward.

Wally saw her coming straight at him, much too fast. He thought he had never seen a girl look so crazed or dangerous or beautiful. He saw her shoot up from the floor and he heard the air sucked screeching into her nostrils.

Chris saw only the surprise on Wally's face.

There was an instant of public disbelief, of denial. And then the explosion. Shouts and applause and bravas poured down from the house and out from the wings and as word raced through the orchestra pit musicians stood up on their chairs and stared.

The tip of the conductor's baton hung on air, paralyzed.

"A triple turn!" The cry ran through the theater. "She did a triple turn!"

"Jesus Christ," Wally whispered, "you could have warned me."

She clung to him, not answering. Her sweat felt like a cold river pouring over his skin.

The conductor rapped his music stand. "Gentlemen— *gentlemen!*" He gave the upbeat. The music began again, giant funereal heartbeats of plucked strings and struck timpani.

Gradually it dawned on Wally what he was holding in his arms.

"Chris," he whispered, and then *"Chris!"*

Her arm slipped off his shoulder, dangling, and then as his own strength gave out she slid to the floor.

\*     \*     \*

They laid Chris on a blanket just beyond the main swirls of backstage traffic. Someone made a pillow of towels for under her head. Her toe shoes were slipped off, her feet propped up on the seat of an electrician's chair.

Steph hung back. A stillness rippled out from the silent body. Dancers watched from a tactful distance, dark and quiet as the shadows of trees.

The company doctor hunched over Chris. He took her pulse, handed her wrist back to her. A thermometer came gleaming from his bag and went between the two rows of small white teeth. Chris had a dreaming, contented look, like a child sucking on a lollipop.

The doctor's every movement was rapid, staccato: the tourniquet, the stethoscope, the listening, the looking, the light flashed in the eyes, the tongue depressed with a wooden stick.

Steph got her courage up and stepped forward. "What's happened to her?"

"Plenty." There was guarded anger in the doctor's voice. "Who are you?"

"I was—I'm her roommate."

"She's asleep."

*"Asleep?"*

"And starved. When did she last eat?"

"I don't know."

"What is it about you dancers? Can you get her to bed and feed her?"

Steph's mind raced. She knew Chris would not accept help from someone she now regarded as an enemy. And she certainly wouldn't feed herself.

"I can put her in the hospital," the doctor said, "but the company won't like it because it raises the insurance premium."

Steph said, "I'll be right back."

"Stephanie." It was Sasha, one hand on the edge of a prop bin, stretching and warming up for his entrance in *Harlequinade*. He had leashed Merde to a light pole and the poodle was snoring softly. "Something wrong with Christine?" He grasped Steph's shoulder, used her as a support to exercise the other leg.

"She's very sick."

A shadow crossed his face. For an instant, shame outweighed arrogance and his eyes dropped, borne down. "Is something I can do?"

The old impulse stirred in her. How lovely it would have been to muffle her face against his chest, to feel his strength holding her up.

"Yes."

"Anything."

He was ugly-handsome, boy-man, gazing at her, flirting with her, even now.

"I need a dime for the phone."

"You want to use the phone in my dressing room?"

"No."

He shrugged, charming in defeat, and then he called to a stagehand and borrowed a dime and closed Steph's hand over it.

She went to the pay phone in the corridor. It was just a phone on the wall, smack in the middle of traffic and hurry, no booth, no privacy. She dropped the dime in the slot and placed the collect call.

People didn't exactly stop and stare but they slowed down and shot the quick glances of dancers running for a cue who've heard a rumor of disaster.

Steph's feet fidgeted. Three rings; four rings. She swallowed. *God, let someone be home!* The sweat was turning cold on her skin and she hadn't the faintest idea what she was going to say.

"Hello?"

"Mrs. Avery?"

Two conversations battled for the same line. The operator was trying to straighten out the collect call and Steph was trying to shout over the operator, over the orchestra.

"Something's happened to Christine?" Mrs. Avery sounded frightened.

Steph felt herself drowning in an ocean of bustle and fortissimo. "She passed out during performance."

"I can't hear you, she *what?*"

Steph waited for a lull in the music. She told Mrs. Avery what had happened. Mrs. Avery spoke in a strangely controlled voice.

"Is there someone to take care of her till I get there?"

"I don't think she'd let me."

"Can you get her to the hospital? I'll fly to New York first thing tomorrow morning. And, Stephanie—thank you."

More dancers had gathered, blocking the wing. Steph pried her way through them. There were stares and headshakes. There was fear and mute acceptance, the knowledge that what had happened to the girl on the blanket could happen to any of them, would sooner or later happen to some of them. There was the guilt of survivors and with it whispered offers of help.

Wally was crouched beside Chris, holding her hand, telling her it would be all right, telling her desperately. Steph stared down at the face, whited-out beneath the make-up. It seemed to her Chris was calling silently for help: *Save me, don't let me die here!*

Steph shook off the thought. *No one's going to die. No one's even going to be sick.*

*Not if we move fast.*

"Wally, she's got to go to the hospital."

A rustle went through the dancers as they strained their collective ear.

"I'll get a taxi," Wally said.

His eyes met Chris's and it dawned on them both at the same time: they were still in costume, still in make-up. They looked like Halloween drag freaks.

"We'd better put on raincoats," Wally said. "And one on her, too."

# forty-six

It was twelve-thirty in the morning by the time Wally let himself into the apartment.

"Anyone home?"

No answer.

*Funny* he thought, *Ellis ought to be home by now*. His eye roved the clothing and old newspapers strewn about the room. Nothing seemed changed since he'd dashed out that morning.

The coffee cup, half full, was where he'd left it, on the mantelpiece of the so-called wood-burning fireplace that didn't burn wood or paper or anything else. Ellis had wanted a fireplace—"Makes it homey," he'd pleaded—and so they were paying a hundred dollars more than they could afford for the run-down, badly heated, leaky walk-up.

Wally sniffed.

The garbage smelled ten hours older. Ellis had forgotten to dump it. Again.

Wally let his ears wander idly over the silence. Someone was walking upstairs: the ceiling creaked right above the louvered doors that would have hidden the kitchenette if the paper bags of garbage hadn't been in the way. A TV was going downstairs, faintly. He imagined he could hear the slow intake of human breath, and then a long time later the release.

When he heard whispers he realized he was not imagining the sound. Anger began crawling along the back of his neck. He strode to the bedroom door. It squeaked open just as he was about to touch his hand to the knob.

Ellis slipped out, hitching one strap of his overalls over his naked shoulder. "Guess what." He looked flushed and bubbling and vague. "We're out of milk, could you run down and get some before the deli closes?"

Wally frowned. "What's that smell? And I don't mean the garbage you forgot to take out."

Ellis shrugged. "Okay, it'll be café noir for breakfast, just like you hate."

"Jesus, it smells like you broke open two dozen poppers. You know I hate that stink."

"I spilled a bottle of liquid amyl." Amyl nitrite and the substitutes sold at sex stores were supposed to add a kick to sex, but they were bad for the circulatory system and most dancers avoided them. But Ellis had his own ideas about dance and sex.

Wally's exhaustion was suddenly gone, like a switch clicked off. He was alert, braced.

"Wally," Ellis said very distinctly, "go get some milk. Go get a sandwich and sit on a bench and eat it. Just go. I'll have this mess cleaned up in ten minutes."

"Who's in there?"

"Look, shithead, you didn't pay the rent this month."

"You brought one of your tricks here!"

Ellis' eyes were frozen and fixed and didn't give a damn. He gave the door a bare-heeled kick. It swung slowly inward. A rectangle of light spread across the bedroom. It began at the foot and traveled along a leg and inch by inch it illuminated Zoltan Tovary sitting naked on the bed, head tilted calmly back, eyes staring and ready to meet any gaze that could be leveled against them.

Wally squinted a moment. He felt two hundred years old. "This is our *home*," he whispered.

"*Was* our home."

"A month's rent doesn't give you the right to—"

"Wally, if you want to get it over with now, fine by me."

Wally realized Ellis had arranged this moment, orchestrated

it. He stood speechless and disbelieving and Ellis hitched up the other strap of his overalls.

"Zoltan and Virginia are getting a separation," Ellis said.

Wally's mind raced like tires grabbing for traction. Virginia—Zoltan's wife. A blonde who was always pregnant, always at rehearsals knitting.

"Zoltan and I are going to move in together. We love each other very much. It's really quite perfect, Wally. I only wish you and I had had something half as good."

Wally stood straight and suddenly alone, feeling failure flake down on him like ice from a winter sky. His mind struggled to understand. Somehow the sex that had brought him and Ellis together now stood between them. The wall that had enclosed them now separated them. For a long black moment he stared into emptiness.

Zoltan rose from the rumpled bed and came to stand motionless beside Ellis. His eyes swept Wally and one eyebrow arched in an ironic flick of recognition.

Wally turned away from their joined hands. He walked across the room and fought to make his thoughts stick together. His eye roamed the walls and he realized that every stain, every crack on them was familiar, memorized. He had never realized it before. The apartment was chipped and bleak and in all the years' arguing who would clean it they'd never cleaned it. The rooms bore the scars of a hundred screeching battles but he couldn't hate the apartment.

It was his home and Ellis was his family.

Now his home and family were lost, taken from him by a man with three children who changed wives as often as he changed the marcel of his fading hair.

Wally lifted his eyes toward Ellis, but Ellis was somewhere else, afloat like a new moon in a cradle of stars. Wally stared a long sober moment at the boy who had dazzled him. He strained to grasp the truth of this instant. It had taken him two years and eight months, it had taken him till now, to see beneath the beauty, to see the mindless crawling thing that lived within that armor.

He didn't hate Ellis.

What he felt was worse. He hated himself. Shame overflowed him like slime from a cesspool.

"All right," he said finally, "I'm going."

Ellis looked at him sharply, wanting something more. Perhaps he wanted the scene to go on longer. Perhaps he wanted to show his new friend that even though he was a boy from the corps he could still cut down a principal. Wally shaped a smile and beamed it across the lifeless space between them.

"You're not angry, are you?" Ellis said, probing.

They stood staring at one another and Wally remembered the long-forgotten loneliness before Ellis. Slowly he shook his head.

In the next moment he was rushing down the dark stairs and out into the street, into the night that was warm with late spring.

\*　　\*　　\*

"Hi there, stranger, what'll it be?"

Wally stared into the smiling shadow of the broad-brimmed cowboy hat, couldn't remember whether he knew the bartender or had tricked with him or what. Didn't want to remember.

"Rob Roy straight up. Make that a double."

He figured tonight he had earned it. He took his drink to the corner stool, downed it in three long gulps.

A chubby man in leather stood eyeing him. "Ready for another?"

The liquor had soaked up some of Wally's anger. He felt quieter now. "Sure, why not?"

The man bought drinks, smiled and talked. Wally nodded and tried to listen, but the jukebox was banging out a disco version of the Infernal Dance from *Firebird*. The music kept edging in on his concentration. Long ago he'd performed in *Firebird* with Ellis. They'd both been in the corps then. The steps began coming back to him. His foot turned out on the bar stool, hooked up for an imaginary pirouette...

His thoughts skimmed back over the past, the years before he'd hooked up with Ellis. He hadn't cruised Central Park in a long time. He glanced at his watch, squinted the hands into focus.

Seven minutes after one.

He thought of the underbrush in the Ramble, the promise of anonymity. The action ought to be pretty heavy there by now. He felt a stirring in his groin. Why not? Tonight he'd earned it.

"Good night," he said to the man in leather.

A hand scooped out after him. "Hey, you're not going!"

Wally waved. The street door didn't want to open in or out, but finally, with a kick, he stumbled out onto the sidewalk.

The park was three blocks away. He managed to stagger reasonably straight lines, considering. He surveyed the cruisers on Central Park West. Hairdressers with poodles on leashes. The safety first crowd. Dullsville.

He took the pedestrian path that cut through the wall and curved down to the lake. It was shadowy, secluded. His eye was caught by a guy sitting on a bench. He slowed down.

"Hey, you." The guy was smiling at him. "Want some fun?"

The guy pulled his penis out of his fly and let it dangle.

*Shit*, Wally decided, *I'm not that drunk*. He kept going. A movement in the darkness tugged at his eye. He glanced back. There were three guys now, staring in his direction. Their heads bent together, nodding. A drift of hard-edged laughter caught him.

He quickened his stride. Steps followed behind him. He didn't look back.

"Hey, faggot!"

The steps were gaining, clattering nearer. He broke into a run.

"Hey, faggot, you dropped something!"

The path dipped down into darkness. Far ahead, atop a steep rise, he saw a single lamp, a bench, a police phone. He ran full out. Heart thumped, lungs burned. Halfway up the rise a hand grabbed the neck of his jacket. Instinctively, stupidly, he held on to the jacket.

And they had him.

"Ya fuckin' scumbag!"

In one instant he was surrounded. One of them punched and missed wildly and another spat in his face and the third brought a beer bottle cracking down on the side of his skull, releasing a hot sticky flow that he knew was blood.

He clawed free, screaming for help. With the last will power in his legs he lunged up the hill. He yanked the telephone from its box.

The wire had been cut.

He stood panting in the circle of light. Two more of them

came out of the wavering shadows.

"Looking for us, sweetheart?"

They grabbed for him. He windmilled his arms, struggling to fend them off, but the others had caught up and someone grabbed him low around the legs. A dozen hands ripped and punched at him. A kick in the testicles knocked the breath out of him. He began choking and crying from the neon-green pain. His vision streaked out in tears and blood. He went down kneeling onto the asphalt.

They dragged him off the path and into the shrubbery, out of the light. One of them yanked his head up by the hair and two others kicked him in the stomach and face. He was screaming. They ripped off the front of his bloodied shirt and stuffed it down his throat. He couldn't get air.

"Look at pretty boy, he shaves his fuckin' chest!"

The shaved chest drove them to even harder punches and kicks.

"Hey, watch this."

The blows stopped. An armlock around the neck held him paralyzed. He heard a match being struck and then came the grinding of a lit cigarette on his nipple.

He realized there would be no help. He knew he was going to die. His gagged mouth tried to shape the Lord's Prayer.

*Our Father who*

The kicks kept coming, head, face, and back, and then they dropped him. He fell on his side. His spine felt like two pieces of glass cutting into one another. They kicked his nose till it was a flap of cartilage. Someone pulled at his wrist.

"Nice watch."

"Bet his boy friend gave it to him."

"Get his wallet."

And then for no reason he could imagine, it stopped. He opened his eyes, blinked through the blood. Someone was standing over him. *Oh, God, more?*

He curled his arms over his face.

"Jesus—they really did a job on you."

Someone crouched beside him. He felt the gag eased from his mouth. Vomit came up in two dark heaves. His mouth tasted of iron and salt, as though he'd been licking ship hulls.

"Can you stand?"

He tried. Couldn't.

Hands helped him up. He was able to move one foot and drag the other. Hands helped him to a bench. A clean handkerchief pressed against his nose, staunching the blood.

"Say—aren't you—?"

Wally shook his head. "Hospital . . . please . . . going to pass out . . ."

And he did.

\*    \*    \*

Wally Collins did not show up at the next day's *Sleeping Beauty* rehearsal. Or the day following.

Sasha partnered Steph instead. He danced full out and he danced brilliantly. In one variation he did a double *cabriole* sweeping up into a double turn in the air, landing smack on the beat in perfect extended fifth position, and he wasn't even out of breath.

"That's not the choreography," Volmar said, to no one's surprise. And then, to everyone's surprise, "But it's all right. Keep it."

When Sasha lifted Steph or placed his hands on her waist to assist a pirouette she felt her heart racing. *It's because he's ahead of the beat*, she told herself. *He's rushing me and I'm nervous.*

Lowering her from a lift, he left his hand slide teasingly along the inside of her leg. "Still angry?" he whispered.

"Still angry."

"Dinner tonight?"

"No dinner any night ever."

After rehearsal she saw him laughing and whispering with Colleen Jackson, who was dancing the Lilac Fairy, and she supposed it was meant to make her jealous.

It did.

She was in a foul mood showering and changing and when someone called her name in the corridor she kept right on walking.

"Hey, Steph, slow down a minute, will you?"

It was Ellis. He looked like the wreckage of a hurricane and Steph's first instinct was to sweep him out of the way. His eyes were yellow and bloodshot and bristles of beard were growing out of a day-old shaving gash and his breath smelled of liquor and mouthwash.

"Wally's been hurt."

She stopped. The tip of a premonition pricked at her. "What's happened? Where is he?"

"I threw him out of the apartment two nights ago and he must have got drunk." Ellis was standing very still, speaking very softly, as though he had put himself together with Scotch tape and the least sudden movement might undo him. "He was attacked in Central Park. He's in the hospital now."

"Oh no." Steph closed her eyes.

"Would you come with me, Steph? Please. I can't do it alone."

*     *     *

A harried nurse directed them down the corridor. There was a smell of rubbing alcohol and disinfectant. Television sets and sickbed visitors whispered through half-open doors. Ellis hung back outside the room.

"Come on," Steph said. "You're his best friend. He needs you."

Ellis just stood looking mutely at her. "If he wants me I'm right here."

The door was partly open. Steph knocked softly and slipped into the room. "Wally?"

The blinds had been angled shut and the room was dark. The figure on the bed stirred. "Steph?"

For a moment she didn't want to believe it was Wally. There was no face, only maplike smears of raw purple stretching across skin and bandage. *Iodine*, she realized with relief, *not blood*.

"Can I come in?"

"Sure. There's a chair around here someplace."

"Found it." She pulled up the steel chair and sat very close so he wouldn't tire his voice.

Great shocks of blond hair had forced their way in fringes through the bandages. The eyes sparkled palely. The eyes and hair were Wally. Her gaze clung to them, tried to ignore the rest.

"Does it hurt?"

"It did," he said. "For a little while."

There were charts hanging on clips from the front of the bed and she wondered why so many. "We were worried," she said. "We missed you."

"I missed you. It's nice to see a friendly face." He tried to smile, and the attempt was heroic on a face so battered.

Something stuck in her throat. He saw her staring.

"Looks that bad, does it?"

"It looks—like it'll look a lot better in two days. Is your nose broken?"

"My nose is okay."

Steph tried to think of something cheerful to say. She remembered a line people said in movies. "How does the other guy look?"

"There were five other guys. I don't even want to remember how they looked."

"I'm sorry. That's lousy luck."

"My own stupid fault. I was drunk. Walking in Central Park at one in the morning. What else can you expect?"

"How do you feel?"

"Like an ass. Like a selfish ass the way I've let you down."

"You haven't let me down." She put her hand on his and gave an encouraging little squeeze. His fingers slipped between hers, clinging. "How long are you going to be in here?"

"Every doctor says something different. Steph, I'm sorry, but I won't be dancing."

"Not dance the gala?"

Wally shook his head. *He's taking it too hard,* she thought. *People dance galas with their teeth knocked out. Alonso dances them blind.*

"You can put make-up over that bruise. The swelling will have gone down by tomorrow—"

"I won't be dancing, Steph." He said it with a firmness that surprised her. "You're just going to have to get used to Sasha. He's a better dancer anyway."

"You're better than anyone in the company and you know it."

"I'm a better partner. He's a better dancer. So watch out. He'll try to steal the gala from you."

"I won't let him," Steph said, just to show she could be firm too.

"That's the spirit." Wally was staring at her thoughtfully,

regretfully. "You know, we would have been a damned good team."

"And we will be. Who cares about the gala? It's just a lot of publicity and the same old *Sleeping Beauty*."

"No. You're a special Sleeping Beauty. I'd love to have danced it with you—just once in front of an audience."

She sensed something in him that frightened her. Not self-pity, which she would have understood. Resignation. It was as if he'd forgotten what it was to be a dancer. Dancers didn't give up because someone smashed their nose in. Dancers survived torn tendons and swollen joints and lost toenails and slipped discs. They survived bad love affairs and failed marriages. They survived.

"We'll dance it, Wally. How hard did they bang you on the head? You haven't forgotten the steps, have you?"

"No—I'm not going to forget the steps. Not ever."

Maybe Wally was just having a bad reaction to the beating. Maybe he was upset over Ellis. *Ellis will cheer him up*, she thought. *That's what he needs*.

Wally sighed. The sound of that sigh bothered her.

"You know, they say a smile is like a turn-out. If you don't practice, you lose it."

He half smiled, every muscle of his face battling bandages and scabs. She wondered how many stitches he'd taken.

"How's that?" he said.

"Shows promise."

His eyes misted over. She hugged him. She could feel the familiar strength in his shoulders and torso.

"Damn it," she said. "I really wanted to dance it with you."

"Thanks, Steph. That's the best review anyone could have given me."

*He'll get through*, she thought. *He's badly scratched and he's argued with Ellis. But that can all be fixed.*

"I brought you something," she said.

"You didn't have to."

"Close your eyes."

She motioned Ellis into the room. He entered hesitantly and stood at the foot of the bed. When he spoke his voice was thick and hoarse as though the words had to fight through clogs in his lungs.

"Hello, Wally."

Wally opened his eyes. Steph knew instantly. *This was a mistake*.

"What do you want?"

"Just to say hello—and I was worried about you—and I'm sorry."

Wally pushed a silence toward Ellis. He turned his face away. "Steph, get him out of here."

"I'll make it up to you," Ellis said. "I promise."

"There's no way you can make it up."

The words poured out of Ellis in a pleading rush. "I'm going to stop playing around. I'm going to stop drinking. I'm going to tell Zoltan to get out. You can come back. I want you to come back. Please come back, Wally."

Wally stared at Ellis. Steph sensed something cruel and final and murderous building in him. She felt helplessly unable to head it off.

"Why don't you go get drunk and get laid," Wally said, "and get lost?"

"Give him a chance," Steph said.

"I gave him a chance. It took him two years—and he finally wrecked me. And if I could get out of this bed and walk, I'd throw him out of here myself. But I can't get out of bed and I can't walk, so I'm asking you nicely, Ellis—get the hell out. You wrecked me, mission accomplished, go wreck someone else."

A cold shock went through Steph. "Wally—is there something wrong with your leg?"

"The leg's fine." Wally's hands fumbled at the sheet and finally managed to throw it to one side. "But the foot's shit."

Steph tried to lock the muscles that controlled her facial expression. The foot no longer had the shape of a foot. It was a bloated mass of plaster and adhesive, as though someone had taken eighteen yards of surgical tape and anchored a telephone directory to his leg.

"One good thing about getting your ankle pulverized, they give you morphine. I'm flying."

Ellis had lowered his eyes, unable to look.

Steph made herself look. She had to show Wally it didn't matter. "Will it—heal?"

"They say in a few months."

She took a deep breath of relief. For a moment she had been afraid.

"I'll walk normally. I won't run very fast, but I won't be on crutches."

"Will you—dance?" Ellis asked.

"Believe it or not, Ellis, I'd be a worse dancer than you. No half *pointe*, no balance, no turn, no *jeté*. No, thank you. Happy about it?"

Ellis stood bulkily beside the bed. For a long moment his face worked, but nothing came out—not tears, not words. And then, very softly: "Wally—I'm sorry."

"Are you? Do you understand? Look at my foot! Take a good look! You did that!"

Ellis slumped and began to sob.

"Don't you come crying to me," Wally shouted. "You still have two feet—*I'll* never dance again!"

"Wally—I'll give up dancing. We can open a business. A school."

"Big fucking deal! You're no good—never were, never will be. I could have been someone!"

Ellis jerked as though each word were a pin impaling him. "Wally—please—let me help—*please*."

Ellis reached his hands out. No one took them.

Steph couldn't even feel pity for him. She felt only anger at the enviers and destroyers of this world, sorrow for the human wreckage they left behind.

"Get out of my life!" Wally screamed.

Ellis backed falteringly out the door. The room was very silent now. Steph stared at the foot and then at Wally staring at her. She remembered his *tour en l'air* and his six unsupported pirouettes and the sensation of leaping across space into the safety of his arms and she thought she would go crazy if she couldn't think of something else.

It was Wally's voice that rescued her. "Steph—would you do one thing for me?"

Steph couldn't answer. The tears were too close. She nodded.

"I'll be watching you on that TV set. Just be the most beautiful Sleeping Beauty that ever was. Promise?"

She didn't want to look at him, didn't want him to see her crying. "Oh, Wally, I'm not that good."

"You *are* that good. You're as good as the best. I danced with them, Steph. I know."

Tears and sniffles came spilling down. She grabbed blindly

for the Kleenex box by his bed. He took her hand.

"Hey—a smile is like a turn-out."

"I can't smile."

"Yes, you can. Smile—and kiss me."

She choked back the sniffles. And smiled. And kissed him. And promised.

# forty-seven

A guy couldn't even piss in peace. The second oboe followed Seymour Harnett out of the meeting and kept on arguing, right there in the men's room of the Americana Hotel.

"So it's my fault the dumb faggot gets mugged?" Seymour Harnett said.

"It's nobody's fault. But now this Russian steps in and he looks like a saint, and we look like shits."

"So we look like shits."

"That's not the attitude, Seymour. Learn from the Russian."

"What am I going to learn? Russian? Toe dancing? Sixty-nine positions?"

"How to get the public on our side."

"Yeah? How?"

"We volunteer to play the gala."

"That's a shitty idea."

"It's our gift to the city. It's our gift to the nation. We send telegrams to the mayor, to the President, to the papers. It's our gift to *civilization*."

"Civilization never gave me a damned thing except tax surcharges."

"Just that one performance. It'll be on coast-to-coast TV. It looks good. *We* look good. Artists. *Americans*."

"N. O. No way."

"I'm going to propose it at the meeting, it'll go to a vote."

"You do that and I'll have your union card. I happen to know you don't cut your own reeds, I happen to know you get them on Forty-third Street."

"And the same guy sells reeds to every bassoon and flugelhorn in New York, including your brother-in-law, which is why his English horn quacks."

Seymour Harnett was so angry he could hardly zip up straight. And sure enough, when he got back to the emergency meeting of the strike committee and asked if there were any motions, the second oboe raised his goddamned hand.

*     *     *

Marius Volmar watched from the orchestra. When he could bear it no longer he bent toward the microphone.

"Can we have Carabosse's entrance again? She comes in stage center, I want the light to pick her up. And where was the flash? Let's put this together."

It was the first stage rehearsal and it was going badly, as they always did. The dancers who weren't dancing kept getting in the way of the ones who were. Electricians wandered the stage with hand-held mikes, dragging wires behind them that were sure to trip unwary feet. Stagehands prowled. The Lilac Fairy was dancing in ski pants and a hooded parka. The pianist diddled at his little upright. Sets raised and lowered themselves for no reason. High on a light pole a blinding strobe began to flash.

Volmar's mind was numb from the effort of not despairing. His heart pumped a steady stream of pain through his chest and left arm.

The grand promenade still did not work. He was down to two principals, Stephanie and Sasha, with no real covers. The new girl couldn't handle the Act One solo and the new boy couldn't handle the *battements* in Florimund's Act Three variation.

The company was a creature living on raw snapping nerves, and Volmar kept whipping it forward toward that slender maybe of a gala. Just when he thought he had it under control, the creature would rebel, and an entire rehearsal would veer wildly off course, as it had today, like a punctured, rocketing balloon.

He still did not know if he had a *Sleeping Beauty* or not. Let alone an orchestra.

He spoke again into the microphone. "Are we ready for that entrance?"

A voice shouted, "Ready!" and he signaled the conductor, and the conductor beat time for the pianist. Three counts before the entrance an electrician dashed across the stage, waving his thumb-indexed score.

"I got a flash coming up! Gimme a flash!"

Four boys came running onstage, dragging behind them the fairy's black chariot. There was no lightning, no puff of smoke.

"Where's my flash?" the electrician screamed, and the cry came back, "Warren's working on the wire!"

Volmar struggled against his anger. He had asked for the wicked fairy, and as a prank they'd given him a brawny stagehand, slouched in the chariot with a can of beer. Volmar grabbed the microphone.

And then the stagehand stepped down onto the stage and pirouetted.

It was a real pirouette. That fat muscle-bound body could pirouette.

*The man was once a dancer*, Volmar realized, *and now he's a stagehand.* Volmar put the microphone down. The pincers gripping his heart relaxed. But he needed to breathe. He needed to move. He pushed up from his seat and walked toward the back of the house.

From several rows away he saw someone in the viewing room at the back of the theater.

"Marius?"

It was Dorcas, sitting with arms clasped on crossed knees. Her face was pale and her huge eyes moved with him.

"We're back on the same side," she said. "There's nothing left to quarrel about now."

Volmar's frown wobbled. "Nothing," he agreed. "Sasha dances the gala."

Dorcas attempted a smile. "Assuming the orchestra lets us have a gala."

"Assuming."

"He'll be good. He'll be as good as Wally would have been."

"He'll be better than Wally could ever have been."

Dorcas stared at him. "You knew that and you still blocked him?"

"I knew it from the first company class."

"But didn't you want *Sleeping Beauty* to be the best you could possibly make it?"

"I wanted it to be mine."

Dorcas arched her eyebrows. "Well—that's human. And it's honest to admit it."

"It's foolish. Foolish to do, foolish to have to admit."

She patted the seat beside her and he sat.

"You'll just have to forgive yourself," she said. "I've had to forgive myself, God knows."

"For loving Sasha?"

"Partly."

"I thought the other women might discourage you."

"Not about Sasha. Anyone else, but not him. It's weak of me, but I *am* weak. And I'm old and I've never had any talent but money. He's young and he's strong and he's got every talent a dancer would sell his soul for." She looked at Volmar. "And you don't love anything about him at all, do you?"

"I'm past tense and he's future and I hate him for that. It's unfair of me, I know."

"Yes, it is," she said. "The only thing wrong with Sasha is that he made us argue."

Volmar shrugged. "Friends always find an excuse for arguing."

"And are we friends, Marius? Still?"

For a moment he didn't answer. "I was thinking of death the other night. At first I was frightened. And then I thought, *Hell won't be so bad—not with Dorcas there to argue with*."

"Do you think they'll let me into hell? I was always afraid of winding up someplace wish-washy—like purgatory."

"If they don't let you in, I'm going to have a very lonely eternity."

"Do you know, Marius, that's the first truly kind thing you've ever said to me?"

\*     \*     \*

Mrs. Avery stood beside the hospital bed and gazed at her daughter. The girl stirred and Mrs. Avery quickly dried her cheeks with the back of her hand.

Chris opened her eyes and looked up at her mother. She saw something in the face that made her sorrowful.

"I've made you unhappy," she said. "All my life I've made you unhappy."

Mrs. Avery shook her head. "No. You've made your father and me happy. Never anything but happy. And there's good news. The doctor says you can leave this afternoon."

There was color in Christine's face and she smiled when her mother bent down to kiss her. Mrs. Avery left the hospital room feeling hope for the first time since she'd arrived in New York.

But the doctor kept her waiting in his office and the wait chipped away at her hopefulness. She was standing when the doctor hurried in. He had one arm still in a smock. Beneath the smock he was wearing the vest and trousers of a beautifully tailored dark suit.

The suit reassured her more than the smile.

"Mrs. Avery."

It was a pained smile. There was a handshake, an apology for the delay. He motioned her to the high-backed chair she had been avoiding. He took an armchair facing her. He had a lapful of documents and he shuffled them and Mrs. Avery felt like a figure in the background of a painting, present but playing no part.

"She's very run down," the doctor said.

Mrs. Avery nodded.

"X ray shows no injuries, no bones broken from the fall. Thermoscan shows no new tumors."

"That's good, isn't it?"

He gave her a long, grave glance. "The autoimmune system is breaking down."

Mrs. Avery did not know what an autoimmune system was.

It sounded necessary, like a heart or a kidney or a lung: but they had machines for those things now, didn't they?

"And the lymphatic system is affected. That much we can tag without actually cutting her open."

"You're telling me Christine is very ill," Mrs. Avery said in a quiet voice. "Is that what you're telling me?"

"It's gone too far."

For twenty years Mrs. Avery had felt she'd been prepared for this. But she wasn't prepared at all. She sat in silence and the doctor, whose time was valuable, permitted her the silence.

And then, tactfully defending her daughter, feeling out the finality of this verdict, she suggested that perhaps there had been an error.

"Mrs. Avery, we have your daughter's records since birth."

Mrs. Avery put out her cigarette with a slow grinding. She sat very still, looking at the doctor. Her eyes remained fixed on him and he took their steadiness as a sign of her realism and self-control.

In fact Mrs. Avery did not feel real at all. Everything seemed so unreal to her that she took this news as one more unreality among many. Children did not die and leave their parents to live on after them. Especially an only child. That was not reality; that was unbearable.

*But Chris is not an only child,* Mrs. Avery tried to tell herself. *We have two other children, two normal and lovely children.*

*But only one Chris,* she thought. *Only one Chris.* Darkness closed over her.

"Is there anything we ought to do?" she said.

"Anything you like. You can take her on a trip. Let her go on dancing. For the next two months or so she'll seem normal. You won't even have to tell her right away."

"And after the next two months?"

The doctor explained that at the present state of medical art very little could be done.

"She wanted to live her life. What else could we have done, Doctor? Kept her in prison with round-the-clock nurses?"

The doctor sighed and Mrs. Avery waited for an answer that did not come. Her hands lay still in her lap. The doctor noticed that they were small hands, smooth like a child's, the fingers shaping an empty nest.

The doctor shook his head sorrowfully. "Our records show she's only twenty."

Mrs. Avery sighed. She knew the doctor was trying to be sympathetic.

He stood and made a dusting movement of his hands. "I'm very, very sorry."

His glance touched her face and her lips in reflex went through the motion of "Thank you."

*        *        *

As Steph stepped out on her mother's floor she saw a man hurrying into the other elevator. Just as the door closed she glimpsed his face.

Marius Volmar.

Steph froze. *It couldn't be. My eyes must have been playing a trick.*

She pushed the buzzer. Her mother came fluttering to the door in a bathrobe.

"Oh, hi, honey," Anna said. "I was just putting on coffee. Would you like some?"

"For a moment I thought I was barging in."

"Barging in on what?"

"I thought I saw Marius Volmar getting into the other elevator."

Anna's mouth was a silent, whooshing O. So it was true.

"No big deal," Steph said. *Why shouldn't her mother have a sex life?* she thought; and then, *But why does it have to be Marius Volmar?*

Anna's eyes sparkled wetly. "Honey, I've been so nervous—and lonely—"

"It's nothing to cry over."

"You're angry at me. I can tell when you're angry."

It flashed through Steph that this was no accident. She visited her mother every Sunday morning. It was their weekly ritual. Anna couldn't have suddenly forgotten what day it was. She had produced Marius Volmar on purpose. She was trying to prove something.

"I can always tell when you have that pout. Don't be angry at me, honey." Anna led the way to the kitchen. She walked as though her back ached. "You know, I'm human too—and I'm not exactly over the hill." From the stove she threw Steph a glance that hinted at all sorts of reproach. "Three years—three years I've been sitting in this apartment. You never phone, you never come over." Anna sat at the table. She poured coffee, shoved cups. "You don't need me any more. I'm not part of your life."

"You'll always be part of my life."

Anna was silent and then she said in a voice edged in bitterness, "After tonight you'll be a star. You'll see me in Bloomingdale's and you'll say, 'Who's that old woman? Don't I remember her from someplace?'"

"That would never happen."

"A lot's going to happen. It's going to happen so fast you'll be dizzy. I'm glad for you, honey, but I've got to be included somewhere." Anna hesitated and then her words came quickly, as though the faster they spilled the less responsibility she bore. "And Marius *includes* me! Maybe only an hour a week, but at least it's every week and I can count on it and he makes me feel welcome!"

"An hour a week?" Steph's face did not change but she spoke with a cruelty so deliberate it surprised her. "Eight to nine when the theater's dark?"

"You're young." Anna knotted her robe more tightly around her. "You don't know what it's like when there's nothing left and you wake up wishing you were dead. You don't know what it's like when you dream about the days when you used to have something to dream about. You learn to settle for what you can get—and if you can get it, you grab it. Why not? Aren't I entitled?" She wiped her eyes with the sleeve of her robe. "Honey, don't I deserve *anything?* Haven't I earned a little something nice?"

"But why does it have to be Marius Volmar?"

"Why not?"

"Because you're trying to use him to push me. I don't need your pushing. I'm fed up with it."

"Pushing?" Anna smiled and shrugged. "Who's got the time?"

"And I'm fed up with your little white lies."

Anna's eyes darkened. Steel crept into her voice. "You calling your mother a liar? When did I lie to you? Go on, when did I ever lie to you?"

"What do you call the way you connived to get me out of Empire?"

"Oh. That."

"Yes. *That*."

"Come on, what are we arguing for?"

"You connived and you've always connived and you're still conniving."

"Well, you just thank your lucky stars *somebody* connived. You're a star, aren't you?"

"You think that justifies it?"

"It justifies a hell of a lot."

"You don't care who or what you wreck. Sometimes I wonder if you even know."

"What do you mean, you and that Danny kid?"

*She's admitting it*, Steph thought. *She's admitting she wrecked Danny and me and she doesn't even care.*

"He was nowhere," Anna said. "He was using you. He would have stepped on you first chance he got. I did you a favor."

A taste of salt and anger flooded Steph's mouth.

"You would have ended up like me and your dad," Anna sighed.

*I'm going to fight her this time*, Steph thought, and her voice was as even as the blade of a sword. "And I wonder about Dad, too."

"What's to wonder?"

"I've always heard your side of it. Maybe there was another side."

Anna pushed up from the table with such suddenness that the percolator almost tripped over its electric cord. She folded her arms and she had the grim taut mouth of a bank guard stationed at the vault.

"Maybe he wasn't such a monster," Steph said. "Maybe he wasn't such a bad dancer, either. Maybe he would have had a career if you hadn't connived and meddled and sabotaged."

A rasping, mirthless chuckle came out of Anna. She shook her head, as though pitying the ignorance of children. "Me, *sabotage?* I stood beside that bastard, I ironed shirts and worked and slaved through thick and thin while he was running off getting lushed, every goddamned minute of that marriage was hell but *I stayed with him* and if you call that *sabotage*—"

"He's in the dance encyclopedias, Mom. Not you."

The words yanked Anna around like a wire. "I *would* have been in the encyclopedias! Critics called me the Duse of the dance! There'd be roles in the repertory today and people would say, 'Anna Barlow created that—*and*—that—*and* that!' I would've had a career, I'd be in Balanchine's *Stories of the Great Ballets*—there'd be a dozen numbers after my name in the index—if it hadn't been for that no-good drunken lush!"

"Maybe that no-good drunken lush would be alive today—maybe he'd still be dancing—if you hadn't—"

"If I hadn't *what?*" The voice was a near scream. "You think *I* pulled the trigger? Well, let me tell *you*, little Miss Know-it-all—"

Anna stopped. Silence exploded.

"What did you just say, Mom?"

Anna's eyes faltered. She sat quickly. She fumbled with a coffee cup. "I said you've got your facts bass-ackwards."

"You said something else."

"I said you've got a performance tonight and let's just relax."

Steph shouted with a strength she'd never known was in her: "Did my father kill himself?"

Anna flinched as though ducking a punch. "I didn't say that."

*"Did he kill himself?"*

"Look, Why upset yourself—"

*"Answer me!"*

Anna's gaze rose slowly to meet her daughter's. The words came whispering and low with no denial left in them. "All right, all right, yes, he killed himself, yes, he was a stinking no-good coward lush, yes, he ran off with the rent money and holed up in some hotel—Aw, honey, why do you want to hear this?"

"I want to *know!*"

Anna was a puddle of bathrobe and tears spilling over the kitchen table. Steph had never seen her mother look so middle-aged and miserable.

"He was with a hooker." Anna's voice was a flat monotone. "He spent his last ten bucks to get laid and it was the last thing he ever did in his life. He had a right. He had a right. I wasn't—

letting him have any. But what did he ever give me except—" She stared at Steph and began pounding the table. "Stop *looking* at me like that!"

Steph couldn't react. She felt a knife had slit her from throat to stomach and every belief she had ever possessed or lived by had spilled into the gutter. "And all my life you told me—"

"I was protecting you!"

"From what?"

"The truth! You weren't old enough!"

"And when *would* I have been old enough?"

"Never! You would never have been old enough! Oh, honey, look at me. Not like that. *Look* at me! I did it for *you!*"

"Did you?" Steph said. "Did you ever do anything that wasn't for you first, me second?"

"All right, I did it for both of us, two birds with one stone, why not?"

"Nothing was because you loved *me*."

"It was *all* for you—the toe shoes when I couldn't afford them, the leg warmers I knitted myself, the lessons I had to go down on my knees and *beg* to get discounts for—and I'd do it all over again, honey, I'm so proud of you!"

"You never gave me a choice. You never even gave me a *chance!*"

"You had the best choice in the world—honey, you're a *dancer!*"

Steph stared at the panic and apology smeared across her mother's face. "And you never even asked if that was what I wanted."

"Wanted? Who wouldn't want it! Of course you wanted it!"

Steph turned and walked out of the kitchen.

"Honey—don't go like that—I wanted to tell you *merde* for tonight!"

And out of the apartment.

Silence eddied through the kitchen.

Hands shaking, Anna telephoned Marius Volmar. It was almost eleven-thirty before she got an answer.

"Marius—Steph knows. She saw you in the elevator."

"No secret keeps forever," Volmar said, and Anna could almost hear the voice shrug.

"And she knows about Marty. She knows how he died."

There was an intake of breath. "You told her? Today of all days?"

"She wormed it out of me. She's jealous, Marius. She's jealous of you and me and she nagged and screamed and it just came out, I couldn't help it."

Volmar sighed. "Anna, Anna, Anna."

"Don't just say Anna Anna Anna, what are we going to do?"

"Stay away from Stephanie till after the performance, will you? I'll think of a way to straighten it out."

# forty-eight

Marius Volmar took the little enamel box from the leather case of his mother's possessions. He slipped it into his pocket. The padding in the corduroy jacket had slid like the silicone in an old strip teaser, and the box looked like another lump, nothing more.

He planned to give it to her before the final dress rehearsal.

She was sitting in the wings stitching ribbons onto her toe shoes.

"Stephanie," he said.

She looked up and a hesitation seized him. Her eyes were cool serene blanks and his tongue stuck to his teeth. It would be easier after the rehearsal, he decided. They'd be alone.

"Watch those *battements* in your Act One variation."

She nodded. He saw that a wall had risen between them. No matter. The little enamel box would break through it.

By two o'clock the company had gathered onstage. There had been no word from the musicians. The rehearsal piano was there and the rehearsal pianist was there just in case.

Volmar took a seat in the orchestra and stared up at the stage and down at the pit. The music waited, neatly laid out on the stands, but by ten after two not a single musician had appeared.

Volmar bent toward his microphone. "We'll rehearse with piano. Prologue, please—omit the overture."

The dancers got to their feet and went listlessly to their places. The piano hammered out the first chords. Volmar watched his girls and boys. He had a sinking impression of clean costumes and dirty toe shoes, movement without joy or jump to it, muscles cold and stiff and knotted with heartbreak.

He opened his notebook, then closed it again and laid it on the empty seat beside him. He sighed. There was no use having the ballet in a notebook: Sleeping Beauty was either there on the stage or she was nowhere.

He had a leaden feeling that she was nowhere.

The rehearsal tottered and staggered, barely maintained a forward direction. They drummed through four numbers of the prologue. Marius Volmar stared sadly at the corpse onstage.

And then he detected a flick of life.

Not on the stage. Below it.

He sat taller in his seat, squinting.

A shadow crept into the dark orchestra pit, and then he made out a clarinetist dropping a weighted handkerchief through his instrument. Lights clicked on at music stands, like the first brave stars on a smoggy night.

A double bass struggled in. The harpist pulled the cover off her harp and a dim curve of gold glimmered. There were voices and shuffling, woodwinds shrilling up and down scales, the pinprick A of an oboe and the whine of strings slithering up to pitch.

The fat gorgeous cacophony drowned out the piano and the dancers stopped dead in their tracks. A little doughball of a dresser came running to the footlights, her mouth full of pins, and her mouth fell open, spilling every one of them.

*Thank God*, Volmar thought, *thank You, God!*

He spoke again into the microphone. "When the orchestra is ready, let's take it again from the prologue, first number after the overture."

The conductor rapped his podium. There was an instant's silence. The baton flicked out a downbeat. Music flooded the stage, warm life-giving music, and the stage burst into a rush of rhythm and color and movement. The dancers danced full out, bold and leaping and alive.

Volmar sank back in his chair, calm and still and exultant. His Sleeping Beauty was exactly as he had dreamed her and she was on the stage where she belonged.

\*     \*     \*

The rehearsal raced forward. Stephanie's *pas seul* and Rose Adagio brought roars of applause from the company.

There was no pain. *Have I gone crazy?* she wondered. She had been used and lied to and manipulated. Her life lay in pieces, like a flung crystal vase, and yet all she could feel was *piqué, chassé,* a leap, a catch, the music surging through her, singing and living through her, making her weightless, lifting her above gravity and time and care.

The company bravaed her Act Three *pas de deux* with Sasha and she smiled at him. *I like him,* she realized. *I actually like the bastard.* She was a dancer and she could afford to like him and she knew she would shine tonight.

After rehearsal Volmar went up onstage. Everything was chatter and smiles and excitement. Except him.

"Stephanie."

She stood staring at him with no particular concern. "Yes, Mr. Volmar?"

Dancers and stagehands scurried past. The newborn premonition of success hung in the air like dust. He would have liked to be alone with her, out of sight of the others, out of earshot. At least in the wings. But he couldn't find the courage to suggest it.

"I'm sorry," he said.

"Don't be. It had to happen."

"It shouldn't have happened that way."

She slipped into her robe. She seemed to care more about the knot than him. "It's not worth an apology."

"I want to make it up to you anyway."

One of her eyebrows lifted and made an angle. "There's nothing to make up."

"I've hurt you."

"You've taught me the most valuable lesson of my life. When I dance nothing can hurt me."

Her thoughts had traveled a great circle that day. She had

passed through every degree of indecision and surrender and somehow come back to where she'd started.

She was a dancer.

Not because her mother or a puppeteer called Volmar wanted it, but because Stephanie Lang wanted it.

"You've helped me, Mr. Volmar, much more than you could ever hurt me. I'm sure people helped you when you were young, and hurt you. And someday when it's my turn, I'll help somebody else and probably hurt them too."

He was standing close enough to smell the dampness in her hair. *Go ahead*, instinct urged. *Give her the box. Give it to her now. You'll never have another chance.*

"It takes a very special sort of person to understand that, Stephanie. And to be able to say it." His fingers fidgeted in his pocket. "I may not have always shown it—I may not ever have shown it—but you're special to me. I'd like to show you just how very special."

"Mr. Volmar, the only thing special about me is that I have a performance tonight. There's a masseur waiting for me. I'd like to nap, I'd like to soak in a tub, and I have to get back to the theater in time to warm up. So would you please excuse me?"

She walked with quick purpose into the wings, leaving him behind like an axed tree.

His heart reacted with a little tremor of shock. He forced himself to breathe deeply. The air was layered with rosin and sweat and body heat. A set squeaked as it flew up. He turned to stare at the naked stage and he saw a gray poodle prowling the cyclorama.

"*Merde! Merde!* Where is my sweetheart, where is my naughty little darling?"

Sasha Bunin came chasing after the dog. He caught it and cradled it and cooed to it. "*Merdoushka moya—nye znayesh kak lublyu tebya?*"

Revulsion made Volmar turn away: was the idiot going to sing *"Ochi Chorniye"* to that animal?

The last dancers were hurrying from the stage, heading toward the showers and home for a rest before the gala. The stage lights had dimmed to a deep dusk and the wings hummed with fading laughter and chatter. Something warm and unexpected gusted through him and his glance edged back toward the cyclorama. An idea hummed in him.

He drew a deep breath, heaved his body erect with the fullness of his lungs. He crossed the stage. "The grand promenade of the guests worked today," he said.

Sasha looked up, surprised.

"You taught them."

Sasha's face darkened. He shuffled nervously. "*Maître*, I did not teach. The dancers asked me. I described."

"You must have described it well."

Sasha tossed out a shrug. "Nothing special. Kirov promenade. Same in *Nutcracker*, same in *Giselle*, same in *Swan Lake*."

"But it's good," Volmar said. "You were right and I was wrong."

There were astonishment and gratitude in Sasha's expression. He seemed shy and almost delicate. *In many ways*, Volmar reflected, *Sasha is a horse. He can pull loads. He puts up with whippings and spurrings. Words do not matter to him so much as the tone of voice. To keep his attention from straying to one side or another, he had to wear blinders. Changes of direction confuse him.*

"This is for you," Volmar said abruptly.

Sasha accepted the little package warily. Volmar had attacked him so often and in such ingenious ways that he dared not think what new attack the tissue paper might mask.

He felt the little package for weight and shape and hardness. His fingers detected no clear menace, but Volmar was a subtle man. He eased the little enamel box out of its wrapping.

His mouth dropped open. There was a mingling of wonder and reverence and dread in his eyes.

The thin line of Volmar's lips could not help arching in a tiny smile. *My jaw must have dropped like that. My eyes must have been just as ablaze and agog when I first touched that box.*

"I have seen one of these," Sasha said. "In the museum at the Kirov."

"Keep it."

Sasha's eyes peeked up timidly. His voice dropped to a whisper. "But, *maître*—I am not worthy."

"You'll learn to be."

Sasha dropped to his knees and seized Volmar's hand and pressed it to his lips. Volmar felt warm and embarrassed. He shook free.

"Now, now, Aleksandr Fedorovich, it's only a box."

Sasha clasped the box to his heart. "Greatest honor Sasha has ever had."

"You'll have other honors. Many, many others."

"Nothing ever like this. Tonight, for thank you, Sasha will dance Florimund like you have never seen."

*Conceited little bastard,* Volmar thought. *Conceited and reliable. Like me. And when I am gone, which may be in a day or a month or a year, he will inherit the company. And he will run it well.*

Volmar smiled and rested a hand on Sasha's back.

*I have found my immortality at last.*

A tranquillity descended on Volmar that he had not known in fifty years.

# forty-nine

Steph was sitting at her mirror redoing her eyes. The dresser fussed with a zipper and warned her not to get make-up on the costume.

The frame of the mirror bloomed with telegrams; the flowers that had been arriving all afternoon overflowed the chairs and carpeted the corners of the dressing room. A knock came on the door, just loud enough to break into Steph's concentration. She blinked in annoyance.

"Lily, would you see who that is?"

As Steph leaned back toward her reflection Mrs. Avery appeared in the mirror. Steph's hand stopped in mid-stroke.

"I'm very busy, Mrs. Avery."

Mrs. Avery's face was haggard, the eyes blank and used up. "Would you see Christine for a moment?"

Steph drew a breath. "No. I have to finish dressing and then I have to warm up." She squinted her eye shut, penciled the brown line above the lid. When she opened the eye again Mrs. Avery had not moved.

There was an odd expression on the woman's face, a trembling effort at control. It touched Steph strangely and she tried to keep her voice gentle.

"I'm sorry, but I need time to get ready."

"Please—just give her a moment?"

Steph tried to control the anger that was pushing against her stomach. "Mrs. Avery, I don't want to see your daughter. Not before performance, not after performance, not ever again."

Mrs. Avery inhaled and then she spoke very softly. "You won't see her ever again. But she'd like to say good-by."

"We've said good-by."

"She's sick."

"I know that and I'm sorry and after five years I've learned that there's nothing I can do about it."

"She's sicker than any of us realized."

"Mrs. Avery, I've given Chris all the sympathy she's ever going to get from me."

"She's going home. I'm taking her tonight."

"Good. She can't take care of herself—maybe someone else can."

"She's going home to die."

The words had a delayed impact. It took them two heartbeats to penetrate Steph's brain and then they exploded. In the shock of understanding she froze. Her mouth fumbled to push out words.

*"Die?"*

Mrs. Avery nodded.

"Does Chris—know?"

Mrs. Avery did not answer. Her eyes were closed an instant and then they opened to stare at Steph with bleak dignity. Her hand reached back toward the door and as it swung inward Steph took a deep gulp of air.

Chris stood in the doorway. Her head was lowered and her hands hung like limp flowers at her sides. A cold shaft of light slanted upon her face and a gentle bewilderment seemed to reach out from her and touch the whole world.

Steph's mouth moved and no sound came out.

The dresser edged toward the door and with a whimpering noise she vanished. Mrs. Avery followed and closed the door.

Chris's pale, soft gaze met Steph's. They stared helplessly at one another.

And then Steph cried, "Chris, oh my God!" and rushed to embrace her friend.

                              *    *    *

Steph's dresser whispered to a wardrobe mistress who was
hurrying to an emergency in the girls' dressing room. The
wardrobe mistress, stitching a rip in a noblewoman's gown,
repeated the whisper.

It rippled past a girl checking her hair spray and brushed a
girl who was testing the ribbons on her toe shoes. She whispered
to two girls who were helping one another with the zippers on
their costumes, and one of them carried the whisper out into the
wings to a boy from the corps who was warming up on a
carpenter's ladder.

A principal wandering by caught the whisper and spread it to
another principal and it eddied through the stagehands and
lighting men and out through the company till it was as much
part of the opening night confusion as the sparking generators
and the dust and the flashing lights and moving sets and the
sound of an oboe in the pit playing the Lilac Fairy's theme.

                              *    *    *

"Why did we argue?" Chris said.

"I don't remember." Tears came to Steph's eyes but so gently
and gradually that there was no spill, only a wobbling around
the edges of the dressing room.

"It was my fault," Chris said.

"No," Steph said, "it was mine." A slender stream of sorrow
twisted back and forth in the gray of her mind and where it
touched a memory there were flashes of movement and color.
She saw Chris flushed and glazed, taking curtain calls after *Do I*
and *Cantabile*. She saw Chris weeping with failure after her
school recital and she saw the pale blond child with one hand on
the bathroom sink, warming up for scholarship auditions. She
remembered all the hopes and terrors they had shared and the
years that had passed like a single yesterday.

"We've let too much get in the way," she said. "We've
forgotten what matters."

"I never found out what matters," Chris said. She radiated
the helplessness and the beauty of a puppy or a baby, of
something newborn and trusting.

She laid her head on Steph's shoulder. Her fingers tightened around Steph's hand.

There was an ache in Steph and fear that came in long waves. But there was something else too. She found herself remembering childhood and Christmas and a time when dance had been not an aching turn-out but a snow-white dream. She found herself remembering that evening when she'd argued with Ray Lockwood.

He'd said there were ballerinas who'd given up performances to let their understudies go on. She remembered saying, "Maybe in books or in movies, but not in ballet."

But now she was thinking: *Why not?*

She saw that this did not need to be the end for Chris.

*I have a life. Chris has—tonight.* WHY NOT?

And in that instant her mind was made up. "Stop talking as though it was over. Nothing's over. Nothing's even begun."

"Oh, Steph, don't try. I know how long I have. Two months, six months . . ."

"You have more than that. Much more."

"Don't. Please. It hurts even to hope. Don't try to make me."

"You have tonight, Chris."

Chris stared at her. "What do you mean?"

"You have as long as the longest memory of anyone sitting in that theater."

"I don't understand what you're saying."

"Dance. Dance instead of me."

Chris swayed and put a foot behind her. "Me—go out there—tonight?"

"You know the role. Take it. You've worked every bit as hard as me." She gripped Chris by the shoulders. "For once in your life take something for yourself! You've spent your life preparing—you're ready—get out there and *dance!*"

Chris stood in wondering denial. "But *Sleeping Beauty*'s your chance."

"No, Chris." Steph slipped out of her costume. She placed it in Chris's hands. *"This* is. *Merde."*

\* \* \*

When Steph came out of the dressing room she was wearing street clothes. "Lily," she told the dresser, "go help her, please.

The back has to be taken in and the waist is loose."

"Yes, miss."

Steph moved quickly through the clusters of dancers. "What's happened?" they asked.

"Chris is dancing Aurora."

"Is it true that she ... ?"

Steph saw the terror in their eyes and she saw that, somehow, they knew. Dancers always knew. "Yes," she said. "It's true."

The dancers waited and whispered and watched and ached.

Just as the curtain was rising on the prologue Chris opened the door. A gust of noise swept past her: stagehands were shouting and the audience was applauding and the music was thundering. The sounds fell against her skin, driving her back like rain. She felt a moment's chill, and then the shiver passed, leaving her refreshed and strong.

She walked swiftly to the warm-up barre backstage. The dancers said hello, which wasn't like them, and they backed off and let her have the barre, which wasn't like them at all. She noticed they were watching her oddly as she began her *pliés*.

She'd missed three days of class, so she warmed up slowly, stretching and bending with great care. There was a trembling instability to her first balance but she conquered it. Her mind and muscles began assembling her entrance. She raised her arm, cocked her foot, shut out reality and imagined the music. Her body fell into the steps.

She was finishing her warm-up when Marius Volmar came hurrying backstage. Angrily, he asked the stage manager what was delaying the curtain.

"We're waiting for Aurora."

Volmar turned toward the rehearsal barre and saw Chris. "What are you doing?"

"Getting ready."

"For what?"

She finished her combination and turned to face him. She had a sudden conviction of herself that was new and terrifying in its sureness.

"I'm dancing tonight."

Marius Volmar had watched the prologue from the front of the house. He knew nothing of the rumors that had swept backstage.

"Where's Stephanie?" he said.

The air filled with something silent and suffocating, like dust hovering after the explosion of a bomb.

"She walked out," the stage manager said.

Volmar jerked as though he'd been struck. "Walked *out?*"

"She told Lily to dress Chris and then she walked out."

Volmar's eyes fixed the man in fury. "Walked out *where?*"

"We can't find her."

Volmar wheeled on Chris. She could feel the rage welling out of him. "Where's Stephanie?"

"I don't know."

The stage manager's thumbs were fidgeting in his fists. "Mr. Volmar, we can't hold the curtain any longer. Do you want me to announce the cast change?"

Volmar gave a negative snap of the head. "No. No announcement."

The stage manager stood wondering if Volmar was actually going to call off the performance. Volmar weighed the idea, but the memory of the Copenhagen *Sleeping Beauty*, of his mother vanishing in the police car, swept through his mind. He stared at Chris in black disappointment.

She was not his Aurora. Was he never to have his dream?

"The orchestra's waiting, Mr. Volmar. We have to tell them *something*."

"Tell them to begin the prelude." Marius Volmar sighed the heaviest sigh of his life. "You'll dance tonight, Christine. And tomorrow you and Stephanie are both fired."

Chris felt ready and serene and, coming down from a pirouette, she smiled at him. *I'm alive*, she thought. *It took me my whole life, but I'm alive*.

\* \* \*

A spot clicked on, stage right, and Anna's hands readied to applaud Aurora's entrance. There was absolute silence in the theater and absolute stillness on the stage.

And one empty spot. Anna's throat tightened.

Aurora stepped lightly onstage.

Anna's heart dropped like a stone in her stomach. It was Chris up there dancing Aurora—not Steph, Chris!

The audience applauded. Anna sat frozen in a rush of shock. *Dear God, something's happened to Steph, tonight of all nights!*

She shot to her feet, pushed her way past jutting knees and surprised faces. She ran up the aisle, stumbled, kept going.

"What's the fastest way backstage from here?"

The speechless usherette managed to point.

Anna plunged down the deserted corridor, through the door marked *No entrance*, up the little flight of stairs. The stage manager tried to block her way.

"What's happened to my little girl? Where's Steph? What have you *done* to her?"

\*     \*     \*

Anna's running footsteps caught up with Steph in the passageway beneath the theater.

"Thank God, I've been looking everywhere for you! Where do you think you're going? Get back on that stage!"

Steph faced her mother. "I'm not dancing tonight."

Anna swayed and recovered her balance. "Of course you're dancing. You can still do Act Two."

Steph's eyes were absolutely calm and that scared Anna.

*"Why?"* Anna screamed.

"Because."

"You're walking out, just like that?"

"Just like that."

"Do you *know* what you're doing?"

"I know what I'm doing."

Anna's voice was a hoarse rushing whisper. "Honey, we've worked our whole lives for tonight! Tonight's your big break! They've got coast-to-coast TV, every newspaper in the world's out there! After tonight you'll be a ballerina! You can dance anywhere, London, L.A., Leningrad, you name it! You'll never have a chance like this again, you walk out now and you're throwing away your career!"

Steph kept walking. Anna caught up again.

"Why, will you just tell me *why?* After all the years I—"

Steph took her mother's hands. "Mom, I love you. I'm grateful for what you've done. I'm sorry for what you've suffered. You wanted a dancer for a daughter, you've got one.

Now let me run my own career and make my own decisions and live my own life."

Anna clutched at Steph but the raincoat slipped from her fingers. She stared in blank disbelief. Steph was gone. Her daughter was gone. All the years, the work, the sacrifice—gone.

Denial swelled in her and with it one last spurt of fight.

"Steph! Wait a minute! I have to talk to you!"

Too late. She turned the corner, breathless, and there was no sign of Steph.

\*     \*     \*

In the viewing room at the rear of the theater, Steph sat unnoticed. She witnessed a dance performance surpassing the beauty of any she had ever seen.

She had worried about Chris's *pas seul*. There was no need. Chris danced it simply, exquisitely.

Sasha became the ideal self-effacing partner. In a hundred subtle and gallant ways he supported Chris. He covered her slips so quietly, so beautifully, that she appeared to be taking virtuoso risks. He let her shine like an angel of lightness and movement and grace.

And she became that angel.

There was perfection that night in Christine Avery, in her figure and face and movement, and in the blaze of that perfection all impurities were burned out. Her leaps seemed to hang in the air. Her turns were lightning fast. Her balances opened like flowers. There were breadth and sweep and poetry in her line. She teased where the music teased, soared where it soared, grew as it grew, from playfulness through suffering to love.

She was Aurora the young girl, Aurora the woman: it was as though Tchaikovsky himself were singing through her.

When Sasha led Chris onstage for their last *pas de deux*, she was wearing the white of a bride on her wedding day. And even in the rush of turns on *pointe* and the dizzying climactic fish dive where Sasha caught her inches from the floor, she was smiling a bride's smile.

Then came the boot-stomping Russian dance, and Chris returned to perform Aurora's final solo: Christine Avery's final solo.

It was a heart-stopping moment: the very mystery of dance itself seemed to unlock, and Chris seemed to float free of gravity and time and all that was earthbound.

It was a moment of sadness for the characters onstage, for all the nobles and the fairies and the Mother Goose figures realized that their beloved princess must soon leave them and go live happily ever after with her prince.

Those in the audience who were sitting very near the stage could see that some of the dancers were crying.

After the closing mazurka, when Chris and Sasha stood embraced and the cast knelt in a circle around them, a whisper swept the first rows: *The defector was crying! And the King, and the Queen, and Puss-in-Boots, and . . .*

But Christine Avery was not crying.

She was smiling with a radiance that lit the theater.

The orchestra thundered out Tchaikovsky's final chords. There was an explosion of applause. The curtain fell, then rose again. Christine Avery came forward to curtsy. As she lowered her head, smiling and swan-graceful and meek, the applause doubled and doubled again.

Another triumph for National Ballet Theatre!

Another triumph for Marius Volmar!

Even the dancers applauded.

There were tossed programs and bravos and shouted questions: "What's her name—Amory?"

"Someone said *Avery*."

"Who *is* she?"

"Whoever she is, she's certainly a star now."

Fighting back tears, Stephanie Lang rose to her feet and joined the standing ovation for her friend Christine Avery.

# GLOSSARY OF FOREIGN AND TECHNICAL TERMS

(Certain definitions paraphrased by permission from *Balanchine's Complete Stories of the Great Ballets*, by George Balanchine and Francis Mason)

adagio: a dance in slow tempo, performed by a ballerina and her partner.

à la seconde: in second position. See *position*.

allegro: dancing that is lively and fast, in comparison to *adagio*.

arabesque: set pose. In its most common form, the dancer stands on one leg with the other leg raised behind and fully extended.

assemblé: a step in which the dancer rises low off the floor, straightens both legs in the air, and returns to fifth position.

attitude: set pose. The dancer stands on one leg and brings the other leg up behind at an angle of ninety degrees, with the knee bent.

ballerina: the highest rank of female dancer in a ballet company.

barre: the round horizontal bar which dancers hold onto for support while exercising.

barrel turn: a spectacular movement in which the *danseur* travels in a circle, executing a series of turns in the air, fully extending his arms and legs while aloft.

battement: any of various movements of the leg executed with a rapid beating motion.

bourrée: see *pas de bourrée*.

cabriole: a movement in which the dancer raises one leg to front, back, or side, then jumps with the supporting leg, bringing it up to beat under the other.

chaîné: a series of rapid turns in a circle or straight line, executed on *pointe* or *demi-pointe*.

chassé: a sliding step. The dancer jumps low off the floor, lands, and the working foot "chases" the landing foot out of position.

choreologist: a specialist skilled in any of several systems for notating ballet movements.

cinq: fifth position.

corps de ballet: the dancers in a ballet company who perform in large groups.

coryphée: a dancer who performs in a group smaller than the *corps de ballet*.

croisé: a position in which the dancer stands obliquely to the house so that when either leg is raised it crosses the other leg.

danseur noble: the male lead and partner of the ballerina in such classical ballets as *Giselle* and *Swan Lake*.

demi-plié: see *plié*.

demi-pointe: see *pointe*.

développé: a gradual unfolding of the leg as it rises from the floor and extends itself fully in the air.

échappé: a step in which the feet "escape" from a closed position to an open position as the dancer jumps upward.

elevation: the ability with which a dancer rises from the floor to perform jumps, and the capacity to remain in the air in the midst of these movements.

en baisse: while bending.

en dedans: turning inward toward the supporting leg.

en dehors: turning outward away from the supporting leg.

en l'air: in the air.

entrechat: a step in which the dancer jumps straight into the air from *plié*, the feet beating, or crossing, a number of times.

extension: a dancer's ability to raise and hold the extended leg in the air.

finger pirouette: see *pirouette*.

fish dive:   see *poisson*

fouetté:   a *pirouette* in which one leg whips out to the side in a *rond de jambe*, then in to the knee of the other leg. The dancer uses the momentum thus gained to turn on the supporting leg, rising on *pointe* with each revolution.

gargouillade:   a jump resembling the *pas de chat*, except that in the course of it each leg executes a *rond de jambe*.

half-point, half-toe:   see *pointe*.

jeté:   a jump in which the weight of the body is thrown from one foot to the other. The *grand jeté* is a swift, high jump in which the dancer pushes off from the floor with one foot in a variety of preparatory positions, holds a fleeting pose in flight, and lands softly on the other foot.

mark:   to indicate ballet movements, for instance by means of a finger shorthand, rather than dancing them full out.

pas:   step.

pas de bourrée:   an intricate step in which the weight is transferred in three movements from one foot to the other. In effect it is a swift traveling movement on *pointe* or *demi-pointe*.

pas de chat:   a light jumping step in which each foot in turn is drawn up beneath the body before the dancer lands again in fifth position.

pas de cheval:   a step in which the dancer's foot paws the ground, like a horse's.

pas de deux:   in general, a dance for two performers. The classical *pas de deux* consists of five parts: the *entrée*, in which the ballerina and *premier danseur* make their appearance; the *adagio*, in which the *danseur* supports the ballerina in a slow, graceful dance; a variation for the *danseur*; a variation for the ballerina; and the coda, a concluding passage for both dancers.

pas de poisson:   see *poisson*.

pas de quatre:   a dance for four performers.

pas de trois:   a dance for three performers.

passé:   a movement from one position to another in which the foot of the working leg passes the knee of the supporting leg.

pas seul:   a dance solo. Also called *variation*.

penché:   a tilting position in which the dancer stands on one leg with the other raised high in back.

piqué: a modifying term indicating that the dancer executes a movement or pose by stepping directly onto *pointe* or *demi-pointe* without bending the knee of the working leg.

pirouette: a complete turn of the body on one foot. Girls pirouette on *pointe*, boys on *demi-pointe*. In the *finger pirouette* the male dancer raises his left hand above the ballerina's head. She grasps his index finger with her right hand while spinning.

più mosso: a musical term indicating a quickening of tempo.

placement: the ability to hold the body in correct position with full turn-out in all poses and steps.

plié: a bending of the knees. *demi-plié*: a half-bending of the knees. *grand plié*: a deep bending of the knees.

point: see *pointe*.

pointe: toe. *en pointe*: on toe. *sur les pointes*: on the tips of the toes. Traditionally, men go no higher than *demi-pointe*, half-toe, where the body is supported high on the ball of the foot and under the toes.

poisson: a position in which the ballerina stands on *pointe*, feet crossed in fifth position, legs pulled back, head lifted, and back arched. When the partner catches or lifts the ballerina in this position, it is called a *pas de poisson* or *fish dive*.

port de bras: carriage, or movement, of the arms.

position: Five fundamental positions of the feet are the basis for all steps in the classic dance vocabulary. They are executed with feet flat on the floor, high on the balls of the foot, or on the toes. In all positions, the feet are turned out. *First position:* the feet are together, making a single straight line. *Second position:* same as first, but with heels separated by a distance equivalent to one foot. *Third position:* one foot is placed in front of the other, each heel touching the middle of the opposite foot. *Fourth position:* one foot is placed in front of and parallel to the other at a distance of one foot. *Fifth position:* one foot is placed in front of the other. The heel of each foot touches the toe of the other so that neither big toe projects.

premier danseur: the male equivalent of the ballerina; the top rank of male dancer in a ballet company.

principal: in ballet companies, the top rank of dancer. The principal dances solo roles only, usually the leading solo roles in a ballet. He or she may be compared to a leading actor in a drama, as opposed to a supporting actor.

relevé: the raising of the body onto *pointe* or *demi-pointe*.

révérence:   a deep bow.

rond de jambe:   a rotary movement of the leg: toe pointed, the foot describes a circle in the air (*rond de jambe en l'air*) or on the floor (*rond de jambe sur la terre*).

sauté:   the word is used as a modifier to explain that a jump is involved in a step or pose.

soloist:   in ballet companies, the rank intermediate between *corps de ballet* and principal.

tour:   synonym for *pirouette*.

tour en l'air:   a *pirouette* performed in the air. The dancer, standing in fifth position, rises from the floor from a *demi-plié*, executes a complete turn, and returns to the original position.

turn-out:   the distinguishing characteristic of the classical dance. Each leg is turned outward from the hip at an angle of ninety degrees, so that the knees are facing opposite directions and the feet form a single straight line on the floor.

variation:   In ballet, the word means simply a solo dance or *pas seul*.